FROM THE
SHADOWS OF
THE OWL QUEEN'S
COURT

BENEDICT PATRICK

Cover design by Jenny Zemanek
www.seedlingsonline.com

Published by One More Page Publishing

ISBN: 9781720082040

CONTENTS

ACKNOWLEDGEMENTS

When going for a walk in the woods, some company is always appreciated. I had a veritable army with me on this particular trek – I hope we weren't too boisterous.

My love and gratitude, as always, to those wonderful, mad individuals I share a home with: Adele, without whom I would be a quivering mess by the end of every day, and our two monkeys, Darcy and Finn.

Thank you as well to my stalwart companions in this writing journey. This isn't the first time we've travelled together, but that does not make your contributions any less important:

My bros Sean, Mark, Connor and Rory, for the craic on Whatsapp, and for those of you lent me your eyes this time around.

Mum and dad, and Jacinta, for the constant support through… well, through the basic hell of existence.

Helen and Craig, who continue to be heroic a little bit every day, and without whom our little family would not survive.

I can't forget everyone else who cast their eyes over this story, or who were available to chat to when times seemed tough: Kat, Ágnes, Graham, Tim (more about you later), Richard.

To my friends and companions over at the Crit Faced Podcast: Phil, David, Timandra and Josiah (if you have not listened to us yet, you have not lived), thank you for the constant fires, and the continuing reminders that characters don't always like to walk the most obvious paths.

A particular thank you to the newcomers to the team, Kathryn, Timy and Alex. Your time and feedback has been invaluable in getting 'Shadows' ready for the rest of the world.

To the cacophony of voices in the Terrible Ten, and the wealth of talent over at Sigil Independent - cheers for the camaraderie, and for the inspiration.

To my elite Reading Knacks, and to the vibrant, enthusiastic community over at Reddit Fantasy - thank you for the encouragement, and for your support.

I can't believe I have never mentioned her before, but a massive shoutout to Jenny for her masterpiece of a cover. Your designs have come to define the Yarnsworld, and are my number one weapon in finding new readers.

To my awesome editors, Alida and Laura, a huge thanks for helping to shape this story.

Finally, I would like to take a moment to remember the editor of the first three Yarnsworld novels, Laura Kingsley, who passed away during the summer. You pulled no punches, and that was exactly what I needed when I was starting my writing career. This book, as well as future Yarnsworld novels, would not have happened without your guiding hand.

BENEDICT PATRICK

CHAPTER ONE

Nascha smiled as the priestess handed over her monthly poison.

She chose not to focus on the thick amber liquid, and instead turned her gaze to one of the few pleasures this ritual trip afforded her. Here, in one of the top spires of the Owlfolk palace, Nascha had found the most beautiful view of the forest below. Holding the fateful cup, she looked out over the White Woods, early morning bringing with it a heavy fog that gave the forest an unnatural look, tall, silver birch trees seemingly sprouting from clouds in the sky. This illusion was broken just before the birch reached the horizon, where they gave way to the dark trees that signified the border of Nascha's home.

"Drink it," the priestess said.

Nascha looked at the older woman. Despite the fact that Nascha had been coming here every month for the majority of her twenty years at the Court, she had not gotten to know any of the priestesses well. From what she could tell, their order rotated the priestesses and acolytes throughout its temples, so very few of the Owl Spirit's clergy spent enough time here for Nascha to forge a relationship with them. In truth, few of them had ever seemed interested in getting to know a simple Court servant, even one who required regular poisoning.

1

"Drink it," the older woman repeated. She did not look directly at Nascha; the priestess' eyes were already fixed on the doorway to the small room, her mind contemplating her next task. Knowing she was unobserved, Nascha pulled a face, looking at the cup again. The amber liquid looked tempting, almost as if it tasted nice, sweet.

It never did.

When Nascha had been brought to the Court as a child, no secret had been made about the purpose of the poison. She had always wondered whether the foul taste of it was simply due to the fact that she knew what she was putting into her body. Perhaps if the priestesses had handed her a fine copper goblet, encouraging her to drink something from the Court vineyards, then maybe Nascha would have convinced herself that the poison tasted good. However, she had always been aware that drinking the poison was a harmful, unnatural act, and despite her acceptance of many things about life at Court, this monthly ritual was hardest for Nascha to bear.

She did not give the priestess the satisfaction of repeating her instruction a third time. Nascha brought the goblet to her lips.

"Give me some," said a voice from the doorway.

Nascha found the priestess' reaction to the newcomer's arrival particularly gratifying. The woman's heretofore stoic face betrayed a wealth of emotions, beginning with anger, finally congealing into a satisfying mixture of shock and fear.

"The length of that staircase is quite unacceptable. Some refreshment would do me good. Give me some," the newcomer, Princess Laurentina of the Titonidae, said again.

Nascha clutched the clay cup, not yet empty, surprised at how possessive she suddenly felt regarding the poison. Its entire purpose was to harm, but like so few things in Nascha's world, the poison belonged to her.

It was the priestess who acted first, rising from her seat to bow before the princess. "My—my lady," she said, clearly unused to interacting directly with a member of the royal family. "My lady, what an unexpected pleasure—"

"Pleasure? Pleasure is the last word I would associate with having to trek all the way up here," Laurentina said, eyes still fixed on the cup in Nascha's hands. "Mother won't be happy to hear I've been waiting, even after I have given both of you a very clear request. Nascha, be a darling and give me that drink."

It was Nascha's turn to experience a range of emotions. She was satisfied to see the look of shock on the priestess' face when the princess addressed her directly. The woman clearly had not expected Laurentina to know the name of a common serving girl, or to speak so familiarly to her. What was overriding that small pleasure, however, was the delicate matter of Princess Laurentina's request for Nascha's cup. Nascha's eyes darted to those of the priestess, and she realised the older woman was experiencing the same conflict. Princess Laurentina had only recently reached her fifteenth year. There were many things about life in the Owl Queen's Court that such a young girl would not be aware of, especially a young girl of royal blood.

Breaking away from the priestess' gaze, Nascha looked at the cup still clutched in her hands. It was clear that the princess did not know why Nascha came up here to drink each month.

How much *did* Laurentina know? She did not know about the poison, that was clear, but did she know anything about Nascha? About why she lived in the Court instead of with her family? They had certainly never discussed it in their time together – their conversations were always about Laurentina, and about the princess' hopes and troubles. In a brief moment of madness, Nascha considered that perhaps it would not be such a bad thing to tell the girl the truth. Despite the vast social gulf that existed between them – a serving girl and future queen – Laurentina was the closest thing Nascha had to a friend. Moreover, Nascha suspected the same was true for Laurentina.

Nascha took a half step forward, ready to explain everything to Laurentina, but then she caught a glimpse of the priestess.

The clergywoman's mouth was open, and she stood rigid, eyes darting between the two friends before her. Something in that nervous look was infectious. Nascha was aware that, although this woman and her sisterhood had no problem in administering the amber potion each time Nascha visited, the priestesses had never been unkind to her. The look of fear on the priestess' face found its echo in Nascha's heart, as she realised with all certainty – though without fully understanding why – that it was not in her best interests for Laurentina to find out her secret. It was Nascha's turn to feel fear, her own eyes darting between the priestess and the impatient look on Laurentina's face. Despite the fact that Nascha thought of the princess as a friend, she had never before refused a direct request from her.

It was the priestess who acted first, the older woman's voice breaking Nascha free from her stupor.

"Drink it, girl," the priestess said, her voice urgent.

Before Laurentina could protest further, Nascha tipped the cup back, and tossed poison down her gullet.

Nascha felt Laurentina's hands on her wrist. The princess had crossed the room quickly, outrage clear on the girl's face, her youthful beauty contorted – as it so often was – by lines of anger.

"How dare you."

At first, Nascha thought the royal girl's ire was directed at her, and this strange friendship they had developed over the last few months was now coming to its inevitable end. Nascha was not really even sure if she would use the word 'friendship' to describe what she had with Laurentina, but the princess had chosen to use that word herself, and Nascha would not dare to argue with her. However, when in the girl's presence, Nascha had always been painfully aware of the differences in their social standings, and what that could mean if they ever came to disagreement.

Such as arguing over a drink of poison.

Thankfully, Laurentina turned to direct her petulant stare at the priestess.

"How dare you," the princess said again.

For her part, the older woman had recovered some of her confidence, either burying her emotions well, or recalling that the girl in front of her was a mere child of fifteen and was not really in a position to challenge a member of the clergy. Not yet.

"That drink was for the serving girl only," the priestess informed Laurentina, "and not fit for one of your lineage, my lady."

Nascha glanced at Laurentina and saw the princess grit her teeth.

"Allow me to fetch you something more suited to your station," the priestess continued, any fear she had originally felt now hidden behind her holier-than-thou attitude.

Princess Laurentina paused briefly, then nodded to the woman. "Bring it quick, then. I don't think I've ever run up as many stairs in my life, trying to keep track of Nascha."

Despite how hard she was working to cover up her emotions, to not let the princess see how worried she had been, Nascha allowed herself to smile as the priestess' eyes narrowed, as if only now fully contemplating the serving girl who appeared to be so important to the princess. The older woman only took a brief moment to do so, however, before taking off to fulfil Laurentina's request.

"Nascha, what are you doing all the way up here?" Laurentina did not look directly at Nascha as she spoke, but instead her eyes tracked the room, a small antechamber in the temple that the young princess was clearly not familiar with. Laurentina's eyes rested on a cushioned stone bench just below the window Nascha had been admiring earlier, and the noble girl threw herself onto it.

"It took me ages to convince the other girls to tell me where you were. Eventually, Sapata in the kitchen told me, but I got the distinct impression the others were not happy with her doing so. Do you think I should have them punished for conspiring against me?" Seeing Laurentina motion for her to do so, Nascha carefully walked to the bench, sitting beside her.

No, the other girls would not have been happy telling Laurentina where Nascha had gone. In general, Laurentina was not well liked in the castle. She was the only child of the Owl Queen, who had indulged her horribly since Laurentina's father died, eventually molding her daughter into the spoiled brat who found no issue with demanding poison from priestesses. The girl's erratic temper was so well known even the nobility were unsure about spending any time with her, for fear of the retribution she might take for any imagined slights. For a servant such as Nascha, the princess' disapproval could be career-ending, if not an actual threat to her life.

"I didn't tell anyone where I had gone, my lady," Nascha said, doing what she could to move Laurentina's thoughts away from petty vengeance. "Just came up here early without disturbing the others, hoping to get this out of the way before I began my duties." This was not a lie. She had not told a soul where she had been going. In truth, she spoke very little to the other servants, preferring her own company.

Seeing the princess purse her lips, Nascha tried to change the conversation. "How is your mother?"

The situation with Laurentina's mother was how Nascha and Laurentina's friendship had developed. Less than a year ago, Laurentina's father had passed away, taken by amethyst fever. That had, of course, been a very difficult time for the princess, but what made it worse was news that the deceased king had given his wife a parting gift: an heir. On the day she gave her husband's body to the Owl Spirit, the queen announced she was pregnant. If the child, due any day now, was male, he would be the heir to the Court's throne.

Nascha had found Laurentina crying in a servant's storeroom on the day of her father's funeral, and had begun their relationship by reprimanding her, mistaking her for a servant shirking her duties. Laurentina, uncharacteristically, had not flown into a rage at Nascha, but instead had broken down in her arms, sobbing her heart out, with Nascha rigid in shock at how familiar the princess was being with her.

Since then, Laurentina continued to seek Nascha out when the princess could find no respite with the rest of her family. As the fuss around her mother grew with the approach of the child's birth, these occurrences had become more frequent. In the last few weeks, Laurentina had sought Nascha out daily, bending her ear about everything in the Court except for what was really troubling her.

"Mother is in labour," Laurentina said impassionately, her eyes distracted by a lone white bird flying over the forest below.

"That must be exciting?" Nascha ventured, adding just enough inflection in her voice to give Laurentina the hint that Nascha was not completely certain how she felt about it.

There was silence in the antechamber for a few heartbeats. Then Laurentina said, "What do you think?"

Nascha was puzzled. "I—I'm sorry, my lady? Are you talking about the birth? If you will be getting a brother or sister?"

Laurentina sighed, looking briefly at Nascha, taking just enough time to roll her eyes at the servant. "No, silly, I mean all of this." Laurentina waved a lazy hand at the world outside the Court, where the mists had begun to dissipate, unveiling the rich earth of the forest floor. "The woods, the kingdom. What do you think it would be like, to have all of this? To rule it all?"

Nascha felt like laughing. What a question for a princess to ask a scullery maid. "I really haven't given it much thought, my lady. My dreams never quite get as big as that, I suppose."

"No, I don't suppose they do," Laurentina said wistfully, her eyes still on the trees below. "It's been on my mind a lot." The princess was quiet for a while, then, and Nascha knew it was best not to intrude on her silence. Eventually, she spoke again. "It would have been mine, you know. I'm only a princess, I've not been blessed by the Owl Spirit, but as the only royal child, it would have gone to me."

Nascha was not too certain if this was true. From what she could tell from the old stories, whichever prince Laurentina took as her eventual husband would become the true source of political power in the Court. Only the queens blessed by the Owl Spirit – those born with white hair – were seen as acceptable rulers of Titonidae Courts. Laurentina's hair was jet black, almost exactly matching Nascha's own, when she remembered to dye it. Again, these were not really questions Nascha spent much time dwelling on.

"Won't it be nice to have a companion?" Nascha ventured, trying to find the best in the princess' situation. "You can spend your time helping to raise him, and when he is older, he will be someone to play with. You won't have to be alone again." Nascha drifted off after saying that, unsure if she had overstepped the mark. It was painfully obvious Laurentina was alone, if only because she had turned to someone as low-born as Nascha for companionship.

Laurentina looked at Nascha. Nascha was surprised at the redness rising on the princess' face, and realised she had made a dangerous mistake in her last statement.

"It could be a sister—"

"It's a boy," Laurentina interjected, her face tightening. "They're certain it's a boy. Prince tomorrow, king the day after that. A boy."

"A brother, then," Nascha said, fearful of provoking even more anger from the princess. "I think it would be nice to have a little brother," she added, becoming increasingly more uncomfortable.

Laurentina was quiet for a moment. Nascha could see the girl's eyes being drawn towards the dark trees that signified the border of her kingdom.

"Are you a good person?" Laurentina asked after a while, her eyes never leaving the horizon.

Nascha looked at the princess, confused. "I—I don't understand. A good person? I... think so. I like to think so."

"How do you know?" Laurentina asked, still not looking at the serving girl.

The question caught Nascha off guard. She was certain the princess was getting at something, but for the life of her she had no idea what it was, and so Nascha did not answer.

"I am not a nice person," Laurentina said quietly, her voice low.

Nascha's eyes darted to the doorway. The priestess had not returned. She was taking an awfully long time.

"I'm sure that isn't true, princess," Nascha said, rising from her seat beside Laurentina. "I am sure you are just—"

Nascha was shocked into silence when Laurentina turned to look at her, the younger girl's brown eyes catching Nascha's gaze and holding it there authoritatively.

"Do you know what I wish?" Laurentina asked, a sad smile creeping across her face. "I am not a good person. I know this. The things I wish would happen, sometimes, when I'm alone. A good person would not wish those things."

"Princess, I'm sure that's not true. I'm sure—"

"Get away from the queen."

Nascha turned to the new voice, jumping in surprise. She was already troubled by where the conversation was going, and having such a moment interrupted by a stranger threw her composure entirely.

She recognised the newcomer straight away. It was Lord Bidzell, one of the lesser nobles of the Court. A lesser noble, but a puppet master who seemed to have his fingers on all the right strings. Whenever something was occurring, whenever there was an event at the Court that invited people to give their opinions, Lord Bidzell always made sure he was somehow in the thick of it. Nascha could sense the man's hunger, always, and that greed emanated from him even now.

Despite the early morning, Lord Bidzell was already dressed in formal gear, the appearance of which was spoiled by his red face, clearly a consequence of his having run up the stairs to the temple. Lord Bidzell was not a young man, but remained in good shape. Nascha supposed that working so hard to gain and retain as much as Lord Bidzell had managed to amass at Court would be good enough exercise.

The nobleman pointed his finger accusingly at Nascha. "Girl, do not make me tell you again. Get away from the queen," he ordered, his eyes never leaving Laurentina's face.

"Yes, my lord," Nascha said automatically, backing away from

Lord Bidzell and bowing as she retreated. She glanced briefly at the princess, and noticed Laurentina's ghostly face.

It was only then that Nascha realised exactly what Lord Bidzell had said.

"I am not the queen," Laurentina said in a small voice, as if she had not already guessed at what had transpired. "You mean my mother. I'm the princess. My mother is the queen."

Forgetting herself for a moment, Nascha raised her eyes to look at Lord Bidzell's face. She was taken aback by the hungry satisfaction that spread across the man's eyes before being covered up by a more appropriate, sombre facade.

Lord Bidzell knelt in front of Laurentina, bowing his head.

"Your Grace," the nobleman said, eyes still looking to the floor, "I bring most terrible news. Your mother—"

"No." Laurentina sprang up from her seat, her movements urgent. "No," she said again, her head beginning to twitch, as if she was losing control over her body. "No, no, you may not tell me." Laurentina's face began to turn red, as it often did just before a tantrum. "I do not hear this." Her voice was shrill, cracked, and entirely too young for a girl of fifteen years.

Lord Bidzell raised his head, seemed to consider Laurentina's words for a moment, then continued. "Your Grace, there has been a great tragedy."

Laurentina gave a cry and ran across the room, clutching herself close to Nascha. Nascha tried to embrace the noble girl who called her a friend, but she could feel herself falling apart as the realisation hit her. The Owl Queen was dead. Lord Bidzell was here to tell them that the queen was dead. The queen – the former queen – had died in childbirth, and now Laurentina was no longer a princess.

The world around Nascha was mute as she contemplated what was happening. Lord Bidzell walked across the antechamber, took hold of Laurentina, and guided her away from Nascha, leading her back down the stairs, to her new responsibilities, to her people.

The queen was dead. Nascha's friend was now queen.

Not taking in what was being said around her, feeling the bitter poison bite away at her guts as it always did, Nascha raised her eyes to look at Lord Bidzell as he guided the new queen through the temple doorway.

For a brief moment, Lord Bidzell paused. He looked at Nascha with narrowed eyes, as if seeing her properly for the first time. Nascha froze, suddenly feeling naked, standing there exposed before him. He had seen something he should not have.

As soon as he left the room, Nascha dashed to a small washbasin, desperate to find out if he had seen anything important. Was he simply wondering – as so many did – how a simple servant could be so close to the princess? To the queen?

Her hands trembling, Nascha lifted them from the rim of the bowl, allowing the water to steady.

There, in her reflection, she saw it. A glimpse of white on her scalp, the roots of her hair that she had not dyed for over a week now.

Too long, leaving too much of her natural hair colour to show.

Nascha fell to the ground, sick with the effects of the poison, sick for Laurentina and the loss of her mother, and sick that someone like Lord Bidzell now knew of her secret.

At evening meal, everyone in the servant quarters was talking about the queen's death. The delivery had been complicated, and neither queen nor son had survived.

There were six young women in the small, enclosed room. Nascha sat in her bed and listened to the others chat at the table, but did not add much herself. The others were not unkind to Nascha, but the attention she received from Laurentina had caused a clear divide between her and her peers. Even before she had earned the princess' attention, Nascha had done her best to keep her distance from them, so as to ensure they remained as ignorant as possible about why she was really at Court. She had been late to the meal tonight; she had been applying and then washing out the sticky substance she used to darken her hair, hoping to avoid any further encounters like the one with Lord Bidzell in the temple. Nevertheless, the rest of the servants knew that Nascha had the white hair normally associated with the Owl Queen, and that created an unspoken gap between her and the rest. This felt slightly unfair to Nascha, as more than one of the girls she shared a room with were true bastards who could draw a direct line between their mothers and members of the Court royalty. It was not uncommon for royal bastards to be given a serving role in the Court, if discovered. The pretence was that this action in some way allowed the girls to better their lives, a small reward for their parentage. Nascha suspected, especially in her case, that the real reason the bastards were all gathered up was to keep an eye on them, to ensure they could not be used by enemies to threaten the line of succession. She had vague memories of her own mother and father, who had been a simple carpenter down in the town, just outside the Court walls. From what Nascha could gather, her parents could not explain where her white hair had come from. She had tried to ask a priestess once, and the woman had surmised that somewhere in Nascha's family tree, a member of the royal house had intruded in Nascha's bloodline, planting a seed that had waited generations before blooming. Nascha had been told that her parents, whose names she did not know, had willingly given Nascha over once the true colour of her hair had been revealed. Without being able to ask them directly, Nascha always wondered if this was true.

"Going to be a right cock-up now, isn't it? The girl hasn't even run a household before, let alone a kingdom."

"Owl's blood, but you're right. What a piss-poor excuse for a queen we're stuck with."

The subject of the serving girls' conversation, after dwelling on the few macabre details of the failed birth they had managed to glean from the ladies in waiting, had naturally moved to discussing rule under Laurentina. Laurentina was not well liked by most, the serving girls especially. Nascha was not surprised they were not thrilled at the new queen.

"Bring me my shoes! Bring me my comb! Bring me my food!" One of the girls strutted around the room, doing a passable impression of Laurentina in one of her moods.

"I can't tell," another said, chuckling, "is this supposed to be what she's like now, or what she's going to be like with a crown on her head?"

"Same difference," the first said dismissively. "Girl's a brat. Put her in charge of a kingdom, still going to be a brat."

Nascha could not really argue with the statement. When the princess – now queen – decided she desired something, she would demand it of anyone nearby, be they servant or noble.

"She just lost her mother," Nascha said softly, unable to help herself. Despite the quietness of her voice, the others did indeed stop speaking.

They turned to look at her, some having the good grace to look ashamed, but the eldest of them regarded Nascha with a look of disdain.

"Suppose you'll be telling her all about us, then?"

The girls knew that was not true. When Laurentina began seeking Nascha's companionship, all of the serving staff – not just the girls Nascha shared a room with – had been worried Nascha was being used as a spy. It had taken her many weeks to assure her roommates, and consequently the rest of the serving staff, that the princess had no interest in anyone other than herself, and that even if she had been demanding secrets, Nascha would never betray her own kind to the nobility. That situation had not changed, and Nascha knew the girls were striking at an old wound, not actually voicing any real concerns.

"Maybe they'll marry her off," another of the servants said, breaking the tension in the room. "Maybe the rest of the nobles will get together, marry her off to some other lordling."

Another squealed in delight. "What about the dark forest? Maybe they could marry her off to the Magpie King."

The rest of the room gasped.

"Don't you dare," someone said, looking in horror at the one who had just spoken.

"It'd be better for all of us, wouldn't it?" one of the others said, laughing at her own words. "Would serve her right, the little bitch, getting stolen away to that nightmarish place, leaving the rest of us to be ruled by some handsome prince or whatever."

"It'd never happen," another said, standing tall, trying to draw the room's attention. "He wouldn't have her. Even the Magpie King couldn't stand our dear Queen Laurentina."

The girls erupted into giggles.

Nascha felt she should stand up for Laurentina. Yes, the girl could be demanding, but she had been nice to Nascha, in her own way. Still, it was only natural for the help to make fun of the lords and ladies. It was their small way of dealing with the massive gulf between the pleasures of the nobility and the travails of everyone else.

"Isn't he dead?" another said. "I heard the Magpie King is dead."

"Don't be stupid," said another. "The Magpie King? It's just a story. Who could really believe someone like that exists? A man with the head of a bird, who jumps around trees, flying through the forest at night? Lot of nonsense."

"Besides, if we got rid of Queen Laurentina, there's no one left in the royal family to rule us. Can you imagine the arguments that would cause?"

"Wouldn't they just send for someone else? From one of the other Courts? Sure there are plenty of other princes and princesses out there looking for a castle to rule."

"He wouldn't take Laurentina anyway, the Magpie King. And not just because she's a brat – and yeah, I agree, she's a complete witch. In the stories, the Magpie King only takes queens with white hair, with the Owl Spirit's gift. There's not a hint of that in our new queen, despite her mother being strong with it. The Magpie King wouldn't be interested in Laurentina."

"We should send him Nascha, then. Wash that junk out of her hair, surely he'd be interested in her."

Nascha shrunk into herself slightly as the rest of the room turned their necks to look. She was glad she had taken the time today to re-dye her hair, but that did little to affect how exposed she felt right now.

"Don't be stupid," Nascha muttered. It was one thing to make fun of Laurentina, pampered high in her royal chambers somewhere above. It was an entirely different matter to make fun of Nascha while she was sitting in front of them, and she would not stand for it. "That's dangerous talk right there, so it is. Don't be stupid."

The eldest of the servants, the one who had spoken last, looked as if she was going to take umbrage to Nascha's words, but the girl instead turned her back on Nascha – clearly meant as a slight – and regaled her companions with a further tale of Laurentina's unsuitability to rule. Nascha, however, was no longer paying attention. She was too busy thinking of Lord Bidzell's gaze earlier that day, the look on his face when he noticed the true colour of her hair. Her anxiety returned. Letting her guard slip like that could cost her dearly.

Then she remembered the changes that had happened today. The queen had died. A new queen was claiming the throne. A new queen, and her friend.

Laurentina. I'm the best friend to the most powerful person in the Court. If anyone like Lord Bidzell tries to threaten me, I'm close to the one person in the world who can protect me.

As Nascha undid her apron, getting ready to begin her evening chores, she felt warmth blossom in her heart, thawing the frost that had lined it since Lord Bidzell had looked at her that way.

Now, with Laurentina on the throne, her friend, Nascha's captivity in the Owl Queen's Court could soon be at an end.

"Shall we swim?"

Nascha drew back from the older woman.

"Bit too cold for swimming," the noblewoman continued, eyes glassy, staring at Nascha but not quite seeing her.

Nascha was in the Court's western tower, tending to the last of her daily duties. Despite the fact that Nascha's Knack – the innate magical gift most of the Owlfolk developed at puberty – was for cleaning, servants at the Court were often called upon to do other tasks. Serving meals to Lady Awenita, the older sister of the recently deceased queen, was one of the least popular of those jobs.

"Full moon tonight," Lady Awenita said.

Nascha glanced out of the window, to the moon that was fading to a crescent. She turned back to Lady Awenita and smiled. "Lovely, isn't it?"

Lady Awenita grinned in response. The queen's sister was, and for as long as Nascha could remember, had always been, mad.

Thankfully, it was a tranquil sort of insanity. The infirm lady's thoughts were trapped in a bygone courtship, presumably when she was much younger. The woman's ramblings unnerved most of the other serving girls, but Nascha did not mind. In some ways, she was jealous of the noblewoman's simple happiness.

"Undress me, love." Lady Awenita's voice dropped low.

Nascha raised an eyebrow as she gathered up the used cutlery. Awenita was no longer looking at her. Instead, the noblewoman's eyes were fixed on an empty space in the middle of the room.

Nascha often wondered who the woman's lover had been. Maybe he had only ever existed in Awenita's mind. Nascha smiled again, gathered her things, and left Lady Awenita to her memories, blowing out the last candle as she left, allowing the moon to enter and paint the room blue.

On a night such as this, Nascha did not need to carry a light, as the stairways in the royal quarter of the Courts were well ventilated, and the clear moon illuminated Nascha's path. She hurried down the stairs, aware she was a lone servant in the royal wing of the palace. She was permitted to be there to tend to Lady Awenita; however, the hour was getting late, and there were too many stories of serving girls who had run into some lordling or other and been taken advantage of. Nascha was determined to never be one of those girls.

"...but it seems so barbaric," came a voice Nascha instantly recognised, seeping through the closed door she was passing. Despite herself, Nascha stopped at the sound of Laurentina.

The queen's chambers, Nascha thought. Laurentina had already been moved into the queen's chambers. Her mother's body had been interred in the Owl Spirit's temple only this morning.

"Isn't there another way, without having to hurt people?" Laurentina's voice had an edge to it Nascha had not heard from the girl before. Despite the amount of complaining Laurentina always did, at the end of the day she had a life in which she did not want for anything. As a princess, she got everything she desired, leaving her to worry only about how quickly she got it. Tonight, however, Laurentina's voice sounded on the edge of worry, a discordant tone that did not suit the princess' shrillness.

"This is the only way," a deeper voice said, answering the new queen. "The history books teach us that it must be so. Do not worry about your legacy, about your reputation in all of this. Ascending royalty throughout the generations have had to commit similar acts to secure their hold on the throne, and they have all been remembered kindly. Your mother did the same when she became queen. This is not an act of evil. This is just the way of things."

Lord Bidzell. Nascha bit her lip, convinced they would not be the only two in that room. Laurentina, despite being queen, was still a girl of only fifteen years. Lord Bidzell was in his forties, and still a bachelor – it would not be seemly for him to be left alone with her.

More than that, however, was Nascha's instant discomfort at hearing the phrase 'act of evil'.

"But… so many of them?" Laurentina said. "When did we get so many of them? And some of them—"

"You must trust me on this. You chose me as your adviser, accepted me when I offered my services. This is my first suggestion, and probably the most important one I could make. You have ascended to the throne quickly, and unexpectedly. The nobility were hoping for many more years of rule under your mother. When you were to finally take the throne, they were expecting a real ruler, raised with the knowledge of how to properly lead them. You are a member of the royal family, yes, but have not been blessed by the Owl Spirit. Forgive my harshness, my queen, but I would rather you were stung by my words tonight than by their swords tomorrow. There are those at Court who would seek to replace you, to supplant your family's claim to rule. We must remove all possibilities of pretenders to the throne.

"This is a list of the bastards we hold at Court, the servants with royal blood in their veins. To protect your legacy, and your life, you must give the order for them to be executed."

Nascha should have stayed there, by the door, to find out more. Any other information she might glean could be critical to her survival.

Instead, she stood, head spinning, eyes unfocussed. Not wanting to be caught vomiting outside the queen's quarters, Nascha stumbled down the stairs and out behind the stables, before emptying the contents of her stomach onto the dirt.

She stood there, head leaning against the wooden frame of the building, gaze drifting across the filth congealing on the ground in front of her, the amber tinge of the poison still evident.

She was not supposed to be sick after taking the poison. She was supposed to tell them if that happened.

Instead, Nascha closed her eyes, willing the walls of the Court to stop closing in so tight around her.

"Get down!" Bradan shouted, grabbing the farmer's shirt and pulling the burly man to the ground.

The man hit the forest floor hard, joining Bradan and the rest of the farmer's family in the bushes overlooking their home.

"What in the Spirit's name'd you do that for?" the farmer said, glowering at Bradan even as he reached for his wife.

Bradan did not look at him as he replied, keeping his eyes trained on the now-empty farmstead, trying not to think about how uncomfortable, how exposed he felt in such a small space with this group of strangers.

"Get out of sight," Bradan whispered again, trying not to lose his patience. "Think I heard something. If it sees us before we see it, we're all dead."

The youngest daughter, not yet having seen ten years in the world, whimpered. The farmer growled – actually growled – but Bradan did his best to ignore him. He was certain he had seen movement in the trees on the other side of the farmland, but he had to be sure.

"It can't come yet. He isn't here," the farmer said. "You promised he'd be here."

"He will be," Bradan said, trying to not let his frustration show. "Trust me, he'll be here."

Please, please be here.

Yes, there was movement in the trees, but it was just a pair of deer, running towards the farmstead across the farmer's small patch of land, the flat green that had been cleared within the heart of the Magpie King's wood.

Those deer were running, but what were they running from?

Bradan's eyes raised to the treetops around him. He had been told to promise that help would come, but if Father did not arrive soon, it would be too late, and Bradan would be accused of being a liar.

Again.

"Bessie!" the farmer's wife shouted suddenly, jumping up from the bushes. This time, to Bradan's relief, it was the farmer who dragged his wife back down to safety.

"Bessie is still in there," the woman wailed, far too loud for Bradan's liking.

"Spirit's breath, we've left one of your daughters inside?"

"No," the farmer said, fixing Bradan with a hard stare, forcing him to look away. "Bessie's the name of the cat."

Bradan sighed in relief. Nothing important, then.

He glanced back up and saw the farmer still staring at him, expectantly. The man's wife continued to wail, a noise that would certainly attract attention once the attack began.

"Missus is awful fond of that cat," the farmer continued, his persistent stare making it clear the situation was not as resolved as Bradan had first thought.

Grunting, the farmer stood up.

"What're you doing?" Bradan said, incredulous. "They're almost here. You can't go back in there for a stupid cat."

That earned Bradan a slap from the farmer's wife on his right, and an elbow in the ribs from the daughter on his left. Two painful reminders of why Bradan tried to keep his own company as much as possible.

The farmer, whose face told Bradan he half-agreed with him, stood resolute anyway, the resigned look of a man who was used to doing things he did not quite agree with.

"Aye, but it looks like I'm goin' anyway," the farmer said, turning to them one last time. "This hero of yours going to appear any time soon?"

There was a pause, during which Bradan prayed with all his might to the Magpie Spirit that his father would suddenly drop from the trees before them. Apparently, the Spirit was not listening. Nothing happened.

"I guess the other option is, you go instead," the farmer said, his eyes never leaving Bradan. There was, hidden deep beneath the man's rough exterior, a glimmer of expectant hope in his eyes.

Bradan almost nodded in agreement. He almost jumped up and strode from their hiding place right then, wanting to do nothing more than play the part of the hero that was being offered to him. However, he hesitated, a memory of his father's disapproving face flashing through his mind.

"No," Bradan said, pushing his own urges deep down. "I'm not strong or foolish enough to stand against them. Have to wait."

The farmer looked away, dismissing Bradan, as so many others had before.

"Up to me, then."

With that, the farmer charged out of the undergrowth towards his home, to reclaim the family cat.

Bradan tensed. He gripped the roots of the gorse bush he had led the family to, eyes fixed on the trees beyond the farmstead, where the deer had run from.

Come on, he thought, willing his father to appear, as they had agreed. *I've done my part, gotten them to safety. Now it's time for you to be the hero.*

The farmer made his way into the house, striding into his home without a care in the world, as if nothing was wrong.

Then the trees on the far side of the clearing exploded.

Bradan had never seen the things that emerged from the hole in the greenery before, but Mother Ogma had told him many tales about them before she passed away. He counted three horse-sized, hairless beavers stampeding from the depths of the wood, heading straight for the farmhouse that still had the farmer inside.

Predictably, the little girl beside Bradan screamed.

Cursing himself for an idiot, Bradan clasped his hand over the girl's mouth, but it was too late. While two of the monstrous beavers ran towards the farmhouse, one of them paused and rose, its giant, sword-like whiskers gyrating in the air as its milk-coloured eyes fixed on their hiding place. A whimper emanated from beneath the fingers held firmly over the girl's mouth. That, apparently, was all the confirmation the monster needed that food was near. Like a dog welcoming its owner's return home, the beaver barrelled across the farmland towards them.

Bradan swore, leaping to his feet, the need to hide now gone.

"Run," he shouted to the woman, dragging her and her daughters to their feet as he himself got up. "We need to get as far away as possible."

"My husband," she said, as she scrambled to grab her youngest child's hand. "What about my husband?"

Bradan hesitated. One of the beavers threw itself at the farmhouse's easternmost wall, causing the roof to topple inward, thatch and beams erupting from the opening like a flower revealing itself to the sun. The farmer could already be dead. Bradan's father had not arrived. Promises had already been broken.

What harm would there be now in Bradan breaking the promise that he had made?

He bit his lip, then turned to the woman. "Run fast. Get back to the village. Warn them what might be coming. I'll get your husband."

The look that passed over the woman's face was an equal mix of relief and doubt. Bradan did not blame her. He had seen creatures of the forest before, but most of them were night-dwelling, and dealt in stealth. The villagers of the forest had grown up with tales and strategies about how to beat them at their own game, how to outwit them. It was an entirely different matter to face these three active forces of nature charging towards them in broad daylight, clearly intent on turning these people into lunch.

Bradan did not blame her for wondering what he could do to stop them. In truth, he had no idea himself.

What was important was that for once, despite his promise to his father to stay well back, he was going to try.

The woman ran as instructed, and so did Bradan, but this time towards the beavers, screaming and waving his arms like an idiot. His first priority was to make sure the beaver charging at the bushes followed him, not the farmer's family.

He succeeded admirably. The monster rushing across the clearing had its eyes fixed firmly on him. Even better, from a certain point of view, one of the beavers busy demolishing the farmhouse turned its head to Bradan as well, also taking an interest in him.

Great, Bradan thought, swiftly changing his own direction and sprinting towards the relative safety of the nearby trees. *Guess I'll take these two, and the farmer can sort that last one out himself.*

He managed to make it past the first trees before the wood behind him exploded in a hail of chipped timber and dirt. Bradan threw himself to the ground just in time for the first beaver to leap over him, charging deeper into the forest, unaware it had just stepped over its prey.

Bradan breathed a quiet thanks to the Magpie Spirit, adding in a further request to keep the beaver running for as long as possible.

Aware that the second monster pursuing him was still unaccounted for, he gingerly peeked his head up from his hiding place.

The other beaver was waiting for him, its horrific face mere feet away from the hole he had rolled into. The creature roared, acrid spittle peppering Bradan's face.

Bradan froze. He knew that was not the reaction needed to save his life. However, his body would not let him do otherwise. As with all of the Muridae, the Magpiefolk who lived in the forest, this was the moment Bradan had spent a lifetime trying to avoid, the moment generations of his people had told their children stories of time and time again, hoping their offspring would never have to experience what Bradan was experiencing right now, facing off against one of the forest's many monsters. Bradan should have known better than to get this close. An image of his father's disapproving face flashed before his eyes, agreeing with that last sentiment.

His father. His father should be here right now. Bradan imagined, for a moment, that his father was indeed descending from the trees, crashing into the monster in front of him. As horrific as the beaver was, Bradan knew his father would make short work of it.

As he was so often reminded, Bradan could not.

Thankfully, instead of taking advantage of its prey's fear, the beaver roared again. That second cry was all the encouragement Bradan needed, and by the time the monster stopped bellowing and was ready to catch him, Bradan had already tumbled away. Behind him, Bradan could hear the beaver thrashing about through the undergrowth, doing what it could to pick up his trail. In the distance, he heard the cries of the first beaver, the one that had initially charged him, now deep in the forest chasing a non-existent quarry. Bradan knew this was the best chance he had of escaping. The beavers would get bored looking for him and head back to the easier prey within the clearing, leaving Bradan to run to the nearby village. In fact, as he thought about it, Bradan realised that was exactly what he was doing. Trained by his father through years of ensuring he was always a safe distance from the danger, Bradan had subconsciously pointed himself toward the village of Meldrum and its fortified walls. He was already making his way to where he would be safe.

But there was nobody else to save the farmer.

Bradan stopped. It was not an easy action to take; it fought against all the training his body and mind had been put through.

But as Bradan realised he was preparing to head back into danger, a secret thrill rippled through him. This must be what it was like to be his father, to know that he was heading out there to make a difference. Despite not having his father's gifts, Bradan yearned for more of this feeling. To be, for once, a hero.

A stupid smile shone across his face. The rushing blood in his body doing strange things to his mind, Bradan leapt back through the bushes. Thankfully, only one beaver remained in the clearing, the others presumably trying to track Bradan somewhere in the forest.

This beaver was within the building itself, having collapsed two of its four walls and all of its roof. The creature's rear was sticking out, wriggling in the dirt outside the farmhouse as its head explored the interior. Bradan's heart sank. If the farmer was still inside, the man would surely already be dead. It was not a large enough building to hide inside once the enemy had broken through.

Then Bradan spotted a small shape making its way around the farmhouse. It was, he realised, that damned cat. The pet was alone, but was not making for the forest, as he would have expected most sensible animals to do. Perhaps if Bradan followed it he would find clues to the farmer's fate.

Hunched low, doing his best to not attract the attention of the enemy in the house, nor to alert the two beavers still in the woods, Bradan ran as quickly as he dared towards the farmstead. The building was trembling, the timber walls bending and cracking each time the beaver threw its weight against them, presumably rummaging through everything it could find inside for signs of food. Staying low, eyes darting to the nearby forest, wary of the monsters out there, Bradan skirted around the outside of the building, where the walls seemed most secure. There, sheltered between two cider barrels, a bloodied gash running down his left leg, was the farmer, the family moggie curled up in his arms, gripping its owner tightly in fear. The farmer looked at Bradan, anger blooming on the man's face.

"You told me my home would be safe," he said.

Bradan had indeed promised this. His father had told him to. Despite having done everything he had agreed to do, despite the extra risk Bradan was taking to save this man, a wave of guilt broke over him. Bradan shook his head, trying to dismiss it. He was not the one who had broken promises. Guilt was his father's due, not

Bradan's. Bradan had done nothing wrong.

Choosing to ignore the farmer's grievance, Bradan grabbed the man, pulling him upward, supporting the farmer's injured leg.

"Don't know how long they'll keep searching for me," he told the farmer, who was gritting his teeth through the pain, still clutching the family cat in one arm. "Your family are safe, and we should be too, if we can get just a short distance away."

The farmer grunted.

At that moment, one of the other beavers burst back through the trees, landing in a cat-like stance at the edge of the clearing, facing directly towards Bradan and the farmer. The beaver held a young deer within its jaws, blood dripping from the corpse, painting the beaver's face with a red smile.

Bradan froze again. He felt the farmer go rigid beside him.

For the second time in as many minutes, Bradan wondered how his father would deal with this. He would probably leap across the clearing in a single bound, grab the beaver by the neck, and twist until it cracked. Not an option for Bradan.

Before them, the beaver stood still, breathing heavily, its eyes fixed upon them. Behind, within the farmhouse, the other beaver's movements became more frantic, as if it could sense something important happening outside.

"This is it," the farmer said. "This is how I die." A hint of resentment laced the man's words. Bradan could not help but feel that most of it was aimed at him.

Bradan looked around, searching for options. "Certainly looks that way," he said, distractedly. At that moment, the building beside them shook again, the beaver inside growling.

The monster in front raised its head, its massive whiskers trembling in the air, its milky eyes not quite looking at them.

Bradan had an idea.

"I think they're blind," he whispered to the farmer. "Pretty sure they're using those whiskers of theirs to listen for us, follow the sounds. That's why I lost the ones that came after me in the forest."

At the sound of his voice, the monster before them plodded forward, confirming Bradan's suspicions. To their left, the beaver invading the farmhouse extracted itself from the ruins, grunting at its companion.

"Fascinatin'," the farmer said, his voice laced with sarcasm.

"Can't see how that makes any difference to us now."

Bradan bit his lip, sending a silent prayer to the Magpie Spirit. Then he turned around and took hold of the cat sheltered in the farmer's arms.

"Sorry, cat," Bradan muttered, not raising his eyes to the farmer's incredulous stare as Bradan hefted the cat over his head and threw it towards one of the monsters.

"Bessie!" the farmer howled, as if Bradan had thrown one of his daughters to the beavers instead.

As predicted, Bessie screeched like a thing possessed, a cacophony of fear and hatred echoing through the small clearing. She continued to yowl as she took off for the trees, a streak of brown dashing through the long grass.

Perfect bait for beasts that hunted by sound.

The beavers took off after the poor cat while Bradan helped the farmer hobble off in the other direction, aware the distraction would last only for seconds.

"You bastard," the farmer said through gritted teeth. Bradan was surprised to see a tear running down the man's weathered face. "You lyin' bastard."

Bradan knew guilt would come later. He valued a person's life far above that of a housecat, but he knew he would later feel ashamed of his actions.

Still, despite the sacrifice, despite the farmer's curses as Bradan hefted him towards the village, Bradan was elated.

He had saved this man. For the first time in his life, Bradan had gone against his father's wishes, and he had gotten to play the part of the hero.

His father was where he had left him: curled in a ball in the back of the cave, cloak wrapped around him like a blanket.

Bradan sighed. He should have suspected this.

"Father?" he said, moving forward slowly, cautious of

surprising the man. It was clearly not one of his father's good days, but Bradan still had to determine how bad things were. If his father was in a particularly poor state, it would not be safe for Bradan to stay the night. The closest village was within his reach before sundown, but whether or not anyone would admit him, especially after the events at the farmstead today, was another matter entirely.

"Son," came a dry rasp from the bundle in front of Bradan, like a whisper from a dream, fallen down the side of the bed after use, reluctant to be found and reused. "Son, how are you? Did you pass the day well?"

"Not particularly," Bradan ventured, unable to contain himself. "There was that beaver infestation I had to deal with. Without the help that was promised."

There was a pause, then the bundle before him sighed.

Slowly, as if aching, his father pulled himself upright, turning to face Bradan. The man looked terrible, even worse than normal. He had always kept his hair long and untended, and it ran down the pale skin of his face in black greasy lines, only the occasional streak of grey infecting it. His father's face itself was drawn, pulled tight across his cheekbones, which was not unusual, but the bags under his eyes were fuller and greyer than normal. The eyes themselves were books into his soul, volumes whose contents had been pulled apart and restitched in a careless fashion, producing a confusing mix of sorrow, self-pity and regret.

"That was today?" his father asked.

Bradan nodded, not trusting himself to speak. He knew he should not blame his father for getting like this, knew the man's... condition was the price of a sacrifice made for a very good reason. However, right now the sting of the farmer's angry words rang hot in Bradan's ears, and he knew his father would sense the frustration in his voice if he spoke aloud.

His father sighed again. He lifted himself to his full height, pulling his black, woollen cloak around him as if to ward off the cold, although Bradan knew the night-time drop in temperature would bring his father little discomfort. No; his father, the man a few people knew as Lonan Anvil, but who was more commonly referred to as the Magpie King, had more insidious ailments to worry about than a chill at bedtime.

Bradan's father made his way to the cave entrance, where he stood in the moonlight, looking out over the forest before them.

He would not look Bradan in the eyes except in exceptional circumstances. It made him feel uncomfortable to do so, a trait they both shared.

"Was anyone hurt?"

"No." Bradan answered straight away, hearing the concern in his father's voice. He did not want him to worry more than he needed to.

"But...?"

"We lost the farm, Father. The farmstead was destroyed, but the family got out in time."

"Good, good," his father said, nodding, absent. "All is well, then."

Bradan bit his lip at this. All was certainly not well. The farmer's livelihood was destroyed, and although their lives had been saved, it had been a close thing.

Bradan was also tempted to tell his father about his own exploits, about how he had stepped up to take his father's place when the farmer's life had been in danger, but he knew better than to mention that. Even when lucid, his father could be quick to anger, especially when disobeyed. On a bad day, Bradan knew even minor upsets could send his father hurtling back into the pit he had been wallowing in all day.

"And you?" Bradan hazarded, allowing himself a small probe into his father's routine. "What happened to you today?"

His father was silent, and Bradan leaned forward to get a glimpse of the man's face. Although his father's gaze was still fixed on the forest before him, he looked puzzled, distant.

He doesn't know, Bradan realised. *He's lost a day.*

This was a bad one.

"Father," he said, "I need you to try hard. Did you leave the cave today?"

His father creased his brow further, and grunted. Then his head whipped around to look at Bradan, and he bared his teeth at his son. His teeth, as they had always been, were filed to sharp points.

"I've done nothing wrong," he snapped, snarling as he spoke. "I would never hurt anyone. You know that."

Bradan involuntarily took a step back, lowering his gaze. He did not want to see the shame he knew would be flooding his father's face after speaking to his son like that. Sure enough, seconds later, his father had whirled around, stomping back into their cave.

I hope that's true, father, Bradan thought. *That you've done nothing wrong. Magpie Spirit help me, let him have stayed in the cave today.*

Bradan wandered in after his father, unslinging his bag from his back, bringing out the smoked fish he had been reluctantly given by the villagers after returning the farmer to safety. "A gift for the Magpie King," he said, trying to add some cheer to his voice, offering the gift to his father.

Lonan sighed, accepting the food. "Don't call me that. There's no royal blood in my veins. I'm just a man."

Bradan shrugged. "Not my words. Some old guy in Meldrum recognised me, gave me this. Think you might have gotten him out of a tough spot a while back. If him thinking you're the Magpie King keeps us in food, why would I argue?"

Lonan raised an eyebrow. "Doesn't make it true." He tore a chunk from the fish, passing most of it back to his son. It was unspoken amongst them both that Lonan preferred fresher food, and would hunt for himself later, but still took the time to sit with Bradan when they were together at meal times.

Bradan chewed at the meat, taking a cup of water offered to him. Now that his father seemed to have calmed, perhaps Bradan could tell him what had really happened today.

"Father, I'm glad you weren't needed today, but it was a close thing."

His father eyeballed him, still chewing. Lonan had probably sensed a change in his heartbeat, letting him know that whatever Bradan was about to say was important. Or at least that Bradan was nervous about broaching this subject.

"The farmer, he went back into his home just before the monsters attacked."

Lonan stopped chewing, looking at Bradan suspiciously. "It is fortunate, then, that he was still able to save himself when they attacked."

"Yes, well..." Bradan lowered his eyes, losing his nerve at the crucial moment. "I helped him out, a bit."

Suddenly he was knocked back to the cave floor, his father having leapt impossibly fast to grab him by the shoulders. One look in the older man's eyes told Bradan he had misjudged his father's mental state. He was angry. Very angry. His eyes seemed to bulge from his head, accusing Bradan with an unstable fury.

"You dare? I told you very clearly to never put yourself in danger."

"You also told me very clearly that you'd be there once I got the villagers far enough away from you. That didn't work out, did it? Idiot farmer gets himself into trouble, you didn't give me much choice."

"You don't have a choice. You were told. I told you. Under no circumstances were you to get close to them. That's my job."

"Something we both agree on, then," Bradan said, daring to look his father in the eyes once more, even though he was visibly shaking at the prospect of speaking back to him.

Lonan's eyes widened, then he sprang off Bradan, throwing himself to the back of the cave, not looking at his son.

Bradan picked himself up, sore, but also relieved he had dared to tell his father the truth.

"Father, I know I disobeyed you, but... Father, I did it. I saved his life, that farmer. He's alive tonight, because of me. It feels... Well, it feels amazing. This must be what it's like to be you, the Magpie K—"

"I am not the Magpie King," Lonan barked. "I told you, I'm just a man. A man who threw away his life to finish a job the Magpie King started."

He raised his head so Bradan caught a glimpse of it in the moonlight, and Bradan was shocked to see tears running down his father's face.

"I gave up a normal life, but the Magpie Spirit has given me one final blessing, and I'll be damned if I'll let the forest take that from me."

He turned to look at Bradan. "When I die, the power of the Magpie King will die with me, and the forest will be a safer place because of it. And I will know I've done all I can to make the world a safer place for my son to live in."

His father looked Bradan in the eye one last time, and Bradan felt that glance like a fist to the gut, so overwhelmed was he by the anger, love and fear he saw wrapped up in it.

"This was a mistake," his father said, making towards the cave opening. "We should not work together on these tasks anymore. I should have known you could not stay away from danger. You're too much like your father."

With that, Lonan took off into the night, leaping silently from the cave entrance. For a normal man, such a jump would have resulted in a tumble down the hillside, with the certainty of broken bones at the bottom. For Lonan, with the Magpie King's powers running through his blood, it was as if he took flight. He soared impossibly high into the night sky, briefly silhouetted against the moon, his ragged cloak billowing out to resemble a pair of black wings, before descending to the treetops far in the distance.

Bradan stood, alone, watching his father disappear into the dark.

How can I be too much like you? Bradan thought, frustration rushing to fill the gap his father had left beside him. *How can I ever be like you, when you've been given the gift to protect people, and I have not?*

TADITA
AND THE
ACORNS

A tale from the fireplaces of the Titonidae

Every Titonidae child knows the name Tadita. Unlike most Owlfolk children, who eventually grow into respectful members of our society, and develop useful Knacks such as blacksmithing, farming, or cooking, Tadita was possessed with an extreme wanderlust from a young age, and her father would spend most evenings roaming the White Woods searching for her, finding her in a new place every night, long after the moon had risen. Despite the worries she gave him, Tadita's father loved her very much, and encouraged her interests, asking questions about her travels and the new sights she had seen as he carried her back to their home, safe in the knowledge that the Pale Wardens would always protect them within the White Woods.

Because of her strangeness, Tadita always seemed to be alone. The other Titonidae would see her wandering along a cliff edge high above them, seemingly chatting to herself, always apart from the other children. "There she goes," they would say, "Crazy Tadita. Off on some wild adventure, all by herself."

As we know, however, Tadita was never alone. Her brother was with her, the one who had wrestled with her in the womb, the one who gave his life so that she could be born. Tadita quickly learned not to tell others that he spoke to her still, not even her parents, but knew he was always close to her. She would wander deep into the White Woods, well away from curious ears, to be able to talk freely with him.

As she grew, Tadita's wanderlust grew with her. Before her tenth birthday, she was the first of her family to leave the shadows of the Ohiyo Court. By the time she was fifteen, she had visited all the Courts of the Titonidae, and stories of her travels had already spread around all of her people as she gained the reputation of being a trusted messenger, a safe pair of hands for letters or packages to send to distant family members or business interests.

However, travelling the length and breadth of the White Woods was not enough for Tadita. She was entranced by the stories of those who visited the Courts from outside, from the neighbouring Leone and Muridae lands, from the dragon men to the north, or the exotic envoys from the distant City of Books who travelled the length and breadth of the world in search of stories. She sought out these visitors and devoured their tales, entranced by a wider world she had never dreamed existed, secretly marking each of their lands on a map inside her mind, promising herself and her brother that they would visit them one day. Visit those lands they did, as she eventually walked the world on paths heretofore unused, finally finding her way to the realm of fairies and never returning.

Before her legendary travels, however, before leaving her homeland for more distant locations, there was one place Tadita was excited to visit more than any other. The forest of the Magpie King.

It had been her father who told her the first tale of that dark place, not long after she had learned to walk. Tadita had been particularly naughty, travelling by herself down the road to the neighbour's stables, urged on by her brother's whispers, as he wanted to see his first horse. That night, after beating her, driven half mad by worry and panic, her father told her of the Magpie King who haunted the neighbouring woodlands.

"And if you wander off again," her father told her, "he will find you, and snatch you, and take you away. He will carry you off to his palace, high on a lonely mountain in the middle of his forest, and you will never see your homeland again."

Tadita could not sleep that night. Instead, aged only three, she had lain in her bed, staring at the night sky through a gap in the thatch overhead, whispering excitedly with her brother about what life would be like if she really was stolen away.

When she grew to womanhood, the promise of that adventure had stuck with her, had matured over time. And so, when her brother finally convinced her to leave home, to head out on her great travels, they both knew the Magpie King's forest would be the first place they would visit.

"Do not go," their father cried, clutching Tadita's hands tightly, as if he were considering forcing her back into their house and locking her into her room. "I love you so much, and could not stand it if anything happened to you. That forest is a dangerous place. You do not know what horrors it may hold for you."

Tadita's eye twinkled at his fear, but she said nothing, instead kissing him goodbye.

The second person to visit Tadita as she left the White Woods was the queen of Ohiyo Court. Tadita was surprised to see her and her Wardens waiting outside of her village, as they had never spoken before, this queen only recently coming into power. However, the Owl Queen had heard much about Tadita and her travels, and was proud to have such a curiosity in her kingdom.

"I urge you not to go, Lady Tadita," the queen said. "I have business in the distant Sand Kingdoms. Remain as servant of my Court, and I will send you there as my envoy. It will be a journey greater than any of the Titonidae in my service have ever taken, and I will see that you and your family are richly rewarded."

Tadita was tempted by the offer; she did love her father, and had always hoped to see the Sand Kingdoms at least once in her life. However, thoughts of the Magpie King's forest, of legends of Mother Web and clever Artemis, reminded her how close she was to achieving her greatest dream, and she declined.

As she walked away, leaving the white-haired queen standing puzzled on the side of the road, Tadita heard her brother give a whistle of relief.

"I almost thought you were going to agree," he said. "They'd have saddled us up with a group of Wardens, and we'd never have had the chance to talk to each other again."

In reply, Tadita just smiled, and began to hum a random tune, which her brother eventually joined in on once he had figured out where she was going with it.

At the edge of the White Woods, just where the pale bark of the trees darkened and knotted into those of the Magpie King's realm, Tadita came across one last figure. It was an old woman, dressed in a simple robe the details of which Tadita could not remember properly after they left her behind. Tadita did not know what was most curious about the woman – the fact that her brother was unable to see her, or the look of shock on the woman's face when Tadita waved to her as they approached.

"If you can see me, child," the woman said, in a voice so fragile it reminded Tadita of crumbling parchment, "then you must indeed be a friend to the forgotten parts of the forest."

Tadita smiled and nodded, ignoring her brother's increasingly panicked questions.

"Where do you go, child?" the old woman asked.

"Into the Magpie King's forest, goodwife," Tadita replied.

The old woman pursed her lips at this, as if tasting something sour. "I do not like that name," the woman said. "They called those woods something else, a long time ago, but I forget that name now…"

The woman's gaze drifted off, as if tracking something unseen and distant. Suddenly, her eyes snapped back to Tadita. "Tell me, why do you travel there?"

"For adventure," Tadita said without hesitating. "To see what others do not."

The woman nodded, seeming pleased with the response. "It is a dark place," she said, "and always has been. Much evil lurks under those trees. If you are to take such a journey, you must bring protection with you."

She offered Tadita her hand, holding three acorns.

"Take these, child. Remember them when the creatures of that forest come after you at night. This gift, along with your own wits, will save you in the end."

Tadita thanked the faded woman, took the gift, and continued on her way, striking up her tune anew as she stepped over the border of the White Woods.

"They're just normal acorns, you know," her brother said eventually, after Tadita had refused to talk about the woman any longer. "There's no magic at all about them. She was just a crazy old woman, handing you some nuts."

She knew her brother was telling the truth, but did not mind. Tadita felt secure with the faded woman's gift in her pocket as she began to explore the Magpie King's forest.

Tadita's explorations of those woods are well known amongst all Titonidae and Corvae. Many tales are told of her encounter with sly Artemis, the trickster of the woods, when he tried to steal away her virginity, but instead she tricked him into lying with a fox. More sinister were the tales in which she encountered many-legged Mother Web, or bargained with Wishpoosh's children for the silver eggs their chickens laid. Few know exactly what happened when

Tadita met with the Magpie King and his queen, but we do know she eventually left the King's palace in tears, and would speak to nobody about the two weeks she had spent with them.

It was after all of these events, when she had begun the return journey back to the White Woods, that Tadita had call to remember the faded woman's acorns.

It had grown late on a winter night, and Tadita had lit a small fire to keep herself warm. She had learned by now that it was not safe to be out after dark in the Magpie King's woods, but the only alternative would have been to knock on a door of a nearby village and beg for a room for the night, and Tadita had had her fill of Corvae hospitality. This one time, close to the forest border, she decided she would risk staying out with the stars.

Not long after sundown, they found her. She was alerted to their presence first by her brother, his gasp in her ear. She looked up, and saw the black figures in the trees around her. At first, the creatures perched on the branches looked like bats, hooding their heads behind leathery wings, although these things were closer to the size of dogs than any bats Tadita had seen before. However, when the nearest one unfurled its wings and raised its head, Tadita realised she was dealing with something completely different. The monster before her – and she had no doubt now that it was a true monster – had no flesh on its face. Instead, perched atop the giant bat body was a clean skull, glinting orange in the firelight. Around her, as if moving to some hidden cue, the other beasts unfurled their wings, exposing their naked skulls. From out of the grinning jaws of each of these skulls rolled a long, tendrilous black tongue, tasting the air around them.

"They're hungry," her brother whispered to her. "Whatever they are, they are hungry."

Looking at the saliva running from each of the monsters' mouths, Tadita could only nod in agreement.

It was then, just as she was accepting death as the only potential outcome, that Tadita's hand came across the acorns in her pocket.

Slowly, trying to startle the winged beasts as little as possible, Tadita lifted the acorns, and threw them onto the hot stones at the edge of her fire.

"What are you doing?" her brother whispered, but Tadita dared not answer him. Instead, she listened to the acorns sizzle as they cooked, smelled the roast nuttiness. The monsters could clearly smell the cooking nuts as well, leaning in closer to the roasting treats, their long tongues almost touching the forest floor.

Finally, Tadita took the hot nuts from the fire, the skin of her hand blistering as she did so, but she dared not react to the pain. Instead, one by one Tadita threw the nuts into the air, and one by one she caught them in her mouth, crunching on them and swallowing the food.

Around her, the beasts spread their wings and howled, jealous of the treat that had been enjoyed right in front of them.

"You fool," her brother hissed. "You could have distracted some of them with the food. Was it worth it to have one final mouthful before you become food yourself?"

Tadita clicked her tongue at him, but still said nothing.

As the beasts readied themselves to fly at her, she bent down to the fire again, as if collecting more acorns to eat. The beasts hesitated, intent on the possibility of more good food, certain this time that they would be the ones to enjoy it.

Tadita reached straight into the fire, and pulled forth a handful of red-hot stones. Despite the burning of her flesh, she did not scream. Instead, just like before, she opened her mouth, and threw the handful of stones into the air, ready to catch them when they descended.

The monsters got to the stones first. Screaming like children being stolen from their mothers, the bat-things swooped down, each of them swallowing one of the red-hot rocks.

Not one of those stones reached the forest floor. Instead, each of the monsters, a burning rock in their gullets, fell to the ground, screaming with agony.

Tadita saw her chance, and fled.

She never returned to the Magpie King's forest. With that adventure behind her, Tadita and her ghost brother went on to achieve great things, paving the way for the Titonidae people to prosper, to make connections with foreign powers, and to become a force to be reckoned with in the world.

However, before her eventual disappearance, Tadita would always shudder when people asked her to speak about her first journey, her journey into the Magpie King's woods.

"There are some places in the world," she would say, "where people should not travel. I have been into that dark forest, and have escaped with my life. Nothing in this world, no promise of treasure nor adventure, could get me to walk under those branches again."

CHAPTER TWO

The White Woods were quiet that morning. Yesterday's mist persisted, but today it was only a gossamer blanket of white, a decorative cloth draped over the land surrounding the Court.

The new queen's land.

Nascha wandered through the woods, all the while staying within sight of the Court, still struggling to process yesterday's events. Laurentina was now queen. The young monarch, closer to being a little girl than a woman fully grown, had only yesterday demanded that a priestess of the Owl Spirit drop all she was doing and fetch her a cup of water. Now Laurentina was in command of all their fortunes. Worse than that, for some reason the man Laurentina was now closest to – the insidious opportunist Lord Bidzell – had Nascha marked for death.

Nascha chewed her lip, bending to pick over another likely piece of kindling, one that had fallen close to one of the forgotten idols that littered the forest. Nascha wrinkled her nose at the shit-stained lump of wood, a lump that was said to resemble a person, if looked at in the correct light. Only three such idols existed within the distance Nascha was allowed to travel from the Court, and she had never been able to find the person within any of them. Indeed, the only reason Nascha was able to identify the idols at all was by the attention the owls of the woods seemed to pay to them, defecating on them seemingly constantly between dusk and dawn. The owls also appeared to drop sticks on the forgotten idols, making them good places to gather firewood, albeit providing an unpleasant experience for the gatherer.

Laurentina would never harm me, Nascha said to herself, repeating the phrase that had kept her awake all night. With Bidzell in the royal chambers with Laurentina – alone, it had seemed, making the whole experience highly inappropriate – Nascha had not dared to approach the princess. The queen.

Today, perhaps, the opportunity might arise for Nascha to have a word with Laurentina, to assure herself that everything was all right.

Finding another stick – her last, Nascha decided – her eyes rose to contemplate the forest around her. The Owl Queen's Court was set high above the White Woods, on a plateau that erupted from the centre of the queen's realm, and from where Nascha now stood the woodland took a sharp dip, affording her a glimpse of the southern half of the Titonidae lands.

On the horizon, clearer than it had been in the thicker fog yesterday, the dark trees of the Magpie King's forest marred the view, summoning within Nascha the deep-rooted dread that had been bred into all Owlfolk children.

That way lay danger.

Nascha turned, this time to glimpse the thin spires of the Court behind her. Her home, the place where only last night a man of power suggested putting her to death.

For a few brief moments, Nascha contemplated running, making for the Magpie King's trees. She knew no Titonidae would dare enter that place to follow a simple servant. Nascha had contemplated running many times as a younger captive of the Court. She had planned her courses of action, stockpiled resources to help her find her way back to her family, or to some distant land where she could be free again. Every time, she had backed down at the last minute, squandering her plots, abandoning her secreted packs of food. The Court worked such aggressive rebellion out of her eventually, but Nascha could clearly remember the burn of shame at knowing her own fear was all that stood between her and freedom.

She felt the same burning in her cheeks today. Tadita felt no fear when she ventured into the Magpie King's realm. Why, then, would Nascha rather risk death at the hands of her own friend than flee beneath those murky boughs?

Because Tadita was a hero, a character in a story.

And I scrub kitchen floors.

Nascha took one last look at the dark forest looming on the horizon, suppressing a shudder. She knew she would never have the strength in her to walk beyond that border.

Nearby, a branch cracked.

She scanned the treeline, looking for the source of the noise. It could be anything, of course, any woodland animal that graced the White Woods – deer, rabbit, squirrel. It could even have been the trees themselves, moved by a small wind. Nascha knew the Court's plateau was well patrolled by the Pale Wardens, and that the chance of encountering any predators or intruders was rare. Despite this assurance, Nascha's gut stirred at the sound. Something inside tugged at her, warning her this noise was not random, warning her that fate was walking through the woods that morning.

Another crack, and Nascha fancied she caught a glimpse of movement just beyond the trees to her left.

"Who's there?"

Despite how certain she was that something unusual was occurring, Nascha was surprised to find she was not scared. It was not that she did not feel fear; that familiar sensation was right now brushing up her back, its light fingers stroking her skin as it crawled to the top of her neck. However, Nascha found she was able to ignore that feeling of dread, to suppress it, spurred on perhaps by her curiosity, perhaps by thoughts of Tadita the explorer, or perhaps just by the knowledge that in spite of this unknown force, she would have to return to the Court, where she might very well be marked for death anyway.

Before her, the branches parted, and a man emerged. He was unlike any man Nascha had ever seen. Whereas the men of the Court, from the nobles down to the lowly servants, were impeccably groomed, as was befitting those living and working with the queen, this man was rough, the stubble of his beard a few days old at least, the edges of his knee-length jacket worn and frayed. He was older than Nascha, that much was clear, but she found it difficult to tell exactly what age he was. His unruly auburn hair was streaked with grey, matching his stubble, and his face held many lines of age, but his eyes... his eyes held a vitality Nascha envied. The stranger locked eyes with her the instant he stepped from behind the trees, his hungry gaze paired with a sly grin, the points of his eye teeth catching the morning sunlight.

"Well, what do we have here?" he said, his voice holding within it a playfulness. Nascha could not decide if it was charming or dangerous.

It was then that she noticed the man's tail, the bushy fur of which matched his own red hair, the tip of which was a grey white.

"You're one of the Vulpe," Nascha said, annoyed with herself for gasping at that realisation. "One of the Foxfolk."

The man gave a grunt of satisfaction, and his grin grew a bit wider, if such a thing was possible.

At the sight of that smile, Nascha felt something akin to a physical force inside her, pulling her towards the man. Something just below her gut, deeper than she was comfortable with, was tugging her to him. Feeling heat rise to her cheeks, not in any way expecting to feel this kind of reaction towards a scruffy stranger, Nascha had to work hard to stop herself from walking towards him.

"Oh, I know what I am, little bird," he said, stepping fully into the clearing. He was moving forward carefully, as if approaching a wild animal, wanting to see how close he could get before it bolted. "I know what I am. But what are you? I took a trip into the White Woods to take a peek at some of the Owl Queen's treasures, but I had not expected to find a jewel so precious."

She raised an eyebrow at the compliment, unimpressed. Nascha had spent plenty of time among noblemen who thought they were a gift to women, and she knew just how little such a compliment cost to give. What she was finding more difficult to deal with, however, was the primal pull taking place within her, as if a hidden force was trying to forge a connection between her and the fox man.

"How'd you get up here?" she said, trying to sound as accusing as possible. "The plateau's perimeter is guarded. No way they'd have let you in without an escort."

The Vulpe's smile became lopsided, and he rolled his eyes lazily, gesticulating absentmindedly with his long fingers. "Oh, you know. I have my ways if I want to move unseen, little bird."

Nascha's heart surprised her by skipping a beat at the words 'little bird'. She was irritated to admit she was attracted to this man, physically attracted. She was not one to lose control like this, unlike so many of the other servant girls. Nascha was not a maiden, of course. Life at Court held many temptations, and she had only gone so long listening to the other serving girls talking about their own explorations before Nascha had decided to pursue lovemaking herself, but so far her experiences had been curious at best, and had left no lasting impression on her. Her draw to this man was different. It was unlike her, and it felt wrong.

"Well," she said, trying to compose herself, "you'd better get out of here quick, then. The queen's Wardens won't take kindly to being fooled, and they never go far from me when I'm allowed to roam outside the Court's walls."

It was a lie. The Wardens could well be close, or not. They cared very little for her, assuming she would never dare leave the boundary of the plateau, where she would be stopped by the plateau guard anyway.

The Vulpe raised an eyebrow at her, stepping forward once again. Three more steps, and she would be able to reach out and touch him.

Her body tingled at the thought of it.

"Allowed? Why would they have to allow you to leave, little bird? What little treasure have I stumbled upon?"

He bit his lip, contemplating her, and she could not help but exhale deeply at the sight of his canine digging into his own flesh.

She raised her head, trying to ape the confidence with which she knew Laurentina would face a stranger such as this. If the Vulpe thought he was faced with royalty, or someone otherwise important, Nascha would damn well give him the best show she could.

"And who are you, to be addressing me so?" she ventured, summoning as much haughtiness as she was able.

The man hesitated at her change of tone, but did not retreat. Instead, he smiled again, and gave a little half bow. "Vippon Vasilescu, at your service… m'lady," he said, eyes meeting with hers again as he raised from his bow. "My troupe and I have been travelling westward, heading for the Magpie's forest, but we heard tell of a coronation in the White Woods."

Nascha nodded. "Yes. The Owl Queen is dead, and tomorrow her daughter takes the throne. What business is that of yours?"

He chuckled. "Oh, you know, just a bit of healthy curiosity. Curiosity, and a possibility of employment. My people are entertainers by nature, and my troupe is no different. When the Vulpe hear of a party, we head towards it, hoping to ply our trade."

Nascha knew this to be true. On three separate occasions, she recalled when other Vulpe troupes had made their way to Court, and their arrival had always been viewed with nervous anticipation. The Vulpe were as well known for their entrancing performances as they were for their trickiness and deceitfulness. Still, she did not recall any of those previous performers having an actual fox's tail.

She glanced at the man's face and was taken aback by how serious he looked now, how deeply he was contemplating her.

When he spoke again, his voice was low, all previous charm gone. "My lady, tell me true – are you a witch?"

Nascha stood rigid, shocked by the accusation. What was going on? The gravity with which he now looked at her warned Nascha there was real danger here. Should she pretend she was a woman of power, and have him attack her out of fear, or admit she was a simple servant girl alone in the woods, and let him take advantage of her inability to protect herself?

Slowly, carefully, never breaking eye contact with the stranger, Vippon, Nascha spoke. "Why would you ask me something like that?"

His eyes narrowed. "Something has drawn me here, away from my troupe. I think it might have been you."

Nascha felt the tug towards this stranger again, and realised the pull was not in her imagination. It was not just a natural reaction to finding herself attracted to this stranger. There was something else going on here, drawing her towards this man. He was feeling it too.

And he thought she was doing this to him.

Nascha could not help but smile at the thought, smile that someone felt that she, the bird in the cage, had some kind of power over him.

Vippon stepped back at the sight of her teeth, his turn to be unsure.

"I assure you, Mister Vasilescu," Nascha continued, not letting the smile fade, "if I indeed had the power of witchcraft, I would use it for purposes other than to draw someone like yourself to me. Furthermore, and please remember this advice if you plan to grace the Owl Queen's Court with your presence, it is not seen as particularly good manners to accuse a lady of witchery if you wish to gain her favour."

Vippon nodded, his grin returning, but he did not approach her further. "Well then, my good lady, I have erred. Because I would indeed value your favour."

The invisible bond tugged at Nascha again, but she resisted it, instead smiling slyly at the Vulpe. She nodded with her head towards the Court's spires.

"The coronation is tomorrow, as I said. I'm sure if you speak nicely to the plateau guard, they will give you entrance." The Vulpe were rarely denied. It was not worth drawing their ire by doing so.

Vippon bowed again, backing away from her, retreating into the greenery surrounding the clearing. "We will do so. Will I have the pleasure of seeing you there, my lady?"

Nascha did not answer. The Vulpe withdrew, and her smile slowly faded as she felt the invisible bond with the man dissipate, all sense of power, of control, leaving her.

She would be at the coronation, yes, but Vippon would be surprised if he expected to find her in a lady's fine clothing.

Laurentina's coronation was a grand affair. It was the first time Nascha had seen the princess – now the queen – since word had reached them of her mother's death. Nascha had not been invited to the actual ceremony, but in a gathering this large, it was her duty to wait on some of the lower tables of the banquet hall.

The high tables were reserved for the royal family themselves, all of whom Nascha recognised. Lord Bidzell was also there. As a nobleman but not a direct member of the royal family, he seemed out of place sitting at the young queen's right hand. Other Titonidae nobility had travelled from the other Courts of the White Woods, and a handful of dignitaries from neighbouring powers were also present. The Leone, the Lionfolk, had sent a warrior woman as their ambassador, a shaven-haired giant clad in polished armour who towered over the Pale Wardens positioned throughout the banquet hall. The Mousefolk had also sent a grey-hooded monk, who must have ridden day and night to travel the distance from the Mouse Queen's palace to arrive in time. Others Nascha did not recognise, including a short, pale-skinned man in what looked to Nascha like a jade dress, embroidered with a repeating pattern of golden books.

None, however, outshone Queen Laurentina. She sat at the head of the table, clothed in a dress of white lace, a headdress of barn owl feathers fanning out behind her, framing her black curls and porcelain face. Nascha had been surprised, perhaps even a little demoralised, at how it had only taken a few days for the fifteen-year-old girl she knew to seemingly disappear completely, looking now the perfect image of a soulless monarch. Her bond with Laurentina had been the only thing Nascha trusted to prevent Lord Bidzell from having his way with Nascha and the other bastards of the Court. Looking at Laurentina now, all thoughts of that bond disappeared. The girl's face was rigid, impassionate. Worst of all, she was constantly looking to Bidzell for confirmation.

Nothing had happened since Nascha overheard their conversation about culling the bastards, but she was determined to speak to the queen as soon as possible, at the very least so she could sleep better at night.

Vippon was there too. His tale about travelling with his troupe had been true, despite Nascha's doubts, and he had indeed approached the Court to give a performance. And so, as Nascha poured watered-down wine for the lower nobility, she had the privilege of watching the actors perform their play, the Fall of the Magpie King.

Vippon himself took on the titular role, his bushy tail popping out from behind the cloak of black feathers he wore around his shoulders, his long, beaked paper mask jutting outward, mimicking the helm of the Magpie King from the stories. It was a popular tale within the Court, although Nascha had never seen it acted before, only heard it being told. It was a complex tale of the final Magpie King, an evil man eventually unmasked as a false heir all along, the true king having been banished to the life of a drunk old man. Eventually, a common villager stole the Magpie King's power for himself, defeating the tyrant in single combat, freeing the forest from his thrall, and forever breaking the hold the Magpie King had on the surrounding lands.

Vippon played the role for laughs. He kept knocking over the scenery, and the other actors, with his long beak and his own tail. When the young villager – played tonight by a dark-haired female, her half-unbuttoned villager's smock drawing the full attention of most of the males present – finally defeated the Magpie King, Vippon howled like a mad dog as his mask split apart, running around the throne room, pulling red streamers from within his mask and throwing them over the crowd.

It was a popular tale with the Titonidae. The Magpiefolk had always had a hold over them, and their king had always demanded the most beautiful white-haired noble females to join him as his queen. Nascha was not sure if the Magpie King had ever really existed, but even if he had, she was thankful his reign was now over, and that the Corvae had been laid low. Laurentina, with her raven-coloured locks, would never have been offered up as tribute to that dark forest, but Nascha's natural hair may have been of interest. Perhaps, if there had still been a Magpie King to appease, then Nascha's presence at Court would have become useful.

At the second round of applause from the assembled nobles, Nascha noticed movement at the high table. Queen Laurentina, seemingly unimpressed by the performance, was withdrawing, accompanied by two of her Wardens. Lord Bidzell, who up until now had been her constant shadow, remained on his feet, applauding the Vulpe.

Hastily, Nascha made her way around the table she was serving at, filling cups to the brim whether more wine was asked for or not, anxious to empty her jug and seek an audience with Laurentina before Lord Bidzell could regain her side.

She hurried from her table, slinking around the walls of the hall, making for the passageway Laurentina had exited into. She had almost made it out of the room before she felt a familiar, invisible tug, yanking her head around to face the performers in the centre of the hall. Vippon was staring right at her, broken magpie helm held in his hands, a brief look of confusion on his face as he regarded her, clearly shocked to find her in servant's garb.

Not letting herself feel the embarrassment that threatened to rise because of how he looked at her, Nascha instead cocked an eyebrow and bowed to the Vulpe, aping the final movement he had given her earlier in the woods. When she rose, the Vulpe was smiling again, and licked his lips as he regarded her, his earlier hunger returning. Nascha felt fear then, in the way he looked at her, like a hunting dog staring at a fawn across a forest meadow. More than that, to her great confusion she felt a secret thrill, knowing what he would expect to claim if he caught her. She did not trust herself enough to resist his advances, if he made any. Perhaps the wine tonight was not as watered down as the other servants thought.

Breaking contact, shaking her head to rid it of the older man, Nascha turned and ran after Laurentina.

"Your Grace," she shouted, upon sight of the white cloaks of the Pale Wardens that shadowed their new monarch. "Your Grace, a moment of your time, please."

The closest Warden turned and readied her spear, standing between Nascha and the young queen, but not before Laurentina was able to catch a glimpse of her pursuer.

"Let her pass," Nascha heard the queen command, and the Warden did so without debate.

For a fraction of a second, Nascha felt overwhelmed by the woman standing before her. The Owl Queen, her face stoic, her painted features less than human, was more imposing than the mock Magpie King that pranced around in the banquet hall. However, Laurentina was only able to hold that regal posture for a heartbeat. From behind the crumbling facade of the Owl Queen, the familiar face of a fifteen-year-old girl emerged, tears springing from her eyes as she leapt forward to embrace Nascha.

"Oh, Nascha," Laurentina exclaimed, hugging the servant girl as she never had when she was only a princess. "Nascha."

Relief. Nascha was overcome with relief. Cradling the queen like this was like exhaling after two days of holding her breath.

This girl will never hurt me, she told herself, feeling the child sobbing into her shoulder. *I am safe.*

"Get your hands off the queen."

The command came from behind Nascha, and the hairs on the back of her neck stood on end as Lord Bidzell entered the passageway.

Nascha, still clutching Laurentina close, very aware of the Wardens levelling their weapons at her, turned to look at Lord Bidzell, draped in his white finery, standing behind her.

It was, however, the queen who spoke first. "What is the meaning of this, Lord Bidzell?" Laurentina said, the grace of her regal voice ruined by the sniffing that accompanied it. "Is it inappropriate for your queen to seek out her only friend in the Court?"

Lord Bidzell, completely ignoring Nascha, his eyes fixed only on Laurentina, lowered his voice, smiling kindly at the young girl. "Your Grace," he said, stepping towards her, hand outstretched, "we have spoken about her before. You have already come to a decision. A decision you agreed was for the best."

Nascha's stomach flipped.

A decision.

Laurentina's grip around Nascha's waist tightened, the girl's small fingers feeling like cat claws digging into her flesh.

Nascha pulled herself back from Laurentina, to look into the girl's eyes. The queen's perfect makeup had been ruined by her tears, and by rubbing herself on Nascha's servant smock. She now looked like a practice doll, a figurine ruined as an apprentice painter took their first steps to learn their craft.

"My queen?" Nascha asked, face creased, throat dry.

The haunted look in the new queen's eyes did not help the churning in Nascha's stomach.

"Laurentina?" Nascha whispered, just before rough hands grabbed her from behind.

"I told you to get your hands off her," Lord Bidzell said as he threw Nascha to the stone floor.

Her lip split as her face hit the ground, and she turned to look at them all, shocked, helpless, a dangerous anger growing in her belly.

"But what have I done?" was all Nascha could ask, her eyes moving between those of Lord Bidzell, Laurentina, even the two Wardens.

Only the queen's face returned any emotion, Laurentina looking every part the wide-eyed, lost young girl that had come sobbing to Nascha in the corridor only moments ago.

Then Lord Bidzell stepped up to Laurentina, took her hand in his own, and squeezed it gently. The queen raised her head to look into the older man's face, and he returned her gaze with a nod, the barest hint of an encouraging smile. In a heartbeat, the facade Laurentina had worn in the banquet hall returned, the young girl disappearing once again, replaced with the cold, impassive face of the Owl Queen.

Laurentina almost looked at Nascha then. Nascha could see it, the small movement of the queen's head, the monarch's eyes moving across the floor, seconds from connecting with Nascha's. Then, clearly having second thoughts about doing so, she looked back to Lord Bidzell, and nodded. Saying nothing more, Queen Laurentina turned and walked away, still flanked by her Wardens, ignoring the wounded serving girl whose clothing the queen had left half her face on.

Lord Bidzell motioned back to the banquet hall, where more Court guards were watching the encounter.

"Take this one away," Bidzell ordered, pointing at Nascha, issuing the instruction as if telling them to pick up a scrap of meat abandoned on a kitchen floor. "Lock her in the Wisdom Tower. The queen has declared her to be put to death in the morning."

"What?" Nascha shouted, eyes wide, incredulous. "She never said that."

The Wardens grabbed her under the armpits, hauling her to her feet. "She never said that," she told them again, weakly, aware they would not listen to her. At that moment, despite the fear, the horror, of what was happening, a small, distant part of Nascha was proud of the fact she was not crying.

Finally, Lord Bidzell looked directly at her, and unfurled a piece of parchment he had kept within his pocket. "She signed the decree last night. All known bastard offspring of the royal line are to be removed immediately, to prevent a possible uprising, for the good of the Titonidae people."

"But," Nascha said, quiet, her voice low, her eyes fixed on Lord Bidzell, "I'm just a serving girl. Spirit's blood, my Knack is for scrubbing floors. What kind of threat could I pose to Laurentina?"

"I don't expect you to understand. The queen takes no pleasure in this, I assure you, but there are already whispers of dissent, word spreading that she is not fit to serve, people looking for alternatives to the crown." Lord Bidzell stepped towards her, lowering his voice so that only Nascha and the Wardens would be able to hear.

"And if those people knew that a bastard existed who carried a portion of the Owl Spirit's power within her, a bastard with pure white hair, a mark of blessing that our Queen Laurentina has not been given? Well, you can imagine what a gift you would be for those who oppose the throne."

Lord Bidzell looked beyond Nascha and the Wardens, back to the banquet hall.

"You must understand, this is nothing personal. But such measures must be taken."

With that, the nobleman walked off, leaving Nascha's mind numb as she was led off to her cell.

She should have been flattered. Her last night of life, and Nascha had been given a room to herself.

The accommodation was hardly luxurious, but neither was it as bad as the dank prison cells she heard villains thrown into at the end of stories. The bed she had been given was passable, at least as comfortable as those found in the servant quarters. This was, however, the first night of Nascha's life she could remember being alone, truly alone, as she slept. Normally there would be a chorus of other serving girls snoring gently, or muttering in their dreams. On the small handful of times Nascha had taken a lover, her partner had always been a visitor to the Court, a servant to visiting nobility, and the encounter invariably ended with them both creeping back to their own rooms, never to meet again. However, there would be no lover coming to her tonight, to whisk her away from her impending execution. The solid wooden door of her cell, with the equally solid bar thrown across it on the other side, would see to that.

As was to be expected, Nascha could not sleep. It was not, however, tomorrow's execution that kept her awake. Nascha's mind would not contemplate that event yet, would not allow her to treat it as real. A small, remote part of her admitted that the arrival of morning would probably plunge her into hysterics, but sunrise seemed so far away right now. Instead, that locked cell door was all that occupied her mind. She sat upright in bed, staring at it, the moonlight from the window behind her painting it an eerie blue.

She had been a prisoner all her life, ever since they had taken her from her mother. When walking the Court passageways, cleaning as she went, she had been under observation from

Wardens and priestesses. Even with the relative freedom of the nearby woods, Nascha had always been aware there was only so far she would be allowed to roam before she was chastised and returned to the cell of her life as a servant. She had allowed herself to accept those chains, as the leash had been long, and she could ignore it if she contented herself with everything it allowed her access to.

But that door. That door cut her off from the world. Right now, in the middle of the night, as the queen's coronation continued many floors below, Nascha convinced herself she could accept that she only had hours left to live, if she were actually allowed to live them, to fulfil so many of those small dreams she had for the future, so many first experiences she had put off, savouring the anticipation, worried that the actual events would dull in comparison.

"I appreciate a session of 'find me, catch me' as well as anyone, little bird, but I will admit, I struggle to think of any I've known who've taken the game to the lengths you have."

Nascha gasped, turning to the silhouetted figure perched on the window ledge, knowing his identity immediately as much from the invisible tug she felt as from the way Vippon addressed her.

So many emotions surged through her as she stared at him, her hand raised to her throat, jaw open. She knew immediately she was saved. The tide of sentiments, those thoughts she had not allowed herself to have, strained against her defences. They threatened to overwhelm her, turn her into a quivering wreck, make her burst into tears and beg Vippon inconsolably to save her life.

Instead, after a few frozen moments, she righted herself, pulled her bed sheet up to cover herself some more, and simply replied, "I guess you've never played it properly, then."

She would not allow herself to be moved to tears in front of this man.

Chuckling, Vippon jumped down from the window, landing in a crouch at the foot of her bed. That alien sensation within Nascha thrilled at the sight of him doing so, realising how long it had been since she had been alone with a man at night. A man she was clearly, inexplicably attracted to. Vippon's fox tail twitched behind him, like a cat's when ready to pounce.

"If I did not know any better," Vippon continued, "I would say you are in danger for your life, little bird."

"Looks like you do have some sense about you, then. They plan to put me to death at dawn, so the rumour goes."

The Vulpe paused for only a moment to contemplate this before sitting on her bed, his hand resting on her foot, still under the covers. She shivered at his touch, separated as it was by the bedclothes.

"I can take you away, if you want. Get you to safety."

She raised an eyebrow. "I had assumed that was the point of all of this," she said, indicating the window he had entered.

Vippon chuckled, looking at the exit, his hand scratching the back of his head. "I'll admit, curiosity drove me more than anything. That and desire, of course."

"Of course," she said as matter-of-factly as she was able, praying silently to the Owl Spirit that Vippon could not see her blush.

"So tell me," the fox man said, leaning closer, his hand sliding up from Nascha's foot to rest lightly on her thigh, "why would they go to the bother of locking a serving girl away like this? Why would you be such a threat to them?" There was a hunger in the man's eyes now, and not just because of the intimate position he had arranged for himself.

Nascha sighed, shifting under the covers, her hand rising to her hair, trying to run her fingers through it, but failing. The dye she had coated it in yesterday left the strands sticky and unworkable.

"It's my hair, I'm afraid. They take exception to my hair."

Vippon cocked his head, his hand remaining on her leg. "Your hair. You will forgive me, little bird, but I cannot believe that. Your hair is one of the least exceptional things about you."

Nascha pouted, shifting on the bed, moving her leg away from Vippon's grasp. "You haven't seen it at its best. They force me to keep it this way."

She considered changing the subject, accustomed to drawing attention away from her natural hair colour. However, nothing she could say at the moment could get her into a worse situation than the one Vippon was rescuing her from. Also – and later Nascha would force herself to admit this was the main influence over what she did next – she did not like Vippon's comments about her looks.

"My hair is normally white, you see. They make me change it."

Vippon, already in close proximity to her, leapt upon the bed, his hands finding her shoulders, his feet placed on either side of her waist.

Nascha felt light-headed, overcome just as much by the intensity of his grip as she was by the strong tug on that invisible link between them.

"You've been blessed by the Owl Spirit."

It was not a question. Nascha looked into his eyes, took a firm grip of their bond, and pulled him closer toward her, so their noses were almost touching.

"Since I was a little girl," she whispered, exhaling as she did so, allowing her lips to curl slightly at either end.

He raised his fingers to her hair, running them through it. She did not mind the tugs, she was too busy losing herself in Vippon's eyes. Nascha had never had anyone look at her with so much... wonder before. It was intoxicating.

"Come with me," Vippon said, his gaze not leaving her hair, his fingers working through it to caress her scalp. "Be mine, and I will take you from this place. I will treat you like the queen you were born to be."

Both of them grabbed at their link at the same time, pulling their lips together, Vippon kissing her roughly, scratching at her face with his stubble as he stole her breath.

"I was wondering when you'd get around to asking," she said as he withdrew.

She pulled aside her bedsheets, wrapping her legs around him to pull him close as his hands worked their way up her thighs and under her shift. She gasped as his fingers found her, and she drew him towards her with an urgency that suggested she still only had hours left to live.

They would not come for her until sunrise, and there was plenty of moonlight to enjoy before then.

"Don't make me tell you again, Knackless — stay out of Meldrum."

The head of the village did not exactly wave his pitchfork at Bradan, but he may as well have, especially with a good handful of burly farmhands standing behind him, almost growling at Bradan as the older man spoke.

"So," Bradan continued, suppressing the urge to start edging backwards from the not-quite mob that had quickly gathered after he had trotted into town less than half an hour ago. "So, you're saying you're not going to give me any food? You're not going to honour the tradition of helping a traveller in need?" He lifted his head to force himself to look the elder in the eyes as he spoke, but upon making eye contact Bradan instantly looked to the ground instead, silently cursing himself for a weak fool as he did so. He was never good with people, especially not in heated situations like this. Funny, because since he began travelling with his father, Bradan had had plenty of practice.

One of the mob members actually spat at Bradan's feet.

The village head looked disapprovingly at the spit, but the act did not change the man's mind. "We fed you yesterday already. It only takes so long before a traveller becomes a squatter. Best you don't show your face around here anymore, Knackless."

Bradan did start to back away then, but did his best to keep his fear from his steps and his voice. "Only reason we came here was to save your people from the monsters."

"Aye, and look how that turned out." Bradan jumped at the voice, despite himself. It belonged to the farmer he had saved yesterday. The man's face was a mess of purple, and his right arm was bound and supported by a sling. The farmer looked at Bradan with eyes that reminded Bradan distinctly of how that cat had looked at him just before he threw it.

"I saved your life," Bradan said, knowing from experience these people would not back down, not even when confronted with unbending reason. Despite that knowledge, Bradan was unable to help the frustration their words brought to boil within him.

"You promised to save my farm. It's ruined now. We'll never be able to rebuild it. What am I supposed to do?"

Bradan shrugged. "I don't know. Isn't it a good thing you've got options, though? Much better options than becoming beaver food, I reckon."

"You reckon you're such a big deal, don't ya? All because of who your father is. Reckon we won't touch you because of him?"

"What, because he's the Magpie King?"

This time it was the elder's turn to spit, and Bradan was surprised by the look of disgust the old man gave.

"He meant a monster," the elder said. "You reckon we're scared of your father because he's a monster."

Bradan paused, mouth hanging open, as if he had just been slapped. He quickly recovered, the realisation that the mob was leaning towards him spurring him into action. He needed to get out of there quickly.

"Well, you are, aren't you?" he said, forcing himself to hold the elder's eye. "Scared of us?"

The villagers grew rigid, and glanced to the trees in the distance, beyond the village wheat fields, as if suddenly aware of how close those dark branches were.

Bradan turned and walked away from the village of Meldrum, before anyone could conceive another flimsy retort. It would come, Bradan knew. This was not the first time he and his father had been treated like this by the villages. It tended to be Bradan who bore the brunt of their bile, with Lonan rarely showing his face in public, much less during daylight hours, but today's rebuke stung more than normal. Ordinarily, it had been his father whose work was going unappreciated. Lonan had not showed up yesterday. It had been Bradan's turn to play the hero, finally, and still he was being run out of the village.

He was halfway through the wheat fields surrounding Meldrum before someone caught up with him. Bradan was not surprised he had been followed. As often as he was run out of a settlement, this moment would occur just as frequently.

"Here, boy, here." It was an older lady, well past her sixtieth year, at least. Her long white hair flowing behind her as she ran reminded Bradan briefly of Mother Ogma, the old healer who had raised him when he was younger, but she had long since passed to the realm of the Magpie Spirit. This woman, her voice low despite the fact that nobody else was nearby, pressed a small basket into Bradan's arms.

The smell of fresh bread from within made his mouth water, but instead he gave the woman a smile of thanks. "Thank you, goodwife. I take it you know my father?"

The villager smiled, head shaking vigorously as she backed away from him, towards the village. "Not me. My daughter. She almost stumbled into Mother Web's nest when she was younger, little idiot. Your father... We all know he's the only reason she survived that night. Passed away last spring, Spirit bless her, giving birth, but if it weren't for your pa, I'd have had ten more years of heartbreak under my belt, and no grandson to ease the pain."

She raised her head, realised she was babbling, then turned and ran back to Meldrum. Bradan smiled, continuing on down the path, inspecting the basket's contents. Bread and salted meat; nothing fancy, but enough to feed him for the next few days. Bradan knew his father would not be interested in this stuff. He found his own food. Anything they were given by the villages was always Bradan's.

Taking a bite of a loaf, Bradan eventually exited the fields, plunging back into the covering of the trees. He chewed, sighing, trying not to let the villagers get him down.

Father must feel like this all the time, he thought. *All the good he does for them, for the whole forest, and they still call him a monster. All I did was save the life of a man too stupid to run away when evil came knocking, and their attitude still bugs me.*

Taking another bite, Bradan thought further about his father, realising he was wrong. His father probably did not care at all what the Corvae people thought of him. For all Bradan knew, his father thought as little of them as they did of him. His mind... his mind did not work the same way as other people's. It could not. It had been poisoned decades ago. He had given it up in sacrifice, taken poison into his blood, accepted the gift of the Magpie Spirit to save the forest, to dethrone a mad king, even though he had known the process would drive him mad.

Bradan's father had abilities well beyond those of a normal man. He had the strength of... well, Bradan had never seen a bear before – as far as he knew, those creatures existed only in stories – but from what Bradan could gather his father had the strength of ten of them. More than that, probably; depending on which stories you listened to, sometimes bears were the height of a man or the height of a house. Funny things, stories, Mother Ogma used to say. They'll tell you two completely different versions of the same fact, and more often than not they'll both be right in some way. Bradan smiled at the thought of the woman who raised him, and kept the smile on his face, fighting against the sadness the memory of her passing threatened to bring with it.

He picked up a stone at the side of the path and threw it into the forest to his right. Bradan could get a decent distance on a throw like that. Could even cause some harm, if he were close enough to someone when throwing. Give them a bump on the head they would still feel in the morning.

His father, however... a stone throw from him would be like an arrow shot. The projectile would penetrate flesh and wood, and would crack boulders. His father had the strength to leap through the air over huge distances, to almost appear as if he were flying, and could land safely after jumping to such heights. He was fast, so quick even Bradan had difficulty spotting his movements when he was in action. More than that, Bradan's father seemed to have some kind of connection to the forest, seemed to be aware of what was happening in it. He would talk about a new seed taking root two villages away, just as often as he would sense the monsters of the forest getting ready to threaten nearby settlements. For all intents and purposes, Lonan was the Magpie King.

Except he was not. Not really. The Magpie Kings of the forest had been a line of rulers who had existed for countless generations. They had been blessed by the Magpie Spirit; they were a royal line whose blood had grown resistant to the harmful effects of the Magpie Spirit's gift. Lonan had stolen that gift, had stolen the black flower that had belonged to the Magpie King's line, and had used those stolen powers to end a reign of terror that had infected the forest for a generation. However, as Lonan's blood did not contain a resistance to the black flower's poison, the process had turned him mad.

There were times Lonan was extremely lucid, times when Bradan was convinced he could have a normal life. For a long number of months after Bradan had begun travelling through the forest with him – after Mother Ogma had passed away, and Bradan had convinced his father to let him join him in the wilds – Bradan did not witness any of the episodes he had been warned of, and he was convinced everyone had been exaggerating his father's affliction. Then one night his father had attacked him, howling mindlessly, eyes wide with animalistic hunger, knocking him to the ground and gnashing his teeth in Bradan's face before realising what he was doing. His father had fled, leaving Bradan to wander the forest for months alone, and when Lonan finally returned he remained distant. They had spent little time together since. Sometimes they shared a meal, but seldom actually spent an entire night in the same place.

And yet Bradan still saw the greatness in his father. Mother Ogma had always made it clear she saw the man as a hero, and Bradan felt the same way. He knew the entire forest owed his father its freedom. He had seen him intervene on behalf of others in dangerous situations, seen him fight off packs of wolves or bandits when they threatened villages or farmsteads. Lonan would also seek out the dangers of the forest, would stand between them and the innocent Corvae villagers when they were threatened. The situation with the beavers was only one example. In his few years travelling with his father, Bradan had seen monstrosities he had only heard of before in stories, such as giant spiders, men with the heads of birds, and trees that had uprooted themselves to attack villages. The forest was a dangerous place, Bradan had always been told. There was much evil in it. But there was also Bradan's father, willing to put himself in harm's way to protect the weak.

Most of the time.

When he was not too busy staring at a stone wall, unable to remember his own name.

Finishing the bread, Bradan decided to save the rest of the basket for later. His father usually provided for them both, but much like with the farmstead yesterday, his presence was never guaranteed. Best to save food, to prevent a day of hunger in case his father did not show.

Reaching a fork in the path, Bradan looked up and wondered what was going to happen next. Last night, his father had told him they were done, they would not work together again. That was not the first time such a promise had been made, but Bradan had to admit he had never actually willingly put himself into harm's way before. He suspected this time would be no different – Lonan would eventually return, either because of concern for Bradan, because he needed him to interact with the locals, or because he simply forgot about the previous meeting. He would return. Probably.

Until then, it was up to Bradan to make his way through the woods. In comparison to confronting the villagers of Meldrum, spending time alone in the woods was a welcome relief to Bradan. He had grown up with mostly his own thoughts for company, wandering through the wilderness close to Mother Ogma's cottage, gathering herbs for her poultices. The other Corvae had never liked associating with him, and he found no joy in speaking to them, either. He never really knew what to say, how to hold their interest, and they certainly had little to tell him that was worth his time to hear. Crop rotations? New weaving patterns? Those were the topics the Knacked of the forest preferred, and they bored Bradan to tears. Over time, Bradan supposed, he had completely lost the art of conversation, especially since Mother Ogma passed away. Instead, he found it a particularly effective tactic to look away from anyone who was trying to speak to him, and the awkward silences he gave eventually convinced them to cut the chat short, which suited Bradan just fine.

He decided to head south, as that was a part of the forest he and his father had not frequented in a good few seasons. The people of Meldrum had hit upon a true issue with those who travelled the forest – seldom were they welcome in the same place more than once every few years. Tradition dictated that travellers through the forest should be helped along their way with food and shelter, but even silver-tongued Artemis had outstayed his welcome on more than one occasion, if the stories were to be believed.

The path forked, and Bradan followed it south. A wooden figurine, hanging from the branches just above, caught Bradan's eye, and reminded him why it had been so long since they had travelled down here. He had entered the Lady's domain. The people of Meldrum and the surrounding villages still worshipped the Magpie Spirit, as had been their tradition for generations past, but since the death of the last Magpie King, some had been turning to less familiar figures to protect them from the dark. A few villages close to the ruins of the Eyrie sent prayers out to the Birdmen, creatures that had been seen haunting the trees of that part of the forest, remnants of the last mad Magpie King's line. Bradan and his father had even come across a new collection of farmsteads that called upon the Bramble Man to help them in times of famine. They left that part of the forest quickly, with Lonan worried the people's madness could be catching. Bradan had even noticed a few spider-like totems inside Meldrum, and fancied that a good number of those people were asking Mother Web for her aid just as much as they called upon the Magpie Spirit.

However, the Lady seemed to be the figure whose presence was rising the most within the Magpie King's forest. When they last visited the southern villages, three of them had converted their places of worship to favour her instead of the Magpie Spirit. The small effigy Bradan was now staring at – little more than a stick figure with rust-red leaves intertwined within it, falling behind as red hair – signified where the Magpie Spirit's worship ended, and where people now turned to the Lady for aid. Based on his previous experience, Bradan had expected to travel for at least a day longer before encountering anything like this. Her influence had spread further.

He walked onward, pulling his thin woollen cloak around him as shelter from the autumn winds. It was early in the season, but he was surprised to find how quickly the forest had taken to the season's death. Around him, many trees were already bare, and… and the ground was empty.

With this many bare trees, especially early on in autumn, there should be a healthy layer of leaves littering the forest floor. Instead, the left of the path was bare, with only brittle twigs lining the ground before him. To the right of the path, there was a gentle dusting of rust leaves, as Bradan would have expected at this time of year, but that did not explain why the forest to his left felt so empty.

Bradan narrowed his eyes, studying the trees. They had not shed their leaves for the autumn. They were dead.

What had happened here?

Unable to help his curiosity, he stepped closer to the copse of dead trees, racking his mind for stories of creatures that would do this to the forest. Most of the beasts that stalked the Magpie King's forest cared little for the foliage, instead pursuing anything living, mostly humans. The larger beasts, like the beavers, or mythical bears, would knock trees over and ruin them, but would not drain them of life like this.

Bradan walked into the centre of the ring of dead trees and placed his hand on one of their trunks.

"What did this to you?" he whispered, puzzled, appreciating the mystery of it all.

For a second, he thought the bark of the dead tree was falling off at his touch. Instead, the tree he was touching reached out, and grabbed him at the wrist.

"Father!" was his first reaction, and he hated himself for shouting it, especially as it was the only word he was able to offer before a second hand – for it was indeed a hand that had grabbed him – unfolded from the tree and clasped itself over his mouth.

Gripped tight now, thin, clawed digits pressing into the flesh of his arm and his face, Bradan's eyes widened in panic as what he had mistaken for the side of the tree pulled away from the dead trunk and dragged him towards the centre of the clearing.

He was thrown to the ground, mouth still covered, staring into the face of the thing that held him. Now it had removed itself from the tree, Bradan could clearly see the legs, arms and head of this thing, but in truth it was more tree than person. Instead of skin, it was covered in bark, gnarled, dry and broken. In place of hair the creature had thin vines trailing from the top of its head, down to its waist. No leaves sprouted from the vines, giving her hair – this creature was female, judging by the withered, distended breast-like shapes formed from tree bark – an aged, pathetic appearance. Her face was the least human thing about her. There were eyes set in the creature's head, green, dully glowing orbs, roughly where a human's eyes would be found. However, that face, lowered to be almost touching Bradan, had no other features on it. Instead of a nose, mouth and cheeks, this thing's face was simply a collection of broken and cracked tree bark.

Despite the lack of a mouth, as the creature bore down on him, bringing her face almost into contact with his nose, Bradan could hear it breathing. Distantly, his body rigid, able to only move it in short fits of struggling, Bradan recalled a story Mother Ogma told him about tree spirits seducing wayward travellers. The spirits in those stories were kinder looking, but the outcome for the travellers had not been pleasant.

"The Lady sends you greetings, little prince," the creature rasped, relaxing her grip on Bradan's face and wrist, but remaining standing astride him, face lowered to his.

Despite his predicament, despite how close to death he was dancing right now, something inside Bradan deflated as the thing addressed him.

"Prince? You've got the wrong guy, sorry."

The creature chuckled. It was more of a hissing sound than anything else, the noise of a strong wind forcing its way through the place where a cottage wall and thatched roof met. It did nothing to fill Bradan with confidence.

"She bade us look for the son of the Magpie King. I am the first to find you, little prince."

Bradan furrowed his brow. He should have known this would

have something to do with his father. "Still mistaken. My father's no Magpie King. He's just a man who tried to do the right thing."

The creature hissed again. This thing was old, Bradan realised. The bark that made up her skin was thick and broken, the kind of growth that took an oak a human lifetime to develop. Her features resembled those of an elderly woman more than anything else, skin sagging and distended, folding under itself as she hung over him. However, none of the aches and pains of an elderly human were present in this creature. The way she stood, poised over him, reminded Bradan of a wildcat hunting a rabbit.

Realising the creature was waiting for him to speak, Bradan asked the question that was foremost on his mind. "What are you?"

It did not laugh this time. Instead, it was the creature's turn to take time to consider Bradan, as if it had not expected to be asked this. Almost, Bradan thought, as if it had never contemplated this question before.

"I am... part of her," the creature said eventually, its gravelly tones hesitant. "We used to be one, I think. Myself, her other servants, and her. She was much diminished, and the moon would allow each of us to come to the fore. Now, however, with her power rising, she can finally set us free again."

The thing became more confident, gathering in speed as it spoke. Bradan became unnerved at the enthusiasm, at its renewed sense of purpose. "I and my brethren are of the new moon, when the night is darkest. We are of the forest when it is closest to death, when life has withdrawn as much as is possible, but hope still remains. Like wraiths, I and my sisters move among the trees, serving our Lady, spreading her messages."

On the word 'messages', the creature, this wraith, flexed her claws, and Bradan got the distinct impression not all of her messages were as verbal as the one he was currently receiving.

Mouth dry, he tried not to focus on her sharp fingers.

"What about me, then? What would someone like the Lady want with me? Got a message for me to pass on to my father?"

"Not the father, no," the barkwraith replied. "Just for the princeling alone."

"I've told you already, I'm no prince," Bradan said, irritated, despite his predicament.

Again, the thing hissed in pleasure. "Are you certain?" It lowered its face towards him, and Bradan could read glee on those haggard features. "Your father holds great power. The power of the Magpie, the power that overthrew my Lady in a previous life. You stand to inherit that power."

Bradan's heart fluttered, unable to help his reaction as the creature spoke his greatest desire. Did this thing know something he did not? Or was it mistaken again, as it had been in calling him 'prince'?

"It doesn't work like that, the Magpie King, his powers. It never passed from father to son, not like a crown."

"Yesssss," the thing hissed, slowing down, "yet the powers remained in the same family for countless generations of Magpie Kings. Why is that, then, she wonders? What might you have, that all the other princelings before you already possessed?"

Bradan's eyes widened. "Poison. Poison in our blood."

The barkwraith hissed in pleasure at Bradan's words. She did not need to speak further, as Bradan had often thought of what she was referring to. The ancient line of Magpie Kings – the power had passed from father to son not because of some hereditary inheritance of those abilities, but because the Magpie King's bloodline had developed a resistance to the poison, to the madness that accompanied the Magpie King's powers. The madness that had stolen Bradan's father's mind.

Bradan was a generation removed from that madness. Perhaps… perhaps his blood contained the resistance that Lonan's did not.

"My Lady sees much potential in you, young princeling," the barkwraith hissed again, drawing Bradan back from his thoughts. "The son of the Magpie King could be a great many things, could mean a great deal to the future of this forest."

As it became more and more apparent that this creature was not out for Bradan's life, he relaxed, despite still being on the forest floor. Instead, he allowed himself to enjoy the emotions the barkwraith was encouraging in him, emotions he had a hard time summoning on his own. Glory, hope. Importance.

He had often thought of this: of being sought out by the Magpie Spirit, of being offered the same powers as his father. This creature and the Lady were right – Bradan did have the potential to be a hero. It was in his blood. It must be – that was how the stories worked. He could become the next Magpie King. A better one than his father, a sane one.

His thoughts were broken as the barkwraith reached out to stroke his face. The proximity of those sharp claws, coupled with the oddly touching gesture, brought him back to the reality that he was sitting on the dirt with a monster towering over him. He was not the Magpie King; not yet. There was still danger here.

"My Lady would make you an offer," the barkwraith hissed.

Bradan's heart went cold. Mother Ogma had told him enough tales of deals with creatures from the forest to know that no good would come of this.

"She sees the potential in you," it continued, "and she wishes to tend to it. It would not do, to have someone in her forest with the potential you have, and to allow that vine to wither and die without ever bearing fruit."

Again, Bradan was confused. "I don't understand. She wants to help me become the Magpie King?"

The thing struck forward without warning, slapping Bradan across the cheek. From behind the bark that covered its face, Bradan could hear a low rumbling, almost like growling.

"Not another Magpie, no," it hissed. "Not that perverse source of power. The forest is moving on, and the people of power within it must move on too."

Here it comes, Bradan thought, face smarting from the slap. *What does it really want?*

"You have potential, but the Magpie Spirit has seen fit not to help you develop it. My Lady, instead, offers you her own boon. Come and join her, join our ranks. She will gift you with powers you have only been able to dream of, powers that would make you more than equal to your misguided father."

As it spoke, Bradan could feel the truth in the creature's words. The Lady was indeed rising in prominence in the forest. Prayers in her name were spoken just as much as those to the Magpie Spirit, and the number of villages coming over to her worship was increasing every year. If anyone was able to raise Bradan up, to make him the type of hero he had always wanted to be, it was her.

The barkwraith leaned in closer. "Imagine," it said, voice lower, "instead of saving a farmer, being able to save the entire farmstead."

Bradan cocked his head. "You were watching?"

"My Lady knows of everything that happens in her domain."

"You saw what was happening, but you didn't help?"

The barkwraith said nothing, but Bradan could hear the low growl begin to develop from behind the bark on the thing's face again.

Not put off by the lack of response, Bradan sat up for the first time. The wraith stepped back from him. "This is why I won't join. Go back to your Lady, and tell her my reason. I help people. My father, for all his flaws, he helps people. Your Lady does not."

"She listens to the prayers of the forest. She rewards those who worship her, who pledge fealty to her."

"Yes, but only as a reward?"

It did not respond.

"I have no interest in joining up with another power looking to claim the forest for itself. You talk of saving people, but only because you know that's what would attract me. This Lady of yours, I've never heard of her doing any good for the people of the forest. She just gathers more to herself, likes to hear people sing praises to her name, but she doesn't earn them. I refuse. I refuse her gifts."

The barkwraith hunched, continuing to walk backwards, seeming more spider-like than human now, scuttling out of the clearing of dead trees.

"She thought you would not accept. Not at first."

Bradan shrugged, standing up, raising his voice to keep addressing the wraith as it moved away.

"So why come after me, then? Why bother, if you knew I wouldn't join you?"

It chuckled one last time before disappearing from view.

"To plant a seed, young princeling. To plant a seed."

The forest was quiet. Bradan breathed slowly, standing rigid, listening for any clues that his encounter was not yet over. Finally, satisfied that the wraith had really withdrawn, he turned and ran back to the forest path.

He was not surprised when, minutes later, after having found the path again, he began to shake. He sat down on a rock and took out some more of the bread he had been gifted earlier in the day.

Spirit's breath, that was close.

Despite his relief at surviving the encounter, a small part of Bradan was aware of what he had just turned down. She had been offering him power, this Lady. That was, essentially, exactly what Bradan wanted. The chance to become important, to matter. But surely there were better ways to achieve that, especially for him.

Especially for someone with his blood.

Contemplative, Bradan stood, squinting as he looked to the treetops, trying to peer beyond the leaves. Not too far in the distance, Bradan thought he could glimpse a cliff face that rose from the forest. He could not see it from this position, but he knew a ruined castle stood atop that cliff, the former Eyrie stronghold of the Magpie King.

Bradan pursed his lips. He had not accepted the Lady's gift, but that did not mean the barkwraith was wrong. Bradan had potential. He got it from his father, from his father's blood. He had shown he had it by risking his life to save the family from those beavers. More than anything, however, Bradan showed his potential through his hunger, through his constant desire to be something... better.

Almost as if he knew he was destined for greatness.

Having finished his bread, a grin on his face, Bradan set off towards the Eyrie, towards the ruins of the Magpie Spirit's temple.

There, he would ask the Magpie Spirit to bestow upon him the same gifts it had given his father.

It was time for a new protector to rise in the forest.

A better one.

BEYOND THE BORDER

A tale from the fireplaces of the Titonidae

All Titonidae children know the dangers of the Magpie King's forest. Its dark trees on the border of the White Woods are a constant reminder of the threat that dwells nearby. However, as is often the way with youth, sometimes children need to see something themselves before they truly believe it.

So it was for Kangee and Catori, two children from the Tanasi Court, which used to be the most southern Court to border the Magpie King's forest. Do not look for the Court anymore, as it is not there, but those dark events are for another tale.

Kangee and Catori, like so many of the Owlfolk children, were fascinated by the tales of the forest, of the fell creatures rumoured to live within, but most of all by the ruler of that murky land, the Magpie King.

"I don't believe in him," Kangee would often tell his sister, after Nanny had tucked them both in and left them in the dark. "A man who can fly, and has a bird's head, and steals children from their beds? Sounds like peasant nonsense to me."

Catori, not impressed by her younger brother's bravado, shivered in her bed. "Nanny says she seen him. When he came to take away the princess, when Nanny was a little girl, she seen him."

"Princess? We've never had an Owl Princess here. There've never been any white-hairs at our Court. That's why papa says we're one of the poorest."

"That's 'cause the Magpie King keeps stealing them, silly."

Kangee stuck his tongue out at his sister, even though she could not see him.

"Well, I still don't believe in any stupid Magpie King."

Like so many Owlfolk children, Kangee and Catori would find

themselves drawn close to the Magpie King's forest, to where the silver birch of the White Woods gave way to the gnarled, knotted forms of that dark place.

It was during one of these moments, when the children had managed to slip away from their nanny during a family walk, that the brother and sister decided to play a game.

"Who's the bravest?" Catori said. "You or me?" She stared at the dark trees at the bottom of the hill, where the Magpie King's domain began. "Who dares to get closest to those trees?"

Kangee scoffed at his sister's suggestion. Unlike her, he was not afraid of stories of a crazy bird man.

"You don't have the guts to beat me," he said, striding halfway down the hill, standing between Catori and the edge of the forest. "You're too scared he'll come and steal you away to be his queen."

Catori bit her lip and marched past her brother, standing halfway again between him and the first black tree. "Don't be stupid," she said, turning back to him once she had stopped. "He only marries girls with white hair. He'd just eat me if he caught me."

Getting nervous now, but not wanting to show it to his sister, Kangee decided to end the game. He marched past Catori, walked right up to the end of the White Woods, and stood beside the final tall birch.

He turned and looked at his sister's now-pale face. "Guess it's me he'll eat first, though, right?" Catori just stared, her eyes moving between her brother and the black trees behind him.

"Right, let's stop this stupid game and get back to Nanny," Kangee said, confident with his victory.

Imagine his surprise, then, when his sister stuck out her bottom lip, clenched her hands into fists, and strode right past him. Just one step further, but that one step was enough to take her from one kingdom to another.

She turned on her heel to look triumphantly at her brother, who was staring with his mouth open, dumbfounded.

"Who's the bravest now?" she said, beaming, the victory on her face stoking Kangee's irritation.

Pushing his fear to the back of his mind, knowing that the worst thing in the world would be to let his sister beat him, Kangee clenched his own fists, and marched beyond his sister – but not just one step beyond, like she had. No, Kangee took five giant strides past his sister, well beyond the border of the White Woods, stepping further than he ever thought he would into the Magpie King's forest.

His chest thumping with elation, he turned to crow at his sister, a smile breaking across his face.

She was not there.

"Catori?" he said, his smile fading, a sickness welling up in his gut. "Catori, where are you?"

He took a step forward, in case she had run back into the White Woods. It was then that Kangee realised he could not see the silver birches anymore. A few more steps forward confirmed his fears. The border back to his home was nowhere to be found.

He could never remember how long he wandered the forest, looking for Catori, crying like a newborn, snot running down his lips. Sometimes he would say it had been just hours. Other times he swore he spent days looking for her before he found someone else.

It was an old man, swinging from the low branches of an oak tree. The man had something red that he kept taking from a pouch at his waist, but he shovelled the food into his mouth so quickly Kangee was unable to tell exactly what it was.

Upon seeing Kangee, the old man startled, fumbled about behind himself, then found what he was looking for and placed it on his head.

It was a mask. A mask of a bird man.

Kangee had found the Magpie King.

At first, Kangee was a little confused by the king's appearance. He had expected some kind of freakish man-bird hybrid, not an elderly gentleman who had difficulty putting his own helmet on. That was why, perhaps, Kangee moved forward after he had been spotted, instead of running.

"Hello there, young man," the Magpie King said, after Kangee took his first step forward. The old man's voice was not particularly threatening, but neither did he seem quite the doddery old man Kangee had first taken him for. "What brings one of the Owlfolk so far into my woods today?"

"I lost my sister," Kangee said, sniffing. His fear of the old man lessening, he stepped forward once more, trying to catch a peek of whatever was in the bag of red. "I ran further than her into the forest, and now I've lost her."

The Magpie King cocked his head. "Sister? Don't suppose she's a princess, by any chance? With white hair?"

Kangee shook his head, and the Magpie King sighed.

"No, I suppose that was too much to ask for. Been a long time since we've had a queen in the forest, and for a moment there I was hoping… Oh, but never mind. These things will come, these things will come, the forest will see to it. There's always an Owl Queen for the Magpie King, if they are patient enough."

"Please, sir," Kangee said, moving forward again. "I was wondering, what're you planning on doing with me? Are you going to eat me?"

"Eat you?" the Magpie King said, not hiding his affront at the suggestion. "I will do no such thing to those who walk in peace through this forest."

Bolstered, Kangee stepped forward again. "Will you take me, then? Steal me away from my family, keep me here to be your slave for all eternity?"

"I should think not," the Magpie King said, chuckling. "Got enough hens clucking around me already, no point in sending another to join the brood. If you were a princess, perhaps I'd make an exception, but… you're not. You're definitely not."

"So you'll help me, then?" Kangee said, eager now, running directly beneath the Magpie King's feet. "If you aren't my enemy, will you help me find my way back to my sister, and to my home?"

The Magpie King leered down from his branch, the point of his long-beaked helm almost touching Kangee's nose. "Help you? Now, why would I want to do something like that? You've already admitted to entering my forest without my permission. On top of that, you have wasted several minutes of my time. Can't you see I'm an old man? Time gets more precious to me with every second, and you've wasted so many of them already. And let's not mention the fact that you failed to bring me a queen, or any other gift suitable when meeting royalty, hmm?

"More than that, though," the king said, dropping down from the branch, age bending him to the same level as young Kangee, "and please don't take this personally – I do so enjoy watching you idiots stumble around my home."

With that, the Magpie King disappeared in a puff of smoke and leaves, startling Kangee and leaving him stricken.

Despite the refusal of the Magpie King to help him find his way out, Kangee did indeed make his way home, several days later. An Owlfolk woman about his mother's age was patrolling the forest border close to where he had entered it, and he cried out in relief when he spotted her, half starved as he was with hunger.

The woman, however, was not as pleased to see him. Indeed, the blood ran from her face at the sight of him, and she clutched him and gave off a high-pitched wail when he finally reached her.

It took Kangee a few moments to realise that the woman was Catori, his own sister. For him, lost in the Magpie King's forest, only a few days had passed. For Catori, it had been considerably longer, long enough for her to become a wife, mother, and then widow, all without the support of her brother.

Brother and sister were able to rekindle their friendship, though they were a mismatched pair, running through the White Woods together, age always chasing after youth. Kangee was the one who looked after Catori in her final years, when her strength left her, and he spent the rest of his days patrolling the borders of the White Woods, warning away any Titonidae children who were threatening to repeat his mistake.

And so, all Titonidae tell their children this tale to warn them of the dangers of venturing near the Magpie King's forest, and of the strange magics that haunt those dark boughs.

CHAPTER
THREE

Nascha had not been a blushing maiden when Vippon had taken her from the tower. One did not spend a life growing up around arrogant nobles and lusty serving girls without picking up at least a curiosity for the more physical pleasures. Nascha had chosen her partners carefully – always those passing through the Court, never anybody too important – but ultimately had decided that sex was a disappointment for her. A lot of build-up, a lot of mystery surrounding it, but overall it resulted in embarrassingly quick half-blind fumbling, and weeks of worry for her moon's blood to appear.

Lovemaking with Vippon was a revelation. That first time together, in Nascha's cell, before escaping through the window, she had invited him into her bed, ready to cover them both up again with her thin sheet, happy to feel but not to be revealed. Vippon instead had pulled the sheet off them, not giving Nascha time to protest. The hunger in his eyes, the desire as he looked at her naked body coated in moonlight – she got caught up in that moment, losing all self-realisation, not becoming aware of her nakedness again until they were both spent.

After that, he had carried her down the Court's walls, his uncanny strength and balance – a part of his gift from the Fox

Spirit, he later told her – allowing him to find footholds despite holding her in his arms as he descended. One of the first instructions he had given his people after bringing Nascha to them, even as their caravans exited the Court on the same evening as their performance, had been to remove the dye from her hair. The substance the Vulpe women had worked into her hair had been foul smelling, and the ladies' hands had not been kind. Nascha had been too swept up in the adventure of her intimacy with Vippon and subsequent escape from death to pay much attention to the other Vulpe. Anytime she spoke to them they would grunt at her in return, and then speak to each other in that harsh language of theirs.

Nascha had a few minutes to admire herself in a cracked mirror after the black dye had been removed. She had always known her hair was naturally white, but as the Court had kept her true heritage hidden, she had never before seen herself with a head of undyed hair before. Wrapped in the knitted robes of the Vulpe, unruly white curls tumbling down her face, Nascha did not recognise herself. She smiled at what she saw in the polished glass. The serving girl, the prisoner in the queen's castle, was gone. She was not certain who she was looking at now, but Nascha was looking forward to getting to know her.

Vippon evidently shared that desire. They travelled for a few hours through the night, Nascha remaining hidden under a bundle of furs in one of the smaller caravans in case of an early pursuit. They stopped not long before dawn, the horses apparently tiring early after their midnight trek. The Vulpe women, still not addressing Nascha directly, brought her back to Vippon, himself working the reins of the lead caravan.

Nascha thrilled at the shock on his face when he saw her, hair now white, and smiled as she saw that hunger grow in his eyes again. He leapt down from the caravan roof, his eye teeth glinting in the dawn light.

"And here I thought I had bedded a serving girl last night," he said softly, genuine awe in his voice as he ran his hands through her newly cleaned hair. Nascha's hair was tangled and naturally frizzy, so the motion was not as smooth as Vippon perhaps would have liked, but Nascha did not care. "Little did I know I had found myself a queen to bring home."

He bent to lift her again, as he had in the tower room just as they had made their escape. Caught off guard by the action, Nascha stepped back, hand raising slightly, as if to ward him off.

Vippon looked at her, puzzled. There was also, she was surprised to see, frustration in his eyes. Almost a type of desperation.

At that moment, she found the link again that had been made between them both in the forest. Vippon clearly had more experience than she did with midnight dalliances, and she had to suspect he had more experience with daring escapes too. When they had first met in the forest, she had actively opposed him, not letting him have everything his own way. Her lack of familiarity with the events of last night had taken some of the fire out of her, and Nascha had allowed Vippon to take charge, clearly a role he was happy to play.

However, on refinding that invisible bond between them, Nascha's confidence returned.

She raised her head slightly so she could look down her nose at Vippon, whilst curving her lips into a half smile. She pointed towards the door to his caravan, indicating with her head that she wanted Vippon to go inside.

His head moved between the door and her finger, puzzled, but not unhappy.

"Go on," she said, motioning to the door again and giving an unseen tug on their link. She was thrilled to see Vippon take two steps backwards at that invisible command. "Go on. Your queen wishes to be waited upon."

His face breaking into a full grin this time, Vippon walked up to the door of his home and opened it with a flourish, inviting Nascha inside.

This time, it was Nascha's turn to take control. When they were alone, without speaking further she undressed herself, Vippon following by removing his own clothing once he realised what she was doing. If Nascha the serving girl had been standing there in front of him, her hands would have automatically made their way to cover her nakedness, as if there was something shameful in revealing herself to this almost-stranger. However, that girl was gone. Instead, Nascha stood in the dull lantern-light, aware of the warm glow reflecting off her exposed flesh, just as it would be reflecting off her newly unveiled white hair. She was also aware of Vippon's eyes on her, eager now, and she was aware of just how much he dangled on her leash, of how much control she had over him at that moment.

"Lie back," she commanded, pointing to the cushioned bed behind him. She was not experienced enough in the bedroom to stop a blush from filling her cheeks, and part of her – the former serving girl – was mortified to feel the blush running down her neck, knowing it would be making her pale skin blotchy. However, this new Nascha – Nascha the rebel, Nascha the explorer, Nascha the free – simply smiled at her lover again, letting her own excitement show through, watching this man lie back on the bed, clearly ready for her.

She acquiesced, giving them both what they wanted, climbing on top of Vippon and lowering herself onto him.

Nascha lost days in that caravan, in her new life. The control she had, the passion they shared, consumed her. The fact that she also drank more than she ever had in her life helped with that. The wines of Vippon's troupe were not the watered down, bitter-tasting stuff the servants were given back at the Court. This drink was thick and rich. Consuming it, lying there naked with a man, not having to do housework for days at a time – this new life took over Nascha, and she allowed herself to succumb to it. She lost days, eventually choosing to never leave the wagon. She was being pursued, of course, so it was best to stay out of view, but there were other reasons.

Outside, the world was imperfect.

Vippon's people tolerated her, but despite her best attempts to strike up a conversation, the Vulpe did not respond. They did not go so far as to dismiss her, but they made it plain and clear – the women in particular – that they were not going to open up to her. This had been especially true when Nascha had spotted them first trying to wash her clothes, none of them clearly having the Knack for it. She assumed they all had performing Knacks, to best contribute to their troupe's livelihood. Nascha had attempted to show them what they were doing wrong, but instead the women got angry, bickering at her in their harsh language, eventually deeming her servant smock beyond saving and burning it, forcing Nascha to rely on Vippon's generosity for new clothing. The Vulpe wine made her head ache in the mornings, and hearing the rest of the troupe bark at each other in their foreign tongue only added to her malady.

Instead, Nascha was content to bed Vippon, drink his wine, then fall asleep, ready to be woken again when he returned from his work outside. Inside the wagon, she was the queen Vippon wanted her to be. Here, she was more important, more adventurous than she had ever been in her entire life. She was certain Nascha and Vippon shared adventures together, under those covers, that Tadita had never dreamt of.

Life, of course, did not allow Nascha to live like that forever. Vippon brought her food, sometimes, often leaving it by her bed after they had feasted on each other, but she had to withdraw to the outside world for proper sustenance. She could not remember how many days they had been travelling for. It could not have been more than a few, surely, but in her wine-aided haze, Nascha struggled to remember a time when she had not lived this way. Pulling on the woollen clothing Vippon had provided and throwing a heavy shawl over her shoulders to ward off the night-time cold, Nascha took one more glance at herself in the mirror before leaving the wagon. Her white hair was wild, tousled, untended. Her face briefly reminded her of Laurentina's – the look of contentment that was only possible when everything you needed in life was handed to you without working for it.

Nascha raised her eyebrows at her reflection in a kind of salute, smiling to see the happy woman before her. Then she ventured outside the wagon, to the campfire and the noise of the Vulpe at their meal.

They were loud, Nascha realised, as she made her way closer to the large fire that had been stacked in the centre of the ring of the half-dozen caravans Vippon's troupe owned. The Vulpe had made no attempts to be quiet for her, had not been worried about disturbing her sleep. Squinting against the glare of the firelight, much stronger than the dull lanterns of her wagon boudoir, Nascha raised her head to the night sky. It was black up there, except for the stars and moonlight. Nowhere near dawn or dusk. From what Nascha could tell, they were surrounded by trees, in the middle of a forest. There were no signs of any settlements nearby.

It was then that Nascha realised where she was. The black branches of the trees above her were more than just silhouettes of the birches of the White Woods against the moonlight.

Her panic forced the rest of the haziness from her body. Wide-eyed now, dismayed, she darted her head around, expecting trouble to burst into the clearing at any moment. The Vulpe did not notice her change in disposition – they did not really notice her at all – and they certainly seemed to have no concerns of their own. They were enjoying their meal and drink, a few couples dancing around the fire, but for most this seemed to be business as usual.

"Vippon," Nascha gasped, eyes roaming wildly for the troupe leader. She found him exactly where she expected, at the heart of the party, on the other side of the bonfire from her, whirling a dark-haired Vulpe woman – not more than a girl, really – around the campfire.

In her panic, Nascha did not pay any attention to the woman in her lover's arms. Instead, she ran to him, stumbling across the uneven ground.

"Vippon," she said again as she ran, louder this time, looking for that invisible link to pull on, but not finding it.

The Vulpe leader looked around at the sound of his name, and his face broke into a grin when he laid eyes on her. He turned to the nearby Vulpe watching him dance, and shouted something at them in their unfamiliar language, giving Nascha the clear impression that he was bragging. In response, the crowd around him cheered, the Vulpe girl bowed to her partner, and left Vippon's arms.

"My white queen," Vippon called to her, walking across the makeshift dance floor with his arms outstretched, pulling Nascha to him as she finally reached him. "Gracing us all with your presence? I should have known the owl would wait until the sun went down."

"Vippon, this is wrong," Nascha gasped, both hands clutching Vippon's shirt.

The man looked at her, confused. "The girl? My cousin, dear Nascha, nothing more. You need not worry about her. We Vulpe, we enjoy life. When my partner is not available to dance with me, I must find another, but I will always return to you, my queen."

She shook her head, frustrated. "No, no. The forest. Vippon, you've taken us into the Magpie King's forest."

She whispered the last bit, not wanting to let the others close by hear. No point in letting the Vulpe panic when they realised the mistake they had made. Better for Vippon to take control of the situation, to lead them to safety before somebody got hurt in the commotion.

Instead of looking concerned, Vippon turned back to the crowd, and shouted at them in their native tongue again.

The bystanders roared with laughter. Confused, red-faced, Nascha felt her frustration growing.

"You meant to come here?"

Vippon chuckled, his face close to hers as he turned towards her. He was lucky she did not slap him for treating her so. He should be explaining the situation, not ridiculing her in front of his people. "Yes, my Nascha, we have been in the forest for over a day now."

She shook her head. "I—I don't understand. This place is evil. The stories—"

"No, no, do not worry. You must be aware that I have my own... connections. My people have made an alliance with the powers of the forest. We will be welcome here, you will see."

Her grip on his chest lessened, but her panic did not leave her completely. Instead, she clung to him while he started speaking to those around him, and her eyes scanned the gnarled, reaching trees of the clearing they had stopped in. At any moment now, she expected the creatures from the stories the servants told each other to step out from between those dark branches.

When they set off in the morning, Nascha told them she wanted to walk alongside the caravans. She could tell the demand did not sit well with many of the other Vulpe. It seemed they were happy enough for their leader to bed a white-haired girl behind closed doors, but they wanted little to do with her out in the open. When she tried to speak to them, the men grunted at her, offering little conversation in return. The women were worse. They stood with their hands on their hips, listening to her questions – have you been to the Magpie King's forest before? Is that girl really Vippon's cousin? – but afterwards would scowl at her, replying with a series of barks in their own guttural language.

"Pay them no mind," Vippon said, when she brought her concerns to her lover's attention. "That is just *Kettu*, our language, how it sounds. You should travel east sometime, to the Vulpe homelands. Our villages, you can hear them screaming at each other from a mile away. Two, on a market day. They aren't angry with you. Why would they be?"

"None of them speak common? Not even your cousin?"

Vippon cocked his head. "My cousin?"

"You remember, the girl you were dancing with last night. Your cousin."

Vippon blinked. "Yes, Ireena, yes. I was almost certain she could speak your language. I'll have a word with her this evening, see if she can tell me what they're up to."

He was the only one Nascha could speak to, the only one who would speak to her, but Vippon's time was limited. He was driving the lead caravan, and on the few occasions he left the seat, he always seemed to be sorting out some small issue, or making important decisions with some of the others. So Nascha was mostly left to herself, trotting alongside the procession, taking in the sights of her freedom. Despite being surrounded by people, Nascha was lonely. Perhaps it was also a combination of the fact that for once in her life she did not have a list of jobs to complete by mid-morning. No serving girl in the history of the Court would have ever believed that one of their number would be feeling nostalgic for the daily toil, but Nascha had to admit that life was certainly simpler when someone else organised it for you.

She did not have much time to dwell on those issues, however, as Nascha kept her mind and eyes busy. She was watching the woods, looking for the creatures she knew lived in them. The beasts Tadita had encountered in her adventures; the skull-headed bats, the fern-wolves and the Bramble Man. Her eyes darted amongst the dark branches as they passed them by, every movement she saw in them a possible hint that a creature was lurking there, each sound from the foliage reminding Nascha of the tales of her childhood: spiders the size of trees, beavers the size of horses, faceless women who would trade your soul for power.

And, of course, a mystery greater than all the others combined: the Magpie King. Part of Nascha thrilled at the idea of coming across him perched on a treetop, watching them, watching her. A shiver ran up her spine as she considered this thought, pulling her woollen cloak over her head to hide her unruly white hair from curious eyes. Not for the first time that day, she considered how similar she must look to the Owl Queens in the stories, the ones promised as brides to the Magpie Kings of the forest.

She drew closer to Vippon's caravan at the sight of the first settlement, a simple farmstead just off the forest road.

"What're they like?" she asked him.

The Vulpe leader, distracted, did not look at her. "What? Who?"

"The forest people. The Corvae. What do they look like?"

He turned to look at her, that confused, slightly mocking smile on his face again. "What do you mean, what do they look like? They're people, like you and I."

Nascha raised her eyebrow at this, her gaze briefly moving to Vippon's tail, which poked out from behind him. The stories had led her to believe the Corvae would be freakish things, not quite human, living in squalor. This building, however, was not unlike something she might find back at the Court. Not as regal as those palace buildings, of course, and nothing like the buildings used by the actual royalty. The Corvae farmhouse was a whitewashed stone building with a thatched roof, reminding Nascha a lot of the servants' homes back at the Court, particularly those linked to the stables. She had not expected anything in the forest to be so clean, so tidy. So normal.

She caught her breath as a figure rounded the building, coming from behind the farmhouse. The first Corvae she had ever seen. These people were legends at home, notorious for never leaving the boundaries of their woods. Unable to help herself, Nascha gasped, raising her hands to her mouth.

The young woman who had rounded the corner paused to move her eyes over the caravan. She wore a long skirt, more colourful than the plain servant smock Nascha had worn at the Court, but not dissimilar. The girl had long, brown hair, most of which was tied in a bun behind her.

The girl's eyes fell on Nascha, and her face changed immediately. The Corvae girl's eyes widened and she let out a yelp, dropping the bucket of pig muck she had been carrying. She ran inside the farmhouse. Nascha could hear – and understand – her calling for her father as she ran.

Immediately, the caravans stopped, one of the Vulpe men

calling from behind to speak to Vippon. A number of Vulpe jogged up to their leader, speaking hurriedly in their own language, gesticulating wildly, as the Vulpe seemed wont to do. They all turned to glance at Nascha from time to time. Vippon had said their language was naturally aggressive-sounding to those untrained in it, but the look in their eyes was unmistakable.

They're talking about me. They're talking about me, and something is wrong.

Nascha's gut tightened. She had felt that tightness before, recently, when Lord Bidzell had first noticed her, when she had first got the inkling that something was going to go wrong for her in the near future. The feeling of freedom Nascha had been enjoying – the feeling she thought represented her new life – disappeared.

"What's wrong?" she called up softly to Vippon, once the others had withdrawn to their caravans.

Vippon's smile was still there, but seemed somewhat colder, irritated.

"They're scared of you," he said.

It was Nascha's turn to look confused. "Those grown men are scared of a skinny woman like me?"

"Not them," he clicked, "the Corvae. Your white hair. They think you're a witch. Keep that hood drawn. We're close to their village now."

Without looking back at her, he flicked the reins and ushered the caravan onward.

For a brief moment, Nascha stood in the roadside dirt, unable to fully comprehend the words her lover had said.

Scared of me? Why would anyone be scared of me?

She turned to the farmhouse and caught sight of two pale faces at the window. Again, the eyes of the Corvae widened, and the faces quickly disappeared.

Nascha stared at the window for a moment more, and then smiled.

It was nice, for once, to be the one someone else was scared of.

She drew her hood down further, doing her best to tuck her hair under it, and walked briskly after Vippon's caravan.

The Vulpe moved from settlement to settlement, performing for the larger, important ones, such as the Court, for prestige, but also entertaining small villages in exchange for food. The Corvae village – Gallowglass, Vippon called it – was an unimpressive affair. It was a ring of about a dozen cottages, with a small stream running through the village green in the centre of the circle of buildings. The Vulpe caravans moved into the centre of the green, forming their own circle of wagons, just like the one Nascha had seen the previous night. It appeared they were expected, as a small contingent of villagers had already gathered to meet them.

As the caravans rolled into position, Nascha caught sight of a movement over to her left, well beyond the group of elders. A small girl in a simple brown dress stood between two of the cottages, staring at the caravans. Two things about the girl stood out to Nascha. First was how serious the child looked. The young woman back at the farm had given Nascha a range of emotions in the few seconds she had been in view, but this child – surely no older than five – stood sullen faced, eyes locked on the gathering caravans. What else stood out was the shock of red hair atop the child's head, a blaze of anger in a forest of calm browns and greens.

Nascha waved at the girl when she thought the child was looking at her, but the little girl did not wave back.

Vippon spoke to Nascha briefly before making his way over to the village elders.

"The others are worried you might put the Corvae off letting us stay here tonight. Keep out of sight, and keep the hood low."

She pursed her lips. "Maybe I could talk to them, let them know I'm just... just a normal person, you know?"

He looked away, distracted. A few of the older Vulpe had already approached the waiting elders. "Just stay out of sight," he said, then left her.

Nascha wrinkled her nose. Now that the joy of freedom and the thrill of the new experiences with Vippon were wearing off, she was becoming increasingly annoyed at how he spoke to her. In fact, life with the Vulpe in general was not living up to her expectations. Hungry for conversation with someone who was willing to pay her a bit more attention, Nascha turned around to find the red-headed girl again, looking to pursue the curious child a bit more.

The girl was no longer there. In fact, the space Nascha thought the girl had been standing in – the gap between the two cottages – was filled by a tree, a small aspen with reddening leaves.

That… that can't be right, can it?

Nascha scanned the rest of that side of the village, in case she was looking at the wrong cottages, in case the girl had been standing in another gap.

There was no child to be seen.

Curious, Nascha walked toward the small tree.

A Corvae woman came out of one of the cottages beside the aspen. She was not unlike the Titonidae, Nascha thought, not unlike the Owlfolk. Nascha bowed her head at the woman in shy greeting, but pulled her hood still lower, conscious of the effect her white hair had on the farm girl earlier. She walked past the Corvae, between the houses, towards the small aspen that marked where the child had stood only moments ago.

So strange, Nascha thought, looking from side to side in case the infant had ducked behind one of the houses when she had not been looking. *Where could she have gone?*

"What're you doing?" came a hissing voice from behind.

Nascha turned, surprised to see the woman from the cottage looking at her, wide-eyed and white-faced.

"Sorry, I was just looking for the girl."

"Girl…?" the Corvae woman began to question, but then her eyes widened further, as if in realisation. The woman raised her hand first to her mouth, then began to make some form of gesture over her forehead, not unlike the one the lower-born Titonidae would make to ward off evil.

"Get away from the tree," the woman said, backing away, as if something terrible was about to happen. "She does not let us touch the tree." With that, the Corvae ran off towards the busier village clearing.

Confused, Nascha turned to regard the aspen again. The woman had seemed terrified, and not, this time, because of her. Was there something about this tree, somehow? Nascha narrowed her eyes, focussing on the aspen, wary of stepping closer to it after the Corvae woman's warning. It seemed innocent enough. Bit of an unusual place for a tree to be planted, so close to these two cottages. It was fine for now, as the tree was still young, but it would need to be dealt with eventually, when its branches began to interfere with the nearby thatched roofs. The only odd thing about it, as far as Nascha could tell, was that its leaves were considerably redder than those of the surrounding forest, although autumn was setting in, and different varieties of trees did behave in different ways.

Rough hands grabbed Nascha from behind.

"What're you playing at?"

Her brief moment of fear disappeared when she found that it was Vippon who had spun her around. The fear, however, melted into annoyance – and not a little alarm – when Nascha noticed how hard Vippon was gripping her shoulders. She could find no trace of the spark that his eyes normally held when he was with her. Instead, this man was just angry at her.

"I…. There was a little girl, and—"

"Didn't I tell you to stay out of sight?"

Her first reaction was to apologise, to grovel, tell him he was right, and then scramble back to her caravan – his caravan – with her head bowed. However, the new Nascha, the girl in the mirror, quickly shoved that emotion away, and replaced it with anger. Anger at this man who thought he had the right to speak to her like that.

"You did. I wanted to find out about the girl."

Perhaps if Vippon had been in a sounder frame of mind, perhaps if his own emotions had not been so heated, he might have noticed the edge to Nascha's voice.

Instead, he gripped her roughly by the arm and dragged her back towards the caravan, not speaking. Nascha, inside seething, did nothing, instead noting the looks of approval from the other Vulpe as they watched Vippon escort her to his caravan, push her inside, and then slam the door behind her before returning to charm the Corvae elders.

A week ago, Nascha would have thrown herself on the bed and cried into a pillow, lamenting her own stupidity at not following orders. Instead, she stood there in the dimness of Vippon's caravan, only a little light getting in through a dirty pane of glass, staring at herself in the mirror.

Slowly, she let the hood fall, allowing herself to see the woman hidden underneath. The white hair, the serious face, the clothes that did not belong to a serving girl.

This isn't going to work, Nascha thought. *He doesn't get to treat me like that. Mister Vasilescu and I need to have a very serious chat about exactly how I am to be treated if he expects me to keep travelling with him. How I am to be treated by him, and by his people.*

She waited until nightfall, when sounds of frivolity burst forth from the village green. The Vulpe had put on a performance, the same one they played at the Court – The Fall of the Magpie King. Nascha sat on the bed, back straight, continuing to stare at herself in the mirror as the crowd of Corvae cheered. She pictured Vippon bowing, his hand swooping generously to the rest of the Vulpe performers.

The celebrations did not stop there. Food would be offered to the guests now, and drink as well. Nascha gave it about an hour after the show before she decided it would be safe for her to join the frivolity without being noticed.

She cracked open the caravan door, Vippon's summer blanket wrapped around her as an extra cloak to ward off the chill of the autumn night. The majority of those attending the festivities were in the centre of the ring of wagons, and although a few Vulpe men were patrolling, Nascha reckoned it would be easy enough for her to make her way unnoticed.

Hood pulled over her head again to avoid alarming any of the Corvae, and to stop any Vulpe from noticing her before she wanted it, she ducked under one of the travellers' caravans and took a look at the party taking place on the green.

It was time to show Vippon she was not a woman who could be ordered about like that.

Much like the other night, a fire was ablaze in the middle of the ring of wagons, and Corvae and Vulpe were dancing together around it. Some kind of string instrument was playing a fast-paced tune, but Nascha could not make out the player. At first, nor could she spot Vippon. She had expected to find him as before, dancing around the firelight with the woman whom she was certain was not his cousin; but it was mostly Corvae up there now, with a few Vulpe men dancing with some of the younger daughters of the village.

She found Vippon, eventually, in the dark of one of the far

wagons, cuddled up with a Corvae girl. Nascha stood there in the shadows, watching them for a while, her fists clenched. Vippon turned to whisper in the girl's ear, and Nascha caught the glint of firelight off his teeth, but never saw the full features of his face. Instead, the young woman on his lap gasped, then clutched at his shirt, pulling him close to kiss him. Vippon's hands disappeared up the woman's long skirt, and Nascha turned away, her heart thumping.

Prick. Complete prick.

She tried not to think of those long stretches of time she had spent in the caravan, drowsy and drunk, wondering when Vippon would return.

Prick.

She stood in the shadows with her back to her lover, imagining the things he was doing right now to the woman only a few steps away from her, his fingers touching her where they had touched Nascha less than a day ago. She was tempted to walk up to them now, interrupt them in the act, just to see if he even cared about being caught.

You don't deserve it though, do you, Mister Fox? I don't think you even deserve to know how you lost me.

Something snapped inside. Turning to see her lover one last time, noting his hands still up the Corvae's skirt, the young woman staring seriously into his eyes, Nascha ducked to make her way under the caravan again.

She was not planning on spending another night in the company of these strangers. The Magpie King's forest might be dangerous at night – although Nascha was beginning to believe those stories were exaggerated – but she would rather risk making her way alone through it than return to the caravan and allow Vippon to touch her again.

Not looking back at the celebrating Foxfolk and Magpiefolk behind her, Nascha took a deep breath, and readied herself to take her first step towards the night-time woods.

However, as she did so, a trio of Vulpe – one woman, two men – rushed up to Vippon, barking at him in *Kettu*.

Vippon dropped the Corvae girl, dumping her unceremoniously off his lap, and got to his feet with a snarl. One of the nearby Corvae moved forward to talk to him, but the Vulpe leader shoved the man out of the way and stormed out of the clearing, followed by those who had come for him.

Spirit's shade, Nascha thought. *They've discovered my disappearance already?*

However, Vippon and the Vulpe trio did not make their way to his caravan as she had expected, but instead moved toward one of the further cottages, and then disappeared out into the woods.

Nascha realised this was the best chance she was going to have. Now Vippon was distracted, she could escape without his heightened senses noticing.

She stood there, looking at where he had disappeared to, not moving.

It was her best chance, but... but Tadita would not have just run off stupidly, without preparation. Whatever had distracted Vippon had bought Nascha precious minutes. She was going to use them wisely.

Heart thumping, Nascha ran back to Vippon's caravan. There, she grabbed a small backpack that lay unused under his bed. Her eyes rested briefly on the lantern that had been their main source of light during their explorations of each other. It was tempting both as a source of light in the dark woods, and also as a means of revenge – she was half tempted to smash it on the ground, allowing the oil inside to catch Vippon's caravan ablaze. Instead, she gave up both notions as being too noticeable, and then dashed outside again.

It would have been easier to just disappear now, and that would be that. However, Nascha's growling tummy told her there were other matters to attend to first. She would need food for several days, at least – who knew how long it would be until she found another village, or made her way out of the forest entirely?

As Nascha left the light of Vippon's caravan, doubt began to settle in as her anger began to cool. Yes, Vippon had angered her, wronged her, but was the right reaction really to run off into the Magpie King's forest in the middle of the night? Certainly her journey through the forest with the Vulpe so far had suggested that the dark folktales the Titonidae told of this place were highly exaggerated, but there must be some truth in those stories. As her passion cooled, uncertainty took over. What should she do?

However, as she exited the caravan, the Corvae nearby began to shout in alarm, joined by a number of aggressive voices speaking *Kettu*.

Vippon had returned from wherever he had been called off to, much sooner than Nascha had anticipated.

For a brief moment, her heart sank, thinking she had missed her opportunity to escape unnoticed, cursing herself for thinking with her belly instead of her heart.

It was then, however, that Nascha caught sight of her lover, back amongst the Corvae, all charm having left his face. It was to Nascha's shame that she felt relief that his anger was not directed towards her this time. Instead, Vippon clutched a Corvae man by the collar, threatening to throw him into the fire.

Nascha knew she should run. She had already squandered an opportunity to do so, and she did not know if the Fox Spirit had given Vippon any gifts that would allow him to track her.

However, as the Corvae man struggled against Vippon's grip, Nascha crept under the caravan, inching closer to get a look at the events playing out in the heart of the village.

He was being watched. It was a sensation Bradan had experienced many times before. Most who spent any time wandering through the forest were familiar with it. Eyes were constantly on you, just hidden from sight. It was nothing supernatural that told him something was out there, just his innate ability to read the forest, in the way a scholar reads a book. The birdsong was more distant than normal, suggesting something unusual – probably dangerous – was close by. There was rustling in the bushes clearly not caused by any of the normal forest residents.

Most of all, as Bradan had been travelling for two days now along the forest path to the Magpie Spirit's temple, he had been expecting something like this to happen.

"I've been looking for you."

He stopped in the middle of the path, aware that evening was already well on its way. Normally by this stage he would have found a tree to crawl up into, to secret himself away for the night, or a nook in a hillside to shelter in, to hide from the beasts that roamed the darkness of the forest. However, he was aware how close he was to his goal – to the Magpie Spirit's temple, where he would ask the Spirit to gift him with the same abilities as his father – and Bradan had wanted to press ahead. He was anxious at being out in the forest at this time of night, he was not a complete idiot, but his natural fear had been overcome by how excited he felt. Excited at the choice he had made, excited at how much his life would change if the Magpie Spirit agreed to his demand, if it lifted him up as a being of power.

However, Bradan had known his father would eventually find him.

He raised his eyes to look at the dark figure on the branch above.

Lonan sat there, hunched, more like a large cat than anything else. Unlike the Magpie Kings of legend, Lonan wore no mask, but instead his face was hidden by the shadows of the lank, dark hair that drooped downward like a hood. His faded black cloak looked new in the shadows of the trees, and it also hung from him, creating the appearance of something unnatural suspended in the air above the path.

Lonan was indeed unnatural. He was the most powerful thing in the forest, and he was mad.

Bradan raised his eyes, not quite looking at his father's face.

"You said you didn't want me around anymore," Bradan said, annoyed at how meek he sounded.

The figure above him shifted, uneasy at Bradan's statement, but saying nothing more.

What kind of mood was his father in tonight? How had he been, for the past few days? Bradan preferred being around him when he was lucid. He liked to think that during those times, he caught a glimpse of the true man called Lonan, the man who had been sacrificed to save the forest all those years ago. Sometimes, however, Bradan was not certain if those calm times were a true reflection of his father's personality. When madness took Lonan, Lonan got angry. Mother Ogma had always said that you got to see someone's true self when they let their anger out.

It occurred to Bradan then that Lonan might not remember sending him away.

"Are you just checking up on me?" Bradan asked. "Or is there something you want?"

"You shouldn't be travelling alone at night," his father said, his voice hoarse. If Bradan had not known exactly who his father was, he imagined this experience would have scared the life out of him. It said a lot that Bradan was used to having conversations like this. "There are bad things out there."

Bradan blew a stray lock of hair from his eyes, smiling at his father's words. "Aren't there always? I've been careful, like you taught me. The forest isn't as bad as it used to be. You taught me that, too."

"I taught you to get to safety before darkness came," his father replied. The reprimand in his voice was clear. Bradan flinched at it. "The moon rose a good half hour ago. You're a clear target out here, making noise like this."

Bradan looked up at the sky, anxious. The grey light was indeed fading quickly, and the sun would soon completely set.

"I know," he said.

How could he explain to his father? There was no way Lonan would allow Bradan to plead the Magpie Spirit for its favour. Bradan knew Lonan would not want his son to risk the same life that had been forced upon him. Never mind that Bradan felt he had it in his blood to resist the poison of the Magpie Spirit's gift. There was no way his father would have similar faith in him.

"I thought I was close to a settlement," Bradan lied, hoping his father trusted him enough to not be studying his heartbeat. He knew Lonan could read a person by how their heart was sounding, and he was sure his own was betraying him right now. "Thought if I pushed on further I'd find a roof to sleep under tonight."

Lonan shifted on his perch, but did not give away any clues that he had picked up on his son's deception.

"Gallowglass is close," Lonan said, indicating with his head beyond the path, off to the left. "Fifteen minutes in that direction, if you jog. Should be able to get there before first bell, but they're not sleeping in their cellars tonight."

Bradan raised an eyebrow at this. It was not unheard of for residents to stay up after evening bell – so unlike when his father had been a boy, and when staying up at night-time was a guaranteed way of getting yourself killed – but it was very unusual for an entire village to be staying awake.

"Some kind of festival?" Bradan asked, unable to recall any particular events that would be happening at this time of year.

Season's Weeping was still many weeks off, and they did not celebrate it in this part of the forest anymore. Only in the west, where the Magpie Spirit was remembered best, were the old festivals kept to so rigidly.

"Outsiders," Lonan said. "Performers from outside the forest, keeping everyone up."

"Vulpe," Bradan said, lip curling as he did so. He hated the Foxfolk, how they swept through the woods from time to time, invariably upsetting the villages they passed through.

Lonan nodded. "Yes. Yes… Vulpe, and something else."

Bradan's furrowed his brow as he realised his father was confused by something.

"What is it?"

"I can't tell. There's something else with the Vulpe, something… something of power. I was on my way to investigate."

Lonan left the words hanging there between them, allowing Bradan to contemplate them, until he picked apart his father's true meaning. Once he realised what his father was getting at, Bradan's heart sank.

"You mean you want me to investigate."

Lonan did not reply, but he did not need to. He did whatever he could to avoid mixing with the people of the forest. Of course he would send Bradan if it meant not having to go himself.

"There should be no danger involved," Lonan said eventually. "Just observe from the outskirts, and let me know what you find. Whatever this source of power is, it has been dormant, and my hope is that it will pass through without causing trouble for us."

Bradan felt torn. He was pleased his father still wanted him, pleased he had either forgotten his earlier words about breaking ties, or had had a change of heart, but Bradan had his own desires to act upon now.

Still, it was getting dark quickly, and Lonan's appearance coupled with the impending gloom had stolen the excitement from Bradan's quest.

Tonight, he would investigate for his father, and find a roof to shelter under. Tomorrow, he would ascend.

Night had completely fallen by the time Bradan reached Gallowglass. Despite his earlier bravado when speaking with his father, Bradan was not comfortable moving in the forest at this time of night. Normally, he would be focussed on finding some hideaway to survive in until sunrise. However, it was clear to Bradan, even at this distance, that his father's report had been correct – a celebration was going on in the village. Getting close to that noise should give Bradan some degree of safety, as most creatures of the Magpie King's forest were put off by large gatherings of people. It was only when travelling in small numbers, away from the light of bonfires, that things became dangerous.

Still, the sight of the Gallowglass cottages, silhouetted by the firelight in the centre of them, gave Bradan turn to pause. It would be safe enough for the Corvae out there, but that did not mean they would not be suspicious of an unknown face emerging from the woods at this time of night. It would probably be better for Bradan if he—

Spirit's breath, someone's coming.

Seeing the four figures – mostly men, judging from their height and gait – breaking away from the ring of cottages and making towards him, Bradan swore and ducked into the nearby undergrowth.

Could they really have seen him from that distance, at this time of night?

Bradan risked another glance at the figures, now seconds away from his hiding place, and his heart froze.

It was difficult to see their features in the night-time, as the moon was particularly obscured by clouds, and the distant firelight was ruining his night eyes, but it was clear to Bradan that one of the men had a fox's tail.

Bradan shrank back into the bushes again, fighting the urge to just break and run off in the opposite direction.

A fox's tail? This Vulpe was a Gentleman Fox, a man blessed by the Fox Spirit, much in the same way as his own father held the gift of the Magpie Spirit in his veins, and the Owl Queens of the Titonidae held their patron's power. This man was clearly the power Bradan's father had sensed, as those gifted with these primal forces cried out to each other over long distances, so the stories said.

Bradan racked his brain to remember as much as he could about those imbued with the Fox Spirit's power. They had a title, Gentleman Fox, just like the Magpie King or Owl Queens. This was not true of all the great spirits of the world, as the Mousefolk queen did not have one, even though the tales suggested she held the totality of her patron's gift to her people. The Magpie Spirit was similarly gracious, gifting only one person at a time. That was why Bradan's father, and all those who had inherited the power before him, were so powerful. Bradan had no idea if this was the only Gentleman Fox who walked the world in his patron's name, or if that gift was diluted, spread among many.

He breathed quickly, able to hear the Vulpes' footsteps now, coming closer. If it was his father approaching, Bradan would have already been sensed, his rapid heartbeat betraying him.

Damn it, why did the stories never tell exactly what the Fox's gifts were? All the tales said that gifted Vulpe should never be trusted, but that was true of any Vulpe appearing in a tale.

The Foxfolk reached the edge of the clearing, two steps from Bradan's hiding place, and he held his breath. They were speaking in that rough tongue of theirs, and Bradan had no idea what they were talking about. To his utmost relief, the group walked past, so close to him, clearly agitated. A glint of metal in the moonlight betrayed the fact that at least one of them had a knife drawn. It was difficult for him to tell, as he did not speak the language, but Bradan got the distinct impression they were angry.

The voices disappeared into the forest behind Bradan. It would be smart now to head towards the village, to the light and heat, and find out more information so he could talk to his father, pass on the facts. The Gentleman Fox would soon be out of sight, and Bradan would struggle to find him again. The man clearly did not have Lonan's powers of perception; he could not hear the forest's heartbeat and sense life within it, but Bradan was certain the Gentleman was a danger to everyone around him. His father would not be pleased if Bradan followed him, especially so soon after his last chastisement.

But, Bradan thought, glancing behind him to where the four Vulpe were disappearing into the dark of the forest, *if danger was anywhere close by tonight, it would be with those Foxfolk.*

Would people suffer if Bradan let them do their own thing, unopposed out there in the dark?

Not in his forest.

Heart pounding, trying to ignore the voice in his head that berated him for his stupidity so soon after facing off against the beavers, Bradan turned and followed the Vulpe, trying to keep as much distance as possible between himself and the pair.

What powers might this man have, then? Lonan had supernatural strength and speed, to match his senses. The Owl Queens – for there were a number of them, from what Bradan could tell – had powers tied to dreams, and to reading people's thoughts. The queen of the Mousefolk, the Muridae… the stories were never really clear about what gifts her patron bestowed upon her, although Bradan vaguely recalled that she had the ability to pass on some of her powers to her subjects. Perhaps this Gentleman Fox was like them, the Mousefolk subjects, briefly touched by a greater being, but only slightly more than a man? A chill running down Bradan's spine warned him that he did not really think this was the case. If his father had sensed this man's gift from so far away, he must be powerful indeed, imbued with whichever powers the Fox Spirit saw fit to ensure the survival of its adopted people. If Bradan upset this man, it would almost certainly mean his death.

He was so caught up in his own thoughts, he almost gave himself away. The Vulpe had stopped, and were now shouting in the tongue of the forest.

"…thought you could hide from me? From me?"

"No, no, please. I didn't mean anything by it—" The second speaker, someone clearly grovelling, was cut off by a cry. Presumably his own, after being hit by one of the Vulpe.

"Oh, Magpie Spirit protect me."

"Magpie Spirit?" one of the Vulpe sneered. "I thought you worshipped the Lady here?"

Another cry from the Corvae man, as he was presumably hit again.

"Oh, yes, yes! My Lady—" Another hit, and the man stopped speaking, instead beginning to cry.

"I should just tell her. Should just let her know how unfaithful her people are. She would do my job for me, to teach you all a lesson in loyalty."

The Corvae man began to grovel, spouting unintelligible words.

"I will not, however," the Vulpe said again. "When you lay your hands on my people, it is my job to stand up for them."

At this, Bradan chanced a peek at what was happening, peering behind the tree he was using for his shelter.

There were indeed only five people there, the four Vulpe – the Gentleman Fox's tail twitching irritably as he knelt to pick up his prey – and the lone Corvae. The victim was young, possibly not even in his twenties. Blood poured down the right side of his face from his eye socket, which was a mess of red, and his features were scrunched into a nest of pain.

The Gentleman Fox grabbed the villager's tunic and hauled him over his shoulder. With that, the Vulpe continued to speak in their own tongue, and turned to make their way back to Gallowglass.

The man needed help. He was going to die, if this Vulpe followed through with his threat. What could Bradan do, however, against someone blessed by one of the great spirits of the world? Even his father would be hard pressed to win against such a man if the Fox Spirit's gift was as potent in this Vulpe as Bradan suspected. Bradan would just be throwing away his own life if he intervened now.

Father, we need you, Bradan thought, not daring to speak the wish for fear of being picked up by whatever senses the Vulpe might have. *There is a life in danger, Father. Please, Magpie Spirit, help him come and protect his forest.*

Bradan shadowed the Vulpe as they returned to Gallowglass, and after they walked into the ring of wagons, he dashed across the village green, desperate to see what was happening.

"Father," he whispered as he ran, as loud as he dared. "Father, come quick. There is danger. A Gentleman Fox is in the forest." His father would hear him, Bradan knew, even if he was a day's travel for a normal man away from the village. For Lonan, he could still travel that distance in time to save this man's life.

If he was listening. If he was lucid. If the madness had not taken him.

As Bradan reached the circle of wagons, the shouts of festivity from around the central bonfire turned to screams. The Vulpe had shown the Corvae their captive.

Bradan threw himself under the nearest wagon, crawling on his belly to the other side, to get a look at what was happening in the clearing beyond.

The Gentleman Fox was standing in front of the bonfire, holding the beaten villager by the scruff of his neck – no, Bradan realised; he was holding him by his hair, hoisting the man's limp body high so the other Corvae could see him.

An older man, a village elder whose name Bradan should have remembered from his last visit a few years ago, stepped forward, towards the Gentleman Fox. The elder was unsteady on his feet, and Bradan realised with a curse that the man was drunk.

"Friend Vulpe," the old man said, confused, more than a touch trembling, "what's the meaning of this? We invite you into our village, into our homes, and you assault us? You bring shame upon the Fox Spirit with these actions."

In response, a Vulpe – a woman this time – jumped forward from the crowd and slapped the elder round the face, throwing him to the ground.

"Shame upon me?" the Gentleman Fox sneered. "It is you who bring shame, Gallowglass. This man," the Vulpe shook the helpless villager, almost spitting as he addressed him, "this lech of a man assaulted one of my family."

A ripple of murmurs spread throughout the gathered crowd, Vulpe and Corvae alike. Several of the Vulpe men shouted, their aggression adding to the tension of the gathering. Some of the more inebriated Corvae ran back to their cottages at the sound, fearful for their lives.

Come on, Father, Bradan pleaded silently, too afraid of the Gentleman Fox's possible heightened senses to call for Lonan anymore. *We need you now, Father. This man needs you.*

"Spare him!" a voice shouted from the crowd, a female voice. "He was only talking to her. He didn't mean anything by it."

A cry went up, silencing the voice. Metal glinted in the firelight, and Bradan could tell knives were being drawn. He could not tell if it was the Vulpe or the Corvae doing so. Worse, it was probably both. The village green would become a bloodbath, and with this being of power involved, the forest folk would not fare well.

"Did not mean anything by it?" the Gentleman Fox sneered. "Let this be a lesson to all the people of the Lady's woods, to all who are host to the Vulpe. Lay one hand on any of us, and Vippon will take revenge upon you."

The fox man raised the villager again, and Bradan realised his intention was to throw the unconscious man onto the bonfire behind him.

Now, Father! Bradan pleaded, but Lonan did not appear.

Cursing under his breath, Bradan jumped out from under the caravan.

"Stop, in the name of the Magpie King!"

The clearing froze, and several of the nearby Corvae gasped at the sight of him, and the mention of the Magpie King's name.

Bradan, for his part, tried not to shirk away from the dozens of eyes on him now. Gone was the cool anonymity of his forest walks. Here, he was the centre of attention.

That included the focus of the Gentleman Fox. The man – he had called himself Vippon – was as still as everyone else, eyes fixed on Bradan, but Vippon was also the first to relax, allowing his mouth to curve into a smile.

Spirit's blood, Bradan thought. *He's taken the measure of me already. He knows I'm no challenge to him.*

"Haven't you heard, pup? They don't worship the Magpie King here. Not anymore."

A wind blew through the forest, and Bradan fancied he heard aggressive whisperings on it, but he was too rapt by the events within the clearing to pay any more attention to it.

"To these people, these are the Lady's woods now. And the Lady will take no kindness to you mentioning his name here."

Two Vulpe sidled up beside Bradan, tensed, ready to grab him.

Bradan did his best to ignore the strangling panic that threatened to take over his faculties as the possibility of physical harm reared its head.

"I'm an envoy from the Magpie King," Bradan said, knowing his growing panic must be clear on his face, angry at himself for not being better at this. "You know me, some of you. You know this to be true."

More mutterings from the assembled Corvae, this time in the affirmative. Bradan was pleased to see the villagers' reaction give Vippon some hesitation, but still he held the villager aloft.

Bradan continued, "He has sent me here, on his behalf, to offer you the opportunity to back down."

Some of the nearby Vulpe barked a laugh at this, but Vippon's face remained fixed in that mirthless half-smile.

"He wishes to give you the opportunity to forgive his subjects for wronging you, and to leave them in peace and be about your way."

For a brief moment, Bradan could almost sense Vippon considering the offer. The Vulpe's arm lowered, the villager moving towards the ground.

Then a shout came from an unseen source. "We don't worship no Magpie Spirit here, boy," the cry came. It was an elderly voice, female again, just a random Corvae opening her mouth at the worst possible moment. "And there ain't no Magpie King out there, neither. Ain't been for years. Just a sad, crazy man, half-baked and ready to beg for his food. We turned you away last time, we'll turn you away now. The Lady'll protect us from this menace. Don't got no need for no false Magpie King."

Inside, Bradan groaned, and Vippon smiled.

"You hear that, pup? Guess you're not welcome here either."

Vippon motioned at the Vulpe closest to Bradan, and they grabbed him, pulling him towards their leader.

A small part of Bradan was pleased to see Vippon drop the villager, who was gathered up by some nearby Corvae, scampering back to their homes with their wounded. However, any pleasure he might have taken in saving the man's life was smothered by fear regarding his own continued existence.

"Guess it's time we taught you a lesson, pup. This is what we do to people who interfere with matters that do not concern them."

Vippon nodded again, and a heavy weight collided with the back of Bradan's skull.

The Vulpe holding Bradan let go the instant the club hit him, and he crumpled to the grass. Any opportunity to escape was lost, however, as he had lost control of himself, was unable to will his arms and legs to crawl to safety. It was as if the blow from the weapon disconnected him from everything except the knot of agony blooming at the base of his skull.

The Gentleman Fox spoke again, this time to his companions, and in their own language. It must have been the order to beat Bradan, as the guttural words were followed by boots to Bradan's gut and face. These new blows seemed to knock some sense into Bradan, as he found he could move again, doing what he could to curl himself into a ball, hiding from the worst of the attacks. He tried to break free, to turn and run, but when he lowered his arms from his face to pull himself up, a Vulpe boot connected with his jaw, snapping his head to the side and throwing him to the ground again.

Curled up in pain, blows beating down upon him, all Bradan could do was cry and scream.

Father! Father!

Perhaps if he had the gumption to shout those words aloud, instead of just screaming them in his head, the pain nursed within them might have been enough to snap Lonan from whatever stupor was holding him back.

Instead, the Vulpe laughed, and stepped back to survey their handiwork. They were not finished with him, Bradan knew. They would be planning to kill him, based on Bradan's knowledge of the Vulpe from the tales, to send a message to the rest of the village. He tasted the blood in his mouth, the loosened teeth, the patchwork of bruises across his body, and he knew there was nothing he would be able to do to stop them.

Then the Vulpe around him shouted. For a brief moment, Bradan thought this was the order to continue working on him, to finish him off. However, the cry was repeated, panicked now, and blessedly his attackers, including Vippon, ran away.

Puzzled, blood pulsing in his head like a crow's dawn cry, Bradan pulled himself up.

There was smoke coming from one of the Vulpe caravans. No, not one of them. Three of the caravans, in a row, circling the western side of the green. Bradan could see flames begin to lick from the top of one, and, not realising he had been holding his breath, allowed himself to breathe at the shouts of the Vulpe as they hastened to gather water from the small stream to save their burning homes.

How did this happen?

Not daring to spend any longer contemplating his luck for fear of losing it, Bradan scrambled to his feet and ran in the opposite direction.

He was not pursued, which was a second blessing, as his beaten body screamed at him as he stumbled across the grass toward the safety of the woods. Something was wrong with his right leg, not letting him put his full weight on it, and it felt like something had pierced the flesh of his chest. Stopping briefly at the edge of the forest, he pulled his bloodied tunic up to see if there was a knife there for him to pull out. Instead, he found an angry swelling growing along his left ribcage, suggesting that damage had been done underneath. Following instructions he remembered from Mother Ogma, a healer by trade, he tried to take a deep breath, and felt a stabbing pain as he did so.

Broken rib, then. Maybe more than one.

He pulled his tunic down, turning to make off into the forest, hoping those fires would keep the Vulpe busy so he could get far enough away as to not be worth pursuing.

As he turned, he caught a shock of white from the trees to the north of the village. Hesitating for a brief second, eyes narrowing, he caught a glimpse of a dark figure running in the moonlight. It was a girl, a woman, he was certain.

A woman with white hair?

He waited to see if the woman noticed him, but she did not look up, and disappeared into the forest a good distance away.

Knowing he could never catch her, and silently thankful for the mysterious figure he suspected was the reason he was still alive, Bradan turned towards the thick trunks that made up the forest before him, and ran into the night.

THE
FOX'S CASTLE

A tale from the fireplaces of the Muridae

Everyone knew the miller's daughter would marry well. Despite her father being of Muridae stock – one of the Mousefolk, like the rest in the village – her mother had been one of the Titonidae, and was treasured by her husband and envied by the men and women of the village for her curious beauty and sharp wit.

The miller's wife, tragically, died in childbirth, but her final words were to tell her husband to look after their daughter as if she was the most precious thing in his life.

"But she is, my dear," he said, clutching his wife's hand tightly, trying to convince himself her pulse was not weakening. "Other than you, she is."

The owl woman smiled, enjoying one final time the shameless devotion that had attracted her to the man.

"More importantly than anything, my love," she said, her final sentence as life left her, "make sure she marries well. As I did."

With that, the miller's wife died.

The miller mourned, but he kept his promise, and did not pass the sickness of his grief on to his daughter. The girl grew into a beautiful young woman, with a long, slender neck and wide, curious eyes. All the young men of the village grew to admire her from afar, but that admiration could not overcome their fear of her father. In his old age, he doted on his girl, but would fly into fearful rages at any man who so much as grinned at her, and had been known to swing the heavy broom that he used to shoo birds from the blades of his windmill at any gentleman callers to their home.

So it was that the miller's daughter remained unmarried by the day of her twentieth birthday, the day the Gentleman Fox came to their village.

The miller's village was on the edge of the Grasslands, well away from the normal roads the travelling folk took with their trains of caravans. As such, all the Muridae people stopped and stared when a man with a long, fine overcoat, with a fox's tail poking out from beneath, wandered down the path into the village. The man, who introduced himself to all as the Gentleman Fox, had long, finely groomed auburn hair, and a dapper moustache that he played with between two fingers when conversing with people. He greeted all who looked his way, and was the epitome of charm to the close-minded people of the village.

However, the Gentleman Fox's charm fell away on sight of the miller's daughter, her sleeves rolled up and her apron spoiled as she helped her father carry a freshly ground bag of flour from the mill. Instantly, an intense hunger took hold of the stranger, and those who him at that moment stepped backward, afraid for their lives.

A heartbeat later, the Gentleman Fox's charm returned, and he quickly put it to good use. By evening, he was dining at the miller's table. By the end of the week, the miller had accepted the Gentleman Fox's request to marry his daughter.

The people of the village marvelled at how this stranger had so charmed the miller, who until then had beaten anyone who even looked as if they were going to suggest courting his girl.

A few evenings before the wedding, when the miller was in his cups, toasting his good fortune at finding such a fine husband for his girl, the people of the village came to him, and asked why he had agreed so readily.

"Only the best for my girl," he said, his eye twinkling. "That was my promise. And who better for her than someone blessed by the Fox Spirit, and someone with a fine castle for her to live in?"

"A castle?" the villagers asked, surprised. They had warmed to the Gentleman Fox well enough, but he had never struck them as royalty, what with travelling the roads by himself; and his clothing, although fine, was nowhere near what they would expect from a nobleman, and certainly not one important enough to live in a castle.

"Oh yes," the miller said, "just up there, in the mountains beyond the river. When he marries her, he will take her away, and there she will wear rich dresses, and will have countless new friends to spend her days with."

"Have you seen it, then, this castle?" the villagers asked.

At that, the miller fell silent, and went back to his drink.

The next day, the miller went to the Gentleman Fox and asked to be taken to his castle, to see it himself.

"Ah, alas, that will not be possible," the Gentleman Fox said. "For you see, as soon as you accepted my proposal, I contacted my servants and told them to refurbish my home, to make it ready for my wife. I would be embarrassed for you to see it in its current state, with rooms unpainted and without a comfortable chair for you to rest on, or a bed to sleep in. It would be better for you to wait until after the marriage, when all will be as it should be."

The miller nodded at this, happy he had chosen such a thoughtful husband for his daughter.

That night, however, he told the rest of the village what the stranger had said, and they remained unconvinced.

Pursing their lips, the bravest among them approached the Gentleman Fox, and demanded that they see the castle. After all, now that the miller's daughter – loved by so many in the village – would be taken from them, many of them planned to travel to the castle soon anyway, to visit the young woman they all cherished so much.

The Gentleman Fox nodded. "Of course, my friends, you are all welcome at my home. However, I had planned for you to visit my castle in grand carriages, a royal procession of my wife's kinsmen up the mountain in style, letting all in my lands know how important you are to me. I have bid my servants procure these carriages, and will have them ready after our wedding. If, however, you would rather visit my home before then, please be my guest to make that long climb by yourselves, and do forgive my servants if they mistake you for common folk, instead of the important guests I had hoped they would be presented with."

The villagers looked at the tall mountain in the distance, and thought of how sore their feet would be at the end of that journey. They also thrilled at the idea of being waited on by the Gentleman Fox's servants, and so turned and smiled at the stranger.

"No," they said, "we will be happy to wait and inspect your castle after the wedding." Then the villagers went back to their business.

One person, however, did not fully trust the Gentleman Fox's tale. The miller's daughter had inherited more than just her mother's looks, but also her shrewd insight. Although she had agreed to the marriage, because it made her father happy, and because the Gentleman Fox made her blush every time he smiled at her, she felt that not all of her intended's story added up. He had the manners of a prince, true, but his clothes were patched and frayed. He spoke of his castle home, but his boots were badly scuffed, and had clearly been resoled a number of times.

Not wishing to concern her father, not wishing to break his moment of happiness needlessly, the miller's daughter took it upon herself to visit the Gentleman Fox's castle, alone.

It was early in the evening, the day before she was due to be wed, that the miller's daughter crept from her home, a shawl hiding her face as she moved through the shadows, making her way towards the distant mountain where the Gentleman Fox's castle lay.

The journey was long, but the miller's daughter was confident that if she pushed herself, and if she did not stop, she would give herself enough time to visit the castle and return to her father before dawn. She tried not to think of the dangers she could face on the way. Her pragmatism, inherited from her mother, told her it was better to risk bears and wolves for one night than to be married to a liar for the rest of her life.

Finally, after a long, moonlit climb, she came upon the castle. Indeed, she was somewhat surprised to find it actually existed. She had expected the notion of the castle to be a ruse, one crafted to steal her from under her father's nose. Upon sight of the tall, grey edifice, she rose her eyebrows, impressed with the truth to the Gentleman Fox's tale.

Still, something felt wrong. Although there was indeed a castle, and although it was the middle of the night, the place felt empty. No flags flew, no guards walked the ramparts. All around her she could pick out only the sounds of the mountain at night, and nothing to betray the inhabitants of the castle.

Her suspicion rose further when she approached the building and realised the castle gates lay wide open.

Gingerly, she crept forward, waiting for the moment when one of the Gentleman Fox's servants would leap from the shadows, grabbing her for the intruder that she was.

Nobody came.

Unopposed, she made her way into the keep. Curious, her

suspicion winning out over her fear of the silence, she crept up the lonely staircase, wanting to explore the rooms above, to see if she could find clues as to the whereabouts of the Gentleman Fox's servants. One by one, she visited each of the castle's rooms. Each and every one of them was bare. Empty. No people, no decor, no furniture. Each of the rooms in the Gentleman Fox's castle held only floors, ceilings, walls and spiders.

After an hour of wandering, unable to comprehend what she was seeing, the miller's daughter realised it was time to make her way home if she was going to appear in time for her own wedding.

However, as she made her way down the great staircase, she spied a room she had not yet explored. Finally, it contained something the other rooms had not: a staircase, leading down.

The stairway was long and perilous; it seemed to circle a dark hole with no bottom, and had no railing separating the miller's daughter from oblivion. Eventually there was an end in sight, a floor of dirt at the very bottom of the staircase.

The miller's daughter descended to find the small room at the bottom lined with cells. It was not unusual for a castle of this size to have its own dungeons, but the young woman was still disturbed by the thought that she would soon be living somewhere that people were also imprisoned.

However, when she looked into those cells, the miller's daughter's concern turned to outright horror.

Each of the cells contained the body of a dead woman. Some of them had been dead for years, but she could still tell straight away they were women.

They were all wearing wedding dresses.

Morning came, and down in the village the Gentleman Fox rose with relish, looking forward to his impending nuptials. He did so enjoy a good wedding. The locals greeted him as he passed them in the street on the way to the church, wishing him a good day and passing on their regards to his intended. As always, he smiled at them, replied with a jolly compliment, and tried his very best not to show the pure contempt he had for idiots such as these, who would invite a stranger into their homes. Still, he could not blame them too much, as they were not the first he had deceived, and – Fox Spirit willing – they would be far from the last.

The Fox Spirit demanded brides as proof of its servant's cunning, and the Gentleman Fox was loath to disappoint it.

As he entered the church, despite the hubbub around it, for a brief moment he felt panic, as if for some reason he expected his bride to not be there, as if this time his deception would be uncovered.

He gave a quiet prayer of thanks to the Fox Spirit when he saw her there, waiting for him at the end of the aisle, blushing beneath her veil. If she was a little red around the eyes, then so what? It was not unknown for a bride to spend the morning of her wedding day crying, or to pass a sleepless night before gaining a husband.

She would have plenty of tears to shed soon enough, in sacrifice to the Fox Spirit.

Vows and rings were exchanged, and things went as planned, although the Gentleman Fox was surprised, and a little put off, by the intensity of his new wife's gaze. Normally in these sorts of situations, these little village girls could not keep eye contact with him, blushing furiously and looking away, aware of what they thought lay ahead for them in the night. However, this miller's daughter was impassionate, but fixed on him, as if daring him to look away first, which he eventually had to do. Could it be that this girl was not a maiden? That would certainly explain why she held no fear of him. Still, it mattered not to the Fox Spirit. A spirit trapped was a spirit trapped, no matter how free that spirit had been before finding its way to his dungeons.

The wedding feast was a humble affair in comparison with what he was used to, but he endured it, anticipating what lay ahead. The Gentleman Fox gave a short, charming speech, earning the tittering laughter of most of the village.

The Gentleman Fox's first sign that something was amiss was when he noticed neither his bride nor her father were laughing.

The second sign was when his wife stood to make a speech.

"I want to tell you all about a dream I had last night – my final night as a maiden, the night before I married such a grand lord, to share with him his land and his castle." The Gentleman Fox shifted uneasily in his chair at her words. He was fairly certain he had married a Muridae before, and the woman had never spoken at that wedding. A local custom, perhaps.

"I dreamt that I visited our home last night," she continued. "That I hiked all the way up to the mountain whilst the moon was high, and found our castle. I wandered inside, and can you guess what I discovered in there? It was empty. The castle was completely empty."

There was a mixture of gasps and laughter from the village, but most were confused by the girl's tale. The Gentleman Fox, however, felt the bristles of his tail stand on end at her words.

"Or I thought it was empty," she said, "until I found my way into the basement."

Feeling his collar tighten around his neck, the Gentleman Fox quietly slid back his chair, doing what he could to exit the feast as nonchalantly as possible.

"And can you all guess what I found there, in that basement? In the home of the man I now call husband?"

All eyes turned to the Gentleman Fox as he moved around the edges of the room, making for the exit at the far end of the building. He smiled and waved at the onlookers, doing what he could to redirect their attention to his wife.

"Brides. A dozen brides, all dead, rotting under his castle. What does it mean, do you think, to have a dream like that on the eve of your wedding?"

The villagers were quiet now, mouths hanging open, looking at the girl in shock, eyes darting between the Gentleman Fox and his wife.

The Gentleman Fox smiled, took a deep breath to give a reasonable explanation and then facilitate his exit, but instead he screamed.

He collapsed to the floor, unable to stand because of the pain that racked his body. He called upon the gifts given to him by the Fox Spirit, planning to use them to leave this cursed place, but found they were gone.

It was then that he saw his wife's father standing behind him, Mousefolk machete in one hand, the Gentleman's tail in the other. The man's face was grim; there was to be no reasoning with him.

The Gentleman Fox did not hear his wife explaining the truth to the village. Indeed, he hardly even felt the heels of the men cracking down on his head and chest.

Instead, his gaze was fixed on the fox tail still held in the miller's hand as it withered away before him, just as the Gentleman Fox's own life left his body.

As his last spark dimmed, the Gentleman Fox knew that somewhere out there, another of the Vulpe – the most charming, most cunning of them – would be noticing a new growth from the base of their spine, something that would in a few weeks sprout to form a bushy, rust-coloured fox tail.

After all, even though this Gentleman had failed in his service, the Fox Spirit's hunger had to be sated somehow.

CHAPTER FOUR

Nascha laughed as she ran. Tearing through the forest in the moonlight, her hood fallen down, her white hair whipping behind her like a thing possessed, she exalted in how out of breath and how free she felt.

I set fire to their caravans. Me! The serving girl!

The people back at the Court would not recognise her, now, even after such a short time away. They would never have dreamt of her doing the things she got up to with Vippon. She certainly would have been the last person they would have expected to set fire to the Vulpe caravans, giving herself the opportunity to escape.

It had not just been about her. She had been shocked by the cruelty of the Foxfolk, how they had treated that young man who had shown up at the end. Nascha had known she could escape without causing such a scene, but the young Corvae would have had no chance against Vippon's enhanced abilities. She had almost left him to his fate, but then the tales of Tadita resurfaced in her mind, and Nascha had realised the Titonidae folk hero would have done something to help before leaving herself. Hopefully the stranger had enough movement left within him to escape in the commotion as well. There was nothing more Nascha could have done for him.

A movement in the trees above caught Nascha's eye, and for a brief moment her muscles locked, her breath held. In that instant, the stories of the things that lurked in the dark of the Magpie King's forest came back to her, and she realised she was alone, by herself, in the deep woods, with nobody else to protect her. For the first time in her life, she was not being kept. She was responsible for herself.

Then Nascha remembered touching parchment to lantern flame, setting the caravan wood ablaze, and laughed again. She clearly had more in her than she thought, this new Nascha.

Perhaps, she thought, *I've changed again. I can't imagine I look much like that girl in the mirror a few days ago, the doe-eyed, often kissed, half-undressed lover of a caravaneer.*

Who am I now, then?

She thought about what she might look like to anyone watching her running, unaware and currently unconcerned about her destination. A streak of white in the forest's blackness. Laughing slightly manically at her defiance of the Fox Spirit's chosen one. Her clothing becoming increasingly more distressed as she caught it on brambles and thorns.

Nascha the hermit? A vagabond?

An adventurer?

She giggled at the thought.

At that moment, a shock of wings from the trees collided with her face, and Nascha gave a cry, throwing her arms up to ward off whatever had surprised her.

Just a bird, she told herself, watching the black and white shape alight on a branch not far away. She grinned again, amused at how quickly she let herself go from brave adventurer to screaming infant. Just a bird, out at night, like the owls back at the Court.

Nascha stopped, saluting with two fingers towards the distant magpie on the low branch, its white head turning to peer at her. She had no idea where she was going. She had no idea where she was. She had been so intent on escaping Lord Bidzell's decree that she had not thought about where the Vulpe would be taking her, had no clue where they had been headed. She dimly recalled a story about a fox man owning a remote castle, cherishing the bones of his former lovers after luring them back there and locking them away. Was that the future Vippon had in store for her? Better to be lost in these woods, surely, than be someone's dinner. At least out here, Nascha was in charge of her own destiny.

"What about you?" she said, turning to address the magpie. "Where d'you think I should head next? Where's my next meal?"

Strange for a magpie to be out so late, Nascha thought. Then again, there probably were not many owls here. They would all flock to the Courts. Perhaps here there was better eating for the magpies at night now the owls were gone.

Nascha paused, contemplating the distant bird, narrowing her eyes. Magpies were not an entirely unfamiliar sight back at the Court. They were, in general, not well regarded, the Titonidae being superstitious of them because of their association with their neighbours, and were chased away as quickly as possible from the palace grounds. Still, Nascha had seen many of them before.

That was how she realised this bird was not a magpie.

Her first clue was that only the creature's head was white, and its body was raven black. The bird looked at Nascha, cocking its head.

She stepped closer, puzzled now. There was something about this bird—

Then she gasped.

The bird had no feathers on its head. No feathers, and no skin. As if sensing her realisation, the bird tilted its beak away from her, presenting Nascha with a side profile of its features, very clearly showing the exposed bone and empty eye socket of its face.

"Spirit's shade," Nascha said.

The creature opened its beak and croaked. Nothing that lacked a tongue and vocal cords should have been able to make a noise like that, but Nascha was more concerned with the echo that greeted it from the distant treetops, an echo that did not fade.

Sensing that things were about to turn, Nascha spun on her heel and bolted away from the dead bird.

She did not have time to contemplate the creature's identity. Vague memories of the evil things Tadita had faced on her visit to the forest flitted through Nascha's head, although they dissipated as soon as Nascha realised she could hear the sound of many beating wings behind her, in the trees above her, accompanied by the guttural croaks that were all these creatures seemed to be capable of.

"Great Spirit, Great Spirit," Nascha puffed, already feeling fire flood her lungs. The most exercise she had experienced for the majority of her life was jogging up and down the stairs to the temple tower. Tonight, she had already sprinted through the forest for a good half hour. She would not be able to outrun these creatures long.

A hot pain in her right shoulder caused Nascha to shout in pain. One of the birds – all of which had their heads stripped back to the bone – had dived at her from above, its sharp claws ripping a line through her woollen cloak. She screamed at it, batting it away, but as she did so she got a look at what was behind and above her. Nascha had thought that maybe half a dozen of the monsters pursued her through the woods. The multiple pinpricks of white against the black of the forest told her the number was in actuality much, much greater.

She spun and ran again, but her breath came short and sharp.

I'm going to die. I'm going to die.

After her experience with Lord Bidzell, a small part of Nascha's brain thought she would be used to the concept of imminent death by now. In fact, part of her was proud of how stoically she had treated her sentence of execution back at the Court.

The acceptance of her demise was not as graceful this time.

"Great Spirit, Great Spirit," she uttered in refrain, glancing to the side now, hoping beyond all hope that Vippon would yet again come to her aid.

As she turned her head to look for her lover, another of the creatures swooped at her, its claws just missing her eye, opening up a trio of fine cuts across her cheek instead.

She batted the thing away, surprised at the anger she felt towards the bird for attacking her.

It's not fair, it's not fair, she thought, feet pounding on the forest floor, flesh and fabric tearing as she dashed through bushes, not allowing them to slow her down. *I was free. For the first time, I was free.*

What price freedom, though? She was not certain it was worth her life. Maybe she would have been better off with Vippon, sheltered in his caravan, under his blankets, her bones eventually decorating the floor of his castle dungeon.

At that thought, the panic drained from Nascha. She kept running, despite her legs and lungs protesting, but she remained deadly serious.

No, she thought, *I would never choose a life like that. Better to be my own woman than to let a man own me and decide when to toss me away.*

If I am to die, better to be at a time of my choosing, because of – for once in my life – choices I made for myself.

Choices like running off alone into these cursed woods.

Realising she was in danger of collapsing from exhaustion, realising the creatures could finish her off whenever the notion took them, Nascha took a deep breath, spun on her heel, and – just before the first of the beasts made contact with her – screamed, "Come and get me, then, you greedy little bastards."

She closed her eyes, gritted her teeth, and a great rush of wind blew in her ears, but the expected impact and tearing of flesh did not come.

Surprised, hesitant, Nascha cracked an eyelid open.

Before her stood a man. Pale skin, lank hair, a dark, tattered cloak draped around his shoulders. In his right hand he held one of the bird-creatures by the neck. His eyes still on her, he squeezed his fist and the bird's head shattered, exploding all around him. None of the other creatures were in sight.

The man before her dropped the bird's body to the floor and, her exhaustion finally overcoming her, Nascha felt herself fall into blackness, not stopping herself from collapsing into the newcomer's arms before blacking out entirely.

There was a lake, Nascha was dimly aware. It was night, and there was a lake. Her mind was foggy, and she shook her head to clear that fog, but it did not move. Was something wrong with her?

The fog lessened, and Nascha realised there was someone at the lake. It was a woman, a woman with white hair. Was that... was that her? Had she died, and she was somehow looking down on her own body, her ghost waiting for the Owl Spirit to take her away?

No. The woman by the lake, she was crying, her face in her hands, her knees in the lake's waters. She was older, this woman, and was dressed in a deep blue robe the like of which Nascha had never worn before. The woman… she seemed familiar to Nascha, somehow.

Then, suddenly, a man in black arrived, leaping impossibly from some nearby treetops, landing softly beside the crying woman. Nascha tried to shout out, to warn the woman of the stranger's arrival, but found she could not. Thankfully, when the woman raised her head to see the newcomer, she smiled, and held out her hand to encourage the man to take it.

Nascha blinked, and the scene began to fade.

Only a dream. It had only been a dream…

She awoke, and it was still dark. Darker than it had been before – there was no moon or starlight to illuminate her surroundings. Somewhere, muted, she heard wind blowing, distant from her. Nascha shifted slightly, stifling a groan, and felt cold stone beneath her. A cave. She was in a cave. Had that man carried her here?

She shivered.

For what purpose had she been brought here? An image of Vippon gnawing on human bones flitted through her mind.

She shifted again, giving a small moan as the cut on her shoulder, the blood only thinly clotted, reopened.

"Welcome back," said a voice in the darkness.

Nascha froze. He was close. Whoever he was, the man who had saved her was within reach of her.

"I can't see you," she said accusingly, annoyed at how her voice shook as she spoke.

There was a shuffling as the figure moved – away from her, thankfully – and sparks blazed briefly to life as flint met flint.

"I forgot," the man said, not quite speaking directly to Nascha. "Forgot she would not be able to see."

The spark caught whatever fuel the man had placed on his rudimentary fire, and soon a weak orange glow filled the cave. It was small, and dry. She could not see the outside from where she was, and supposed the cave must be deep, based on the lack of light from the night sky. Nascha tried not to think of the tales she had heard of Mother Web and her brood, the giant spiders that were said to live under the ground in these woods.

"Thank you," Nascha said softly, not expecting the stranger to hear.

Instead, the man cocked his head sharply at her words, still not looking at her. "Fine," he said, "fine."

There was silence between them for a few moments, filled only by the high winds outside, and in the firelight Nascha got a better look at him. He was much older than her, but it was difficult to place his age – perhaps in his fifties, his face a landscape of ridges and valleys. His hair, as Nascha had previously noticed, was long and unkempt. His skin was pale and uncared for, looking almost clammy. He stood over the fire, hunched, pulling his tattered cloak over his shoulders. Nascha realised he was sweating, although there was no way the heat of the fire could have made him do so.

"You're a witch," the man said. There was no menace in his voice; it was just a statement, but still it shocked Nascha.

"I am not," she said, standing up in protest, some of her own fire returning.

He turned to look at her. The pupils in his eyes were large, almost overcoming all other colour, but what shocked her the most were his teeth. They were sharp, pointed, like an animal's.

The man considered her for a moment, then said, "Your hair. White hair. White hair for a witch, that's what they say in the villages."

There was something about this strange man. Something... familiar?

"Well, where I'm from, nobody particularly likes being called a witch, thank you. Not really a good conversation opener. Not a good way to make friends."

At her use of the word 'friends', the man turned away again, back to the fire.

"Friends. Something I've never been that good at. Even before... I'm sorry. I didn't mean to offend. The Owlfolk. You're one of the Owlfolk. That's what I should have said."

Nascha nodded, a bit embarrassed now.

"A queen."

"What?"

He turned back to look at her again. "Your white hair. A sign of the royal family." Again, another statement, not a question.

She shook her head. "Not me. Not really, anyway. My ma was a seamstress, they tell me. A proper one, not the indecent kind. Da was a huntsman. They loved each other, I guess, or were faithful, at least. I can't really remember them. When word about my hair spread to the Court, I was taken away. Put where they could keep an eye on me. They reckon, somewhere in my family history, one of the nobles came to play. Left a seed that waited for generations to bloom. Gave me my hair, and a job at the Court, but no crown. Just a servant."

The man smiled at that. "Not quite a queen, then. I know how that feels."

Nascha expected him to elaborate, but instead he continued to stare at the fire, its light casting long shadows on the cave roof.

"Nascha," she said eventually. "My name's Nascha."

"Why were you out after sundown? Surely the Titonidae know the dangers of this place."

Nascha blew at a lock of hair that had fallen over her face. "I didn't have much of a choice. Found myself in a situation, and needed to get away fast. Also, I didn't think the forest would be as bad as the stories made out."

"Yes, I've been guilty of that mistake too, in my youth." Again, the man offered no more information.

"Who are you?" Nascha asked him, more intrigued than worried by what his answer might be.

He looked back at her, the flames casting an amber glow over his black eyes.

"Lonan. They call me Lonan."

"Are you... I thought you might have been the Magpie King."

"There is no Magpie King," Lonan said quickly, turning away. "Not anymore."

Nascha let out a sigh of relief. "Thank goodness."

He turned to look at her, quizzical.

"I hear he had a thing for girls with white hair," Nascha said, attempting a joke.

Instead of a laugh or even a smile from this strange man, Nascha was rewarded for her jest by a tug towards him. She was so surprised by the invisible force pulling at her, she almost fell into the fire. Lonan clearly felt it too, as he jumped up from the fireside, backing away from the unexpected sensation.

"What was that?" he said, clearly unnerved, on guard. Nascha was reminded that seconds ago she had been accused of witchcraft.

Across the firelight, their eyes met, and she felt the tug again, almost physical this time. Nascha nearly stepped towards Lonan. Instead, he moved away, turning from her, walking to the back of the cave.

"What are you doing to me?" Lonan said.

"I—I'm not doing anything," Nascha said. "I think. It just seems to happen, sometimes."

It felt exactly the same as when she had first met Vippon. Like last time, she was drawn to this man, invisibly, yet Nascha found this even more difficult to explain than with the Vulpe leader. There was no attraction here. This man, Lonan, there was nothing appealing about him. He was old, like Vippon, yes, but wretched, and miserable. He had none of the Vulpe's charisma, and she should have felt nothing but revulsion and suspicion for him.

Yet the pull remained. Even though it was no longer tugging at them, it was still there, between them, a taut link, and clearly Lonan felt it too.

Finally, he looked at her again. "Something inside me is... drawn to you." He glanced at her head. Her hair. "Something inside you. Perhaps you inherited more from the Titonidae nobility than just your hair colour. I'm not the Magpie King, but I am the closest thing the forest has to one now. The Magpie Kings of history were always drawn towards those with the Owl Spirit's gifts..."

Her hand found its way to her hair, threading her fingers between her messy strands. She shook her head. "Can't be. I've never had anything like that before. Surely I'd know by now if..." But then Nascha remembered the poison. The poison they had forced her to drink each month, to stop her from having any children. To stop her from developing any of the gifts of the Owl Spirit.

The poison she had thrown up against the side of the stable when she first heard Lord Bidzell suggest her death.

She looked up at Lonan again, her mind reeling. Was she developing powers of some kind? Perhaps that might explain why she had felt a connection with these powerful men, a connection she had mistaken for attraction with Vippon. The part inside her that was a sliver of the Owl Spirit's power recognised a kindred spirit in these people. Looking at Lonan, at this wretched figure before her, part of Nascha felt repulsed at what had happened between her and Vippon. Had she really been attracted to him, or had she been tricked by whatever in her blood made her feel this way?

And then, eyes meeting with those of this stranger she was invisibly being pulled towards, Nascha felt something new. Lonan was not involved, this time, not really. Instead, something else looked at Nascha through the older man's eyes. His pupils widened, the skin and muscles of his face otherwise unmoving, and Nascha had the uncanny sensation that it was no longer Lonan looking at her. The unseen link between them changed, and she felt something else take hold of that bond, something far away, distant.

Something that had noticed Nascha, and taken an interest in her.

Lonan shook his head, dismissing the bond between them, turning away as if oblivious to the other entity looking through his eyes. Despite being no longer bound to Lonan, however, Nascha still felt connected to something else. The bond that had joined her to Vippon and Lonan had changed; it no longer pulled at her, nor at whatever else was connected to it. Instead, the link seemed to be some kind of guiding thread, joining Nascha with whatever else was out there. She shuddered as she felt a presence along that bond, searching down it, making its way slowly towards Nascha, like a spider creeping down its web towards its prey.

"You aren't like normal people," Nascha said, voice low, trying to suppress her horror at the sensation of being hunted out. "You're stronger. You move quickly."

Lonan grunted in acknowledgement, but said nothing, still turned away from her.

"Where do you get your powers from?"

He waited a moment before replying. "The Magpie Spirit. Mine are the gifts of the Magpie Spirit."

A ripple of familiarity vibrated along the invisible thread. Whatever was making its way down it was far away, very far, but Nascha had no doubt it was making its way towards her, now.

She had to get out of this forest as quickly as possible, and as far as she could from this man, and from anything to do with the Magpie Spirit.

Lonan stiffened, his head darting to the side, as if he had heard something. Oblivious to Nascha's thoughts, almost as if he'd forgotten about her presence, he marched out of the cave.

Her mind reeling from her experience, the bond with that distant force persisting, unbreakable, Nascha ran after him.

The sun was beginning to rise over the forest. Nascha gasped at the view before her. The cave Lonan had carried her to was set halfway up one of the many small mountains that rose from the forest, and as such, Nascha had a good view of the land from above. It seemed to her as if there was dark green in every direction, tumbling before her like a bear rug on a nobleman's chamber floor, the treetops waving in the dying winds. She turned north to get a glimpse of the White Woods surrounding the Owl Queen's Court and could not find them, the horizon ending in the dark green that was so pervasive.

"There's something out there," Lonan said, looking at the woods before him.

For a moment, Nascha thought this man could feel what she was feeling, that he was talking about the thing that had given him his gifts, that was now searching for Nascha. However, instead Lonan pointed to a clearing in the trees a few miles from them, where some Corvae roofs peeked through the canopy. The presence looking for Nascha was much further away than that, for now. Further than the forest borders, she thought, as another vibration ran down that invisible link.

"There is something in the forest. Something powerful, moving."

Nascha looked at the few visible rooftops, but could see no evidence to support Lonan's statement.

"You'll be safe in the cave," he said, crouching, tensing. "Stay, until I return."

Nascha gasped as Lonan leapt from the cave mouth. For a moment she thought he was actually taking flight, and that he would soar through the sky all the way to the village. However, after travelling about half the distance between the cave and the village, Lonan descended into the treetops, and disappeared. The Magpie Spirit's gifts did not include flight, but apparently his strength was considerable.

She stood there for a moment, watching the sun rise, eyes remaining on the spot where Lonan had descended to the trees. The tranquillity of the moment was ruined by the dull tremors reminding Nascha that, somewhere out there, something was coming for her.

Stay?

That's the last thing I want to do in this cursed place. Time to get out of this forest once and for all.

Noting the location of the distant village – Nascha's only landmark in the sea of green – she gritted her teeth and began her descent.

Bradan ached as he plodded on through the forest, aware that he was probably being pursued, aware that at any moment Vippon and his Foxfolk could come bursting through the trees and take him down. His insides suffering, bones grinding as he moved, Bradan knew he would be defenceless if he was attacked. His father – seemingly distracted by some bout of madness – would be his only chance, but Bradan was convinced Lonan was not coming tonight.

Bradan pushed through the trees, and was greeted with a sight that caused him to let forth a sigh of relief. It was the Magpie Spirit's temple.

He had been here a number of times in his life, so the tall building was familiar enough. It sat at the base of the cliff that was home to the Eyrie, the Magpie King's ancestral home. However, unlike the Eyrie – those unclaimed ruins nobody lived in – the temple had been somewhat repaired since Bradan's father's time.

Taking a few seconds to check if anyone was waiting for him, aware that pursuit could be mere moments behind, Bradan staggered forward, sending a quick prayer to the Magpie Spirit, hoping the doors would be open to him. The last time he had visited the temple, it had been unoccupied. The Lady's influence had spread to this part of the woods by then, and the smattering of religious hermits who had adopted the repaired temple as their own had abandoned it, though they remained scared enough of the stories of the Magpie King to leave the building itself in good enough repair.

Bradan almost fell against the double doors, and, to his relief, they opened for him.

Inside, the temple was clean, but empty. Pews of wooden seats were arranged in rows, facing the back of the room. The altar itself was dominated by an old totem pole, each face of which depicted a different version of a magpie. The same bird, but mirrored dozens of times, each visage showing a different aspect of the being the people of the forest had once unanimously dedicated themselves to.

Bradan staggered up the aisle and collapsed at the altar, just beneath the totem pole. The majority of the temple was dark, but clean. In the back of his mind, Bradan realised someone must still be tending to it, regularly sweeping away dust and cobwebs. He knew enough about the Lady to know that anyone who did so would be encouraging her wrath, so it showed true dedication to the memory of the Magpie Spirit to continue this small favour. The walls of the building, once lined with woodcarvings showing the legend of the first Magpie King – or so Bradan's father had told him – were now plain, simple wooden panels, presumably replaced by the Corvae before the Lady's influence had spread. This totem pole, scratched and disfigured from years of neglect under the rule of the false Magpie King, was the only thing that remained of the original temple, other than the pews themselves.

Lying on the ground, sore, exhausted, aware that at any moment the Vulpe could catch up with him, Bradan raised his eyes to the carved faces of the Magpie Spirit.

He rarely prayed. Not properly, despite having come to the temple in the past. Certainly, during moments of anguish and extreme emotions, he'd let slip a quick request to the Spirit, asking it to save him. Anyone in the forest would do the same in such situations. But now, exhausted, quivering in anticipation, Bradan stared up at the totem pole and prayed.

"Magpie Spirit, please," he began, faltering, unsure of how to continue. "My father. My father, he is ill. He is the one carrying your gift, he is the one protecting the forest..." Bradan thought about his father, huddled in a cave somewhere, muttering to himself, engaging in conversations that only he could hear. "He has tried so hard to protect your people, to be there for them when help was needed, but... he is ill."

Bradan looked up expectantly. "The forest needs a new protector. Needs someone to be blessed by you, to carry your gifts without the madness that so often comes with them. My father, he tried hard, but the poison has overtaken his mind. The line of the Magpie King is dead, and their immunity to the poison disappeared with it."

He sat upright now, preparing his final gambit. "But I – I am the son of one who has been cursed by your gift. Out of everyone else here in the forest, I am the only one with a chance to contain your powers, to accept the black flower and to fight off its poison. Great Magpie Spirit, I am ready to claim my birthright. I am ready to step up and protect my home, and to allow my father to rest."

He stood now, fists clenched, his exhausted body renewed as his heart beat in anticipation. Blood – blood that carried the gift of his father – raced through his body.

"Great Magpie Spirit, I offer myself before you. Give me the powers of the Magpie King. Allow me to become the protector of the forest, and I and the rest of my line shall serve you until we are cleansed from this world."

Somewhere in the rafters, wings fluttered.

Bradan thought for a moment that this sound heralded some visitor to the temple, some avatar of the Magpie Spirit that had come to raise him up, to empower him. Instead, the fluttering settled down again, probably just a nesting bird disturbed by his speech.

No other sounds came. No response to Bradan's pleas. The energy that had sustained him, held him aloft to make his petition, left his body, and he collapsed with a sob, no longer able to summon the strength to hold himself upright.

Hating himself for begging, he turned his tear-filled eyes again to the totem. "You're losing the forest. The people, they're turning from you. Forgetting about you. Look at this temple – clean, but empty. I could bring them back. Give me power. Let me be a light for them; return your greatness to their eyes. My father can't do that. He is terrified of their gaze."

He paused for a moment, trying not to shudder himself at the thought of the eyes of the villagers of Meldrum on him, but he shook his head, dismissing them.

"I could be a Magpie King to walk in the light, to chase away the pretenders to the forest, to bring all of the people back to you."

The totem did not respond.

"Give me the gift. Give me my gift!"

Again, nothing.

Bradan opened his mouth to plead anew, but no words came out. Instead, he heard a high-pitched keening echoing around the dark chamber, and realised it was coming from him. Horrified at the noise he was making, he did not shy away from his anguish. He was beaten, pursued, and now he had been rejected by both his father and his god.

Sobbing, Bradan lowered his head to the temple floor, and allowed exhaustion to overcome him.

He was standing upon a cliff edge, overlooking the forest.

Bradan realised almost immediately that he was dreaming. His body still ached, but the pain was remote, distant, as if the injuries of his flesh held little importance here.

He could clearly see the forest spread out before him, despite the lack of moonlight in the purple sky. The forest itself was too uniform, too perfect, as if it were a stitched quilt, a fuzzy remembrance of a forest in the mind of a creature that had not visited it in a very long time.

The slope he stood on was steep, and the steepness did not appear to abate until the forest floor a very long distance below him. Bradan suspected that if he tried to descend that way, he would very quickly stumble and fall to his death. If, of course, it was possible to die in a dream.

Bradan did not want to find out.

It was only when he looked to the distant horizon that Bradan saw anything that threatened the uniformity of his dreamscape. The sky out there was darker, somehow. At the horizon, the dreamlike purple haze did not continue, and an inky blackness seemed to swirl up from just beyond the forest boundary. Bradan's eyes were drawn to this blackness, and they widened when he realised the blackness was moving, growing. An empty feeling in his gut told Bradan this was something he should fear. It was only then that he considered why he had been brought here. This no longer felt like a normal dream. Desperately, he racked his mind to think of which of the creatures of the forest invaded dreams, but he could only come up with the notion of the Owl Queens, and this did not feel like their touch.

The blackness on the horizon grew further, and Bradan realised – as he had expected – that it was coming closer, approaching him, spreading across the purple night sky, fouling that dreamlike light, seeding it with the stuff of nightmares.

He fell to his knees when the blackness coalesced into a shape he recognised. It was a colossal bird, its wings flapping only sporadically, making its way across the forest. This creature was easily the size of the Eyrie itself, the Magpie King's former castle. Possibly bigger.

"Magpie Spirit," Bradan whispered, aghast, but this time he was not using the deity's name as an expletive. He was addressing the creature flying towards him.

Unable to act, both because he was trapped on this mountainside, and fear and awe kept him frozen, Bradan continued to kneel, rigid, as the black bird came closer. Finally, it stopped, just out of his reach, its wings beating but not seeming to affect the bird's motion. Bradan got the impression it would hang there in front of him just as well if its wings were still.

This is it, Bradan thought. *The Spirit itself has come to bless me. My father has never been afforded treatment like this.* Bradan's chest almost burst, his heart pounding, his blood charged with a lightning storm of excitement. *I'm going to ascend. I'm going to be the next Magpie King.*

He knew he should be standing tall. A proper Magpie King would rise to his feet, facing this unknown, ancient force with confidence, assured in his blood right. But this thing before him, the great Magpie Spirit, was vast. It was larger than any animal Bradan had ever seen, or could ever conceive. It was impossible. Bradan knew, somehow, that what he was looking at was just a fabrication, just a sliver of the true force that was worshipped by his people, and had been for generations. So he knelt, overcome with awe, waiting for the Spirit to address him.

It did not. The being hovered impossibly before him, and

Bradan felt the Spirit's gaze narrow, focussing in on him, contemplating him.

He felt exposed. Naked. Alone.

Finally, when he felt he could take the waiting no more, Bradan shouted, "Great Magpie Spirit, tell me: have you heard my prayer? Have you come here to bless me, as you did my father?"

The colossal black bird did not answer, but moved closer. Bradan could see himself reflected in the black of the thing's eyes.

After another series of agonising minutes, Bradan spoke again. "Great Spirit, will you not speak to me? Have you come here to gift me, so I can best protect your people?"

Finally, the Magpie Spirit spoke.

"You are not of the line of kings I established here. Yet you still contain traces of me."

The Spirit's beak did not move, but its words echoed about Bradan's head like a thunderclap in a cavern.

Bradan, face creased in confusion, shouted, "No, my father is the current... he is the one who took your gift when the line of the Magpie King fell."

"The line of the Magpie King fell?"

Bradan opened his mouth to respond, but his jaw hung there, slack, as he realised what the Magpie Spirit was saying.

"You—you didn't know? But... but it was many years ago. Decades. The Magpie King was betrayed. My father, he sacrificed himself to rid the forest of the betrayer..."

The Spirit was motionless, unresponsive.

"But that was so long ago. Before my lifetime. You didn't know?" Bradan shouted at the Spirit, but it continued to watch him, not showing any inclination to answer his questions.

Bradan felt a heat rise inside as the implications of this revelation hit him. "But... where have you been? You're supposed to watch over us, to protect us from harm. We're your people, and we've needed you. We've been praying to you, thinking you were helping us. Where have you been? Where have you been?"

The Spirit moved then, swooping toward him, and Bradan screamed as that great beak descended upon him and into him. The world of the dreamscape shattered, and that purple sky was replaced with... Bradan's life.

Images from his own past blurred around him. Early memories of Mother Ogma teaching him how to make a poultice to keep wounds clean. Meeting his father for the first time, and how scared he had been of him, how long he had cried in his bed afterward. The other children in the village making fun of him, calling him 'scarecrow'. The day he realised his Knack was never going to develop. Knackless. The first time he met someone whose life his father had saved. More tears, better tears. Pride at being told how much he looked like his father. Mother Ogma's last words. Heading into the night to find his father, convincing him they could share a life together. The first sign of the Lady's presence spreading, the first of her shambles Bradan saw hanging in the trees. The villagers' dirty looks when Bradan mentioned the Magpie Spirit and the king. The barkwraith meeting with him in the woods. The Lady becoming more powerful. The Lady. The Lady. The Lady.

Bradan screamed. At the back of his mind, he was dimly aware of what was happening. The Magpie Spirit had invaded his thoughts, was tearing through them to find out about events in the forest over the last few generations. Its search had begun with Bradan's own life, but clearly became fixated with the idea of the Lady of the Forest and her rise, revisiting any mention of her over and over again, those replays becoming more frantic, forceful and angry. Bradan had been attacked recently, his mortal frame still broken and bruised from the assault by the Vulpe. However, their attacks were nothing compared with what the Magpie Spirit was doing now. The deepest parts of him were being invaded, his most precious, tender memories being groped at, held up for display, bringing back the pain and joy of those moments in equal measure.

It was the most terrible thing Bradan had ever experienced.

Finally, the Spirit broke contact with Bradan. He was back on the mountaintop, exhausted, spread out on the ground. He was not surprised to find that he was sobbing, and could not stop himself.

The Spirit hovered there for a moment longer and then, finished with him, it turned to go.

"Wait," Bradan croaked, reaching out for the retreating deity. "What about me? What about the Magpie King? My father is trying his best, but he is not fit to hold that power."

"And neither are you," the Magpie Spirit replied, not deigning to turn to look at him again. "Perhaps in time, but not now. Now, you are not worthy."

The Spirit moved toward the horizon.

"Wait," Bradan screamed after it. "Wait!"

He was woken by a rattling from the rooftop. It took Bradan a moment to realign himself, to realise the purple sky was gone and he was back on the floor of the temple. Outside, a wind raged, battering the wooden shingles of the temple roof.

Bradan continued his sobs from his dream. He did not know how long he had slept for, but clearly the rest had done little for his physical injuries, as any movement still felt like spikes of bone tearing at his insides. What was worse, however – even worse than the rape of his mind by what he'd previously thought was a benevolent being – was the ongoing, haunting echoes of the Magpie Spirit's last words.

You are not worthy.

Breathing heavy, his anger a fuel for his abused limbs, Bradan stood upright, tears still streaming down his face.

"Not worthy?" He had not meant to shout the words, but as he fixed upon the eyes of the nearest totem magpie, he could not fight against the rage inside. "I'm not worthy? My father is not the only one who has given his life for this forest. If I'm not worthy, then who? Tell me that, Magpie Spirit," he said, spitting as he addressed the totem pole. "Or do you care so little about your forest that it means nothing to you that you're losing it?"

Neither the totem pole nor the Magpie Spirit responded. Bradan had not expected them to. Instead, he shouted at the empty temple, the rage in his voice echoed by the rising winds outside.

The Vulpe must not have pursued him, he realised. Otherwise, they would certainly have caught up with him while he was sleeping. Perhaps they chose to pursue that white-haired woman instead, the one who had saved him. He hoped she was all right.

Face curdling, Bradan chided himself for thinking of someone else. Clearly the Magpie Spirit did not think him worthy of becoming a protector, so why should he bother trying to be one anymore?

Sick of the sight of the place, unable to remain within the mocking glare of the carved magpies, Bradan forced himself to stay upright, and took halting steps towards the temple door.

He pushed it open, struggling against the force of the winds from outside. The half light that surged into the temple's darkness told Bradan that sunrise was not far off.

Outside, the wind was alive, picking up the leaf fall and tossing it into the sky, snatches of red and brown flying through the air, as aimless as Bradan now the promise of his ascension had wilted and fallen.

There, waiting for him just beyond the treeline, was the Lady's barkwraith. If it had the mouth to do so, Bradan was certain it would be smiling at him.

He stood in the mouth of the temple for a few moments, rigid at the sight of it. He was not fearful of the creature, he was just… contemplating it. He was angry at the Magpie Spirit, angry at its rejection, angry at how pointless his life was now that he would not be rising in his father's place.

Something inside him snapped into place. As purposefully as his injuries allowed, he strode across the clearing towards the barkwraith at the edge of the wood.

Not giving it a chance to address him, Bradan spoke first. "Tell the Lady I am hers. Tell her if she gives me power to protect the people of the forest, gives me the strength to no longer have to hide in the shadows, then I am hers."

The creature just nodded, then pointed west. "She waits for you in the village of Ebora. There, she will give you her gift."

Bradan stared at the thing for a few moments longer, his eyes containing all of his fury, glaring at the barkwraith as if his pure hate would be enough to scorch it, to set it on fire.

Then Bradan turned on his heel and headed west, on to Ebora, to force his way into legend.

THE GIRL
AND THE
LAKE

A Lost Tale of the Corvae

The Owl Princess had run away from home that night. She had been arguing with her father, as often she did. Their arguments ranged from many subjects, such as how to properly clean the kitchen, what had really happened to her mother, and which distant land the traveller Tadita had visited first. However, that night the argument had been the one they most often had – the argument that all other arguments stemmed from, where the rift between father and daughter truly came from. They had been arguing about suitors, about whose hand the princess would accept in marriage.

When her father sent her to her room, that had been the final straw. A girl of sixteen, the same age as Tadita when she had left home, the princess had gathered up her white hair, hidden it under a cloak to protect her from prying eyes, and crept out of her father's castle, slinking away into the White Woods.

Although she had often thought about leaving home, about escaping the eventual fate of being handed off to some distant prince, the Owl Princess had no idea of where to head next. She had spent her life being waited on by the servants of the Court, and had very little idea of the world outside her father's realm, or how to survive in it.

That was why, on the night she fled her father's home, she found herself at the small lake that lay just beside the border of the Magpie King's forest.

The princess, exhausted from hours of travel, lay by the side of the lake, her toes wrinkling in the water, staring up at the cloudy sky, contemplating her future, her anger with her father cooled by the lake's water and the night breeze.

That was when she heard the sobbing.

Her first inclination was, as she had been taught, to run away. Although she was still well within the White Woods, the princess was aware of how close she was to the Magpie King's forest, and was aware of all the stories the Owlfolk had been told of that place. In particular, she was aware of how the Magpie King coveted the Titonidae nobles born with white hair, and – despite her father's promises that the Magpie King had not been spotted in his lifetime – she pulled the hood of her cloak further over her head, ensuring no stray locks of hair gave away her identity.

As soon as the princess reached the undergrowth of the forest, however, she hesitated, looking back. The sobbing was distant now; it had not followed her, but remained just as mournful as it had by the lakeside.

It would have been a simple thing for the princess to retreat then, to slink back to her father's home, to return to a life of nobility, royal weddings, and doing her duty.

Instead, the Owl Princess returned to the lakeside.

She eventually found the source of the tears. It was a young man, sitting by the side of the lake not too far from where she had rested her feet. A heavy, worn black cloak draped his shoulders, pulled all about him as his frame shuddered, a cry escaping his lips. From this distance, the man's hair was long and unkempt, and his face was pale, reflecting the dim, cloud-veiled moonlight.

"Why are you crying?" she asked the man, announcing herself as she stepped from the trees towards the shore.

He leapt with a start, with a speed that frightened her. When he stood to look at her, she saw that he was thin, sickly, and that his clothes were soiled. He bared his teeth at her with a snarl. She could not help but notice the fangs in his mouth, and she felt sick, knowing she had made a dreadful mistake. She glanced back at the forest behind her, wondering if he would give chase with the same speed if she just turned and ran.

The man rubbed at his eyes, as if frantic to remove his tears before she spotted them.

"You shouldn't be out at night," he said. His voice sounded cold, but was laced with the sadness of someone who had been interrupted while grieving, someone not quite prepared to speak to another human being. "The forest is dangerous. Go home."

She should have obeyed him. However, being a princess, the girl was not used to being commanded, and she took exception to the man's tone. Also, a small part of her was intrigued by his story. Who was this strange boy? What in the world could have brought him low, to such a state?

The princess took a step forward, her head held high. "How dare you," she said, adopting her best regal tone. "How dare you talk about my father's forest, as if you knew it as well as I did. The only danger here is that which you bring with you."

The man looked about himself, confused, as if seeing the forest around him for the first time.

"Your father's forest?"

A small part of her, distant, knew she should not do it, but the princess could not help herself. She stepped forward again, pulling back her hood, allowing her white hair to betray her royal heritage. "My father is the Owl King, and this is his land. The land that, one day, I will rule."

She had expected the strange man to be impressed. Frightened, possibly. Instead, he was only confused.

"This is the Owl King's forest?" He spun around again, as if noticing the white of the birch around him for the first time. "I've come so far?"

The princess coughed, bringing his eyes back to her. "You do not know where you are?" She stepped towards him once more, her fear dissipating as her curiosity took over.

His eyes widened, as if noticing the princess for the first time, and he took a step back from her, fearful, his hand raised.

"Do not come closer," he said, his voice raised, urgent. "You do not know... You cannot trust me. You have no idea what I might do. I do not know."

Ignoring his advice, worrying about how frantic the young man was becoming, the princess stepped forward again. "I think you are ill, boy. Let me take care of you."

She reached out, wanting to lay her hand on his shoulder.

"No!" he shouted. Then, to the Owl Princess' shock, the boy crouched, and leapt into the air.

She stood agog as he disappeared into the greyness above them. For a brief second, far off in the distance she fancied she could see a black shape descend from the sky, down into the dark trees of the Magpie King's forest.

The princess stood for a few moments longer, unable to move or speak. Then, in shock, she turned herself around, to make her way back to her father's home. She slunk past the Court guards, past the maid sleeping outside her chamber, and climbed back into her own bed, without disturbing any others, or letting them know she had been gone.

For the rest of that night, however, the princess did not sleep. Instead, she spent the final hours of night-time staring at her ceiling, thinking about the strange boy from the Magpie King's forest.

It was a few days before the princess summed up the courage to make the journey back to the lake. She followed the same routine as last time, not letting any others know she had left, hiding her hair from prying eyes. However, she did lower her hood when she got to the lake, where she found the stranger waiting for her.

"You should not have come back," he said as she approached, his muscles tensed.

In response, she just smiled, and offered him some of the wine she had stolen from her father's cellars. He refused it, but he did accept her company. They sat together by the moonlit lake, and she talked to him of life at the Court, of her squabbles with her father, and her hopes for the future. For his part, the tattered man was guarded about his own past, but as she continued to return to the lakeside, night after night, the princess began to piece together his story from the snippets he gave her. He was strong, had been given gifts – that much had been apparent from the first night she met him – but those gifts came at a price. He had distanced himself from his people for fear of hurting them. When he told her this, he became angry at himself for returning to speak to her, realising he was putting her in harm's way by spending time with her. After that night it was a month before she found him waiting by the lake again.

The night he returned, he embraced her, telling her through his violent sobs how lonely he was, how it both relieved and terrified him that she kept coming back to the lake. For her part, the Owl Princess was fascinated by this special, tortured man who felt so fragile in her arms.

It was not long after that they became lovers.

Their lovemaking was awkward at first, both unsure of the act, but eventually it became all the princess lived for. At day, her father would parade suitors before her, and she looked on them with sleep-clouded eyes, all the time thinking of her tattered man by the lake. At night, she came alive in her lover's arms.

All that changed the night he came to her wrong.

The princess knew straight away that something was different about her beloved. He did not greet her with the sad smile and open arms she was used to. Instead, he was hunched like an animal, his eyes darting around the lakeside as she approached. He was sniffing the air, but tensed when she stepped into the moonlight.

"My love?" she said.

When he turned to her, she saw his face was covered in blood.

With a gasp, she ran to him. "What has happened? Tell me, what is wrong?"

He leapt towards her, then, and it was not a friendly movement. He stood two steps away, tall, threatening. His face, which should have been so familiar, was alien to her.

And then the princess remembered her beloved's fears, about how dangerous he was, and she wondered who owned the blood that was smeared across his face.

"Beloved," she whispered, "what have you done?"

"Me?" he said, his voice two stones rubbing against each other. "I have done nothing."

The doubt must have been clear on her face, as he stepped forward and hit her.

As a princess, she had led a sheltered life, and had never been harmed before. When she looked back on that moment, she supposed it had been just a small tap, but it was enough to send her onto her back, her mind reeling.

"I would never hurt anyone," her lover screamed at her, standing over her. "Never!"

She answered only with a sob, unable to otherwise voice her confusion and pain.

The hurt in her voice must have made some kind of connection, as it was as if a cloud had lifted from her lover's face, allowing him to see the horror of what he had done.

"I would never…" he whispered. Then, taking one last glimpse of the princess lying beaten on the ground, he ran.

That was the last she ever saw of him.

She eventually recovered from the blow, making her way home, shocked, silent. She did not sleep that night, lying looking at the ceiling, unblinking.

Eventually, the princess returned to the lake, looking for her lover again, wanting an explanation, wanting desperately to find a reason to forgive him. Despite her cries, he never revealed himself again, not even when she shouted across the silent lake, telling him about his child that would soon be born.

Her father found out about the baby, eventually, and was of course beside himself with anger. He hid his daughter away, hoping to keep her misdemeanour secret. Her sister, also blessed by the Owl Spirit, took to the throne instead, ensuring the family line continued to rule the Court.

On the day of the child's arrival, the princess hoped her lover would return to see his son. Instead, an old Magpiefolk woman approached the king, offering to take the child back to the forest, where she claimed it belonged. The Owl King, happy a solution to his problem had presented itself, willingly accepted.

The princess was not given the chance to say goodbye. The loss of her child, and of the man she loved, broke her. There were those who whispered of her returning to rule, of her desire to rise up against her sister, who had taken the throne from her.

Nothing could be further from the truth. To this day, the princess rests still in her tower, receiving few visitors, almost forgotten by her family. She is not, however, lonely. While her body has become infirm through atrophy, her mind is far from that tower in the Owl Queen's Court.

She still dwells by that lake, in the moonlight, safe in her lover's arms.

CHAPTER FIVE

Nascha found herself almost skipping through the forest. She struggled to remember how to, at first. It had been so long since she had attempted it. Since she had been allowed. Dimly, she recalled holding somebody's hand as she skipped through a village, but she could not recall who it had been. A woman, of that she was certain, but not her mother – Nascha had been taken from her before she could walk. She was now finding the whole process of skipping to be a little bit ridiculous, but that emotion was eclipsed by how liberating the whole experience was. She no longer had to do what other people said.

Stay here until I tell you to. That was what Lonan had said to her this morning. Told her to do.

Thinking of his command, Nascha pulled a face, more for her own benefit than for that of any woodland creatures that might be watching.

Until I tell you to.

Nascha had had enough of being told what to do, thank you very much.

She did not doubt that the forest was a dangerous place, and she did not doubt that Lonan knew how to be safe in it. But she also knew that everyone she had put her faith into before had let her down, and she knew that allowing his words to imprison her in that cave would have felt too much like being back at the Court, or in Vippon's caravan. She would take her chances with the wood, but she would be more careful this time. No more going out at night.

This time, she would stick close to the settlements. And above all, in the Spirit's name, get out of this forest before it killed her.

As if it sensed her thoughts, the distant entity Nascha suspected was linked to the Magpie Spirit and Lonan's powers made its presence known again, another tremor running down the invisible thread that bound her to it. She had hoped that distancing herself from Lonan would have broken the link, but it seemed to have made no difference. That presence out there could still sense her, and was still coming for her. Nascha pinned her hopes on leaving the forest, and leaving the place of the Magpie Spirit's power. Hopefully then, when she was outside the forest's border, the link would be broken.

Thank the Spirit – the Owl Spirit, not the Magpie – that Lonan had drawn her attention to the nearby village before he had left. Otherwise, Nascha would have been just as aimless as she had been when fleeing Vippon.

The trees thinned before her. It had been over an hour since she had climbed down from the cave she slept in last night, and she had seen no sign of Lonan since. She hoped he would not make the connection between Nascha's disappearance and the village he had told her about, as she did not want to see that man angry because of her disobedience.

Not that he had any business telling me what to do in the first place.

Painfully aware of her white hair and the commotion it might cause among the superstitious Corvae, Nascha pulled her hood over her head again, her hair already tied behind her back with some thread she had salvaged from her dress. The Corvae had been spooked enough when they glimpsed her white hair when she travelled with the Vulpe. Nascha had no idea what they would do to a lone witch they found travelling the forest, but she was certain she did not want to test them. At least, not until after breakfast.

Her face broke into a smile as the village came into view. It was much like the last one she had entered with the Vulpe – a break in the trees, a rough ring of whitewashed cottages, a central green – but Ebora had a few noticeable differences. First, there was a larger

135

building at the eastern side of the village, one that was at least three times the size of any other Corvae building Nascha had seen so far. It had a large bell suspended in an open tower over the double door entrance. Nascha was used to hearing the sound of the evening bells of the forest by now, and she supposed this was Ebora's own warning for when night approached. The purpose of the rest of the building confused her, however, especially as it seemed to be decorated with colourful flowers, tied into wooden posts all along its front wall.

What had made Nascha smile, however, were the trees. The village green did not have a stream running through it, as Gallowglass had. Instead, there was a central ring of short trees, separating the cottages from the flat green of the middle. Nascha did not recognise the type of trees, but it seemed at first to her as if they burned, as if nature had set them alight in celebration of its own beauty. She blinked, and realised that it was simply the colour of the leaves. The turning of the season had painted most of the other forest trees dull browns or faded orange, but the trees within Ebora were a bright red.

Nascha stepped forward to further appreciate them, but then stopped. Something about the sight was troubling her. Something familiar.

With a start, Nascha realised she had seen trees like these before. The small aspen, sheltered between the cottages of Gallowglass, where she had lost sight of the little girl.

Nascha's eyes moved between the trees, and she realised they were identical to each other.

They were also, as far as she could remember, identical to the one back at Gallowglass.

Her joy at seeing something bright piercing the gloominess of her surroundings faded as she remembered the fear on the face of the Gallowglass villager when Nascha had approached that small tree. Without understanding the reason for that reaction, the sight of so many fiery aspens in front of her unnerved Nascha, and instead she moved away from the central ring, to the gathering of people at the northern end of the village.

It was a surprise to Nascha that she had not been challenged yet, but as she approached the crowd at the northern end, she realised it was because everyone was so busy. A man and a woman were standing on top of a table – seemingly pulled out of the kitchen of one of the cottages – and were barking orders at the gathered villagers. At the command of these people, Corvae were running all over the place, children carrying baskets of fruit and vegetables, laughing as they ran, an old man pulling on the reins of a donkey, swearing at it, trying to convince it to stop taking a bite out of the pie on the long table he was dragging it past.

A feast? Nascha thought, getting close enough to get a better glimpse of the long table.

Sure enough, there were already plates and cutlery aplenty decorating it, but very little food appeared to have arrived.

Finally, someone noticed Nascha's approach. A woman, older than Nascha by at least ten summers, double-took at her, then fixed her with a curious stare. Nascha suddenly felt very aware of how she had intruded upon these villagers, and that she had crept up on them unannounced. She also became very conscious of her hair tickling the back of her neck, and sent a quick prayer to the Owl Spirit to ask that her locks stay where she had put them.

Instead of shouting in alarm, the village woman rolled her eyes and marched over, hobbling on her lame leg.

"Another one?" the Corvae exclaimed, not really seeming as if she expected a response.

The woman had a shrill, overloud voice, reminding Nascha of the matron back at the Court. "Just a sniff of a feast, and you outsiders come running, don't ya?" The woman grabbed Nascha by the arm, and pulled her with no little force away from the feast table.

For a moment, Nascha thought the woman meant to shoo her from the village altogether, but instead she found herself being led to a smaller table, just a few steps away from the main one. This table already had a few scruffy occupants: men with overgrown beards, or women with unkempt hair. All of them were a rough contrast to the much tidier villagers. Nascha guessed these people were like her, from outside the village, possibly living alone in the forest somewhere.

"Thought you all would have had a lick of sense, staying away from something like this, but I guess food is food, after all. I'd probably risk my neck at a wedding for a bite to eat if I was you."

"A wedding?" Nascha repeated, unable to hide the excitement in her voice. Of course, it made sense – the feast table, the holy building decorated for the ceremony. Back at the Court, weddings were one of Nascha's favourite celebrations, where nobles and servants alike were encouraged to let their hair down and enjoy the finer things in life. It was at the queen's nephew's wedding when Nascha had first allowed that visiting squire to undress her.

Nascha looked at the table of vagabonds again, then raised an eyebrow. It must be custom here in the forest to feed outsiders during a wedding celebration. Back at the Court, these people would have been marched out of the woods for daring to approach a feast.

The Corvae woman looked at her with a raised eyebrow. "Aye, a wedding. Damn, you didn't know?" Suddenly, a dark shadow passed over the woman's face. "Wait, how much do you not know?" The woman gripped Nascha's arm. "Are you from this part of the forest?"

Nascha's heart beat a little faster. Was she that easy to see through?

"I… I guess I'm not, no. I've been to plenty of weddings, though, so I know what to expect—"

The woman's face was white now, but she was not looking at Nascha. Instead, her gaze drifted across to a man and woman making their way from the feast crowd towards the decorated temple at the east end of the village. Nascha frowned as she saw them.

The woman's white dress clearly highlighted that she was the bride, presumably leading her husband-to-be to the temple for their marriage ceremony.

It was then that Nascha noticed something unusual about the pair.

"Why are they…" She drifted off, and turned back to the Corvae woman, whose hand was still on Nascha's arm. The woman herself was shaking – just like the soon-to-be married couple were.

"Why are they so afraid?" Nascha asked in a hushed voice, dreading the answer.

"Oh, you poor thing," the Corvae woman said, her arm gripping Nascha's wrist tighter. "You have no idea." She pulled on Nascha, no longer leading her towards the side table, instead pulling her to the edge of the village clearing. "Come," the woman said, voice shaking. "Come on, quick, before—"

Behind Nascha, a child screamed. The woman turned before Nascha had the gumption to, and Nascha was treated to a look of pure horror on the villager's face.

Behind her, Ebora had grown quiet. Where moments before there had been the hustle and bustle of wedding preparations, now there was just silence. Dread soaking her heart, Nascha slowly began to turn to see what was happening.

"No," the woman whispered harshly, her fingers digging further into Nascha's arm.

Nascha almost cried out in pain, but then stopped herself. The Corvae woman was rigid. The woman was holding her breath, her eyes wide. She was doing everything she could to stop herself from moving. A primal part of Nascha realised that if she wanted to survive whatever was happening behind her, then she should do the same.

The whole time, the woman's wide, unblinking eyes were no longer on Nascha, but were looking over her shoulder, at whatever was happening on the village green.

"She does not like it when we move," the woman whispered, struggling to keep her lips still. "If you move, you attract her attention. You do not want to attract her attention."

Nascha, confused, looked at her guide, but said nothing in response, not trusting that she could manage to whisper with all these wild emotions running through her body. Instead, Nascha listened, struggling to hear anything over the sound of her own heart beating, as if it were pounding away inside her head instead of her chest.

Behind her, out in the centre of Ebora, something was moving. It did not quite sound like footsteps. More a sort of… rustling? Whatever it was, it was moving through the village green, and judging by the amount of noise it was making, it was something of a decent size. Much larger than those birds last night.

Lonan had mentioned a presence moving through the forest. Spirit's Shade, Nascha had walked right into its path.

She looked into the eyes of the Corvae woman, trying to peer at the reflection in the woman's eyes, trying to get some clues as to what was moving through the village. Somewhere in the distance, Nascha could hear the muffled cries of a child. Presumably, a parent was smothering the infant, willing to risk suffocation instead of drawing the ire of whatever was now walking through Ebora. Eyes narrowed to better focus on the reflection in the woman's eye, Nascha made out a large shape moving between the red aspen trees of the village green. It was… was it covered in fur? Or was that leaves? Whatever it was, it was much taller than the small trees decorating the centre of the village. She thought, perhaps, the thing could be almost as tall as some of the buildings.

The desire to turn around to look at it was maddening, as was the desire to make a run for it and hope she was not noticed. The only thing stopping Nascha from doing so was the talon grip on her arm, and the sweat dripping from the Magpiefolk woman's brow as she fought to keep herself from trembling. If that woman could remain still, even though she could see the horror on the village green, then Nascha should be able to do so in her ignorance.

Briefly, she thought of Lonan, the man with the Magpie Spirit's gifts. Would this be something he could deal with? Would he turn up again, drawn to her by that invisible string, once again saving her life before the forest took it? Or was this creature beyond even his strength?

The thing reflected in the Corvae woman's eyes stooped out of view. Behind Nascha, there was a collective sigh, a brief rush of relief, and the Corvae woman herself relaxed, but only slightly. Nascha turned to look at the scene behind her. At first glance, there was nothing out of the ordinary, other than the clear discomfort of the collected villagers of Ebora. Looking fearfully at each other, they broke off in small family groups, and one by one, without speaking to each other, the families walked slowly towards the church.

It was then that Nascha noticed the small autumnal trees that decorated the village green. They were gone.

In their place, exactly where the trees had been just moments ago, stood a dozen small, red-headed girls.

The image hit her like a slap to the face. Nascha's mouth hung open, her mind reeling from what she was seeing.

Unspeaking, she turned back to the Corvae woman, her own face a question, her features white.

The woman still did not look at Nascha. Instead, her eyes were on the church, where everyone else in the village was making their way to.

"Here in Ebora, we worship the Lady of the Forest. Weddings are sacred to her, a covenant that has existed since she first ruled the woodland many generations ago."

The woman turned to look at Nascha, a tear running down her cheek as she kept speaking. "My brother is getting married today.

The Lady has joined us, to bless the union. As she always does. She waits for us, inside her church."

For a brief moment, the woman looked directly into Nascha's eyes, her wide gaze a cry for help, looking for a way to escape whatever lay ahead of her.

Then the Corvae woman shook her head, breaking the eye contact. "I must go and attend the ceremony," she said, pulling up her skirts and starting to move across the green, ignoring the red-haired girls that were standing solitary throughout the village now. "I must attend, but you should not. Leave us, outsider."

With that, the woman left, making her way across the green, past the unmoving children. She paused for just a moment before entering the church, staring at the black doorway, summoning up her courage. Then the woman took a deep breath, ducked through the entranceway, and disappeared.

Nascha stood rigid, eyes unmoving from the church. She could not believe what was happening here. The forest was haunting her. Every choice she made in here sent her to another perilous situation. She had entered sharing the bed of a murderer. When she escaped him, she was almost eaten by the things in the night. The man who saved her wanted to keep her locked up in a cave. And now, some being terrible enough to scare an entire village into silence was invading a holy building.

Unable to cope with the overwhelming sense that this forest was out to get her, and that it was only a matter of time before it succeeded, Nascha allowed her gaze to wander from the church doorway, drifting over the red-headed girls that stood in the village green. Suddenly, Nascha froze.

One of the girls had turned, and was staring right at her.

A second later, Nascha felt two hands grab her roughly from behind.

"What in the Spirit's name are you doing here?"

The young woman's hood had slipped from her head without her noticing. That was how Bradan had recognised her, even when he was hiding in the bushes beyond the tree line, well away from the centre of the village. As such, she was the first thing he saw upon arriving at the large glade that held the village of Ebora.

The woman with the white hair. Did she have anything to do with his escape last night? Bradan had to know.

The white-haired woman was watching a villager make her way across the green, towards an overgrown church at the far end of the settlement. It was then that Bradan noticed the other figures standing out in the open. Although they resembled small girls, Bradan recognised them for what they were immediately. Cursing under his breath, he quickened his pace, trying to ignore his battered body's complaints, making an arrow line towards the white-haired woman.

"What in the Spirit's name are you doing here?" he shouted as he spun her around by the shoulders. He had not meant to do so with such force, but his recognition of the Lady's Children had set his arms shaking, unable to control them properly.

The woman looked at him in shock. Her face, despite already being quite pale, was completely drained of colour. Either she knew what the Children were as well, or she had just seen something else to scare her wits away from her. Her white hair, however, stood out for him. For most living in the forest, white hair meant an elder, a witch, or a queen. Bradan could rule out elder and queen straight away. From the helpless, slack-jawed expression on her face, Bradan reckoned this woman was no witch either, but there were plenty of tales about the acting abilities of the witchfolk, so he decided to remain guarded.

Removing his hands from her shoulders, he repeated his question. "What're you doing here?"

The repetition seemed to break the woman from her reverie. "You! You were there last night, with Vippon." He saw her eyes glance over the swelling in his face, confirming her statement.

Bradan nodded. He was surprised how good it was for someone to recognise him, and not have their expression instantly curdle into one of disgust. He wanted to talk to the woman some more, find out what she had been doing with the Vulpe, why she had saved him, but there were more pressing matters to attend to.

"What're you doing here? This place isn't safe. There's something going on here—"

"You're telling me," the woman interrupted. Bradan saw a flicker of irritation cross her face. Ah, there it was, an echo of the reactions people normally had when dealing with him. "I saw your 'something going on' make its way into the church over there, followed by all those poor villagers."

Bradan looked at the church with renewed awe, and more than a little fear. "She's in there? The Lady?"

The woman broke eye contact with him, looking slightly sheepish. "Lady? I don't know about any lady. I didn't see what it was, exactly, but it was big, and they were all terrified of it. Spirit's Song, I was terrified of it, and I don't even know what it was. And then all these girls just showed up—"

"They're her Children," Bradan said, looking at the red-headed girls again. Now three of the Children were looking his way, and he could not tell if that was something he should be worried about. "Well, kind of. They're not human, of course. She's not human," he added, in case he had not made the situation fully clear already.

"Yes, I did manage to figure that one out for myself, thank you," she said. The look she shot him was properly scathing, and he could not help giving an inward sigh on seeing it.

He had clearly inherited his charm from his father.

Bradan looked again to the church. If the Lady was already in there, that was also where she wanted him to be. His skin tingled at the thought of meeting her, as if a hundred tiny spiders were dancing all over him. The notion that taking the Lady up on her offer might not be the best choice in the world once again forced its way into his head, but for the umpteenth time that morning he pushed the doubts back. He was certain this was a bad idea. He was also certain this was the only way he would ever be able to rise in power to take his father's place.

"You've got to get out of here," he said to the woman, his eyes not leaving the church. "It isn't safe."

To his surprise, the woman hit him, slapped him on the arm.

He jumped, shocked at the violence, and saw that she herself was caught off guard by her own reaction. She hesitated for a brief second, and Bradan thought she was about to apologise. However, she seemed to think better of it, and instead took a deep breath, her face reddening.

"It's not safe? Well, thank you for letting me know. Spirit's name, what would I have done if you, a gallant knight, hadn't been passing by? A giant tree monster and some crazy tree children aren't safe? Good to know. If only you'd been around a few weeks ago, what a series of revelations you might have been able to give me about my life. Perhaps you could have advised me on all the fantastic choices I've been making recently."

Bradan rubbed his arm, staring at the white-haired woman, the red in her cheeks a stark contrast to the paleness of only a few moments before.

He shook his head, caught off guard by her passion. "Who are you, anyway?"

"I'm Nascha, of the Titonidae. And I'm trying to get out of this damned forest alive, thank you very much."

"Well, Nascha, stay away from that church. If you're wanting to stay alive, that's the best advice I can give you."

Nascha seemed shocked by Bradan's words, but he quickly realised they were not why her eyes had widened. She was staring beside him. Slowly, Bradan turned to his left. One of the Children was standing there.

The girl wore a simple dress, one he had initially thought was black, but now saw it was a dark green. The thing that wore the face of a girl had an expression of complete seriousness, perhaps even irritation.

It was looking at Nascha.

"You are invited," the Child said to Nascha. "You are welcome to attend our festivities."

The thing turned from Nascha, briefly locking eyes with Bradan, then returned to its place on the green.

"That's it, then," Bradan muttered. "Guess you're coming with me." He nodded, indicating the church.

"You? I didn't hear it say anything about you."

"I already got my invitation," he said, not looking at the owl woman in case he gave away any hint of his purpose.

"Look," he said, more authoritative this time, turning to Nascha. He raised his arms and almost grabbed her by the shoulders to impress how important it was for her to listen to him, but the thunder on her face as he raised his hands made it clear that would have been a very bad idea.

"Look," he said again, trying to find the words to explain in such a short space of time. He started walking towards the church, beckoning for Nascha to follow. "We've got to be really careful here. I don't know if the White Woods have any stories about the Lady—" Nascha shook her head, to indicate she had no clue. "—but from what I gather she can be very… particular. There's a long list of stuff you can do that would draw her attention. Her attention tends to be a very bad thing."

"I had gathered that," Nascha said under her breath. Bradan realised the fire had gone from her voice. Her eyes were locked on the dark doorway the two of them were rapidly approaching, and the red in her cheeks had faded again.

"Don't look at her. Unless she gives you permission, unless she looks at you directly, don't look at her. She doesn't like that."

Nascha nodded, exhaling deeply.

"Honestly, don't make a sound if you can help it. Especially if she is speaking. Just… just don't say anything, or do anything that might disturb her. She… she sees herself as very important. Much more important than us. You know the way you swat at a fly buzzing around your head in the heat? She sees us a bit like that. Although once she starts swatting at you, she would keep going long after you were dead, not stopping until there was nothing recognisable left. Yeah, I guess she has a bit of an anger issue as well."

"So, don't make a sound," Nascha repeated, a nervous smile briefly flitting across her face.

Bradan returned the smile. They were right outside the church now. Taking a deep breath, he turned to the doorway and offered Nascha his hand.

He stood for a second, expecting her to take it, and looked back when no contact was made. Nascha was staring at his outstretched hand, suspicion clearly etched across her face.

Idiot, he thought, feeling the blush burn on his cheeks. *I haven't held hands with a girl – with anyone, really – since I was a child. Why'd I do that?*

He almost withdrew his hand straight away, but instead took a deep breath, looked into Nascha's eyes, and gave a small smile.

"Hello," he said.

She was taken aback, taking a half step away from him, but then mirroring his smile with a confused grin of her own.

"My name's Bradan," he continued. "There's a very big chance

I might die in there, and it'd make me feel a bit better if someone would hold my hand as I walk in."

She paused only briefly, gave her nervous smile again, nodded, then took his hand. An unexpected shiver went up Bradan's spine as she touched him, and he cursed himself for a fool for thinking about things like that when about to meet the Lady.

Not speaking to each other, Bradan and Nascha walked side by side into Ebora's church.

The front door led into a small stone hallway, itself not much longer than Bradan was tall. Walking slowly through the passage, his eyes adjusted to the dimmer light inside, mostly cast by candlelight from the room beyond.

The church was packed, he realised, despite the complete silence that haunted the space. There were simple wooden pews lined up on either side of the church aisle. These pews contained what seemed to be all the villagers of Ebora, all dressed in their best clothing. Each and every one of them was standing still, stiff, facing the front. At first, Bradan thought something might be wrong with them, some kind of spell cast to render them so still. However, as he took his first step into the room, he took a quick look at the man standing to his left. Tears were running down both of the villager's cheeks, and his knees were shaking. He was terrified. The whole village was rigid with fear.

Walking slowly up the aisle with Nascha, nobody reacting at all to their presence, Bradan scanned the room, searching for signs of the Lady. At first, he thought drapes were covering the tall windows set into the church walls, but Bradan quickly realised that large leaves had grown to cover the openings, a collection of foliage dense enough to block out almost all the morning light, letting only a sluggish green hue make its way into the room.

The church cannot mean that much to them, if they let it get so overgrown, Bradan thought, puzzled by the condition of the place. The rest of the building – neat pews, altar littered with various harvest goods – seemed in good repair, but the windows were covered in greenery, and the upper parts of the walls and the entirety of the ceiling were covered in… vines?

A chill ran up Bradan's back. There was no sign of the Lady, but she must be here somewhere. He glanced around again, but saw nothing to give away her presence. The bride and groom stood at the altar, rigidly facing forward like everyone else, silently waiting for some sort of signal. He saw a space a few rows from the front – closer to the events than he would have liked – and he motioned for Nascha to head in there, sidling up beside the elderly couple that already occupied it. The front row, just two pews ahead, held a family; a father, mother and two children. The children were clinging close to the adults, their parents' clothes scrunched up where the children gripped them. The boy, a sandy-haired thing, could not have been older than four. How he knew to keep this still, this quiet, was beyond Bradan's comprehension.

Bradan looked to the side, at Nascha. Her big eyes were roaming over the details he had just been focussing on – the family in front of them, the vines above. Where did she fit into all of this? Had the Lady known the owl woman would be in Ebora when she had summoned Bradan here? Somehow, Bradan did not think so. Nascha did not feel like someone who had been… tainted by the Lady. What, then? He looked at her white curls and thought of the legends of the Owl Queen, consort to the ruler of the forest. He realised then that they were still holding hands, and he blushed furiously, looking away from her. She kept gripping his hand, though, and he made no effort to let go.

A man walked out from a side alcove. He was elderly, and his robes and woven decorations dangling around his neck marked him as a holy man, maybe a priest of some kind. It did Bradan no good whatsoever to see that this man too was terrified. The priest glanced briefly at the congregation, but then lowered his head in shock, visibly trembling as he made his way to stand between the betrothed.

He had seen something behind them all that had made him react like that. Was the Lady behind them, watching somewhere from the back of the church? Bradan felt a maddening urge within him to turn around, but fought against it, fearing the attention he would draw to himself.

Just in time, he realised Nascha would have made the connection too. He squeezed her hand tight as her head began to turn. She froze, but shot him a look that would have curdled milk.

"Don't look," he whispered, loud enough for only Nascha to hear. He hoped. "Don't draw her attention. Don't move. Don't look behind."

The holy man stood between the couple, shaking, seemingly unsure what he was permitted to do next.

A padding of feet up the aisle from behind Bradan made the hairs on the back of his neck stand up. It was one of the Children.

"You may proceed," the thing said, then padded back down the aisle again.

The priest nodded, and continued to nod, as if it was a nervous twitch he had just developed. He looked at the congregation, doing his damnedest to make sure his gaze remained lowered.

"People of Ebora," he addressed the crowd, his voice wobbling, "we are gathered here today for a joyous occasion…"

The words the holy man was reciting were familiar enough to Bradan. This was the patter the holy people of the forest had given out for generations whenever a marriage took place, with a few additions and amendments made. Where Bradan was used to hearing about the Magpie Spirit, today the ceremony mentioned 'The Lady', 'Our Gracious Lady', or 'Our Glorious Queen'. So familiar was the ceremony to him, his attention began to drift, past the holy man, past the stricken faces of the wedding couple, looking around at the gathered villagers, looking at their faces, trying to piece together any further clues about what was happening.

He gleaned nothing else about the situation, found nothing new, until the moaning began. Again, Bradan fought the urge to turn around as soon as the sound started. This time, it was Nascha who gripped his hand, either to warn him against turning, or just a reaction to stop herself from moving any further.

It was a low noise, made by a human-sounding voice. Definitely female. A few things struck Bradan about the sound, the groans that continued to travel throughout the church. First, their source was high up, from what Bradan could tell without turning to look. It sounded as if the moaning was coming from somewhere close to the roof at the back of the church. Secondly, it was definitely not a sound of pleasure. At best, something behind him was in discomfort. Very possibly, it was in pain.

The holy man stopped at the sound, but when it became clear the noise was not going to cease, he continued the words of the service, his voice lower, hesitant at first, pausing to see if his continued speech would meet with any punishment.

He stopped again, however, when the first cry came. This was clearly a cry of pain, the moaning breaking into an anguished, wordless yell of agony. The cry lasted for only a few seconds, then returned back to the groans, sounding more fraught now, the owner's distress clearer.

Bradan looked at Nascha. Her eyes were wide, searching for his, silently asking what was going on. He truly had no idea. Bradan had never heard nor experienced anything like this before.

If only he could turn around to look. Then he would know.

The church was broken by another cry. The entire family in front of Bradan jumped. The sandy-haired boy gave a yell, and his father gripped the child by the back of his head, forcing the boy's face into the man's side, doing what he could to muffle the child's screams.

Behind him, Bradan heard a number of the congregation gasp. He felt it too. The child's sound had not been appreciated. From the back of the church, the cry of pain faded back into a moan again, but one that was now laced with irritation. The thing behind him making the noise – the Lady, perhaps, although why she would be in pain Bradan had no idea – was becoming angry.

In front of Bradan, the sandy-haired boy struggled against his father. Everything had clearly been too much for the child – the terror of the church, the strange noises behind, and now his own father hurting him. The four-year-old boy had broken; he was crying, screaming. Muffled as he was by his face being forced into his father's clothing, with the rest of the church silent save for the moaning from above, even those muted cries stood out.

Spirit, please, make him stop, Bradan prayed, willing something to happen to make the child's cries cease. Bradan looked up at the priest. He had stopped the service again. The man was transfixed, looking towards the aisle, tracking something moving up it. Behind Bradan, to his right, just behind his field of vision, he could hear something moving.

It was getting closer.

Nascha's nails bit into his skin.

The child continued to scream.

Bradan stood rigid, feeling helpless.

Somebody make the child stop!

Movement to Bradan's right caught his attention. Terrified, not daring to move any part of him that could be seen by whatever was watching from behind, Bradan strained his eyes, looking to the church floor. There he saw, moving toward the front of the church like a snake stalking its prey through the grass, a vine, growing impossibly quickly along the floor. Bradan could not take his eyes from the tip of the vine. It was barb-like, sharp, like a spike, like a weapon. It was moving purposefully up the aisle, making straight for the crying child.

Please, don't hurt him, Bradan thought, praying again, but this time to his imagined version of the Lady in his head.

Time seemed to slow – the opposite of what Bradan wanted to happen – as he stood frozen, watching the spiked vine inch forward.

Is this what he had signed up for? Is this who he was signing his life over to? A creature that would kill a child just for irritating her, for making noise when it was scared?

Nascha's grip grew tighter, and he realised she was tensing. The sharpened vine had reached the boy's pew, and was now worming its way along the back of the wooden seat. Bradan realised, to his horror, that Nascha was getting ready to do something. She was not going to stand by and let this child be harmed.

Bradan had no doubt that in doing so she would be punished instead. She could very well be putting herself forward to be killed.

He squeezed her hand tight, enough to feel the joints pop within his grip.

"Not yet," he said, risking a whisper. The vine did not seem to notice, but Nascha's eyes met his. She was scared, but determined. He felt stupid shooting a quick smile at her, but he could not help but be impressed by how she was willing to put herself in danger to help this child.

"Not yet," he said again. He did not tell her why. Not because he thought something was going to come to help the child. Not even because he did not want to see Nascha harmed. It was because some morbid part of him wanted to see what the Lady was willing to do. Last night, he had promised to enter into her service, even though he knew his father did not approve of her, and that she was an unknown force within these dark woods.

What she did now with this boy would tell Bradan exactly how much of his soul he had given up when making his promise to her.

Finally, just as the sharp vine crept behind the back of the boy's father, mere inches from where Bradan's hand gripped the pew, the child spotted it, pulling back from his father's grip just enough to catch a glimpse of the tendril snaking towards him. The infant's keening reached a fever pitch, matching the moans of pain that still sounded from somewhere behind Bradan in the back of the church. The child tried to pull away but his father, otherwise rigid, gripped him tight. The man's shoulders briefly shuddered, and Bradan realised the father was sobbing uncontrollably.

Without thinking, realising this was the last possible second he had to act, Bradan's hand snapped out to grab the vine. His hand clasped over the tendril – about the size of his own wrist – and he immediately went rigid again.

What had he done? He had interfered with the Lady's judgment. The vine tried to progress onward, raising its sharp tip to look at the boy, but Bradan held firm – more through the rigidity of fear than through wanting to protect the child – and it could not tug past him.

Nascha squeezed his hand again, and gripped him tight. Bradan prayed to the Magpie Spirit that his body obscured the Lady's vision, that she could not see what had stopped her weapon from finding its target.

The tip of the vine in Bradan's grip raised itself from the bench, and Bradan was reminded of a scorpion's sting priming to strike. It turned, sightlessly searching, and plunged back down, sinking into the wood next to Bradan's hand. If it made contact with his own flesh, it would find no difficultly in similarly skewering him.

The child must have realised this too, as he gave a final squeal, then went limp. The boy had passed out, and the absence of his screams felt like an instant release. Without meaning to, Bradan relaxed, letting go of the vine, cursing himself for a fool a half second later. Thankfully, at the cessation of the child's cries, the searching tendril stopped in its path, seemingly no longer interested in harming the child, flopping harmlessly onto the pew as if it were just another piece of decorative foliage. The noise was gone, and that was all the Lady wanted.

The Lady.

Her moans from the back of the church still dominated the room, even though the priest had begun the service again. Her cries rose in pitch every so often, screaming briefly, then relaxing back to groans, ebbing and flowing, suffering what seemed to be increasingly regular patterns of intense pain.

With a start, Bradan realised what was happening. She was in labour. The Lady was giving birth. What they were all hearing was a forest goddess experiencing the pain of labour.

He began to breathe heavier. What could a being such as her possibly be giving birth to? And why here, at this wedding ceremony?

As if waiting for Bradan's moment of realisation, the screaming from behind him reached a new pitch, and culminated in a screech that made Bradan feel that something back there was dying, having the life ripped from it violently. The howl ended in a tearing sound, a wet splash, and then the Lady was silent.

Instantly, the room relaxed. The priest, his complexion slightly less pale, finished the service, making some sort of holy gesture between the bride and groom that Bradan did not recognise. The bride was even able to manage a slight half-smile to her new husband as they were formally wed.

With a small gesture, the priest indicated to the congregation to turn around. Bradan's head shot around, meeting first with Nascha's eyes. They held each other's gaze briefly, as if shoring each other up, preparing themselves for the sight that awaited them behind.

Then, together, they turned to look at the Lady of the Forest.

She was huge. More than twice the height of a person. This, however, was nowhere near her most dominant feature. She lay against the back wall of the church, her face clearly visible, even though she was on the other side of the building from Bradan. Other than her face, however, and her legs, very little of the Lady resembled anything human. The back wall was a collection of autumnal foliage, all spreading out from where she lay against it.

Her face was beautiful, clearly, but there was nothing about it that Bradan would call attractive. Her striking, motionless features were fixed in a gaze at the wall across the church from her. She did not seem to be exhausted by her recent labour, or at all interested in the people who gazed up at her. The glowing candles, placed on the altar on the opposite side of the room from the Lady, emphasised the crevices of her face. He could not tell how human her skin really was, but right now, in that flickering, shadowy light, she looked far, far removed from Bradan's definition of that word. If Bradan had not spent the last half hour hearing her birthing pains, he would have assumed she was a statue, carved years ago and now overgrown with foliage.

The plant life on the wall flowed from her, most striking of which was the shock of red colour that burst from her head. At first glance, Bradan had assumed that it was simply red hair, like that belonging to the Children he had met outside. However, he quickly realised that none of the strands that fell from the Lady's head were actually hair. Instead, they were thin vines of ivy, each leaf as red as the blood that ran through Bradan's own veins. More leaves, this time in much more muted autumnal oranges and browns, flowed down below her neck, forming a dress worthy of this woodland goddess.

He could not see her arms anywhere. Instead, sprouting from her leafy dress came the thick vines that covered the ceiling and walls of the church, spreading her influence throughout the building. However, her legs were clearly visible. Her dress parted close to where Bradan imagined her waist to be, and the Lady's bare legs were exposed, open wide and straddling the entranceway to the building.

And all around that entranceway, clearly having been dropped from her womb to the church floor, was the issue of the Lady's labour.

There, pooled on the church floor beneath the resting goddess, green vines still sprouting from between the Lady's legs, was a multitude of fruit. Bradan could not name any of that uncanny bounty, although many of the fruits birthed from the Lady looked vaguely familiar, reminding him of others that he knew. There were fist-sized orbs that almost looked like apples, except for their unusual colours of purple and orange. Some were long, elongated produce in a variety of colours that Bradan assumed one would have to peel before getting to the edible flesh. Others looked like no fruit he had ever seen before, adorned with unusually shaped leaves, or garishly coloured growths.

He blinked, trying to take in what he was looking at. The Lady, this gigantic wood-woman, had given birth to vines of garishly coloured fruit during the wedding ceremony. The fruit lay where it had dropped from her, covered in viscous amniotic fluid, spilling down the aisle from the entrance to the church.

Bradan turned to look at Nascha, and she had a similar look of befuddlement mixed with horror on her face. The villagers of Ebora, however, did not seem fazed. They had experienced this before.

Bradan and Nascha stood and watched, hands still held, as the bride and groom made their way down the aisle toward the exit.

However, instead of making their way out into the daylight, away from this harrowing scene, they stopped by the Lady's produce. The groom stooped, and plucked a red fruit from one of the vines still attached to the Lady. The goddess, not moving, gave a moan of satisfaction as he did so, a deep, rumbling noise that reverberated around the small building. Wiping off some of the sticky, sap-like residue that coated the recently birthed fruit, the groom offered it to his wife. Bradan was shocked to see the young woman smile at her husband then, almost blush. Wordlessly, joy-filled eyes locked with her husband all the while, the woman leaned forward and took a bite from the overlarge berry. All around them, the Lady again gave a moan of pleasure.

Then, red fruit still clasped in the groom's hand, a dribble of sticky fluid still running down the bride's chin, the two of them held hands and left the church to enjoy married life together.

One by one, the families of Ebora followed them. The groups at the back of the church left first. None dared to make eye contact with the Lady, all of them remaining sombre in her presence, but before leaving, each of them plucked one of her fruits from her vines. Bradan noticed the younger members of the congregation, those who were more daring, raised their hands to take the fruit that hung higher than the rest, coming dangerously close to reaching under the Lady's dress, sap still dripping from where the bounty had poured from her. There were no moans of pleasure to accompany the acts this time, but a general sense of satisfaction saturated the air. The sickly-sweet smell of the birthing fluids hung in the air like honey from a ruptured bee hive, and Bradan felt his head grow light. He had to get out of that building, out into daylight again.

Pulling on Nascha's hand, meeting a little resistance at first, Bradan dragged Nascha down the church aisle, pushing past others to get to the exit.

"I don't want to," Nascha whispered, angry at him, Bradan realised. "I don't want to take that stuff from her. It's disgusting."

"Everyone's doing it," he whispered back. "Just grab one so we can get out of here."

They were at the front of the line now, next to take the Lady's gift. Beside him, Nascha hesitated, and Bradan could feel the gaze of the other villagers boring into the back of his head. More worrying than that, he could feel a growing uneasiness in the air, as if something else that was watching him was becoming aware of Nascha's resistance.

Feeling a panic rise within him, Bradan bent down and picked off a ripe yellow orb the size of a baby's head. He handed it to Nascha, forcing it into her arms, despite her reluctance. Shooting him a look of pure hostility, Nascha finally accepted the fruit, and left the church.

Bradan breathed deeply, thankful this experience was almost over. He took a second to look at the offerings remaining to him, and then reached out to take what looked like an off-white apple that hung from one of the higher vines, still dangling at shoulder height beside him.

No. Not that one.

Bradan jumped back at the sound of the voice. Although he had never heard her speak before, it unmistakably belonged to the Lady, the deep, soft sound of it reminding Bradan of a powerful river cutting through a forest valley, beautiful to look at, but doubtlessly treacherous to step into.

He looked at the villagers still waiting in the queue behind him. They seemed annoyed with him for acting so strangely, but otherwise had not reacted to the sound of her voice. They had not heard it.

He raised his head, daring to look at the Lady's face.

She was staring right at him.

Her face was rigid, impassionate and unmoving as before, but she had craned her neck to stare down at the pitifully small man standing beneath her.

I have another gift for you. Higher. Her face did not move as she spoke, but Bradan felt every word she said in his gut and in his groin.

He raised his eyes, to where her legs emerged from beneath the folds of her leaf dress. Just below that gap, hanging from the vines that sprouted from between her legs, he spotted a luminous yellow apple, waiting for him.

Aware of the eyes of the villagers on his back, Bradan stood on his tiptoes and reached up, fingers brushing against the apple that was just out of his reach.

No. Higher.

Bradan froze in his reaching. His eyes moved upwards to where the vines sprouted from beneath the Lady's dress. There, the sappy residue of her birth still dripped down those green chords. He felt a hum of satisfaction in the air as his eyes rested there.

Taking a deep breath, Bradan grabbed one of the nearby pews, and dragged it across the flagstones of the church floor. Behind him, he heard a mixture of grumbling and incredulity. The remaining villagers were no longer annoyed at him for taking too long. They were now wondering why he had not yet been killed for disturbing their mistress.

Bradan clambered on top of the pew and reached upwards again. His hand briefly brushed the yellow apple that he had originally reached for, and hesitated beside it. Then he pushed further, moving his hand under the Lady's dress, pushing aside the moist vines that sprung from between her thighs.

His face reddened as he heard gasps from behind him. He wriggled his fingers, using them to push aside the wetness that dripped from the Lady, travelling further upwards, trying to find whatever gift she had for him.

He glanced back up at the Lady's face, keenly aware of the intimateness of his touch. Her previously impassive face was smiling back at him. It was the smile Bradan supposed a wolf gave a rabbit just before pouncing on it.

Moving aside the unseen green folds, Bradan's fingers found something different, something round and smooth that he could perfectly fit his hand around. Anticipation fuelling him, he plucked it, quickly withdrawing his wet hand, along with her gift. A sigh of intense satisfaction echoed around the room, and Bradan could tell from their astonishment that this time the villagers had heard it.

Bradan, however, was too concerned with what he now held. In his hand was a plum, its skin perfectly smooth, still wet with the Lady's fluids.

In his hand, he held what he needed to rise in power, to become a protector of the forest to rival the great Magpie King.

THE OWL QUEEN
AND THE
SERPENTS

A story from the fireplaces of the Titonidae

This tale takes place long ago, before the combined forces of the Corvae and the Lionfolk removed the threat of the Serpents from their lands forever.

As was to be expected, the Titonidae had taken the Magpie King's side in the conflict, aligning themselves with that dark ruler and his Owlfolk bride.

As was also to be expected, there were reprisals in response to that alliance.

The Ayuhwa Court was experiencing an era of prestige, their current ruler a queen fully blessed by the Owl Spirit, her white hair and powers to walk through dreams proof that she was one of the deity's chosen ones. Unfortunately for the Court, their star would fall after her reign, as the queen was past childbearing age and had produced only sons to carry her line forward. However, the oracles had been consulted, and it had been discovered that the Owl Queen would reign for decades to come, despite her age, so the Ayuhwa nobility were content to enjoy her protection during the Serpent War, with plenty of time to prepare for the Court's inevitable decline.

Despite having a fully blessed Owl Queen for protection, the Serpents' eyes did not pass over the Ayuhwa Court when it came to seeking out targets during the conflict.

The assault against the Court was an insidious one, and began small. Murals appeared throughout the height of the Court's spires, decorating buildings of notable nobility, falsely accusing them of fraternisation with the enemy, making clear threats against businesses if they continued to support the Owl Queen's reign.

The owners of the graffitied buildings came to the throne to petition their queen into interceding, asking her to root out the Serpents from their midst.

"Our mother is old, and we do not wish to bother her with such small matters," the queen's sons told the petitioners. "Some paintings on the sides of buildings? This is not what the Owl Spirit gave Mother her gifts for. Some soap and hard bristles should be enough to take care of those without Mother's help," the princes suggested. "Show your support for your queen by solving your problems yourself. The Serpents will withdraw when they see you have not been cowed by their slander."

Muttering, the petitioners withdrew, and carried out the princes' suggestion, cleaning the graffiti from their buildings.

For a while, all was well.

However, some weeks later the same buildings were broken into. Windows were smashed, or doors pulled off their hinges. Businesses were set afire, the goods and property destroyed. The homes of the nobility were ransacked, treasures stolen, and those found inside were treated poorly. All properties broken into had the same message left within them – speak out against the Owl Queen, oppose her rule, or continue to suffer.

Again, those who had been mistreated found their way to the Owl Queen's throne, to ask their ruler to intercede against the Serpents. The princes again spoke on their mother's behalf, this time drawing their swords in anger. "These Serpents go too far. Mother, let us take charge of this. Rest yourself, and we will deal with the attackers for you."

Quietly, the queen agreed. The princes took to the streets of Ayuhwa with their guards, visiting places of ill repute, questioning those they found there until they were given names of Owlfolk who had aligned themselves with the Serpents. The guilty parties were rounded up, taken to the market square of the Court, and dealt with in a public execution. The princes were hailed as heroes, and returned to their mother, who had prepared a great feast in their honour.

For a while, all was well.

Then people began to die.

The first time it happened – the son of a noble house found strangled in a back alley – it was thought to be a cruel joke. Despite the markings left on the man's body claiming that his death was retribution by the Serpents, most thought it must have been a local rival taking advantage of the recent conflict, trusting that the Serpents had already been dealt with. However, as more bodies appeared – a lady stabbed in her bedroom, a fishmonger gutted like one of his trouts – it became apparent that some of the Serpents were still at large. All in the Court feared for their lives.

"Please, Your Majesty," the petitioners said upon their third time visiting the throne room to speak to their queen. "Please employ your gifts, and rid us of this threat."

The princes stepped forward to speak on their mother's behalf, but the Owl Queen stood first.

"I shall walk the Court tonight," she told those assembled, "and tomorrow the enemy will have been dealt with."

"But Mother," the princes protested, "you are old, and we do not wish to bother you. We can deal with the Serpents instead. Give us one more chance."

The Owl Queen smiled at her sons' enthusiasm, but shook her head.

"You have tried, my sons, but I cannot put your pride before the lives of my people. Tonight, I walk the Court."

That night, accompanied by her Pale Wardens, the Owl Queen walked the spiral stairs that linked the spires of the Court together. As she did so, she reached out with the Owl Spirit's gift, and walked through the dreams of her people.

Rarely had the queen chosen to employ her powers in this way, because of the great strain it put upon her. However, that night, she saw what lay within the hearts of all her Titonidae. She visited spurned lovers, felt the anguish of their broken hearts even as they slept. She saw the dreams of expectant parents, felt the hope they had for their offspring, and she smiled when she brushed against the dreams of those not yet born, resting peacefully in their mothers' bellies. She saw the dreams of those haunted by events from their past, either what had been done to them, or what they had done to others. These dreams were the hardest of all for the Owl Queen to bear, and she made a note of many Titonidae she would have to send her guards to visit in the morning, to question them about what their dreams held.

But first and foremost, she rooted out any who dreamt of the Serpents. There was no mercy for those Titonidae. She found all who had aligned themselves with that foreign power, and the executioner's axe did not stop that night until the Court had been purged of their menace.

Finally, as morning broke, the queen returned to her palace, exhausted, and waited in the dining chamber for her sons to rise, ordering the servants to prepare a fine breakfast for them in celebration of ridding the Court of evil.

The princes, who had been bitter about their mother's decision, were somewhat mollified by her eventual success.

"So, that's it, then?" the eldest said, taking a gulp of the fine wine his mother had poured for him. "The Serpents are truly gone?"

The queen nodded in the affirmative as she poured drink for her other sons.

"I do wish you'd let us deal with this, Mother," the youngest said. "How will the people have faith in us when you are gone, if you keep showing us up?"

The queen did not answer as she made her way back to her throne, watching her children enjoy themselves.

The princes shared looks as they enjoyed their meal.

Eventually, the servants left, and then the princes stood and drew their daggers.

"Mother, we are sorry," the middle child said, his face showing genuine anguish, "but this is for the good of the Court."

"We had hoped letting the Serpents in would force you to step down," another explained as they advanced on their mother, "but clearly we are beyond that now."

The queen moved her gaze between her three sons, seeming unconcerned for her safety, instead filled with an overwhelming sadness at the sight before her.

"Why?" was all she asked of them.

"Your loss will leave the Court weak," the eldest explained. "We have always known this. But how much weaker will the Court be if you keep belittling us in front of our future subjects?"

"For the good of the Court, it is better if you are removed now, while their trust in us is not completely lost."

"It will be seen as a final attack by the Serpents before withdrawing from the Court," the youngest said. "Mother, please believe us, this truly breaks our hearts."

"Oh, I believe you," the queen said, unmoving on her throne, tears running down her face. "I believe you all too well."

It was at that moment the eldest prince raised his hand to his throat, giving an uncomfortable cough. The middle child did the same, a look of panic breaking over his face.

The youngest of them, also the smallest, collapsed to the ground. He was already dead.

The remaining princes, realising what was happening, realising only now that their mother had not eaten or drunk anything with them that morning, dropped to their knees, faces turning purple, daggers forgotten as both hands clutched their closed throats.

"I never enjoy walking the Court," the queen told her dying sons, her tears running freely now. "What I see there always haunts me. I see all the good of our people, but I see all of the bad, too. Yes, walking the Court allowed me to find the Serpents in our midst, but do you know what else I saw there, my sons?"

The middle child collapsed to the floor, lifeless, and blood vessels broke in the eyes of the eldest as he forced out a final cry of distress.

"Each of the Serpents dreamt of their masters to the east, of the promises of riches and power that would be given to them if they succeeded in overthrowing me. But, my sons, each of those Serpents dreamt of the three of you as well."

And so it was that the final son of the Owl Queen of Ayuhwa Court died, ending that royal line decades before the final Owl Queen of the Court fell.

Since then, new nobility have risen to power in Ayuhwa, but they have never since had an Owl Queen in power. Perhaps one day a new white-haired queen will rise, and then the people of the Court will have to guard their dreams again for fear of what their queen may discover about them.

CHAPTER SIX

Eventually, Nascha spotted Bradan coming out of the church. He looked bewildered, his eyes roaming the village green, not really looking for anything in particular. However, Nascha saw him raise his eyebrows at the sight of her, leaning against the wall of one of the nearby cottages, waiting for him.

"You took your time," she said when he reached her. She was annoyed with him for taking so long. More specifically, she was annoyed at how anxious she had been when he had not come out of the church right behind her.

The boy – young man, really – seemed lost. "What?"

"What took you so long? How come you weren't right behind me?"

He seemed confused at her question. Eventually, his eyes moved to her empty hands.

"Eaten your fruit already?"

Nascha scrunched her face up at the suggestion. "What? No chance. I threw it away. You know where that came from, right?"

Bradan's forehead furrowed. "I don't know if that was such a good idea." He turned behind to look at the wedding party, and Nascha followed his gaze. The celebrations over at the banquet table had begun, and the villagers were tucking into their gifts, different coloured juices running down their chins, visible even at this distance. "I'm pretty sure she expects us to eat them."

"I'm not eating anything covered in that stuff, or anything that comes out of..." Nascha lowered her voice, leaning conspiratorially towards Bradan. "Anything that comes out of lady parts."

Bradan's face reddened, a reaction that gave Nascha a small amount of satisfaction. She noticed a small plum in his hand. His hand – his entire arm, for some reason – was covered in the same gunk all the fruit was coated in.

"If you're so worried about upsetting her, eat yours. I'll go get something from the dining table instead."

He looked at the plum, and for a brief moment Nascha thought she spied an expression of growing fear cross his face. However, after a second he took his eyes from the plum, and stuffed it quickly into his pocket.

"I'll have it later," he muttered, still not looking directly at her.

Having survived the immediate threat, Nascha felt exhausted, drained of all energy. She slumped to the ground, her back against the whitewashed cottage wall.

"What was that?" she asked Bradan, her eyes not leaving the celebrating villagers. "Just what in the Spirit's name was that thing?"

"The Lady of the Forest," he replied, an edge of curiosity in his voice. "You've not heard of her?"

Nascha became aware of his eyes on her, and she spotted them resting on some stray strands of white hair that had betrayed her by falling out from under her hood.

Hastily tucking them back, she said defensively, "You don't seem to be from around here either."

He nodded, his eyes lowering again. "I... I travel around a lot. In the forest. Not like those Vulpe friends of yours."

Nascha could not help the bark of a laugh that escaped her throat at his words. "No friends of mine, I can assure you. Certainly not now, anyway."

"So it was you who set fire to the caravans."

She eyed him, trying to figure out what he was planning on doing with that information.

If you think you can blackmail me, forest boy, you're going to find you crossed the wrong witch.

There was a commotion over by the church, and both of them

turned their heads to look. The remaining villagers had left the building. They seemed disgruntled, talking amongst themselves angrily, and all of them were looking over at Nascha and Bradan.

"I need to get out of here," they both said at the same time.

Nascha turned to look quizzically at Bradan. She wondered briefly what he thought he had done to attract the ire of the villagers, wondered if it had anything to do with his soiled clothing, and also wondering if it was half as bad as being born with white hair.

Bradan moved first. "I think we'd better go, before they stop grumbling and start acting."

"Go? Together?" Nascha instantly regretted the mocking tone in her voice – she had automatically laced her words with it to hide her surprise.

Bradan's face reddened, and he broke eye contact with her, looking towards the trees behind the cottage they were resting against. "I didn't mean together. I just mean if neither of us are from here, and we both reckon we're no longer welcome in Ebora, then maybe it's time we moved on. Going separate ways, of course."

Nascha hesitated. "I don't know where I'm going. I don't know what to do next."

Bradan looked at her, and nodded. "You know what? Me neither. Why don't we get out of this village, and then I'll see if I can help point you in the right direction."

For the briefest of moments, Nascha thought he was about to offer her his hand, like he had done upon entering the church. She knew then that she would have taken it without hesitation. Instead, Bradan nodded, then turned and walked out of the village, with Nascha following close behind. She hated him a little, then, for not doing what she had expected. She hated him even more for how much he reminded her of Vippon, Lonan, and Lord Bidzell – he was someone she needed to survive in this world. But she hated him most of all for catching her in a moment of weakness, and then not letting her succumb to it.

She strode on, channelling her annoyance into her feet, pounding the forest earth harder than normal.

Spirit's breath, what was that thing? The Lady of the Forest? She cast her mind back to the creature in the church, standing astride their only way out. Nascha did not shudder. Her feeling of dread was well beyond that simple expression of emotion now.

"I'm going to die here, aren't I?"

"What?" Bradan asked, turning from his own quiet contemplation. She had noticed that, as they walked, he was playing with something in his pocket. That plum from the tree woman? *Owl's bane, he must be starving if he was contemplating eating something squeezed out from down there.*

"I'm going to die," Nascha said matter-of-factly, "in this damned forest. First some fox people, then some birds with skulls for heads, finally that thing back at the church. Is there anything in this cursed place that isn't perfectly designed to kill people?"

Bradan exhaled, hand still fixed firmly in his pocket, and turned to look at the trees ahead of him. They were heading west, as best as Nascha could discern. She had no idea what lay in that direction. Spirit's blood, she had no clue where the village she had left the Vulpe caravans in was, let alone Laurentina's Court. Other than those few landmarks, there was very little in the wider world she had much knowledge of, outside of stories. The Lion King's Castle, the Sand Wastes, the City of Swords – she had no idea if they even existed, or just made a good tale to tell around the campfire.

She had no plan for what to do next.

"The thing in the church – you knew her?" she asked, quickening her step to catch up with Bradan. "Called her the Lady?"

He looked uncomfortable. "I've never seen her before, but I've heard about her. Would have been happy passing my entire life without having to experience that, but... there's been a shift of power in the forest. You've heard of the Magpie King?"

Nascha nodded, her mind casting back to the man who had saved her from the dead birds.

"Well, he's dead. More or less, anyway."

Nascha's forehead creased, thinking about her saviour from last night, but she just nodded.

"I've heard the stories. It's true, then?"

"Yeah, before we were born, but not much longer ago than that. Thing is, the Magpie King served a purpose. As you've already encountered, this forest is not a safe place."

Nascha laughed in response.

"Well, his existence used to counter that. He was something the people of the forest could rely on, to protect them from harm.

Without him.... well, you've only been here a few days, and you've had a few run-ins with some of our more unfavourable neighbours. Imagine spending your entire life under these trees."

Nascha did shudder this time. As she did so, the path in front of Bradan began to lower, and cut into the earth below. As they kept walking, descending, she realised they were walking into a large basin cut into the forest floor, like those she found close to the few waterfalls she knew of back in the White Woods. The sound of running water nearby confirmed her thoughts.

Not distracted by the change in scenery, Bradan continued speaking. "Well, some of the more powerful beings of the woods have begun to take advantage of his absence, not just by expanding their habitat, but by expanding their influence. The people of the forest, who once worshipped the Magpie Spirit together, are now fractured. Some worship giant spiders, some beavers, and some... well, the most popular of these new powers is the Lady. And that scares me the most, because I have no idea where she came from."

"Which do you worship now? The Magpie Spirit?"

A hint of darkness – perhaps anger? – passed over Bradan's face, but he quickly restored a calm expression. "I certainly believe in the Magpie Spirit. I believe in them all, really. I've met most of them. But I've not met one yet that would particularly inspire me to worship."

"Why stay here, then?" Nascha asked. "Why stay in this Spirit-forsaken forest if there's nothing holding you here, if everything wants to kill you?"

At that, the path opened up ahead of them, presenting Nascha with a proper view of the basin they had descended into. It was an almost perfectly circular indent into the forest floor, an indent about the size of the two Corvae villages Nascha had seen so far. The waterfall that had created it fell from the small cliff opposite her, a cliff that surrounded her now, marking the boundary of the sunken basin, a wall of rock the height of one of the great oak trees they so admired back at Laurentina's Court. The sound of the waterfall crashing into the pool below echoed around the basin. Nascha got a brief glimpse of a family of red squirrels foraging on the forest floor, but they quickly disappeared when they heard her gasp. For the first time in a long while, Nascha noticed birdsong coming from the treetops nearby, a sound that felt alien to her in a place that so far had done its very best to kill her, or at the very least scare her to death.

"It's beautiful," she muttered, in genuine awe.

Beside her, Bradan smiled. "Well, you know, the forest still has a few things to recommend it." He strode forward, toward the waterfall pool. "They're not likely to come this far away from their village to pursue us. We can rest here, then think about our next steps. The most pressing concern is what we're going to do for shelter come nightfall."

He walked toward the pool, but stopped a bit further downstream from it, washing the Lady's filth off him in the running water.

Not wanting to intrude on him while he was bathing, Nascha sat on a rock some distance away, staring at the greenery all around her, contemplating the birdsong.

"I want to get out of here," she said eventually.

"Sorry?" Bradan walked back towards her, his cleaning finished. He sat down with a thump beside her, handing her some stale and battered bread he had in his knapsack.

She took it without acknowledgment. Nascha was too busy contemplating the future, trying to work out what exactly she was hoping for from life. "I'm free. For the first time ever, I don't belong to anyone. But dying here in this hellish place would be a sorry way to celebrate that freedom. I want to get out of here, get out of this forest. Find some civilization, somewhere I can be safe. Safer, anyway. Somewhere I can make a name for myself, without having to rely on anyone else for food or protection."

She was aware of Bradan looking guiltily at the bread in her hands.

"Did you have anywhere in mind?"

Nascha shrugged, giving a little laugh. "I have no idea. I've seen more of the world in the past day than I have the rest of my life combined. Are the Sand Waste cities real? Are we closest to the Lionfolk kingdoms? I just need to go somewhere I can make my own way in the world."

"We're closest to the Grasslands, where the Muridae – the Mousefolk – live. They've got plenty of towns, and cities too, I've heard, larger than any settlements in the forest."

Nascha smiled, her eyes becoming distant. "I heard stories of their boats. Do they really have lands over the seas, and cities there too? Is it possible to travel that far, and still find people?"

Bradan shrugged. "I've certainly heard that's true. Guess you'd need to travel there yourself to find out for real."

Nascha contemplated the idea of travelling on water, giddy at how uncanny a feeling it must be to trust the liquid surface beneath you. She thought about stepping out onto a flat, featureless land, so different from the forest kingdoms she had spent her life in. "It must be nice," she said wistfully, "to see something so different."

She turned to Bradan, serious now. "How do I get there? How do I leave the forest, to get to the lands of the Muridae?"

He looked up, thinking. "A couple of days' travel to the south, I think. As many as four if you stop off at villages on the way, for nightfall. Could shave it down to two if you went direct, but I don't think I need to tell you how dangerous that would be. Staying in the forest at night, I mean."

Nascha turned, facing the direction Bradan had indicated. South. She was staring at one of the cliff walls of the waterfall basin. It seemed high, too high for her to climb, she thought. But then, she had never tried climbing something so high before. Perhaps it was something she was capable of, she had just never trusted herself enough to try it. South, then. A few more days and nights of terror, and then freedom. Perhaps.

"I could take you," Bradan said. Nascha jumped. She had not been expecting him to say anything, and was too lost in her own thoughts.

She turned to look at him, her face a question. He blushed at her gaze, and lowered his eyes. That was a few times already he had looked away from her, unable to lock eyes with her for any length of time. She gave a half smile as she realised this.

"I know my way, I mean. I know the safe places, where you can rest at night outside of the villages. Two days, I think. I could get you there in two days, and at the forest border you could find your own way. Like you wanted, you could protect yourself."

Nascha chewed her lip. She had just been wishing for a life of independence, a life without having to lean on someone to get her through the hardships, and now she was contemplating putting herself into the hands of another stranger. Still, she would be an idiot to throw away her life for simple, worthless pride.

She narrowed her eyes. "What's in it for you?"

Bradan seemed genuinely confused by the question. "I... I

don't really know what I'm doing now, either. My father, we work together, mostly, but we've been having disagreements. And I had a plan I was pursuing that didn't really work out. Plus, I also… also…"

He took a deep breath, then looked right at her, and Nascha could not recall ever before seeing a man as serious as Bradan was right then. "I want to help people," he said earnestly. Hungrily. "There aren't enough people out there helping others, and I want to be one of them. Spirit knows I have no other calling in life. Let me… I'd like to help. I want to know what it feels like to really help someone. If you let me help you, then I give you my word that I'll not stop until you are safe beyond the borders of this forest. Whatever other responsibilities I have, bargains I've made, I'll put them aside until you're on your way. I promise."

She was in awe of him then, baring his soul to her. The weight of the promise he had just made, and the sincerity behind it, was more than a simple palace servant deserved. She smiled, readying herself to say something encouraging in acceptance of his offer.

Bradan's head snapped upward, his eyes tracking the rim of the basin cliff.

Nascha's blood ran cold.

She rolled off her stone into a crouch beside him. Her eyes darted all around the basin, looking for whatever had spooked her companion. Was it the Lady, come after them from the village? The villagers themselves? Her stomach churned at the thought of a more personal pursuit. Had Vippon caught up with her, seeking revenge for her betrayal?

"Up there," Bradan said in a hushed tone, his stance crouched like hers, mimicking a spider, as if ready to pounce. Nascha wished he would draw his sword, and then realised Bradan did not carry a weapon. Just like her, he was defenceless against whatever the forest was about to throw at them.

A flash of white caught her eye, just at the south lip of the basin, high at the top of the surrounding cliff.

"I guess this place isn't as safe as you thought."

Bradan's face turned red, his eyes still training the cliff above them. "I thought we'd be fine before nightfall. Most of the things here only come out at night. I thought we'd be safe."

Another flash of white caught Nascha's eye, this time coming from the north.

"There's more than one of them," she said, trying to not let her panic rise. "They're surrounding us."

Bradan grunted in acknowledgment. "Doesn't matter if they surround us or not. All they need to do is cut off the path down here. We've no choice – no way we can scale those cliffs in any decent time. We have to go out the way we came in."

To the north, a white figure stood up at the lip of the basin, and Nascha's heart fell to her feet. The figure – no, there were two of them now – grabbed hold of a rope, and holding onto it began to descend the cliff face. Bradan swore, pointing to the west and south. Figures moved down the cliff there also.

"Nothing to the east yet, but I'm sure they're waiting for us there. We've no choice, though – look at those weapons. We've got to outrun them." Bradan grabbed Nascha's hand, starting to move, but then he stopped. Nascha was standing rigid, not budging despite Bradan's force, eyes locked on the figures coming to claim her.

Soldiers dressed in dark chain, long spears held in one hand, white feathered cloaks over their shoulders. These men and women were members of the Pale Wardens. Lord Bidzell had sent his men into the forest after her, to bring her back to Laurentina's Court.

"No," was all the protest she could manage. Staring at these figures from her past, from a fate she had thought to have escaped, Nascha was rooted to the spot. The Nascha who had taken it upon herself to set fire to the Foxfolk caravans and who had turned to face a swarm of demonic birds – that Nascha was gone. Once again she was the quiet serving girl, but this time she was not at home in her comfortable castle prison. This time she was in the middle of a monster-infested forest, with no allies worth talking about, and with a score of potential executioners moments away from reaching her.

"What're you doing?" Bradan said, yanking on her arm again. "We've got to go, they're coming."

"For me. They're coming for me. They're from the Owl Queen's Court."

Bradan hesitated, still gripping her arm. "The Court? What're you, some kind of runaway princess?"

In another life, Nascha would have laughed at that statement. Instead, she turned to look at Bradan with an expression of utter horror.

"No, a serving girl. They're here to kill me."

Bradan paused briefly, then set his jaw and tugged Nascha again, moving towards the basin exit. Behind them, at the southern ledge, the first Warden made it to the basin floor, and Nascha heard his chain jingle as he ran towards her. She did not look back, however. Her eyes were too busy scanning the upward slope leaving the basin, looking for the eventual trap.

There was no trap to suddenly spring, however. A trap required deception, luring unsuspecting prey into a situation they did not anticipate. The Wardens did not bother to mask their intentions. Nascha saw a figure in white waiting for them at the very top of the path, also cloaked in feathers, but this time the guardsman's plate was painted as white as the cloak on his back. Lord Bidzell. Lord Bidzell himself had pursued Nascha into the forest.

Bradan stopped. He did not advance further towards Bidzell, but now their escape route was cut off, with four of the Pale Wardens slowly making their way up the path behind. The closest two had their spears already lowered, ready to strike. To their sides, the rock walls of the path were far too high. They might be able to climb them, but any one of the Wardens would be able to cut Nascha and Bradan down long before they could reach safety.

Lord Bidzell himself did not draw his weapon. Unlike the other guardsmen, Lord Bidzell had a twin-headed axe, not a spear, slung over his back. The man walked slowly down the path towards Nascha, his pace steady, methodical. Bradan gripped Nascha's hand, but otherwise he did nothing. There was nothing for him to do. No way they could be saved now.

Lord Bidzell stopped some fifteen feet away. The Wardens did the same just behind. Sighing, Lord Bidzell raised his hands to his head, taking his helm off and holding it at his side.

"You gave us quite a chase, girl. But now we have found you, we can end this foolishness."

"Did Laurentina send you?" Nascha shot back. She was shaking, but tried her damnedest to hide it from her voice. "Does she know you've come here to kill me?"

"I've told you before, she signed the papers. I am merely her servant, following her order. I am trying to protect my queen, to ensure her reign is a successful one."

"You could've left me," Nascha said, almost crying the words. "I had gone, slipped away in the night. Give me a few more days, and I'll be far from here. I'll take off over the sea, never to come back to these lands. Lord Bidzell, give me my life, and you'll never see me again. That'll be the end of it."

Bidzell shook his head. "I'm afraid not. Word of your existence has reached the ears of those who would take... exception to Queen Laurentina's rule. The only thing that will sate their urge for revolution now is your corpse. If they believe an alternative with even a hint of royal blood exists, they will leave no stone unturned to find a pawn they can bring to the playing table."

Lord Bidzell took a step closer. Inside, Nascha felt rage build. There was no way out of this, she could see it now, and this man had hounded her from the moment he set eyes on her. She did not want to end like this, hiding in fear. If Lord Bidzell was finally going to have his way and kill her, she would stand up to him, face him without tears, just as she had chosen to face the birds the night Lonan had met her.

Nascha stepped towards Lord Bidzell, and drew back her hood. She was surprised to see the nobleman's eyes widen, and for the first time since she had known him, she felt his self-confidence fade away. Behind her, from the Pale Wardens, she heard a number of gasps, followed by low muttering between the men.

"You removed the dye," Lord Bidzell said, his face transfixed on her hair.

Nascha's eyes moved to the curly white locks that fell upon her shoulders. A glance to her side told her that even Bradan was arrested by the sight.

"The queen," she heard one of the Wardens whisper behind her.

"That's not the queen," Lord Bidzell shouted at his soldiers. The clear anger with which he addressed them gave Nascha a glimmer of hope. "She's just the offspring of some lord's get, a seed sown long before any of us were born. Nobody of consequence, nothing important about her, except the colour of her hair. The most important thing about this serving girl is the threat she poses to the throne. Maybe now you all can understand why none back at the Court can be trusted to see her."

Nascha felt the moment slip away, the invisible power her presence had over some of those assembled fading. Lord Bidzell had broken the spell cast by her appearance. She was a potential queen no longer.

Still, the confidence that moment had given her did not fade. She had meant to face him, and she was going to. Beside her, Bradan was muttering to himself, looking at the cliffs on either side, as if contemplating scaling them. She let go of his hand, and he quickly relinquished his own grip in response.

Nascha kept her eyes fixed on Lord Bidzell. Her legs shook, but she made sure defiance was clearly etched on her face. Not wanting him to gain the satisfaction of knowing how scared she was, she took the next step, bridging the gap between them by walking towards him.

The nobleman's eyes narrowed.

And then, for a brief instant, Nascha saw.

She saw Lord Bidzell back at the Court, in the former queen's shadow. The queen's gaze always turned to others, never really accepting his advances towards gaining respect in her eyes. Nascha saw the queen on her deathbed, and felt the anticipation Lord Bidzell had experienced at that moment. She felt the frenzy inside him that had drawn him to Laurentina as soon as the queen had passed. His dream – it was his dream and desire Nascha was experiencing now – of standing at Laurentina's right hand, to finally be the one casting the shadow, to become the most loyal and important member of his queen's Court. She also felt his growing dread at the discovery of Nascha, of the fear that what he had achieved in such a short space of time could be taken away from him just as quickly. She felt his acceptance of what he had to do, how it felt so right for him to do it that the life of a servant did indeed rate considerably lower for him than his own advancement.

The vision lasted for a literal blink of an eye. One moment Nascha saw her foe standing in the forest before her, the next she saw inside his mind. One more blink and she was back to the forest, with almost no time having passed.

Unable to help herself, overcome by the rush of information, the assault on her senses, Nascha stumbled forward. Bradan ran to catch her, grabbing her just before she hit the forest floor.

"What happened?" the young man asked, his face pale, breathing heavy.

Nascha did not look at him. After invading Lord Bidzell's mind, she should have been confused herself, perhaps even fearful. Was she really the witch that so many of the Magpiefolk seemed to take her for? With that potential truth, she should be terrified.

Instead, Nascha raised her head, locked eyes with Lord Bidzell, and smiled.

"Sitting at Laurentina's right hand? Really? I never imagined your dreams were so… small."

Lord Bidzell opened his mouth to retort but then froze before speaking. He looked at her, incredulous, as if only recognising her as a person for the first time.

Behind them, Nascha heard the clink of armour as the Wardens tensed into fighting formations, ready to storm forward and take the lives of these untrained, defenceless escapees.

"My lord?" one of the female Wardens called. "Shall we finish this?"

Lord Bidzell stood for one more moment, his eyes still trained on Nascha. Then he nodded. "Let's get this over with."

A clink of metal sounded as the Wardens moved forward, their spears lowered, ready to kill. Nascha turned back to Bradan, and was surprised to see the young man smiling. She had already grown used to seeing him look so persistently serious that the pure smile on his face did not seem to fit. Still, that smile brought with it something Nascha thought had run out. It brought her hope.

"He's here," Bradan said, still smiling, his eyes slightly manic. "Took him bloody long enough, but he finally came."

Behind Bradan, the guards advanced. They were almost on him, but the forest boy did not seem concerned. Nascha just shook her head, not understanding what Bradan was talking about.

She understood a lot better when Lonan dived from the cliffs above, shattering the formation of the guardsmen with his impact.

"Lonan," Nascha said, her smile now matching Bradan's. "You came back."

"You know him?" Bradan shot at her, confused and – amusingly – a bit irritated.

"You know him?" Nascha countered. At no point had Bradan mentioned his association with a crazy magpie man.

Lonan, however, said nothing to either of them. He was too busy dealing with the Titonidae he was sending tumbling back down into the forest basin. A couple of the Wardens he flung against the stone cliffs, and Nascha was convinced they were killed instantly, the impact being strong enough to shatter skull and spine. However, a number of them groaned as they rolled away, bruised, possibly broken, but still alive.

Nascha looked to Lord Bidzell, and saw the nobleman ready his axe, focussed on the new attacker. She tensed, ready to take advantage of the situation.

For the second time in as many days, the man who was not the Magpie King had saved her life.

As if sensing her thinking about its servant, the power linked to her by an invisible thread hummed, reminding her of its existence. Nascha realised distantly that the thing out there hunting her was much closer than before. If she was not quick, it would not be long before she discovered what she had made contact with by looking into Lonan's eyes. She suspected that was something she did not want to happen.

Relief came like a hammer to Bradan's chest as he saw his father plummet from the cliffs above, scattering the assembled Pale Wardens, pushing them back down the steep path, their chain and helmets clanking as they fell. As the Wardens scattered, Lonan dashed back into the forest again. Having seen this tactic before, Bradan knew his father would be repositioning himself out of sight of the enemy, preparing for a new assault.

Bradan loosened his grip on the Lady's plum in his pocket. He had been so close to taking it out, so close to using its power to ensure that both he and Nascha survived the encounter. So close to breaking the promise he had just made to Nascha about getting her out of the forest safely. Now, blessedly, his father had taken that choice away from him.

"Get ready," Bradan said to Nascha, gripping her hand tight. He pointed himself at the leader of the Owlfolk warriors, readying for what he knew was about to come. "Get ready to run." The nobleman Nascha had called Lord Bidzell stood rooted to the spot, having only enough gumption to put his helm back on when he too realised what was about to occur.

Bradan's father exploded from the forest behind Lord Bidzell, impacting the nobleman with enough force to send him careening through the trees, a white comet disappearing behind a clouded sky. Lonan did not speak, did not turn to address the two of them. He just bellowed once, took a glance at the half dozen white-clad warriors who until now had been assembled unseen in the nearby woods, presumably to protect their lord from outside attackers, then leapt off after them.

Seeing their opening, Bradan tugged at Nascha, and ran.

He came. Father came.

Having been abandoned by Lonan against the Vulpe and the Lady, Bradan had not even considered he would show again. At the back of Bradan's mind there was a tickle of concern over how easy it would be for his father to calm himself down once the Pale Wardens were taken care of, but he could not focus on that now. Best to use this opportunity to put as much distance between themselves and this Lord Bidzell as possible, in case his father's protection proved just as fickle.

"You know my father?" Bradan asked Nascha as they dashed together. He was ahead of her slightly, and he knew that if not for him tugging her along, she would not be keeping this pace. He was not surprised. A life inside a castle, even if it was a life of servitude, would not prepare a body for moving through the forest like this. After all she seemed to have been through over the last few days, Bradan was surprised she was able to stand. If he was not already injured – his ribs still ached where the Vulpe had kicked and probably broken them – Bradan knew he would be becoming frustrated at her slowing pace.

"Your father?" she responded, clearly shocked. Bradan could feel her eyes on him, looking for some sort of family resemblance. "Your father is the Magpie King?"

Bradan smiled at that, despite his exhaustion. "He doesn't like to be called that. He's no king."

"He has power, though."

"Yes. Power that came at a price. I'll ask again: you've met him?"

"He saved my life. Last night."

Bradan thought for a moment, ribs tightening as he remembered his own predicament last night, his beating at the hands of the Vulpe. "Yeah, he's got a habit of doing that. Watch out, though. This gift he has – it's taken its toll on him."

"Yeah, um, I did kind of notice. Still, if he got rid of those Owls, he can't be all bad."

As if on cue, Bradan heard a noise above. He looked up just in time to see his father bounding through the treetops, leaping from branch to branch overhead. Then – and even Bradan struggled to track his father's progress as he did this – Lonan landed in front of them, an explosion of leaves heralding his arrival.

Bradan stood with one arm in front of Nascha. He was fairly certain his father would never hurt him, even during one of his more extreme bouts of madness. Nascha, however, he had no idea about, even if she was no stranger.

"Father," Bradan said, wary. "Thank you for saving us. How... how are you?"

Lonan was breathing heavily. He was not looking at either of them, instead staring at the ground he had just landed on, panting.

Not a good sign.

"Lonan?" Nascha tried, from behind Bradan's protective arm. At her voice Lonan did actually raise his head. Bradan tried to not get annoyed at the fact his father reacted more to this owl girl than to him. Instead, Bradan looked for shifts in his father's temperament as his eyes moved from Nascha to Bradan, as if seeing them both for the first time.

"You know each other," Lonan said.

"Yeah, we met earlier. Seems Nascha here has a talent for getting into trouble, and for getting rescued from it by our family."

Nascha responded by shoving Bradan's arm out of the way, shooting him a dark look, and striding over to Lonan. Bradan really wished she had not done that; he was not convinced his father was in the best of moods, although he had to admit that the fact they were able to have a conversation with him at all meant things were not as bad as he initially thought.

"You saved me again," Nascha said to Lonan softly. The girl stopped a few steps away from Lonan, much to Bradan's relief. "That's twice now I owe my life to you. Thank you."

Lonan shook his head and began to pace away from Nascha, his head raised high, searching through the air, as if smelling something. "It was an accident. I didn't know the Owls were abroad tonight. There've been a number of events in the forest of late. The Lady has been stirring, and I've found myself hounding a band of Vulpe from the woods."

"What?" Nascha exclaimed, almost shrinking into herself at the mention of the Foxfolk. "Are they gone now?"

Lonan shook his head, pacing as he spoke, his fists clenched. "They aren't alone. There's someone of power with them. I tried to break them, tried to cut them off from their goal, but... I dare not face him directly. I have no way of knowing which of us would prove the victor. I'll continue to shadow them, to try to figure out what their goal is—"

"It's me," Nascha said, resolute, if not shaken. "They want me. Their leader, a man called Vippon—"

"He has power," Lonan said.

Nascha nodded.

"He's a Gentleman Fox?"

Nascha seemed confused by this, but Bradan was able to respond this time. "He is, Father. I met him last night. He's definitely received the Fox Spirit's blessing. You were right not to face him."

Lonan's eyes briefly rested on Bradan's wounds, but if his father was concerned for him, he did not show it. "Why did you face a Gentleman Fox by yourself?"

Bradan shook his head, irritated that this was what his father chose to focus on. "He would have killed someone."

"He could have killed you."

"Well, he didn't. And I saved someone's life. Again." Bradan paused, giving his father time to respond to that statement.

"I've told you before," Lonan said, and Bradan was surprised by how deep his father's voice became, almost thunderous, "stay away from situations like that. This is no longer your life. These are things for me to deal with."

"But you don't deal with them, do you? I called for you as soon as I saw him, but did you come? Did you even hear me?"

Lonan did not respond, but looked increasingly uncomfortable. Beside him, Bradan was aware of Nascha shifting backward, wanting to remove herself from the family squabble.

"It was your job to save that man, yes. But I was the one who eventually stepped up to do it."

"Is this about last night, or is it about the Meldrum farm?"

"Both, Father. Both. You're the closest we have now to a Magpie King—"

Lonan spat at the name, just as Bradan had expected he would.

"Well, you are. The closest thing the forest has to a protector, but look at you. Half mad half the time, completely missing out on situations that gravely need someone like you."

Lonan turned around to look at Bradan again, and Bradan was shocked to see how wretched he now looked. Bradan hesitated for a moment. This was clearly painful for his father. He could stop now, spare his father more pain.

But…

But then things would never change. Change was coming, whether Lonan wanted it or not. Bradan felt the thing in his pocket, the plum, throbbing, as if somehow calling him to it, as if there was any chance he had forgotten it was there.

"I don't blame you, Father. I know about the poisons working against your mind. Spirit, I'm surprised you've done half the things you've been able to with your life, with madness running through your veins. But that's why someone else needs to step forward, to take up the mantle. Just like you did."

Lonan raised his fist towards Bradan. "Not you. You will not have to live a life like this. I promised."

"Why not me? Surely I'm best suited to this. I'm your son, your blood runs through my veins. Look, I'm already out there helping people. Imagine if I had power like yours – what more could I do?"

Lonan fixed his eyes on Bradan, and Bradan fancied a dark look blossoming on his father's face. "You can't survive this poison, son. One generation of endurance of this illness is not enough to protect our family's minds. The real Magpie King had countless centuries of resistance built up against the Magpie Spirit's gift. More than that, their blood was mixed with others gifted by the Great Spirits." Lonan nodded towards Nascha. "The Owl Queens, the strength of their blood mixed with the king of the forest. You don't have any of that. I won't live to see my son fall like I have."

Bradan took a deep breath. "Not the Magpie Spirit, then. There are other sources of power in the forest."

Lonan turned to look at Bradan, and Bradan wished he had said something else. His father's mouth moved, silently repeating the last words Bradan had just said, and Bradan had to lower his eyes from the intensity of the older man's glare. Then the lines on his father's face darkened, and anger and fear began to spawn from those cracks.

"What have you done?" Lonan asked. His voice was low, but

Bradan felt they must have heard it all the way on the other side of the Grasslands. "Tell me what you've done."

Nascha looked between them both, confused. "Bradan? What's going on?"

Bradan shook his head. "The Magpie Spirit rejected me, Father. Looks like I'm not good enough to follow in your footsteps. Maybe you already knew that."

Lonan stepped forward, the threat clear in his movement. "That's not what I smell on you. Something has its hold on you. Something with its claws around your neck, ready to squeeze." His father hunched like a cat, and, unbidden, Bradan recalled memories of his father attacking beasts that threatened villagers throughout the forest. "Who do you belong to now?"

Bradan inhaled deeply, the plum in his pocket pounding like a drum. "I belong to nobody. Yet."

"Yet?" It was Nascha, this time, who spoke. "Bradan, what is it? Is this something about those powers you said were rising in the forest?" She stared at him, and then Bradan saw something horrible. He saw realisation dawn on her face, and quickly behind it came disgust. The young woman raised a hand to her mouth, and took a step away from him. "Is this… does this have anything to do with the Lady?"

"The Lady?" Lonan growled, stepping right up to Bradan now. "You would not dare have dealings with her."

Bradan did not answer, his head swimming. It took all his strength to stand tall there, looking up into his father's face.

"Bradan," Nascha said weakly, disbelief in her voice, "you can't belong to her. She was going to kill that child, Bradan. She's horrible."

Spirit's blood, he wished she wasn't here right now.

Unable to cope with the look Nascha was giving him, Bradan focussed on his father instead. "I'm my own man, remember? We've gone separate ways."

"You will not be beholden to her," Lonan shouted. The whites of his eyes stood out in the darkness, and Bradan could tell his father was inching closer to the madness that so often took him. Not the madness that left him a meek, harmless wreck crying in a cave somewhere. The other kind. The dangerous kind.

"I'm not beholden to anyone."

The plum throbbed harder, as if disputing that fact.

"Is this why you took so long to leave the church?" Nascha asked. "You were speaking to her?"

"You sought an audience with her?" This was Lonan again, bellowing now.

Bradan had had enough. His father had abandoned him, said he did not want him in his life any longer. He had no right to make demands like this. "Yes, I sought her out. I was left no other choice. You didn't want me anymore. Never even let me do anything meaningful when we did travel together. I asked the Magpie Spirit to give me power, and it told me I wasn't worthy. She was my only option. The only voice that would listen to me. The only person who saw what I could be, what I was doing. Father, with her gift I can be something special. I can help people, like you always wanted to. The way you never can, because of your condition."

Lonan hit him.

Bradan's neck snapped back as he flew through the air, and Nascha screamed his name as he impacted against a tree some distance behind. He saw none of this, however, as he momentarily blacked out when his father backhanded him across the face.

"No! No!" Lonan screamed, leaping towards his son. "You do not belong to her. You are not hers, you are mine. You are mine!"

Lonan slapped Bradan across the face again. From the depths of his stupor, Bradan knew his father was not using his full strength. He was not trying to kill him, thank the Spirit; the first blow from someone suffused with the power of the Magpie King would have been enough, if such intent was behind it. However, Lonan was indeed trying to hurt him, and of that he was more than capable.

"Not hers! Not hers! Not hers!" Each pronouncement was accompanied by a slap across the face, jolting Bradan's head from side to side. His mouth felt twice its normal size, his cheeks engorged, filled with saliva or blood. Bradan became increasingly aware of a dull pain blooming from his right shoulder, where it had hit the tree his father had thrown him against. Try as he might to raise his hand to defend himself, Bradan found he could not. His ribs, already broken by Vippon last night, he could not feel either, a pain so blinding his body had numbed itself to escape.

"Look what you're doing," Bradan heard someone cry, a female's voice.

Mother? Mother, is it you? After all this time?

In front of Bradan, he saw a white cloud floating, pushing itself between him and his father.

Funny, he thought. *Funny a cloud would be this low. I wonder if I can reach out and touch it?*

His eyes focussed better, the pain in his head starting to feel more real now, and Bradan realised Nascha had run over to them, throwing herself in front of him to protect him.

That's not a great idea, is it? His father could toss her aside as if she was a dandelion stalk, cut through her like pruning weeds from a garden. Bradan looked at Nascha's unruly white hair, thought again of a dandelion, and laughed.

Funny. S'funny.

"You're killing him. What could the Lady do to him that's worse than what you're doing right now? You're going to kill your own son."

Bradan was aware of his father stepping back, and a look of horror growing across the older man's face.

"I didn't…" Lonan said. "I would never…"

"But you did, Father," Bradan managed to croak, pushing past the agony Lonan had inflicted upon him. Despite everything, Bradan managed to push himself up. His legs, blessedly, ached only mildly, unlike his face, head, shoulder and ribs.

Lonan was continuing to step backward, shaking his head, looking at his hands.

"No, I would never. Not my son."

"But you did, Father. Look at me." As Bradan said that, he could feel the blood from the wounds inside his mouth dribble from both ends of his lips. He wanted to be sick, but fought to keep it down.

"I'd never…"

"How many times did you tell me that?" Bradan asked. "When we travelled together, when you left in the middle of the night, and when I questioned you when you returned? I asked if you'd hurt anyone, and you told me you never would."

Lonan's face was long, drawn, his mouth hanging open, distraught. It broke Bradan's heart to see him like this.

"Is this what 'never' looks like, Father?" Bradan indicated his ruined face, his broken lips. "How many innocents in the forest have you 'never' harmed?"

"No…"

"This is why I need power, Father. This is why I'm so desperate to find a way to become a force for good in the forest. Because, dear Father, someone needs to protect the people of the forest. Someone needs to protect them from you."

Lonan just looked at his son and shook his head vigorously, manically, his hands raised protectively in front of him, fingers splayed in horror, as if Bradan was the false Magpie King returned from the dead to claim back his title and take Lonan's life.

Then, with one final, fearful glance at both Nascha and his son, Lonan turned and ran off into the night.

THE
LION KNIGHT'S QUEST

A story from the fireplaces of the Leone

This is a tale of long ago, when chivalry was still alive in the Leone kingdoms, when King Reoric still held the throne.

In this age, the title of Lion Knight was held by a woman, the strongest of all her people. On the day her quest began, the Lion Knight travelled to Mount Bastille, the chateau from which the king governed the Lionfolk lands.

"Your Highness," the Lion Knight said, kneeling before her ruler, "I have been called upon a great quest."

King Reoric sat forward on his throne, excited at his subject's words. It had been too long since the Lion Spirit had given his people a challenge, and all Leone longed for the chance to prove themselves once more.

"A conflict is brewing to the west," the Lion Knight explained, "in the Coastal Duchies. I am being called to represent our interests there, to ensure we do not lose more of our kingdom, that our borders do not reduce further."

This was of great concern to King Reoric and the assembled Leone nobility. The Coastal Duchies had been conquered early in the settlement of the Leone kingdom, but the people there were strange, and were often looking to break away from their betters. If the Duchies were lost, the Lionfolk would lose their link to the sea, and that was a loss King Reoric could not bear.

He drew his great sword, Weatherfang, and presented it to the Lion Knight, displaying great trust by putting the fabled blade into her hands.

"Do us proud," he said to his subject, and the Knight's hands shook with pride as she took the weapon from him.

The Lion Knight travelled alone from Mount Bastille, as was

the way of her order, with no squire or page to wait upon her, to make her life easier, to soften her through luxury. She journeyed through the rich, green vineyards of the true Leone lands, travelling ever westward, until the clean country air was stained with salt. Then the lush Leone countryside gave way to the shallow dirt of the Coastal Duchies, and the Lion Knight knew she was drawing close to where the Lion Spirit had summoned her.

It was as if an invisible thread was linking her to her destination, a thread that hummed at her, letting her know that a strong presence waited for her at the other end.

Finally, the Lion Knight met that presence. The invisible thread ended at the edge of a chalk cliff, where the dirt of the Duchies gave way to the rocks and surf of the sea far below. There, waiting for her, was the power she had sensed along the thread.

A man sat on the edge of the cliff, twin bone-white daggers in his hands, one of which he was using to pick something from between his teeth. Unlike the Lion Knight, who wore polished steel plate, as befit her station, this man wore a simple peasant tunic, although unlike the smocks of most of the Duchyfolk, this man's clothing had been bleached pure white. Other than his unusual garb, the only other noticeable feature of this man were the white feathers he had tied into his hair.

"Well met," the man said upon sighting the Lion Knight, leaping up from his place of rest, an irritating smirk breaking across his face. "I was wondering when you'd make it. Allow me to introduce myself – they call me the Gull Knave."

The Lion Knight recognised the man as one aligned with a Great Spirit, but his title was unfamiliar to her.

"Those of us born in the Duchies have been unhappy with the king's rule for some time," the Gull Knave explained, as if reading the Lion Knight's mind. "We reached out to other powers, to free us from your grasp. The gifts given to me were the answer we received."

"I am to fight you, for the crown to keep control of these lands," the Lion Knight said. It was not a question. Such battles between the great powers of the world were not uncommon in those times, and the Lion Knight had already defended her king's honour against the Magpie, Wolf and Serpentfolk during her service to the throne. Rarely did the Great Spirits of the world take part in these conflicts themselves, for fear of the devastation such an event would cause.

The Gull Knave nodded, twirling a knife around the fingers of each hand. "Let's get to it then, eh?"

This confident stranger annoyed the Lion Knight, and she stood tall, refusing to draw her blade.

"This is not the way of things," she told the upstart. "We cannot just battle out here in the wilderness, away from all others. There must be witnesses to our duel, so there is no doubt of the victor afterward."

The Gull Knave smiled at her, picking his teeth with his knife again. "No fear there," he said to her, grinning all the while. "The way I fight, there will be no doubt who has won."

"Nevertheless," she responded, "there must be witnesses. We will wait for them."

The Gull Knave rolled his eyes, but went back to his perch on the cliff edge, ignoring the Lion Knight, staring out to sea. The Knight found a tall ash some way back from the cliff, the Gull Knave still in clear view, and leaned against it, standing sentry, waiting. The thread that had led her to this spot still thrummed, and she could feel others travelling along it, other people of power.

It was not long before they arrived.

Out of the trees and onto the cliff edge walked the Magpie King and his Owl Queen bride, walking hand in hand, as if enjoying a romantic stroll through the countryside.

The Lion Knight stood straight, shocked by the sight of the royals.

"Your Graces," she addressed the king and queen of the dark woods, as was proper. "I had not expected someone of your station to join us today. We are honoured."

The Gull Knave nodded at the king and queen in recognition, but otherwise only stood and prepared to fight again.

"We have been summoned to witness by our patrons," the Owl Queen told the pair waiting at the edge of the cliff. "This summons has taken us far from our lands. Let us be quick about this, then, so we can all return to our kingdoms."

The Lion Knight bowed in response, and the Gull Knave chuckled. While the Magpie King and Owl Queen watched, the Knight and Knave readied their weapons, preparing to fight.

"This contest of champions is for the future of the Coastal

Duchies," the Owl Queen declared, as the Lion Knight locked eyes with her foe. "May your Spirits bless you with their gifts, and may you use them wisely."

The combatants circled each other, each trying to read their opponent as the battle began. The Gull Knave ducked and weaved, leaping forward to needle the Knight with his twin blades, jumping back before she had a chance to respond, a multitude of small cuts decorating her skin as a testament to the man's speed.

"You have no chance against me, girl," the Knave crowed after opening up a particularly nasty cut across her forehead. "Two dozen of us competed for the Gull Spirit's gift. I already killed two dozen to get this far. Your notch will be a very small addition to that number. What do you say to that?"

The Lion Knight, however, did not respond. She had not killed two dozen men, despite having held her position for the best part of a decade. However, she had more than enough experience to know when it was time to shut up, and when it was time to strike.

In one movement, while the Knave was waiting for her response to his jibe, the Lion Knight dove forward, bringing Weatherfang up in a vicious arc, opening the Knave up from groin to throat.

The man collapsed to the ground, gasping, his daggers forgotten.

The Lion Knight stood before her enemy, her face emotionless.

"You must finish him," the Magpie King said, his first words since arriving. "Such a combat should be to the death."

The Lion Knight looked upon her foe, and felt pity. "He may still die," she replied, eyes not leaving the Knave. "But if he survives this wound, he will deserve to. I choose to give him his life."

"That is not your choice to make," the Magpie King said, a note of irritation now detectable behind his mask. "You must kill him. So it has been decreed."

"No," the Lion Knight said one final time, before turning to leave the cliff.

"If he lives, you will not have won. The Coastal Duchies will rise up against the Leone again."

"They will rise up again whether this man dies or not," the Lion Knight said before leaving. "But if I kill this man now, at your insistence, then I will truly have lost. Good day, and I thank you both for your witnessing."

The Lion Knight strapped Weatherfang to her back again as she left, preparing herself for the lonely journey back home. In the back of her mind, she was aware of the thread still linking her to the Gull Knave, his heartbeat weak along it as the fallen man fought for survival.

In his own way, the Lion Knight realised, the Knave had been brave. He and all his people had true conviction that what they were doing was right. That was the only way they could have attracted a Great Spirit to their cause. It troubled the Lion Knight greatly that so many of the King's subjects were unhappy under his rule.

Then, suddenly, the thread linking the Lion Knight to the Gull Knave snapped.

She turned around in shock, but no sound accompanied the Knave's death. Still, the Lion Knight held no doubt as to what had happened.

She stood there, awaiting the murderer's arrival.

Not long after that, the Magpie King and the Owl Queen, still hand in hand, strolled past the Lion Knight. The long sickles that dangled from the Magpie King's waist were clean, but the Lion Knight still knew they had recently been used.

"Such a combat must end in death," the Magpie King said in reproach as he and his wife walked past. "So it has been decreed."

A similar invisible bond linked the Lion Knight to the king and queen, and it faded away as the trial ended, the powers of the world no longer needing such a thread to exist. Still, the Lion Knight was sickened at how calm the King and Queen were at their recent deed, how simple it was for them to needlessly take a life. It sickened the Lion Knight to know that, someday, she could very well be bonded to such people again.

"The Great Spirits of the world will not be denied," the Magpie King said as they strolled from sight. "Do not cross them again."

CHAPTER SEVEN

It was Bradan who had insisted they keep travelling, much to Nascha's surprise. She had expected his injuries to stall whatever plans he might have had for getting her out of the forest, but he clearly had other ideas.

"You heard him," Bradan said, referring to his father, not looking her in the eyes when he said his name. "He said the Vulpe were abroad. Think about that. We've had my father hounding them for us, keeping them from your trail. Can't imagine he's still bothering them, the state he's in now. No clue about those Pale Wardens either, if they've been put off following you. Guess it depends how much they've been hurt. Any idea? If this Bidzell is alive, is he the type to back off once he's been warned?"

Nascha thought back to Lord Bidzell, to the brief glimpse she had into his dreams, to the hunger she felt there.

"If he's alive, he's coming for me," she said after a while.

Bradan hobbled onward, continuing to lead Nascha south. When nightfall eventually came, he urged her to find a tree to climb. She found an ash with its branches low to the ground, one she was confident she would be able to make her way up. Watching Bradan climb after her was painful. The man was clearly in agony. The rising bruises on his face were not the only marks his father had left on him. Anytime he shifted his weight the wrong way, his hand went to his side, and his face showed brief flashes of pain. He only used one hand when climbing. It took him the best part of an hour to achieve a height Nascha managed within a couple of minutes. However, he would not hear her protests.

"Spending the night in the forest is foolishness. If there were any homes close to here, we'd be making for those. If I knew of any safe caves or other shelters nearby, I'd be taking you there. As it is, with me slowing us down, this is our only option. So shut up and let me climb."

His directness shocked her, and she felt her anger rise. It was his own fault, this stupid forest lad, that he got himself beaten up, not hers. He was the one who had angered his father, not her. And, honestly, from what Nascha had seen of this Lady, Lonan had every right to be angry at his son for making a bargain with her. She was not just some ambivalent forest force, prone to lashing out at whim. She was clearly evil. Evil and selfish. Anything that threatened young children for being frightened of something that was making grown men cry was evil, as far as Nascha was concerned.

Finally, Bradan managed to make it up to the top of the tree, finding an arrangement of branches he could collapse in without having to exert too much effort to keep himself from falling. He lay there for a while, panting, just looking up at the cloud-covered night, watching the orange and red of the sunset disappear from the sky. Nascha could not help but pity him then, despite his poor choices. Nobody expected their father to almost beat them senseless. What kind of life must he have had, living in a place like the Magpie King's forest with a father so on the edge?

"It's not his fault," Bradan said, as if reading Nascha's thoughts. He turned to look at her, and she could see how upset he was. More than that, however, she saw desperation in his eyes, as if he had to share the words he was about to speak. "My father, he gave his life for the forest. You heard the tale about the false Magpie King, the madman who broke the line of the royal family and ruled the forest for decades of darkness and fear? My father was the one who overthrew him."

The revelation did not shock Nascha, although she had not known the truth until Bradan had spoken the words. However, from what she had seen over the past few days, it all made perfect sense, like a child's picture puzzle fitting together out of seemingly disconnected parts.

"He gave up his sanity for the power to protect the forest," Bradan continued. "He's a great man. He just… he can't control himself when he gets like this."

Nascha did not know what to say. She wanted to tell Bradan that a father who beat his son almost to death is not a 'great man'. Instead, she sat, unspeaking.

"You wouldn't understand," Bradan said eventually, giving a sigh of exasperation. Clearly he had wanted a response from her, and she had upset him with her silence. "He gave up everything. All the future he had imagined, gone in an instant. How could anybody understand what that's like?"

"I get it," Nascha said, trying to remove any scorn from her voice, trying her hardest to imagine how Bradan was feeling right now. "The night my Knack came, it was like that."

Bradan looked back at her, frowning at the comparison.

"The place I grew up in, the Court, was my prison. A prison of sorts, anyway. As a very young girl, I had no idea, really. Just thought I was another servant, thought I was the same as everyone else. Then, one day, I asked them why I had to dye my hair, why it had to be black instead of white, like the queen. That was the day they took me aside and told me I was a mistake, a threat. That I was lucky to be alive, and if I ever did anything to upset anyone at Court, the easiest thing for them to do would be to feed me to the owls to get rid of another problem in their lives. I was eight, I think.

"That was when I realised I had to escape. For years I planned to do it, backing down at the last minute, lest they catch me and punish me for my attempts. I bound together rope ladders from soiled clothing at the laundry, but eventually hid them under bushes in the Court gardens. I dug a tunnel in the stables, giving up when, after a month stealing time to dig, I had only managed to make a hole big enough to hide my boots in. I stole keys from as many doors in the Court as I could, keeping them hidden up one of the chimneys in the kitchen, too scared to try them out for myself. Even though I stopped just before I made each escape attempt, I kept the items I hoped to use to free myself from that existence. I loved stories of Tadita – do you know Tadita, here in the woods? – and fancied that one day I would throw off the shackles of the Court and become like her. Free.

"Then my Knack arrived.

"It came when I was thirteen, when I had been tasked to scrub the kitchen floors for the umpteenth time. I stood back, looking at my work, marvelling at how the constantly soiled flagstones shone after my brush and bucket had passed them by. I took so much pride in my work. Then a passing cook pointed out that my eyes were glowing, that my Knack had come into play.

"I have a Knack for cleaning. Specifically, scrubbing."

Nascha looked at Bradan, hoping the hidden moon still showed him how ashamed she was, embarrassed of her Knack.

"How could anyone with a Knack for scrubbing hope to follow in Tadita's footsteps? That was when I realised I was destined to remain at the Court for the rest of my life. I had taken too long to escape, and now my life had been planned for me. I was to be a cleaner, a servant, for the rest of my days."

Bradan propped himself up, groaning slightly, to look at her. "Not anymore, though, right?" he said. "Now you've got something else going on. You did something to that man, Bidzell, back there, didn't you? Got into his head. Are you turning into some sort of Owl Queen now?"

Nascha bit her lip, thinking back to that moment when she had invaded Lord Bidzell's waking dreams. Nothing like that had ever happened to her before. Perhaps Bradan was right – perhaps there was something happening to her.

Thinking about it a moment longer, she shook her head. "They did stuff to me, back at the Court. Made me take poison every month. I thought it was to make sure I never have any children, never pass on the colour of my hair, but I reckon they were trying to stop me doing things like *that* as well." She could vaguely sense the part of her that had woken when she had entered Lord Bidzell's mind, but it was a malformed, incomplete part of her. She imagined using that echo of the Owl Spirit's gift was a bit like how a cripple felt in a foot race – it was possible to catch the others off guard, to give a burst of speed at the most unexpected moment, but there was still no chance of winning. "Maybe if I hadn't been poisoned my whole life, maybe then I could have been something, but whatever is inside me… it's ruined, Bradan. They ruined it. It came out when I was angry, but I don't think it's a part of me that'll get any better."

They were both silent for a long while. The moon briefly peeked out from behind the clouds, the white light it cast making Nascha hate it. In the distance, they heard an owl hooting, and Nascha thought briefly of home, of the sparse landscape of the White Woods, of her quiet walks beneath the trees gathering firewood. For the first time, and much to her surprise, Nascha found herself missing her former life.

"What about you?" she asked Bradan eventually. "What's your Knack?"

It was an odd thing to ask. It was not quite intimate, but it was certainly a personal question, akin to asking someone if they were in a relationship. You would find out eventually by spending time with them, but bluntly asking often felt as if there was purpose behind the enquiry.

However, Nascha decided they had been through enough together for such concerns to no longer matter, and besides, she would rather suffer a little embarrassment than endure another moment's silence, waiting for something below to catch their scent.

Beside her, in the dark, Bradan shuffled uneasily at her question, and she felt she had overstepped the mark. Perhaps she had stumbled into some Corvae taboo she had been heretofore unaware of.

"I don't have one," he said eventually. "My father's the same. We don't have a Knack."

Nascha laughed. "Oh, I say. Pardon me, Your Majesty."

She turned to smile at him, and was surprised by the hurt confusion on Bradan's face.

"What? Your Majesty?"

"Yeah," she said again. "No Knack. You know, like nobility."

Bradan shook his head. He had no idea what she was talking about.

"Back at the Court, they call Knacks peasant magic. Nobility hardly ever develop them, and even when they do, they tend to keep it quiet. The uppity ones claim it shows that the nobles are better than the rest of us, that they don't need Knacks to make their way in the world. Me? I reckon it's just because the nobles never bother to focus on any one skill long enough to become gifted in it."

Bradan nodded slowly. "It's always been... I've always been ashamed of it, I guess. Reckoned something was wrong with me."

"You've honestly never heard of this before?"

He shook his head, face now expressionless.

She shrugged. "Well, there you go, Your Majesty. Guess you and your da must be something special after all."

She smiled at Bradan, expecting one in return. Instead, he looked thoughtful, his gaze drifting away from her. Eventually, they returned to the rigid silence she had feared, flinching at every noise that came from below, all the while expecting the Owls, Vippon, or just some forest beast to find them.

As the silence invaded the space between them, Nascha became aware that had been the longest conversation she had had with someone in years. Even with Vippon, on the times he would lie with her afterward in his caravan, they would speak very little. She had not minded, instead contenting herself to roll away from him, basking in the warmth of their lovemaking, or – on those rare occasions – lie with her head on his chest, listening to him breathe in and out, her hand playing with the grey-specked hair on his chest.

Nascha woke with a start, realising Bradan was gripping her arm. She had not meant to fall asleep, but sensing the urgency in his grip, she was immediately alert.

It did not take her long to hear the voices below.

They were Vulpe, judging by the unfamiliar words. The few days she had spent in their company had only been enough time to pick up the most basic of their phrases. From what she could gather, the two below them – a man and woman – were relaxed, almost bored, although it was hard to tell. *Kettu* always sounded aggressive to her.

She looked at Bradan.

Vippon? he mouthed.

She shook her head. The man's voice below was considerably rougher than that of the Vulpe leader's.

She felt crippled by the inability to speak further. Up here, lying on their backs, there was no way of knowing if the two below were alone or not. She was also unclear as to the extent of Vippon's abilities. Tales of the Magpie King said he was able to sense danger in the forest from miles away, could sense the single heartbeat of someone in distress. If that was the case for Vippon, then they were already as good as dead, although Nascha suspected that if his senses were that strong, then he would have already found them.

A slap came from below, and the voices of the Vulpe raised. They were arguing. Nascha looked at Bradan, feeling – not for the first time in her life – trapped.

Then, to Nascha's shock, she heard a moan from below. A moan of pleasure. The heated voices lowered, the female Vulpe now letting out small, encouraging murmurs, the man speaking briefly, hurriedly, in between bouts of… doing something else.

Despite the fear of the situation, Nascha could not help but laugh, a notion she quickly tried to suppress. She caught Bradan's look and raised an eyebrow at him, smiling. He turned away. She assumed he was blushing in the dark, and Nascha's smile deepened. She felt a little bit of that control she had had over Vippon when she met him for the first time in the White Woods.

"I guess Vippon's not there, then," she said, daring to whisper now she knew the Gentleman Fox and his senses were nowhere close by. "Unless they're happy with him watching."

"But they also know we're somewhere nearby," Bradan replied, composing himself. "Otherwise they wouldn't be here. How long until they think of looking up?"

The sounds from below told Nascha things would not take long. She had to admit, Bradan was right – the Vulpe had caught up with her. Vippon might not be close, but he must not be miles away either.

"What do we do?" she asked.

Bradan seemed unsure.

"Keep moving," he said. "I've got a few ideas. There are a few hills ahead, and if we get over them, there are some places in the forest where most sane people would not dare to follow us."

Nascha raised an eyebrow again, her face considerably less suggestive than before. "Doesn't sound reassuring."

Bradan shrugged. "I said I had some ideas. Never said they were any good. Don't worry, though, got something else up my sleeve if that doesn't work out."

Nascha hesitated before asking the question she had been dying to ask since the confrontation with Lonan. "Has this got anything to do with what you said to your father? About making a deal with the Lady?"

Bradan looked uncomfortable, but did not respond.

"You can't seriously want to take her side?" Nascha said, the noises from below becoming more urgent, thankfully, the Vulpe's passion drowning out her own raised voice. "She's a monster. Look at the state she had gotten those villagers into. That child sitting in front of you. What would she have done to him if you hadn't grabbed that vine?"

He did not meet her eyes. "I don't think she's like that. She's ancient. She doesn't… I don't think she really understands people. Maybe… I think I might be able to help that, to change her."

Nascha's face soured. "Really? That sounds pretty impressive. How long've you had that Knack for?"

He looked at her then, eyes cold this time. "I don't really have a choice, do I? You saw my father. I have to do something, to stop him before he hurts someone. If he hasn't already. I've tried the other routes. She's the first one that spoke back to me, who actually found me worthy of her time, and power."

Nascha shook her head. "Not good enough. It's not worth throwing your life away to save a few people, with no guarantee of the eventual outcome."

"It was good enough for my father, when his time came to make the choice. I'll do it for him, just like he did it for everyone else."

Below, the Vulpe lay gasping together, both their passions spent. After a few brief seconds, their arguing began again, as if nothing untoward had happened, and their raised voices travelled away from the base of the tree Nascha and Bradan were resting in.

"We'd better go," Bradan said. "And I'm going to need you to help me down."

Despite his fears, it was actually easier for Bradan to descend than it was to ascend. At least this time, when he misstepped, the direction he travelled in was always down, and there were more than enough branches on this ash for him to catch himself on before doing too much damage. Still, by the time they reached the bottom, Bradan had received a fine new collection of bruises to add to the many he already had. Now that the sun was rising, Nascha got a good look at his face. The left side of it was purple and misshapen, the worst bruising from a fight Nascha had ever seen. When he smiled, it was pitiful.

"Got to keep going," he said. "They won't be back here for a while, but they know roughly where we are now. If they know anything about the forest, it won't take a genius to guess where we're going."

"And where's that?"

He paused before he replied, as if choosing his words carefully. "We call it the Razortree Nest. Fun place."

"I'll bet. Okay, lead on, Your Majesty."

He snorted at the honorific and turned south, hobbling onward. It became obvious to Nascha then how painfully slow their progress was going to be. Bradan's beatings, both at the Vulpe camp and at the hands of his own father, and his toil climbing the tree last night, had worn the man down. His right leg in particular seemed to be giving him problems, and this time Nascha found herself ploughing forward, only stopping to wait when she was just about to lose sight of him, aware that only Bradan knew where they were headed.

"Sorry," he muttered to her, more than once. "I'll move quicker, sorry. Just taking a while to get loosened up."

He was not, however, loosening up. If anything, Bradan was getting slower. Even if they were not being pursued, Nascha knew there was no chance they would make the two-day schedule Bradan had promised. Worse than that, if Vippon's crew thought at all to double back, they would have no chance to outrun them.

It was about midday when Nascha noticed movement to their left. She gave a gasp, trotting back to Bradan, who continued to hobble onward.

"You spotted him, then," Bradan said, his words choking out from him, giving voice to an agony that had been hours in the making.

"Him?"

"Vippon. He's been shadowing us for the last ten minutes, far as I can tell."

"Ten minutes?" Nascha's heart sank. She had hoped it had been her imagination. "Why hasn't he done anything yet?"

She looked in the direction of the movement she had spotted. For a brief moment, a lone figure stepped out from between the trees, a good thirty feet away. It was indeed Vippon, dressed in his ever-present waistcoat, his red tail twitching behind his back. He smiled at her, waved, as if doing nothing more than greeting two strangers passing close by on a leisurely walk, and then stepped behind the trees again.

"He's playing with us," Bradan said, his teeth gritted, continuing to plod onward. "The bastard knows he's got us, and he's playing with us."

Nascha stared at the blank space in the woods that had briefly held her former lover. Then, panting, she jogged to catch up with Bradan. "What do we do, then? How can we get past him? What tricks do you have up your sleeve?"

Bradan laughed, but there was no mirth in that noise. "Tricks?" He shook his head. "Well, we've scared my father off, so that trick is out. I guess I've just got one left to play."

Bradan reached into his pocket and pulled out the plum the Lady had given to him back in Ebora. It was a simple object, but Bradan handled it as if it would attack him, as if it was a body part he had discovered in his pocket instead of a simple fruit.

It only took Nascha a moment to realise what was happening.

"That's the Lady's gift."

Bradan's eyes flicked up to her, but he said nothing. His gaze returned to the plum and, taking a moment to swallow, he raised it to his mouth.

Impulsively, Nascha grabbed at the fruit, folding her hands over it, pulling it back from him. She was surprised by the aggression he responded with, how he pulled back against her with one hand, shoving her away with the other. For a brief moment, a look of rage flashed across Bradan's face, reminding her of Lonan as he had beaten his son.

"I don't want it," she said quickly, hoping to disarm him. "Just don't... don't eat it. Not yet."

His anger withdrew, and he lowered his hand, still clasping the plum, looking exhausted. "I honestly don't want to, but what choice do I have? He's got the gifts of the Fox Spirit, and we have nothing left. Only someone with power can hope to face him. If the Lady keeps her promise, this'll give me that hope."

"Just wait. I don't... I don't want you to do this just for me. I don't think I'll be able to forgive myself if you turn yourself into a shrubbery or a little red-haired girl on my behalf." She took a deep breath. "Vippon and I, we have a history."

Bradan raised an eyebrow at this.

Face reddening, she continued. "I might be able to talk some sense into him. If not, the Razortree Nest can't be far away. If I can't reason with him, eat the damned thing, and get us both there as quick as you can."

He took a moment to consider her offer, then nodded.

Nascha took a few steps away from him, pointing herself

towards the part of the woods she reckoned Vippon must be skulking in.

"Vippon. Vippon, we need to talk. I've come to surrender."

"Surrender, little Nascha?" Vippon emerged from behind an aspen no more than ten metres away from her, much closer than Nascha had anticipated. She could not help but step away when he showed himself. The older man smiled at this, a grin at once winning and sinister.

"Well, thank goodness for that. I would have hated to have to chase you all over the forest."

She ignored his jibe. "My friend here is hurt. I was hoping you'd have somewhere he can rest. And we can talk."

Vippon made an exaggerated move to look over Nascha's shoulder, at Bradan. "Oh, your friend, is he? We've met before, your friend and I. I do believe it would be my pleasure to help him recover from his wounds, however they have been inflicted on him."

Vippon indicted with his head in the direction Nascha and Bradan had already been travelling. "My people have made camp in that direction, a few hours from here. Not quite as fine as the camps you may remember, unfortunately. You see, we have had a few small disasters since the night you left us. I know this might shock you, but a number of our homes were consumed by flames that night – however did that happen? We've also been hounded by the ghosts of this cursed place. I should have listened to you, my dear. It seems that some stories are not quite ready to die.

"Keep walking in the direction you're going, and you'll find us soon enough." With that, Vippon walked south, soon disappearing behind some more trees.

"That's it?" Bradan asked. "He just wants us to follow him?"

Nascha shrugged, trying to ignore the clear tension in her shoulders. "Probably beats carrying us back to his people. Can't imagine he'll leave us alone too long, though."

Sure enough, Vippon emerged from the trees some distance ahead, waved them to follow him, and disappeared again.

Over the next few hours, Vippon appeared to them again, always at a distance, not always directly in front of them. More than once Nascha spotted him off to the side. Once, he came from behind, barging right past them, flashing Nascha one of his winning smiles as he shouldered Bradan out of the way to get through.

Nascha pursed her lips at the cheek of him, but said nothing. The man might not have enhanced hearing, but she did not want to risk putting him in a foul mood by saying something in the heat of anger. She suspected it would be difficult enough to get them out of this situation alive. Best to start off on the right foot, and see where things took her.

They came upon the Vulpe camp as evening drew near. Just as Vippon had suggested, it was much changed since Nascha's time with the troupe. The caravans numbered only three now, instead of the half dozen they had been a few days ago. In place of those lost homes, hastily erected tents had been put up in the protective circle formation they were still adopting. More obvious to Nascha, however, were the glares she received from the other Vulpe upon arrival. Men and women stood mid mouthful, shocked to see her step into their temporary home. Just before any potential violence could erupt, Vippon walked forward.

"Look who I found, everyone. My little queen, whom we all feared was lost. We should celebrate, celebrate Nascha's return to us."

None of the other Vulpe moved. Instead, their eyes tracked their leader. Vippon did not seem concerned that they were not acting upon his instructions. Instead, he motioned to Bradan.

"And look, here is her protector. Some of you may recognise him. Or some of you may recognise the shape of your own feet, imprinted on his flesh. Who would like to step forward and say hello?"

Two grizzled Vulpe stepped forward at the same time, eager to finish off what they had started with Bradan back in Gallowglass.

"Wait," Nascha shouted, waving her hands at the Vulpe, then turning to Vippon. "We have to talk. I'd like to talk to you. Alone."

Vippon returned her gaze, and for the first time since their reunion, all mirth had left his face. Instead, Nascha was greeted by a cold stare from the lover she had jilted, from the man whose homes she had burned. She remembered how violently he was willing to protect his people back in Gallowglass, and all moisture seemed to suddenly leave her mouth.

"Yes," Vippon said, his voice a low monotone. "Yes, I do think we need to talk."

He turned and marched to a caravan at the far end of the circle, expecting her to follow.

"My friend," Nascha said, calling after him. "You must promise he'll be safe without me." Vippon turned around, chewing his lip, his eyes moving from Nascha to Bradan. After a moment, he nodded. "Show this young Corvae the hospitality of the Vulpe," he said to his companions, the false joviality returning to his voice. "He is our guest, for as long as little Nascha here is with me."

Nascha's heart fluttered with that phrase, and all the implications of it. Vippon had granted Bradan guest rights at his campfire, but only so long as Nascha was with Vippon. That could mean so many things. Also, from what she could gather, guest rights for the Vulpe were different from the guest rights Nascha had expected during her time at Court. They persisted only so long as the guest did not offend their hosts. Bradan would be all right. Probably.

Sparing a quick glance at Bradan, who slumped beside the campfire, exhausted, with no Vulpe paying him much attention other than to shoot him hateful glances, she followed Vippon into the caravan.

It was, of course, not his. That one, Nascha had burned. Another Vulpe must have offered to give Vippon theirs until he could build or buy a replacement. Inside, the decor was sparse. Nascha noticed a few of the items that had been decorating the walls of Vippon's former home – a mask in the shape of a blazing sun, an intricately etched bone dagger – many of which were now smoke-stained, if not outright burnt in some places. Unlike his previous caravan, which had always been heavily incensed, this one smelled of burnt peat. The interior was dominated by a double bed, not unlike the one Nascha had spent so much time in only a few days ago.

Vippon paced to the other side of the room, staring out of the small window that looked to where the horses would be hitched when the caravan was moving, his back to her. As her only other option would have been to sit on the bed, which now seemed such an inappropriate place, Nascha stood, waiting in awkward silence, unsure what to do next.

She and Bradan were somehow still alive. Vippon had helped them, in a way, by taking them further south. They must now be close to Bradan's Razortree Nest. However, Vippon was angry. His was a people who lived for revenge, and Nascha had no illusions as to his intentions regarding her and Bradan's lives right now.

She was exactly where Vippon wanted her, and without any kind of plan for escape.

"I'm sorry about your caravans," she said, unsure of how otherwise to begin the conversation.

Vippon stiffened slightly, but still stood looking out of that small window.

"I… I felt there was no other way to get away from you. You did not strike me as the kind of man who would easily let me go."

Again, he did not turn. Instead, Vippon began to speak, his voice distant and wistful. "I grew up in the shadow of the mountains. The Loamsfold, you will not have heard of them. They're far to the east, well beyond the Titonidae or even the Mousefolk lands."

Nascha shifted, hands clasped in front of her, unsure whether or not he expected a response.

"My family were Vulpe, too, but they did not travel like me and mine. We lived in homes like this, as all our people do, but my mother and father had grown comfortable making their living from the mountains, and the lake that collected the rainwater from them. They could fish, and my father traded his art for what he could not find for himself. My mother, I think, had even planted a small garden outside of their caravan."

He laughed at this, chuckling to himself.

"Imagine that, a bed of roses curling around the wheels of a Vulpe caravan."

His mirth died, and he continued.

"I was adventurous, restless. Unlike my family, I had not experienced the travelling life, but I had it in my blood. We had no other Vulpe around us. The other children, the ones I should have grown up with, were seeing the world with their families. I wanted to see it with them. Every day I would leave the confines of that small home, alone, and I would roam far afield, travelling further each journey, pushing my restraints. The prison my parents had made for me."

He still did not turn to face Nascha, but Vippon leaned forward and gripped the edge of the windowsill. Nascha could see the whites of his knuckles, and as he gripped the wood tighter, Nascha fancied she could see it start to crack, thin, irreparable lines sprouting from where his fingertips touched the wood.

"It was on one of those journeys that I found him," Vippon

continued. "The Gentleman Fox, and his castle. It was high in the mountains, far above where I had grown up. He did not seem surprised to see me. He was lying on a rock outside his home, stripped naked to the waist, a pipe in his mouth. "Little one," he said to me, "I've been wondering how long it would take you to get here. Won't you come and join me for a while?" he asked. I looked at the castle, and was unimpressed. All it seemed to me was another prison to lock myself away in, something rooted hard to the mountainside, immovable, rigid. That was not for me.

"However, that cunning man – the first ever man I had met with a fox's tail – he looked at me with a twinkle in his eye when I told him what I thought. Then he took me by the hand, led me to his courtyard, and showed me his caravan.

"I never saw my parents again after that day. I imagine they are long dead now, buried in the same garden my mother took such pride in, far below that castle that now belongs to me.

"And that man, that man who took me from my family and gave me this life…" Vippon was silent for a moment, and Nascha could feel the tension from Vippon permeate the room. The air around her was thick with it. "That man taught me many things, but one more important than anything else."

"What was that?" Nascha asked, playing the role expected of her.

Vippon turned around, and Nascha's heart stood still at the sight of his face. All charm had fallen away from it, all his rage as well. Instead, Vippon reminded her of Lord Bidzell when he had first presented Nascha with her execution papers. She was not a person to Vippon anymore. She was a problem to be dealt with, a growth to be removed.

"We are always alone. No matter who they are, no matter how close you allow yourself to get to someone, they will betray you in the end. And he taught me, when they stab you in the back, let the world see what happens to those who cross you."

What Nascha noticed more than anything was the knife in his hands, and the unforgiving look in his eye. She tensed, knowing she had no chance against his gifts.

"You betrayed me—" Nascha began, raising her hand in protest, but he was not listening.

He lunged at her, his blade and free hand both reaching out for her throat.

Nascha was not fast enough to avoid him. Even if Vippon had been a normal man, the knife was easy in his hand; he had a lifetime of practice with it. Nascha was more used to holding a broom.

However, as Vippon leapt at her, an image rushed into Nascha's mind. It was the face of a man, an older man, older still than Vippon. Whereas Vippon's hardness was offset by the man's natural charm, by the cheeky smile that held back the overall sense of danger one had when looking at him, this face that appeared in Nascha's mind had none of that charisma. This man's face was cold, cruel, and hungry.

Vippon screamed, although not in rage. He raised his arms to protect himself, moving the point of the knife away from Nascha. His leap still brought him into contact with her, impacting upon her and careening them both toward the caravan door, which they crashed through, spilling out and down the steps to the grass. Vippon was on her now, and could easily have finished her off, but he rolled away, shouting, swiping at the unseen face. He got to his feet a few paces from her, his eyes wide and white, his hair dishevelled, his knife held ready to swipe at his unseen assailant.

His eyes flicked to Nascha, filled with an equal mix of outrage and fear. "How did you—?"

Vippon stopped speaking as his eyes turned to look at the camp behind Nascha. It was only then that Nascha realised there was noise from behind her, sounds that belonged more on a battlefield than in a Vulpe campsite. Still on the ground, Nascha spun around, unable to believe things were getting worse.

The Pale Wardens were attacking the Vulpe. Despite everything, Lord Bidzell was still coming for her.

Close by, a Vulpe man gave a cry as a Warden spear pierced his gut, the foxman crumpling pathetically to the ground as life left him. Vippon howled, leaping at the Warden, a single bound taking him all the way across the campsite. Nascha did not wait to see the outcome of that fight. She pulled herself upward, and ran back to the fire to find Bradan.

Vulpe and Titonidae clashed all around her. Although the Pale Wardens were the best fighters of her people, they were tired, and more comfortable fighting on battlefields and in fair fights. The Vulpe outnumbered their enemy almost two to one, and brawls in campfire half light were their specialty. Nascha gave a small yelp as a Vulpe woman leapt on top of a Warden, not giving the white-clad soldier time to pull his spear from the Foxfolk man he had just wounded. The woman's move sent both of them tumbling in front of Nascha. Overhead, the air was punctuated with deadly whistles as arrows were exchanged between both sides.

Bradan was not at the campfire rock where Nascha had left him. Desperately, aware of how exposed she was here, aware that in moments Vippon would come back for her, Nascha spun on the spot, looking for her travelling companion.

He was on the ground just beyond the protective ring of Vulpe caravans. Lord Bidzell was standing over him.

Nascha walked towards the man, otherwise unsure how she could save her friend. Bradan seemed to be conscious, but his eyes were closed, his face a patchwork of pain. There was no wound Nascha could see, but Bidzell's axe was drawn, and his face – helm lost – was no longer impassionate when he looked at her. He was angry. Angry, and possibly… scared.

"How did you do it?" he asked, more emotion in his voice than Nascha had ever heard before.

Nascha shook her head. She had no idea what he was talking about. She kept inching forward, her eyes flicking between Lord Bidzell and Bradan. "Do what?"

"Back then, with the Magpie King. Those things you pulled from my head. How did you do it?"

Nascha knew what he meant, but she truly had no answer to that question. Instead, she shrugged.

Lord Bidzell shouted in disbelief. "You weren't supposed to have her gift. You're just a servant girl, little more than a slave. You had the white hair, that was all. You were never supposed to have power."

Nascha thought of the potion, the poison that would keep her from ever having children, would stop her from spreading her bastard line. The poison that was to suppress her from displaying any more of the Owl Queen's abilities. The poison she had not properly taken this month, instead throwing it up against the side of the stables.

Nascha thought of that poison. She thought of the images she had summoned for Lord Bidzell and for Vippon, ripped from their dreams. She thought of the look of horror on both their faces when she had done so, and she smiled.

Lord Bidzell actually took a step away from her at that moment, seemingly forgetting about Bradan. Taking a breath, he lowered his axe at her. His hand was shaking.

"I was right to hunt you down, then, even more right than I knew. You aren't just a threat to Laurentina's rule. You're a threat to our entire way of life, to all the nobility of the Titonidae, in all the Courts spread throughout the White Woods. If the Spirit would bless someone as low-born as you, then what does that mean…"

He ran towards Nascha, and she tried to focus on him. She looked into Lord Bidzell's eyes as he levelled his weapon at her, tried to see behind them, into his hopes and dreams, just like the legends of the Owl Queen said that one gifted by the Owl Spirit could.

Nascha reached, trying to find something she could summon from his mind to protect herself with.

She found nothing.

There was no power there, nothing for her to wield. She thought again of the amber poison the priestesses had given her, every month since she first received her moon's blood. As she had said to Bradan earlier that night, they had ruined that part of her.

At the final moment before impact, Nascha threw herself to the right, tumbling to the ground. Lord Bidzell was no Gentleman Fox, so Nascha had a chance here, but he still had decades of training behind that axe arm of his. His weapon missed its mark, but as she dived he swerved to follow her, and Nascha screamed as the edge of his weapon sliced a gash across her right shoulder, not killing her as he had hoped but still opening her flesh, causing Nascha more pain in that single moment than she had ever experienced in her sheltered life.

She crumpled to the ground, half moaning, half screaming, her body rigid as she tried to hold herself as still as possible, not wanting to disturb the horrible wound on her back. She was all too aware that keeping still would play exactly into Lord Bidzell's favour, but she could not help herself. It just hurt so much. She was not a warrior. She was not one of the Vulpe, used to the roughness of the road. The only thing in her life that had caused her callouses was hard scrubbing on the Court flagstones. Her body and mind were not equipped to deal with her being opened up like this.

She was still moaning on the ground when Vippon careened

into Lord Bidzell, sending them both crashing to the ground. Dimly, past the wall of pain, Nascha supposed that Vippon – with his Spirit-enhanced strength – would have killed Lord Bidzell there and then, had not the remaining Pale Wardens flocked to their leader like ducklings to their squawking mother.

A shadow moved in the foreground, and Nascha saw Bradan crawling across the dirt towards her, but all the while she was focussing on the white blurs just beyond the campfire clashing with the foul-voiced shadows.

"We've got to get out of here," Bradan croaked, his hand finding hers in the dirt. Despite the heat of the fire, he was cold, and in the moonlight his sallow features and sweat-drenched hair reminded Nascha – for the first time – of his father.

For her part, Nascha could not respond. She tried to shift, but felt the open wound on her back tear more, felt the dampness of her dress where her own blood smeared against her skin.

Not taking no for an answer, turning backward to briefly check that both groups of pursuers were still too concerned with each other, Bradan pulled himself to his feet, then grabbed Nascha under her armpits and hauled her up too.

She screamed.

She felt no shame in it. Her wound stretched, and more wetness from inside her dripped down her back.

"Bastard. You bastard," she said, looking Bradan in the eyes, gasping as if she had just sprinted through the forest.

He nodded, looking half dead himself.

"They took us pretty far south," he said, ignoring her insults. "The Nest can't be too far. They'll never follow us into her land."

Despite her pain, Nascha pulled up short at Bradan's words. "Her land?"

He looked sheepish, then, as if caught doing something he should not have been.

"Bradan," Nascha said, trying to push past the pain, realising that to do otherwise would be to put her life in the hands of whichever of the Vulpe or Titonidae won their fight. "Bradan, whose land are you taking me to?"

He did not look her in the eyes. "The Razortree Nest is the home of the Lady of the Forest. Only those who are invited are permitted to enter it. They'd never break her border, for fear of incurring her wrath."

Bradan's eyes briefly flitted up to look at Nascha's face, and she was certain Bradan was aware of the more immediate wrath he had stoked.

Lowering his eyes again, he shifted away from the Vulpe camp, heading south, just as the half moon rose over the campsite.

"C'mon," he said, moving away from her, his every step a mess of pain. "We don't know how long it'll be before one of them wins, or if they give up and start to look for you again."

Bradan hobbled off, turning just at the edge of the clearing to look back at Nascha.

She was dimly aware of the fighting all about her, of the Pale Wardens and Vulpe locked in conflict that could end within moments, with neither victory working out well for her. She thought of the Lady in the church, of the spiked vine inching closer to the child sitting in front of them.

As blades clashed behind, she gritted her teeth against the pain in her back and did her best to follow.

Only those who are invited are permitted to enter there? she thought as she ran.

Why do I feel we're not going to be any better off in her land than we were in the Vulpe camp?

Bradan could not see properly. That made running through the moonlit forest a particular difficulty, though with all the practice he had had recently, Bradan thought he should have been an expert at it by now.

It was his exhaustion, he knew. He had pushed his body too far, taken too much punishment. He could think of half a dozen of his father's hideaways within a day's travel of here, nooks or caves that promised shelter and a small store of food, enough for him to rest for the week or so it would take his body to do some proper healing. Right now, with his pain and discomfort heightened, any of those hideaways were a promise of luxury.

The reason he did not choose to crawl to any of them ran about a dozen steps behind him, each of her footsteps accompanied by a grunt of pain.

Nascha. The woman had seemed an irritation at first, a pine needle lodged under his fingernail just when he had cast his former life aside, when he had decided to join forces with the Lady, to protect the forest and his father. She got in the way, she judged him for decisions he had already resigned himself to making. The plum in his pocket throbbed like a human heart now, as it had been doing ever since the Vulpe leader had appeared to them in the woods. Bradan was keenly aware that surrendering to its promise now would bring an end to his suffering, and to his helplessness.

He turned briefly to look at her running behind him. Nascha had given up trying to cover her white locks, and they tumbled all about her as she struggled forward, the tips stained dark red with her own blood.

She would hate him if he became the Lady's creature, he knew. Her reaction to the Lady's activities back at Ebora made that perfectly clear.

Lonan, also, was not happy with Bradan's choices. Unhappy enough to beat him up, a not-insignificant contribution to Bradan's current state. However, oddly, Bradan was more concerned with how Nascha felt about him than his father.

Hoping to find the doorstep to the Lady's realm as they continued to run, he took another look at her. Nascha's eyes shot up, glaring at him through her pain as she limped behind him.

He turned away, gasping. He was not infatuated with her. He was almost sure that whatever hold she had over him, it had nothing to do with romance, although admittedly that was an area he had very little experience with. Still, it had been like a physical blow when he realised that Nascha and Vippon had a history, and a recent one at that. It should not be any of his business, of course. Nevertheless, it troubled him to think of her with someone like that.

No, more than anything, Bradan was sad to admit that Nascha was probably the person he was closest to in the entire forest right now. Despite their years of travelling and working together, he and his father had never developed a strong bond. Other than Mother Ogma, few in the forest had given Bradan the time of day, wanting to distance themselves from the boy linked to the Magpie King's shadow.

Nascha was the first person in a long time to talk to him, to have a conversation that was more than a few sentences. She asked him about himself. Spirit's blood, he couldn't remember the last time someone had asked him something personal like she had last night.

He was not about to throw away something like that, someone who… someone who might actually care about him.

In his pocket, the plum pulsed again, its cries adding to the agony each footstep sent through his body.

The Lady would not be denied, of course. Bradan's fate had been sealed as soon as he had accepted her gift. But he would do this thing first before giving himself up. He had promised to get Nascha to the forest edge, to safety, and that was a promise he planned to fulfil. More so, he wanted to see her look of thanks, to see a grateful smile from her, instead of disgust. The plum would come after Nascha had fled the Magpie King's forest.

The Lady's forest.

Spirit damn them all, whoever owned this blasted place.

Behind him, Nascha gasped again, and Bradan slowed to allow her to catch up. He could see her back covered in red. That nobleman had caught her badly with his axe.

"We can't be much farther," he said, trying to encourage her. "Just a few more minutes, then we can rest."

In truth, Bradan had no idea if they were even travelling in the right direction. They were heading south, of course, but Bradan had never actually been to this part of the forest. He had seen it from afar, once, from a hill some distance off, and his father had pointed the Nest out to him, warned him of the Lady's spreading influence. Perhaps if it had been daylight, and if Bradan had been in a fit state to climb a tree to recreate that experience with his father, then he would have a better idea. Still, it seemed a mercy – albeit a short-lived one – to let Nascha think relief was close.

She did not respond, and Bradan fancied he could hear a growl come from her throat.

"Just a few more steps, and then—"

Light bloomed.

This was not the sight of the sun rising, gradually chipping away at darkness's shell until it leaked through over the course of an hour or so. A moment ago it had been dark, the witching hour of the forest, and then a step later the forest around them brightened, a hazy yellow pallor flowing through it, almost like a flower unfurling its petals. Bradan stopped, frozen, feeling Nascha do the same beside him. He turned to look at the path they had been fleeing down, and just a step behind them, the yellow light ended, the forest quickly disappearing into dark again.

They had crossed into the Razortree Nest.

Despite the fear he should have felt, Bradan gave a sigh of relief, his exhaustion ruling his senses.

"We've found it," he told Nascha, who was already threatening to collapse on the path under her feet. "Come on, let's get clear of the darkness, then we can rest."

Not wanting to give Vippon a tempting sight worth taking a few steps into the Lady's domain, Bradan literally pulled Nascha onward, the Owlfolk girl swearing at him. He wanted to get further into the Nest, until the night-time was no longer in sight. Once the darkness of the forest – and hopefully the border their pursuers would not dare cross – was out of sight, Bradan carefully lowered Nascha, and then collapsed to the ground himself.

They lay there for a time, allowing the pain to take over their bodies.

It was Bradan who chose to move first, spurred on by a soft moan from his companion when she shifted her weight.

"Let me have a look at it," he said, and she did not protest. He crawled around her prone form, biting his lip at the sight of the thick red line etched in her skin. It was not the deepest wound he had ever seen, but there was not really a lot of Nascha to cut through, and this one would leave an angry mark. Luckily, it seemed to have been done with its bleeding, the blood now having clotted to form a seal over the worst of the wound.

"You'll live," he told her, "and you'll have a good story to tell your grandchildren."

Nascha snorted at this, causing Bradan to smile too.

Don't think about where you are, he told himself. *Don't think about what the Lady will do if she finds you both here. Nascha needs to rest. You need to rest. Just a few hours, and then you can make for the edge of the forest.*

"What… where is the light coming from?" Nascha asked, her throat sounding dry.

Bradan looked up at the yellow glow. His body was telling him that night-time had only just begun, but in here it was… well, it was not quite daylight. Although Bradan thought of the sun as yellow, normal daylight allowed the world to show off its variety of colour – blue skies, green trees, flowers a multitude of shades. This was not what the light within the Razortree Nest was like. This yellow light seemed wrong somehow, almost sick, coating the surrounding forest in its illness.

He shook his head. "No idea. This must be her, somehow. The Lady. Father never told me of this. Hopefully we won't find out."

"Mother does not like the darkness."

The voice came from beside Bradan, and he yelped as he rolled away from its source, thudding his shoulder into a rock by the side of the path. Beside him, clad in a dress of green leaves, stood another of the Lady's Children, one of the small girls with red hair. Just like the others, the girl looked at them impassionately, without blinking.

Damn. The Lady knew they were here.

Of course she did.

"Mother is a creature of growth. She has spent too much time in the dark already. Now she is growing again, she has decided it must always be daylight for her."

"Don't think she got the daylight quite right," Nascha mumbled beside Bradan.

He almost kicked her in response.

The Child turned its head sharply to look at Nascha, an angry glare on the girl's face.

"Mother has summoned you. Come."

The girl turned and began to walk away.

"Wait," Bradan said, aghast at the thought of having to move again so soon.

The girl turned, fixing him with her stare.

"We're injured," Bradan said, racking his brain to think of a way to get the thing to understand. The Lady, as Nascha was so ready to remind him, did not seem to care about the suffering of others. "We would not want your mother to have to wait for us to crawl all the way over to the other side of the Nest. Also, we are hardly a fit sight for someone of her station. Surely it would not be appropriate for broken things such as us to approach her?"

Spirit, please, make this work, he thought, just before it occurred to him that praying to the Magpie Spirit in this place might be a very bad idea.

The Child fixed her stare on him for a moment, then reached

out her arm toward him. Without saying anything, the girl ran one of her fingers along the soft flesh of her underarm. To Bradan's horror, the Child's flesh parted, causing thick green liquid to well up from the cut.

"Drink it," the Child commanded them. "It will revive you. Sustain you long enough to behold Mother's majesty."

"No chance," Nascha said immediately.

The Child's eyebrows furrowed in a snarl of anger, and Bradan stepped forward.

"You are too kind," he told the creature before him.

He glanced at Nascha, wrinkling his nose at her. *Idiot, Nascha. Just because it looks like a little girl, doesn't mean it is one. You said you thought this forest was trying to kill you. Do you have to keep encouraging it?*

He bent his head to look at the sap welling from the Child's cut. If there was any other way, he would not do this. However, this was not just to revive him. It was to mollify this extension of the Lady before it killed him, or Nascha, or both.

"Just a drop," the Child warned. "It does not belong to you. Too much, and the debt you owe will be one you will be repaying your whole life."

Nervous, Bradan extended his tongue, dipping it quickly into the liquid on the thing's skin.

It did not matter that he only made contact for a moment. As soon as he touched the sap, Bradan felt as if a dozen rooted creatures flowed from the Child's arm, burrowing their way through his tongue, down his throat, then worming their way throughout his body before he had time to draw a breath. There was no pain at their passing, but he was captured by an intense discomfort, and recoiled from the Child as whatever was now inside him burrowed through him, splitting up, making their way through his body to his wounds. One of the things reached his shoulder first. There was a flare of heat, and then his pain was... dampened, somehow. There was a dull ache there still, but his wound no longer restricted his movement. Similar for the pain in his ribs. It was his face that most disturbed him – it felt as if something was churning just under his skin, as if something would surface from a hole in his mouth and crawl around on his tongue. Instead, the warmth spread through his face, and the ache of his tender jaw and cheek bones subsided.

Shocked by these sensations, Bradan noticed Nascha watching

him. He nodded at her. "It's fine. I'm fine. You should take some. Make your back feel better." *Don't be an idiot. Stop making it angry. Just take some.*

Thankfully, she listened to him this time. Bradan watched as the Owlfolk woman hesitantly mirrored his actions, dipping her tongue into the sap on the Child's arm. Nascha stepped back in shock too, and Bradan was treated to the sight of what looked like green roots threading about the cut on her back, pulling her flesh together.

Wide-eyed, but now much more able to walk, Nascha tottered over to stand beside Bradan.

"If you are done," the Child said, seemingly oblivious to Nascha and Bradan's uneasiness with the healing process, "then it is time to visit Mother."

As they wandered deeper into the Nest, Bradan marvelled at the unrealness of the place. Except for the sounds of their own footsteps – the Child made no noise as she travelled – the Nest was eerily silent. No birdsong, no wind in the branches, nothing. All the familiar smells of the forest, which Bradan had become accustomed to throughout his life, were gone too. If he could choose one word to describe the scent of the place now, it would be 'sterile', like one of Mother Ogma's knives, boiled in water before cutting into a patient, painfully clean. The plant life here was nothing like that in any other part of the forest. The trees around them were more like overlarge shrubs than proper trees, their giant, dark green leaves protruding in all directions.

"I've heard," Bradan said to Nascha, as they followed the Child down the path, "that the leaves of this place can cut a person just by brushing against them. They also say the leaves are coated in a poison that kills instantly."

Nascha raised an eyebrow. "Is that really true?"

He shrugged. "I'm not going to test it. Are you?"

They wandered onward, and autumn leaves began to fall, even though there were no trees above for them to fall from. The orange fragments floated lazily on the warm breeze, and Bradan eventually noticed they were not falling at all. The leaves were suspended somehow, drifting in the air, but never coming into contact with the ground. The Child was happy to ignore this phenomenon, walking past the sight, leaving her two followers to gape at the magic while hurrying to keep up with her.

Then, finally, they reached the heart of the Nest, where the

Lady dwelt. It was a circular grove of trees, and the goddess walked among them, seemingly preoccupied with whatever she saw in the branches above. The Lady was dressed the same way they had seen her back in the church – dress of leaves, long red ivy for hair, bare legs and feet – although this time, of course, she was no longer rooted to a church wall. Unimpeded by that village building, the Lady towered above them, more than five times as tall as Bradan was.

The air felt thicker here, as if it was more difficult to pass through. He became aware that both he and Nascha were breathing heavier, and it was not just at the sight before them. Bradan also noticed, climbing among the trees just outside of the grove, on the edge of the shadows beyond the clearing, almost a dozen barkwraiths like the one that had first delivered the Lady's message to him. They were scurrying about the trunks of the surrounding trees, their legs and shoulders bent in such a way to suggest overlarge spiders scuttling in the darkness.

The Lady did not look at them. Above, she sighed, then moved to tend another of the nearby treetops.

The Child turned to them, her back to her mother. "Mother bids you greeting. She demands to know why you, Bradan Anvil, have not yet made use of her gift?"

In response, the plum in his pocket gave a thud, and a spike of pain rippled through the leg it was held against.

"Ah, I, ah, I have it here," he said, withdrawing it from his pocket. He could feel Nascha's eyes bore into it, and chose not to look any further at her, for fear of what he would see in her eyes.

"We know," the Child said dismissively. "That was not the question. Why is it still in your pocket? Why have you not yet eaten it?"

That was a good question. Receiving the Lady's gift would certainly have made their journey so far considerably easier.

"I, um, I have a prior obligation," Bradan said eventually, not planning on drawing any more attention to Nascha than he had to. Still, the truth would help here, in measured quantities. "I wanted to remove myself from obligations with others before pledging myself fully in service to the Lady."

Nascha tensed beside him. He could almost sense her anger at his words.

The Child shook its head. "None should be more important to

you than Mother. You should drop all other obligations for her. She is not patient. She has waited far too long to reclaim her rightful place in the forest."

The Child stopped speaking, and Bradan was not certain how to respond, so instead he waited. Nascha shifted away from him. He tried to ignore the feeling of doom growing inside, as if he was standing with his toes on the edge of a precipice, knowing he was expected to dive off it.

"She demands you take the gift now, and join with us."

Bradan looked down at the plum, the gift. It made sense. The last few days had almost killed him. He would have to be the biggest idiot in the forest to die with the promise of immortality in his pocket.

But if he took it, Nascha would hate him. She would never let him lead her through the forest, or at the very least she would do so, but resent him for it.

"One more day," he said, looking into the Child's eyes, pleading. "Please, my Lady," he said, shifting his gaze to the giant woman standing above them, cooing to something in the treetops. "My Lady, one more day to deal with my affairs, and then I will be yours forever."

Above him, some birds fluttered about the Lady's head. That was what she was tending to, up there, he realised. Newborn birds, learning how to fly.

She did not look back down at him.

"She does not care about human affairs, and neither should you."

"The Magpie King cares about human affairs," Nascha said, stepping forward defiantly.

Bradan almost swore. Instead, he grabbed Nascha by the arm, pulling her back.

"What my companion means, my Lady," he said, hurriedly, praying that he could smooth over this slight, "is that human affairs are an important part of the forest. I would not feel comfortable tainting my service to you if I was still beholden to another. Furthermore," he said, finally succeeding in pulling Nascha back, despite her protests, "my final service will be to remove this one from the forest. She is happy to leave, and I think you will agree we will be better off without her. She does not understand how to act around such greatness. She does not understand that things in the forest have to change."

"Things in the forest have to revert," the Child said quickly. "They have to change back. Back to how they were, before the Magpie Spirit darkened these borders."

"Before the Magpie King?" Nascha said.

Above them, Bradan could hear a humming noise. He realised, after a moment, that the Lady was laughing.

"Hasn't the Magpie Spirit... hasn't it always been here?" Bradan asked.

The Child clucked her tongue, her face darkening.

"Those are the lies the Magpie Spirit would have you believe. No, silly man, the Magpie Spirit was not part of the original forest. It is not, from what we can tell, even from our world. It, like so many of its ilk, has come from somewhere else, from somewhere... beyond. It tempted the hearts of men by taking forms that were familiar to you, and planted its seeds to steal the forest away from those who created it. It stole the forest from Mother. Finally, however, she is rising in power again, reverting the forest back to its proper way."

Bradan's head was swimming. Where was the Magpie Spirit from, if not from the forest? His people were worshipping some kind of invader? This information went against everything he had been taught, everything any child of the forest had been told. *Damnation*, he thought, casting a glance at Nascha, who was rubbing her own forehead in confusion. *This is news for anyone who worships any of the Great Spirits of the world.*

"Seeds," he said, focussing on one thing, trying to understand what the Child was saying. "You said the Spirit planted seeds. What does that mean?"

The Child laughed this time, a hollow, mirthless sound, echoing the humming from the Lady above. "The thing you call the Magpie Spirit, it, along with its brethren, took the forms of animals – Owl, Fox, Mouse, Dragon – and spread throughout the world. Unlike Mother, they are not content with just one part of this land we live in. They want it all, and they do not like to share. The thing you call the Magpie Spirit scours the globe, searching for power, leaving Magpie Kings in its wake, hoping they will take the world for it, and turn men to worship it."

"Magpie Kings. There's more than one Magpie King?"

The Child cocked its head. "You did not really think it was only interested in this small forest?"

Bradan knew he looked shocked. He could not help it. Even trying to contemplate life outside of the forest was difficult enough for him. Trying to contemplate other Magpie Kings, out there in the world, doing the bidding of the same creature – his mind just could not cope.

The Child sneered. "They have been successful, for the most part. The creators of the world, the original gardeners, the great Ladies – they have mostly been destroyed. Like Mother's sister, who tended the White Woods. Some have simply been reduced, like Mother was for so long, forced into hiding, sending their servants to worry at the enemy, hoping to someday rise in power again to reclaim what is rightfully theirs. Oh, in some remote parts of the world, I am sure there are one or two Ladies who have endured, and who even now hold sway over their original dominions, free from the machinations of the invaders. But they must be few, so few. Mother has certainly lost all contact with them. And believe me, the Magpie Spirit and its ilk, they ever hunger, ever wish to spread their influence further, to claim more hearts of men. Left unchecked, it would not be long before they claimed the hearts and souls of all who live on this little globe, floating through space, lonely throughout all the cosmos."

The Child walked towards Bradan now, laying a hand on his chest. Despite the affection in the gesture, her face remained emotionless.

"That is why Mother has called you here. In her great seclusion, she has realised why the Magpie Spirit was able to take the forest from her. It was the people of the forest, that infection that Mother had allowed to fester unchecked, that the invader used to claim the forest's soul, using his Magpie King to sway them to his side. When the people turned from her, so did the rest of the forest.

"Where the Magpie King has been the herald of the thing you call the Magpie Spirit, you will be Mother's messenger. You will inspire the hearts of men, you will encourage them to turn back to the great Lady who is ultimately responsible for all you see around you. With you at her side, Mother will expel all traces of the Magpie Spirit and Magpie King from her realm, and all will be right again.

"So, son of the Magpie King, now you understand. You must eat this fruit. Now. Do not delay any further, or Mother will anger."

Bradan took this moment to look above him. The Lady, her

expression now displeased, pinched her fingers at something in the air. There was a brief cry, and then a black shape fell from above, landing on the grass close to where Bradan and Nascha stood. It was a crow, dead now, crushed by the brief grip of the fickle goddess.

"You would not wish to displease her," the Child said. "She does not abide those who make her wait."

"She will abide," Nascha said, stepping forward. "This time."

Bradan should have been scared at Nascha's actions, but by now he was too numb. There was so much about the world he did not know. He felt insignificant in the face of all the Child had told him. Was it even all true? If it was true, what did it mean for them?

Though Bradan did not react, the Lady did. Finally, she bent down to regard them, Nascha's comments goading her into action. The Lady's face was not like Bradan remembered it from the church, teasing and encouraging. The Lady was angry now. Her lips were curled back into a grimace, and her eyes, each of which were the size of a normal person's head, were narrowed and focussed upon the two humans before her.

The goddess' attention snapped Bradan out of his distracted confusion, realising he had much more immediate dangers to deal with. The truth behind the Magpie Spirit meant nothing if they did not make it out of the Nest alive.

Nascha, although nervous, remained firm. "You heard Bradan. He has a job to do, a promise he wants – needs – to honour. That's what you want, isn't it? Someone you can trust. Well, I've only known him a short time, but I can tell you, out of all the people I've met in my adventure in the forest, this is the only one I feel I can trust completely. He says he wants to honour his promises, and you want to turn him from that path? I say you're being foolish."

The Lady snarled. All around Nascha, vines began to break from the earth, whipping around in the dirt in semi-frenzy. Creases formed on the Lady's face, the texture of the bark that made up her skin cracking under the strain of her anger.

"Oh, you can huff all you want, but you know I'm right. If you make him break his promise now, can you really mend the flaw you'll make? If he breaks the promise he made to me, surely that means he could do the same to you someday, doesn't it? That's not a door you can ever close again, once you convince someone to be untrue to themselves. But if you let him leave here pure, his conscience unblemished, well… well, then you've recruited someone who will stand by your side until that filthy Magpie Spirit and all its totems and prayers are not even a memory in the forest anymore. Isn't that worth waiting a few more days for?"

Bradan watched Nascha in awe as she spoke. She was no longer a quick-tempered, impetuous woman who was well out of her depth in an unfamiliar world. Nascha was commanding, confident, almost…. almost regal.

Unbelievably, the Lady rose again, turning her attention back to the trees. The vines around them calmed, retreating back to the warmth of the earth.

"Mother does not like her," the Child told Bradan.

He chuckled. "She seems to have that effect on a lot of people," he said, ignoring the glare he knew Nascha would be shooting him. In truth, he was touched by Nascha's words, and had no idea of how to look at her after hearing them.

He straightened up, becoming more formal. "Tell my Lady I will rid the forest of this pest, as promised, and shall be back as soon as possible to enter her service. I anticipate our reunion with much enthusiasm."

And more than a little fear.

The Child nodded, and the Lady began to walk away from them, disappearing deeper into the Nest, the barkwraiths following on the trees behind her, scuttling through the darkness in her wake.

"The end of your quest lies a day's travel to the south," the Child told them, pointing in the direction Bradan was planning on going anyway. "You have been commanded to take the girl to the edge of the woods, and to return to Mother before sunset tomorrow. I will see you then, brother."

The Child said nothing more, but turned and trod off through the woods to follow the Lady.

Bradan knew he should be thankful that he survived the experience, that he was travelling once more with Nascha, so close to delivering her from the life she had found herself trapped in.

Instead, inside, Bradan was gripped with fear. He was only now realising the enormity of the situation he had bound himself to. He knew so little about this Lady, about her intentions, about how long a leash she would allow him while in her service.

And, more than anything, he was disturbed by how the Child, the small, wild girl with leaves in her hair, had called him 'brother'.

THE FIRST MAN
OF THE
FOREST

A forgotten tale of the Corvae

This tale takes place in the early days of the world, before the Magpie came to the forest, when animals still spoke, and when people could still hear the songs trees sang to each other through the Green.

Man had only recently come to the forest. They slunk in from the darkness outside, recognising the forest for what it was – a place of plenty, where nature's bounty could be harvested all year round. It was a dangerous place, but for many, those risks were worth taking, for the better lives they could make for themselves there.

There were no villages back then, as there were not enough people living in the forest to fill them. Instead, those who chose to remain within the forest borders made their own solitary homes. Some were little more than tents, animal skins stretched in place to keep the worst of the weather at bay. A few made their own buildings of wood and mud.

A few woodsmen plied their trade amongst those early people of the forest. Any fool could cut a tree down with an axe, but it took proper skill to pick the best trees to fell, and to turn that wood into something useful.

One such woodsman claimed to be the bravest man living in the forest, but his friends called him a blowhard, saying he had no way of proving this was the truth, and that he should just shut up and go back about his work.

Humiliated, the woodsman vowed to prove the people wrong. He took up his axe, and travelled deeper into the woods. Finally, after hours of travel, he found what he had been looking for – the tallest tree in the woods. This was an oak that had grown well beyond the rest of the forest canopy, and that the woodsman had always admired from afar. Up close, he saw it was as ancient as it was tall. It would take five men, arms outstretched, fingertips touching, to be able to form a complete circle around it.

Surely, he thought, if I chop down the oldest and tallest tree in the forest, then those idiots will have to admit that I am the best of them. And so he took his axe and began to chop.

Back in those days, people could still hear the song of the trees, so the woodsman was used to a gentle whimpering as he went about his work. However, he was used to felling much smaller, thinner trees, and had worked his muscles to such size that most trees of the forest would take only one swing of his axe before they fell. This oak took three, and from the first gash he cut into it, a terrible scream sprang from its roots, echoed by all the greenery close by. Unnerved by the sound, the woodsman worked quickly, silencing the ancient oak's death cries.

However, the dying screams of the oak had woken the Lady of the Forest, the ruler of this land the people had stumbled upon. She had heard of these humans, had caught whispers of them upon the song of the forest, but this was her first time being called to deal with them.

She came upon the woodsman as he was preparing to haul the oak back to his home, to show off his accomplishment to the other forest dwellers. The Lady had known the old oak well, as it was almost the same age as her, and she knew anger when she saw what had happened to it.

The woodsman, however, foolishly did not know fear when the Lady revealed herself. These were the early days of the world, and man had not yet learned to fear the dark things to be found within it. Furthermore, up until this moment, everything the woodsman had encountered in the forest so far he had been able to deal with using the blade of his axe. He did not expect the Lady to be any different.

Sensing his foolishness, the Lady decided to make an example of this man.

"In killing this tree, you have spat in my face," the Lady told him, singing through the forest's Greensong, her words of anger chorused by the trees around her. "I call you a coward for doing so."

The woodsman roused at the Lady's words, incredulous that

anyone would dare accuse him in such a way. His beard bristled, and he rose to confront the Lady, axe in hand.

"I am the bravest man to be found within this cursed forest," the woodsman said. "Take those words back, or feel the bite of my axe."

The Lady smiled. "You are a coward," she said, "and a weakling."

The woodsman's eyes almost popped out of his head. "You dare?"

"I challenge you," the Lady said, rising up out of the ground on the roots she had for legs. "A challenge to prove my words are true. You will get three swings of your axe against me, and then, after, I will get to use your axe against you."

The woodsman stroked his beard at the challenge. He knew that most trees in the forest could not survive one strike from his axe, and he had just felled the largest with three. Surely a woman made of wood would fare no better.

"I accept," he said, readying his weapon, "although would urge you to reconsider, for your terms will surely mean your death."

The Lady said nothing, but smiled, and presented her neck to the woodsman.

The woodsman raised his axe, and all around him the Greensong of the forest held its breath, the song of the plant life silencing in anticipation of the first strike.

The woodsman made his first blow.

He fully expected the Lady's head to fall off at his strike. To his amazement, his blade did indeed embed in the wood-woman's neck, but only a chip of wood broke from the wound, a steady flow of thick green sap running down the head of his axe. All around, the Greensong erupted into a chorus of triumph, the surrounding trees singing with pride that their champion had withstood the first blow.

The Lady, the woodman's axe still lodged in her neck, turned to the man.

"Is that all you are capable of? Surely I was correct when I called you a weakling."

The man's face turned red, and he began to sweat.

"You have seen nothing yet, demon," he said, yanking the weapon back, taking his second swipe.

There was an almighty crack, and the Greensong held its breath again. The Lady's head was turned at an impossible angle, her neck clearly broken. Still, the Lady smiled at the woodsman, batting her eyes at him innocently.

"One swing left, human. Then it shall be my turn."

Taking a deep breath, filling his lungs to bursting, the woodsman swung a final time. The Greensong burst into a mourning wail as the Lady's head was struck clean off her shoulders, rolling down the path to the woodsman's cottage.

The woodsman breathed a sigh of relief, and took a cloth from his belt to clean the sap-like blood from his axe.

It was then he realised the Lady's headless body was moving.

Casually, as if the loss of its head had been a minor inconvenience, the Lady's body strolled down the path, retrieved her head, and walked back to the woodsman, her head held snugly under one arm.

"And now," the Lady said, her decapitated head smiling as if nothing was amiss, "it is my turn."

Around her, the Greensong tremored in anticipation, the singing of ash, aspen and oak escalating towards what promised to be a triumphant crescendo. The Lady placed her head back atop her shoulders, then reached out for the woodsman's axe.

Trembling, face pale, he relinquished his weapon, and knelt before the Lady, preparing himself for her blow.

The Lady paused, holding the axe above her head.

"It appears I may have been wrong when I called you coward," she said, thoughtful. 'I had expected you to run, once your death was inevitable."

The woodsman gritted his teeth, his eyes clenched closed. "I am many things, my Lady, but a coward is not one of them."

The axe fell, just as the Greensong reached its crescendo.

The woodsman felt blood run down his neck. Searching with his hand, eyes still closed, he realised the Lady had held her blow, the blade of the axe opening only a shallow cut on the back of his neck.

Doing his best not to cry in relief, the woodsman began to shake in shock.

"Tell me," the Lady asked, her voice cold, "have you learned anything from this experience?"

"Yes, my lady, yes," the woodsman said, the fire in his blood at the promise of a new life making his words rush from him. "I have learnt there are things to fear in this forest. I have learnt how small, how unimportant, I really am."

The Lady nodded at the human's words, and then pursed her lips.

"I too have learnt some things from this encounter."

"Yes, my lady?"

"For one thing, I have learnt that men are brave. This is not a good thing, as bravery can often lead to recklessness."

The woodsman nodded frantically in agreement.

"Have you learned anything else, my lady?"

"Indeed I have," the Lady said, before raising the axe and, with her second blow, chopping the woodsman's head clean off.

His head also rolled down the path, but his body did not stroll after it. Instead, after the few seconds it took for the rest of his frame to realise it was no longer alive, the man's body slumped to the ground, spilling his vital fluids into the soil, food for future generations of the forest.

All around the Lady, the Greensong praised her triumph over the invader.

"You may be brave, but I have learnt that men are still fools. Fools, it seems, who cannot count."

With her third blow, bringing the number of her swings equal to the woodsman's, as agreed, the Lady embedded the man's axe in his own chest, leaving it there as a warning to those who found him. It was an unnecessary blow, as the man was clearly dead, but the Lady found satisfaction in keeping her end of the bargain, almost as much as she found satisfaction in ruining the corpse of her foe.

Then, wordlessly, with the praise of the Greensong echoing behind her, the Lady returned to the heart of the forest, where she would contemplate how to deal with this new threat that was continuing to infest her land.

CHAPTER EIGHT

Renewed by the Child's sap, Bradan felt better than he had in days, especially once they left the yellow-lit Nest and stepped beyond the Lady's power.

Nascha visibly relaxed too. The last few days had taken their toll on her, but leaving the Nest seemed to wash all of the emotional burden away, as if nothing out here in the dark forest could be worse than what they had just left behind.

Bradan looked about himself. They were in a stretch of the forest that was unfamiliar to him, although he had a fair idea of where they were in relation to their goal. In the east, the sky was still black, no hint of the sun wanting to rise. After all the events they had experienced in the last few hours, Bradan had lost his sense of time, and had no idea how far away morning was.

"Which way?" Nascha said. Bradan was glad she was being short with him. The last thing he wanted to do now was to get into an argument with her over his agreement with the Lady.

He nodded south, the direction they had been heading since he had agreed to take Nascha away from the forest. "Down there. A good day's travel, I reckon, and then you should be free of this place."

Nascha did not look at him. Instead, she hugged herself,

shivering. "Good. Good. I don't belong here. I need to get further away, to find happiness, wherever it's fled to."

He realised he should say something in response. Something to inspire her, to make her feel better about herself, better about the forest. It was his home, after all, and Bradan knew he would always belong here, always be bound to it.

"Let's go, then," he said instead.

They began walking through the trees, keeping their distance from each other, Bradan leading and Nascha following a few steps behind. The border of the forest and the Muridae Grasslands was marked by the foot of the Pisha Hills, a wooded expanse of raised land that ran for hundreds of miles in either direction. Once they passed over them, at the other side Nascha would gain her freedom.

Not long after leaving the Nest, they heard a crashing in the distance from somewhere behind. Both of them turned on the spot to face where they thought it might be coming from. It was the sound, Bradan thought, of trees falling somewhere in the distance. He had no idea how far away it was, or what might have caused it.

"What was that?" Nascha asked.

Bradan chewed his lip, and shook his head. "No idea. Never heard anything like that in the forest before."

"Could be Vippon."

"Or the Pale Wardens. Or, knowing our luck, both of them."

Nascha gave a mirthless laugh. "Sounds about right. Come on, no point in giving them less ground to cross."

They began to climb, the land growing steeper, and the charms of the Child's sap began to wear off on Bradan, his legs aching much easier than he had anticipated.

"You don't need to do it, you know," Nascha said, after almost two hours of travelling in silence.

"Sorry? Do what?"

"Join the Lady. I saw how much you shook when you took out that plum. You're scared of her. You don't need to join with her. Nobody can force you to eat that fruit."

Continuing walking, Bradan took the plum out of his pocket. Ever since their visit to the Nest, its throbbing had not been so painful. Instead, it was almost as if it was constantly humming, a dull buzzing in his pocket, reminding him it was still there.

"I don't know. I think there's a pretty good chance she'd kill me if I spurned her. You did say she's the type to do stuff like that."

"Some things are worse than death, Bradan. I don't know why you'd even consider taking her up on that deal."

"I want to." He turned to Nascha, and gave her a reassuring smile. "You know, I actually do want to do it. Am I scared? Yeah, sure I am. Who wouldn't be, wouldn't be scared of change? Especially when I've no real idea what it'll do to me."

He looked at the plum one more time, contemplating its sinister potential, before returning it to his pocket. "But I've wanted this for so long, Nascha. To have the strength to really make a difference here, like my father has, like he always wanted to. You've no idea… You can't understand what it's like to want something like that all your life, and then actually be handed it. Back in the church, when the Lady gave me her gift, that was one of the scariest experiences of my life. But Nascha, it was also one of the happiest. I'm finally going to mean something. Something other than the son of the man who isn't quite the Magpie King."

She was quiet for a while after that. "I think you're something without her hands on you, Bradan. And I'm worried about what kind of something you'll become under her shadow."

They were about halfway up the hill now. Turning to glance at the forest spreading behind him, Bradan saw the greener leaves of the vicious shrubbery of the Nest. Beyond that, he thought he could make out gaps in the foliage, clearings that signified where the Corvae villages were. And on the horizon, jutting from the forest like one of the Pale Warden spears, was the cliff face that held the Eyrie atop it, the Magpie King's former home.

Movement below caught Bradan's eye. A line of white figures snaked through the trees, not far away from where Bradan and Nascha had exited the Nest that morning.

"He's found me," Nascha said, her voice tight. "That bastard won't give up."

"It took us hours to get up here."

"He'll be quicker."

"Not quick enough, though. Come on, you're almost there."

They turned and continued their climb. Bradan tried to quicken his pace, but the northern side of the hill was littered with scree, and the more hurriedly he tried to move, the more he found himself slipping down it. At times, he tried to glance behind, to get a glimpse of the Owlfolk hunting them. He was disturbed to see that Nascha was right; Lord Bidzell and his men reached the northern foot of the hill much faster than they had. It had taken Bradan and Nascha almost three hours of climbing to get to where they were now. Bradan reckoned the Pale Wardens could do it in one, if they kept their pace up. Worse than that, for one brief moment Bradan fancied he saw a brown shape bounding through the trees in the distance, making its way towards them. It might have been his imagination, but a tightness in his own gut formed when he thought of Vippon catching up with them just before the border.

He turned and faced the hilltop, seeming impossibly far away. He had no idea how to judge how fast a servant of one of the great Spirits could travel, but if that was indeed Vippon continuing to pursue them, Bradan reckoned there was just as much chance of the Vulpe leader catching them as there was the Owlfolk.

He could tell by Nascha's face that she had seen it too.

The plum began to pulse again in his pocket.

Of course. Of course. That was the whole point of seeking her gift. To protect people.

He smiled at Nascha. "You'll be all right. We're almost there. You'll not have to see them again."

He had expected her to question him, or to at least seem glad that he was remaining optimistic, but instead, she looked angry. She was glancing at his hand – his hand inside his pocket, cradling the plum she knew nestled in there.

"Don't expect me to be happy about any of this."

Bradan was quiet until they reached the top of the hill. There, the two of them stood for a moment, looking out over the view that lay before them. The forest continued down the hillside, but at the bottom the woods soon reduced, filtering into the flat, wide Grasslands that were home to the Muridae people. Bradan felt overwhelmed by the sheer emptiness of the land ahead of him, the plains of brown grass unbroken save for a few small settlements in the distance. He and Nascha had travelled for only a few days in the Magpie King's forest, and had experienced a good number of life-threatening adventures. Looking at the Mousefolk kingdom, Bradan felt he could travel for weeks in the Grasslands without experiencing anything of note.

"Come with me," Nascha said, her hand finding his, her gaze still cast out over the Mousefolk lands.

229

Bradan was shocked at the suggestion. He honestly had never considered it, had never thought of fleeing his home. Now, with the emptiness of the Grasslands before him, Bradan knew he would never be happy living somewhere like that, so alien to what he was used to, was comfortable with. Not even to spend a life with Nascha, whom he realised he would miss dearly.

He turned to look at her, and then picked out noises in the distance, somewhere lower down the hillside they had just climbed. "They're coming," he told her, trying to not show sadness in his voice. "If I don't head back there and deal with them, they'll never let you get away from here properly. Your Pale Wardens in particular. If they followed you into the forest, what's to stop them from following you onto the plains as well?"

She shook her head. "We could find a way. You've gotten us this far, haven't you? I can't believe that if you threw that plum away and ran down this hillside with me, you wouldn't find a way to save us."

Bradan blushed, lowering his eyes. He had not done enough to deserve such praise.

"I… I made a promise. To you, but to the Lady as well. I can't just run away from that. And from my father. It's not just that I'd miss him – and I would. If I leave, how will I know he's all right? More importantly, who will there be to save the forest from him? After what he did to me, tell me you don't think he wouldn't harm someone else as well. I'm sure he's probably already done stuff he regrets. With the Lady's gift, I'll be in a position to stop that happening."

"If she lets you."

He nodded, trying to avoid the obvious fact that Nascha was referring to – he had no idea how much control the Lady would have over him. "This is my only chance. I've got to take it."

"And what about my chance? How am I supposed to get along out there by myself? I'd never have survived all that stuff in the woods without you helping me. Who's to know if the Grasslands are just as bad? Worse, even."

Bradan shook his head. "Wait, I helped you?" He could not stop smiling at her words. "Nascha, I just pointed you in the right direction. You're the one who has been saving my life all this time."

Nascha said nothing, instead shaking her head to try to get her hair under control, brushing the white locks away from her face using much more aggression than was necessary. Bradan almost found it funny that she seemed to have no idea what he was talking about.

"Think about it. Who got the Pale Wardens to back off when they first came for us? What about my father, when he was beating me? And you're the one who convinced the Lady to delay my service to her. Spirit's blood, Nascha, even before we met you saved me from Vippon and his troupe. The Grasslands will be no problem for you. I've never... I've never met anyone who has been able to do what you've done. You've stood up to gods, Nascha. You don't need me."

He took the plum out again, visibly pulsing now, and showed it to her. "So let me have my time. This'll let me do what you've done for me. I can save you, and help save the forest too."

She stared at the plum, eyes wide, and then raised them to look right at Bradan.

He almost reached out to touch her hand. He thought it was her hand he was going to reach for. Perhaps, however, it had been her cheek, the soft line of her jaw that curved right below her ear.

What stopped him was the tension in her neck, her whole body held rigid, her eyes narrow and cold as she looked at him.

"Fine, Magpie Boy, have it your way. Go off and become a tree. Maybe you're right. Maybe I'll be okay. But I guess you'll never know, will you?"

With that, Nascha spun round and stormed off down the hill, towards the Grasslands, and freedom.

Bradan knew he should call after her. He knew he would never be happy leaving things this way, that they should be parting as friends. He also knew that pursuit was close, and he was Nascha's only chance of getting free of the forest for good.

Also, damn it, he did not understand why she was angry with him. He had gotten her this far, hadn't he? Just like he promised. And he had pretty much agreed to give up his life – to take the Lady's gift – to make sure her enemies stayed away from Nascha. Enemies who had both attacked Bradan already. She had no right to treat him like that.

In his hand, the Lady's plum pulsed. It was time. He had fulfilled his outstanding promise, and the Lady was done with waiting.

Bradan turned away from Nascha, plum still in hand, and marched back into the Magpie King's forest to face his destiny.

Nascha tripped down the hillside, tears of fury stinging her eyes, trying to ignore the ache in her legs that had been a constant companion during her flight over the past few days.

Idiot! Stupid man. Stupid boy. Throwing his life away like that.

She thought of Bradan, and immediately in her mind the form of the Lady of the Forest loomed over him, her palms extended, a hungry look on her face.

Nascha shook her head, banishing the image, as well as her tears.

If he was intent on throwing his life away, she would not care any more about him.

Instead, Nascha would focus on what was immediately happening to her. She was out of the forest. She was free. With that idiot selling his soul for power, even Vippon should not be able to pursue her.

She surprised herself by swearing out loud as soon as she allowed her thoughts to return to Bradan.

Idiot.

We're both idiots.

She knew she should be excited. Before her, the vast plain of the Grasslands stretched out.

Her mind could scarcely contemplate such a wide expanse of land without any trees on it. She had known such things existed, of course, but to actually see them…

Off to the west, Nascha could swear the horizon was shimmering. Could that be the sea? Nascha had always wondered what the sea would be like…

Tripping down the hillside, she allowed herself a smile. Breathing heavily through exertion, she realised the only sounds around her now were the sounds of the surrounding landscape, of her own movement, of her own heartbeat. She had spent so long in her life with only these noises to accompany her, but she had almost forgotten their comforting emptiness in her short time travelling with Bradan. Even when they had travelled in silence together – which had been often – she had been aware of his movements close to her, his soft coughing when his throat was getting dry, the way he worked at a piece of bread stuck between his teeth for what seemed like hours at a time, sucking noisily on them to free the lodged piece of food.

Spirit's blood, Nascha had missed the silence of being alone.

As she stepped over the forest border, as well as losing the sounds of a companion, Nascha felt a weight lift. The sense of being watched that had riddled her since peering into Lonan's eyes faded. Having left its kingdom, the Magpie Spirit could no longer see her. She gave a small whoop of joy when she realised what had happened. The oppression that had been hanging over her lifted, and she felt true freedom when she realised even that invisible remnant of her time in the forest had left her.

Bradan had been right – she was strong enough to make her way in the world. Before he had said the words, she had not realised what she had been capable of, what she had already done on her own. The powers she had stood up to in that forest, anything the Grasslands had to offer must pale in comparison with them. She had spent her life dreaming of adventure, dreaming of being more like Tadita, being brave enough to make a life of her own. How blind she must be to not have realised she had already been living that dream. And now, thanks in part to the forest boy, her path was clear. Find the Muridae, get them to point her towards a ship, sail west and never return to these cursed shores.

The hillside was still lightly wooded, the Magpie King's forest encroaching slightly onto Muridae lands. Nascha stumbled through one of the denser patches of trees, eager to distance herself from whatever conflict would soon be erupting on the other side of the hills.

In was in this patch of trees that Nascha came upon the owl.

There was no dramatic entrance, no flapping of wings or warning screech. Nascha just lifted her hand to move aside a low-hanging branch that was in her way, and she realised an owl was resting upon it, just a few inches from her fingertips.

She froze, staring at the creature in wonder.

This was not like the owls of the White Woods, the large barns and browns, those vicious predators that ruled the tall birches of her childhood home. The owl before her now was much smaller than them, just slightly larger than a man's fist, and was a dull, dusty brown. Nascha's mind quickly went to tales of owls of the Grasslands that burrowed under the earth instead of nesting in trees, and she wondered if this was one of them.

She had spent her life around creatures like this, and knew she should not be in awe of them by now, but for some reason this one captivated her. The tiny brown creature sat just above her head, looking right at her, its open eyes blank and enquiring.

She smiled at it.

"Hello there," she whispered, not wanting to disturb it, but also oddly conscious that she was standing still for too long. In a strange way, it felt rude.

She had thought she was alone in the Grasslands, but suddenly this creature had appeared, a curiously familiar presence. Something that took the edge from this new experience, that made the idea of travelling through this new land bearable.

Just like Bradan had for her in the forest.

"Do you fancy travelling together for a time?" she whispered to the owl.

It flew away from her.

Nascha was surprised at the cry of agony that came from her lips as the bird disappeared. For a brief moment, she had felt she had another living thing to share this new life with, and had allowed herself to relax. Now it had gone, the fear of the unknown was overwhelming.

With the owl gone, the absence of company, the pervading loneliness, was painful.

She stood rooted to the spot, unable to will her feet to continue. She realised, after a moment, that she was straining her ears, trying to catch sounds from behind her. Bradan. She was listening for Bradan. Listening to get any kind of clue about what he was going through. He had probably given himself over to the Lady already. As soon as Nascha's back was turned, she was certain he would have wolfed down the gift, and would even now be unrecognisable to her. She did not think she could cope with running back to him and finding a stranger in his place.

But there was a chance Bradan had taken his time. There was a chance that, even now, he was still weighing his options. Some part of him must realise that what he was doing to himself was wrong, even if he was doing it for good reasons.

There was a chance that her friend – her only friend in the world – was still alive.

Not daring to glance at the freedom of the Grasslands, of the adventure and possibility she was turning her back on, Nascha spun on her heel and began to run back up the hillside.

Bradan's heart was thumping harder than he had ever thought possible.

He had come upon the Pale Wardens not long after Nascha had left him. He had run down the hillside at a fair rate, doing nothing to disguise the sound of his progress. The Wardens had quickly picked up on his presence, and Bradan could hear their shouts as their captains – possibly even Lord Bidzell, although he could not be sure – commanded their men, ordering them to fan out in order to find him. However, they were in Bradan's forest now; they had not caught him unaware, and – thanks to the Lady's Child – he was more or less uninjured. Because of all that, despite their superior numbers and training, Bradan found he was able to run rings around them, all the while leading them on a merry dance back down the hillside, away from Nascha, giving her enough time to get away.

Eventually, he knew, they would catch him. He was aware they were trying to circle around where they thought he was, jumping from bush to bush like Artemis teasing Mother Web, throwing stones at their helms when he was worried they would give up interest and head after Nascha instead. It would only be a matter of time before they succeeded in trapping him. Worse than that, Bradan was convinced the brown figure he had spotted before had been Vippon, leaving his Vulpe behind and pursuing Nascha by himself. Bradan knew his distractions would not last long against the Gentleman Fox. However, Bradan had a different plan to deal with him.

The plum in his hand was screaming now, as if the Lady was fully aware that his bargain with Nascha was complete and he was free to join her service. In truth, Bradan was not certain why he had not immediately taken her up on that offer. He almost had, when Nascha had disappeared over the border. However, just before his tongue had touched the throbbing skin of the fruit, the look of anger and disgust on Nascha's face had flashed through his mind, and he had lowered his hand again.

Just a little more, he promised himself. *A little more time trying to see what I can do by myself. I will give myself over to the Lady, after a little more time.*

It was time. Time to take the plunge, and sell his soul.

But then, as Bradan raised his hand to his mouth yet again, he saw her. A white streak of madness careening down the mountainside. It was Nascha, her white hair flowing free of her hood, half falling, half running down the hill, seemingly not caring if anyone could see her.

What is that idiot doing? She was free. We won. Why'd she come back?

Bradan swore, lowering his hand. Taking a quick moment to ensure no soldiers were lying in wait directly outside the shrub he was crouched in, he sprinted towards her.

He was rewarded by a most amazing sight. Nascha's face broke into a smile the moment she saw him. Oddly, it widened even further when she saw the plum in his hand, and she gave a whoop of joy at the sight of it.

Not able to fathom what was going on, Bradan was totally unprepared for the embrace she greeted him with. The force of Nascha hitting him, arms outstretched, knocked them both flying backwards, tumbling together partway down the hill.

"What in the Spirit's name are you playing at?" Bradan hissed, aware there was no way the commotion could have gone unnoticed. He was thankful to see her, yes, but also confused, and more than a little nervous.

It was just then he realised he was no longer holding the plum.

Panicking, he flipped onto his back and scrambled in the undergrowth, desperately searching for his lost prize.

"Bradan," Nascha tried to say, grabbing at his leg, but he ignored her.

"I've lost it," he said, his voice raised much higher than intended. "Damn it, where is it? That's our only chance."

"No, it's not. Listen to me—"

Bradan spun on her, tears of frustration in his eyes. "No, it is, damn you! That was my only chance to save you, to protect everyone. You've made me drop it, and in a few seconds they'll be on top of us, and it'll be over."

It was the wrong reaction to give her. From their short time together, Bradan already knew she would react with anger. If he was lucky, it might even push her away from him again, and she might make it back to safety.

If only he could find that plum.

However, instead of being angry, Nascha smiled at him, resting a hand on his cheek.

Bradan froze, unsure how to react. He could not remember the last time someone had touched him so tenderly.

"It's not our only chance, Bradan. Just like you told me – look at all the things I've done, all my victories travelling through the woods. But look at yourself, too. You fought off a Magpie King, took on the Lady of the Forest, survived the Vulpe. Bradan, anyone else would be dead by now. Together, we can beat this, without you giving yourself up to the Lady."

Then she added to his shock with the single fat tear that fell from her eye at that moment. Her face turned strangely serious. "I... I've always been alone, Bradan. Except for the last few days travelling with you. I don't think I could go back to being lonely again."

His hand joined hers on his face, first resting gently against it, then holding it firmly. He smiled at her, then. He had been ready to die for the memory of friendship. He was much more willing to die for the possibility of keeping it.

"How very touching," came a gruff voice, just before the butt of a white-painted spear took Bradan in the gut, knocking him away from Nascha. He only just managed a cry before a boot followed where he had already been hit, expelling all air from his lungs, winding him.

Gasping on the ground like a dying fish, Bradan was helpless as the Warden, a smug smile painted beneath her helm, whistled for her companions to come to her. Through his tears of pain, Bradan was aware of Nascha shouting his name, moving to get to him, but the Pale Warden's spear point was in her path.

More white figures appeared from the undergrowth, all with spears levelled directly at Nascha. They had given her too much space last time, taken too long to gloat, and she had escaped. This time, it would be quick, and final.

Lord Bidzell was the last to emerge. He wore no helm now, and he held his left arm limply at his side. Bradan was dimly aware that the rest of the Pale Wardens – considerably fewer in number than when they had first assaulted them back at the basin – were similarly disarrayed. Most of their armour showed signs of combat, dried blood, chips or just plain clear blade marks marring what was once well-kept uniform.

Bidzell's face was contorted, lines of fury etched all over it. "Lower your spears, idiots," he said, addressing his guards. Gingerly, looking somewhat foolish, they followed his command.

Then, to Bradan's infinite shock – and Nascha's too, judging by the look on her face – Lord Bidzell took two steps towards Nascha and knelt, bowing his head.

"Lower your spears, or you might hurt her. The Spirit's own fury would not keep me from taking the head of the man or woman who harms one hair on the head of the Owl Queen."

ARTEMIS
AND THE
OWL QUEEN

A tale from the fireplaces of the Corvae

It was during the reign of the first Magpie King when sly Artemis walked through the woods. He moved, as always, with a sack slung over his shoulder, an apple in his hand, and mischief in his eye. Mischief aimed particularly at the Magpie King, whom Artemis hated above all others. Long had Artemis stirred trouble in the Magpie King's kingdom, but Artemis wanted to achieve more than that.

All Corvae know of how Artemis was eventually successful, how he stole the source of the Magpie King's power, forever changing how the king's gift passed from father to son.

Before that, however, Artemis tried to punish the king in another way.

He tried to steal his wife.

Artemis came upon the idea during Season's Weeping, when he watched the king and queen together from afar, how tenderly the Magpie King looked upon his bride as they celebrated the festival along with their people. Artemis knew then that stealing the king's woman would be a sure way to break his heart, and therefore his spirit.

Not long after the festival, clever Artemis began his plot. Under cover of midnight, he climbed the tall cliff beneath the Eyrie, the Magpie King's home. As she was sleeping, he crept into the Owl Queen's chambers, and stole a lock of her hair.

Just before leaving, Artemis stood in the window, watching the queen's covers gently rise and fall with her breath. She was truly lovely, the Magpie King's bride.

Artemis would enjoy taking her from him.

Excited, his heart racing, Artemis skipped through the forest, his prize clutched in his hand.

When he had been observing them, Artemis had realised the queen doted on her husband just as much as he was besotted with her. He knew no straightforward seduction would convince the queen to share his bed, but clever Artemis had discovered an alternative method to win the queen.

Finally, he arrived at his destination. There, surrounded by a ring of dark oaks, stood a pale Heartwood tree. As Artemis had travelled through the forest, exploring the Magpie King's kingdom, he had heard many tales about the Heartwoods. Of most interest to Artemis, however, had been the Heartwood's ability to change people's lives. Change them, by making someone fall in love with them.

The sun rose, but Artemis found no rest. Instead, he was working away at the bark of the Heartwood, carving his name into it. When he was done, he stepped back to admire his work, at the same time cutting off a lock of his own hair. Then, to complete the spell, he wove his hair and that of the Owl Queen together, letting the knot dangle from the Heartwood's branches, sealing the queen's fate.

Despite his exhaustion, Artemis could not sleep. Perhaps it was the daylight, intruding on his respite even under the folds of his cloak, which he held over his eyes to try to block out the light. Perhaps it was the excitement of finally having the opportunity to hurt his long-time foe. Or perhaps Artemis was simply anticipating the hours of delight he was planning to have in the Owl Queen's chambers.

Daytime remained restless, and as night fell, Artemis hurried back to the Eyrie, beginning his climb of the cliff before the sun had fully set.

When he reached the window, the queen was already in her bed, her covers pulled up, her soft breathing the only sound in the room other than the pounding of Artemis' own heart.

Silently, wordlessly, Artemis crept forward to chance a look at his intended conquest before waking her.

"Darling," the queen whispered in her sleep, eyes closed, face tightened. "My beloved, where are you?"

Artemis grinned at her words, and knelt closer to her face.

"Who are you speaking of?" Artemis asked. "Who is your beloved?"

"Artemis," the queen said, still asleep, but red now rushing to colour the pale of her face. "Artemis the trickster. Artemis the clever."

Artemis shuddered to hear the words, and felt his own passions rise at the sound of her voice, at the desperation he could hear in it.

However, Artemis could not help himself. Before enjoying his victory, he wanted to hear more.

"And why Artemis?" he asked the sleeping queen, grinning all the while. "Why is he your beloved, now?"

She squirmed under her covers, and for a heartbeat he wondered if he had pushed things too far.

Then, however, she responded. "He is so handsome," she said, "and so clever. And so much fun. Nothing like my husband."

Artemis almost gave a whoop of success, and turned to look around him, wishing dearly that the Magpie King could hear the words coming from his wife's lips right now.

"Tell me," Artemis said, hands on the bedsheets now, quivering in anticipation. "If your beloved, if this clever, handsome Artemis was here, right now, what would you do? What would you want him to do?"

"What would I want him to do?" the queen muttered, brow furrowed, and a sinner's smile crossed her face, a look that almost made Artemis spend himself there and then without having to touch the beautiful woman before him. "If Artemis was here, I'd want him to…"

He could not make out the final words, although from the look on her face, the Owl Queen seemed to take much pleasure in saying them, rolling onto her back, the bedsheets falling away, revealing her thin, cotton nightgown.

"What was that?" he said, leaning closer, agonising at having missed the queen's desire. "What do you want?"

"If Artemis was here now," the queen said, whispering low so Artemis had to almost touch his ear to her mouth to hear the words, "I would want him to scream."

As exhausted as he was, as flooded with desire, Artemis' reactions had been honed by a lifetime of distrust, and so it was that he was able to fling himself across the room from the queen before she grabbed a proper hold of his hair, or before her knife found his throat.

"How?" he gasped, slipping across the polished floor as he made for the window, looking on in shock as the queen – clearly awake, clearly angry – sat up in her bed, murder on her face and a knife in her hand. "I bound us with Heartwood. How did you resist me?"

"Foolish man," the queen retorted, otherwise unmoving, her knife still pointed at him. "My husband and I are not just linked through our marriage, through our promises to each other. We have both been gifted by Great Spirits, and the bond that runs between our patrons is unbreakable. You cannot undo that as easily as you can trick your way into a peasant's bed."

He had been made a fool of tonight, but Artemis was not a large enough fool to believe he had any chance against the Owl Queen, her fury rising, her faculties unclouded by his tricks.

He nodded at her, gave a wink, and then darted through the window, descending the castle to the forest below.

Although he put a good face on it, Artemis' pride was much wounded by his defeat at the hands of the Owl Queen, and he resolved with greater enthusiasm to find a way to truly hurt the queen, the king, and their family.

It was not long after that night that Artemis made good on his promise, but that is a tale for another time.

CHAPTER NINE

"You're mad," Nascha said to Lord Bidzell through gritted teeth. "I thought the forest was taking its toll on me, but it's turned you mad."

He raised his head to look at her, smiling. She had never seen a more tired smile.

"Not mad, just slow. I did not want to admit the truth, even though it has been clearly presented to me since the first day I saw your true hair colour back at the Court. You are indeed this generation's Owl Queen, and a powerful one too, I'd wager, to be able to invade my dreams when I am not asleep."

She felt like a caged animal, even with the guards' spears now lowered. Nascha was painfully aware of Bradan, her friend, lying wounded on the ground, just out of her reach. What she wanted more than anything right now was to grab him and get over that mountain range, over the sea, and away from this hellish place and these hellish people.

"All right, then, you've got me. I am the Owl Queen. And I command you, my faithful subjects, to step the fuck aside and let me past."

The Warden who had initially knocked Bradan away from her looked to Lord Bidzell for confirmation, and the nobleman shook his head, chuckling.

"No, I'm afraid not. The name will cause some confusion, I see. It will have to be changed. We cannot go about calling you 'Queen'. You are not of royal blood, and you would use the power that title brings with it for your own ends. You are clearly, however, blessed by the Owl Spirit, although I could not guess at her reasons for it. We will need a new title for your kind. Owl Witch, perhaps? Yes, that would suit you well, you and your station."

Nascha gritted her teeth, but in some ways felt relieved by this further turn in Lord Bidzell's thinking, as it brought her back to familiar territory. This was much more what she would expect from the Court.

"It has long been a shame for us to know that Laurentina was not touched by the Spirit in the same way as so many of her line before her, and there are those at the Court who worried we had fallen from favour because of it. However, your presence back home will help prevent that plummet, and will bring power to the throne." His smile broadened. It was an ugly looking thing, as if pure greed was bulging behind his face, distorting his features as it tried to seep through from beneath his skin. "Power to the throne, and to those who control you."

Nascha felt the flame of hope within her lose fuel and begin to dim. That was his play, then. To take her back, use her to gain even more for himself, and keep her there, as before, a prisoner.

"And what if I don't want to come with you?" she asked, eyes darting around her, trying to find some way to regain control of the situation. She desperately tried to reach whatever it was that had allowed her to make contact with Lord Bidzell's and Vippon's minds, but the flicker of the Owl Spirit's gift within her was silent. Lord Bidzell was wrong – she might contain echoes of power, but it was no more than that. Perhaps the poisons had destroyed that part of her. Perhaps her diluted blood had never been capable of anything more than freak spurts of power. Best not to tell him that now, though. The thought that she might be worth something to him was probably the only thing keeping her alive.

"If I don't want to come, what will you do then?"

Lord Bidzell smiled thinly, drew his axe, and pointed the blade of it at Bradan. "Well, then, I think you would make me do something regrettable."

Nascha's eyes widened. On the ground, Bradan was recovering

from his blow, sucking air through his teeth, staring in desperation. She knew he was not looking at her to save his life. He was wanting her to run.

She gave a small shake of her head. Not this time. Not again.

Nascha took a deep breath, stood up tall, and clenched her fists. "I am Nascha of the Owl Queen's Court, bearer of the Owl Spirit's mark, favoured by her gift. I tell you all now that this man, the one known as Lord Bidzell, is a traitor to the Owl Spirit, and to the Court. The Owl Spirit will reward whosoever holds him back from his actions." As if from nowhere, a sudden wind – a fairy wind, they called these unbidden gusts, back at the Court – flew out of nowhere, sending Nascha's white hair into a flurry, streaming behind her like a cloak.

The Pale Wardens hesitated, just for a moment, at the sight of Nascha before them, staring in confidence at her attackers.

It was Lord Bidzell who spoke first. "Such grace," he said in almost a whisper, but to Nascha's dismay he remained smiling. "I see the queen in you, and her grace. It must run thick in your blood."

"This has nothing to do with my blood," Nascha said, not able to hide the malice from her voice. "This is just what happens when you threaten human beings. This is someone forced to stand up for the life of their friend."

Lord Bidzell nodded, motioning for his soldiers to move towards Bradan. "Perhaps you will learn more obedience when I remove this whelp from your sight."

Two of the Wardens levelled their spears at Bradan, raising them to strike. Nascha could sense – perhaps with some dull echo of her gift – that there was no pantomime here. They were going to kill Bradan.

He looked at her again, eyes pleading.

Run, he mouthed.

She did not get the chance. In a gust of fury, a brown shape bounded into the clearing, a glimpse of white, pointed teeth shining in the moonlight.

Vippon grabbed Nascha roughly, his short dagger already drawing blood at her throat. Another bound and they both disappeared, leaving Bradan alone with the Titonidae.

"After him, you fools!" Lord Bidzell shouted at his guardsmen.

Bradan could do little more than lie on the ground and watch, still winded after the blow to his gut.

The two Pale Wardens ran off in the direction Vippon had taken Nascha.

Bradan was distraught. He had seen the knife, and he already knew the hatred the Gentleman Fox had for Nascha. He had no doubt she was already dead. Vippon would not toy with her again after their previous escape.

Snarling, Lord Bidzell turned on Bradan, pointing his axe at his neck. "Should never have wasted my time with you," the nobleman said. "The fox gets the queen, and I get nothing?"

"Not nothing," Bradan gasped, finally able to speak. The axe blade cut a line on his throat, drawing blood. Bradan could feel the weapon vibrating, trembling with Lord Bidzell's anger. "I'm the son of the Magpie King." It was a gamble, but one Bradan was willing to make for his life.

"The Magpie King?" Lord Bidzell scoffed, but did withdraw his weapon slightly. "He's dead. His line was snuffed out before you were born."

"It didn't die out," Bradan said, sitting up, ignoring his body's screams of pain. "It got diverted. My father wears the helm now, and I will do so too, when I come of age. I may not have inherited his strength yet, but my knowledge of the forest is better than yours will ever be. You need me, if you want to find her before Vippon kills her."

Lord Bidzell snarled, but raised his axe, holding it upright instead of in an attacking position. "You'd better not betray me, boy. Magpie King or no, I am losing my patience with all who stand before me. Lead on, but remember I'm close behind."

Bradan nodded, wincing as he picked himself up. Angling himself in the direction of where Vippon had bounded off, giving a short, silent prayer to the Magpie Spirit, Bradan ran after his friend, Lord Bidzell in close pursuit.

Nascha was in pain. It did not come from the knife held roughly at her neck, even though it was cutting into her. The blade was sharp, and the pain from that wound would come later. It was Vippon's other hand, his fingernails digging into her skin like a hawk's talons, gripping her roughly as he leapt through the trees, moving at speed away from the Titonidae.

Vippon suddenly released her, throwing her violently against a nearby tree. She heard a large crack upon impact, but was unsure as to whether it was the tree that was damaged, or her own head. She was certainly disorientated enough for it to have been her – it felt like someone had lit a bonfire in the back of her mind, and her vision was distorted by the waves of heat rolling from it.

"I've had enough of you," Vippon growled, swiping at her with his blade.

In her daze, she was only dimly aware of it coming towards her, just enough to fall to avoid it, raising her hand to protect her face as she did so. A red line of pain opened up all along her forearm, something wet and hot flowing from it.

"Nobody insults me like you have. Nobody."

He kicked her in the face. She was not expecting it, and had no way of stopping it. The explosion was in her mouth this time, and her head hit something not far behind it.

Only distantly aware of the world around her, Nascha spat out the stones that had gathered in her mouth. They may have actually been teeth.

Vippon gripped the hair on the back of her head, pulling her upright. She spat blood at him and raised her hand, trying to find his eyes with her fingers. He easily batted her aside, then backhanded her across the face in punishment.

She tried to lift her hand again, but her body would not respond this time.

"I would have made it quick, to begin with. Another wife for

247

the Fox Spirit, another bride to decorate my halls with. Instead, you will have to serve as a warning to any who would dare to cross the Vulpe in the future."

He drew his knife to her face this time. She felt the point of it pierce her skin just above her temple, coming to a stop when it hit bone. Then Vippon began to carve a line down her face. "You should thank me, little queen. After I'm done with you, your name will be known from sea to sea. I'm going to make you famous."

As the knife blade peeled more flesh from her skull, Nascha's mind retreated inside itself. Dimly, she remembered the gaze of an older man, making love to her, locking her in the same firm embrace that Vippon held her in now.

Bradan peeled through the woods, branches slapping at his face, roots doing their best to trip him. Despite what he had said to Lord Bidzell, he was running aimlessly, with little clue as to where Vippon might have taken Nascha. He was vaguely aware of white shapes that haunted the forest nearby. The Pale Wardens, running in the same direction, shadowing him. They must be becoming aware by now that there was little direction to his flight, but he did not care. He only had hope left, and his hope was that this was the path Vippon had taken, and with the Pale Wardens running with him, they cast a wide enough net that Bradan was convinced they would find her.

Unless Vippon had doubled back on himself. Unless Vippon had done something to cover his tracks. Which, of course, would be so like one of the Vulpe to do. Bradan tried to dismiss the notion with a shake of his head. He was ungifted – he cursed the plum that lay hidden at the bottom of the mountain somewhere – and he had no time to spare before Nascha's life was taken. Bradan was casting his lot on this one gamble, and hoping desperately that it paid off.

A scream from one of the Wardens to the left brought hope to

Bradan's soul. Without slowing, he grabbed the smooth trunk of an aspen and spun himself around in the direction of the cry, sending another prayer to the Magpie Spirit that Nascha was still alive. Bradan burst through the greenery separating himself from the cry, just in time to come upon his father, a Warden held in his hands, the woman's back bent impossibly over his father's knee.

The dying woman turned towards Bradan, a pathetic mix of pain and misery flitting briefly across her face as the light in her eyes dimmed.

"Father," Bradan whispered. He had not the heart to tell him that she was on his side, that she was helping to rescue his friend. Instead, Bradan was focussed on the fact that the tide was finally turning. They had power now to match Vippon's – to more than match it. With the gifts of the Magpie King at his disposal, it would take moments for Lonan to find and overpower the Vulpe leader. Nascha had a chance.

Bradan's hope died, however, when he looked at his father's face.

The man's skin seemed tauter than normal. The bags under his eyes had collected more misery and despair, hanging on his face like pestilent growths on once-healthy crops. Lonan's pupils, now fixed on Bradan, had narrowed to pinpricks, almost indiscernible in the deep, dark blue of his father's eyes. Lonan was breathing heavily, like a wolf on the hunt, his tongue half hanging out of his panting mouth. Unusually, his father did nothing to hide the filed points of his teeth, and his gaze as he tracked Bradan, moving slowly through the woodland towards him, made Bradan feel he was looking at a complete stranger, not the man who had sworn to look after and protect him.

"Father?" Bradan ventured again, speaking as tenderly as he dared take the time to do so. "Father, are you well? We need you now, Father. Nascha is in trouble. She may already be dead."

Lonan said nothing. His tongue flicked quickly to his lower lip, where Bradan only now noticed a dark liquid staining some of his face. Lonan continued to breathe noisily.

Bradan did not like the way he was looking at him.

Finally, his father spoke. "You are hers, now."

It took a moment for Bradan to realise what his father was talking about. His own mind was so focussed on freeing Nascha, he had almost forgotten the last encounter with Lonan. It had seemed so long ago.

Bradan shook his head. "No, Father, I gave her up. I threw away her gift—"

"Liar!"

His father leapt forward, closing half the distance between them. Bradan was keenly aware of his father's long fingers, pawing at the earth in front of him, working it like Bradan sometimes pulled at his own clothing as a nervous tick.

"No, Father, it's true. I had... I had almost joined her, but Nascha changed my mind. I got rid of her gift."

"Don't lie to me, boy. I smell her on you. More than that, I feel her approach. She is coming here, and will arrive soon. She expects to find a servant. Instead, she will find only your corpse. If I cannot save your life, at least I can save your soul."

She's coming here? Spirit's shade, that's the last thing we need. "If she's coming, Father, she comes with vicious intent—"

Bradan was about to tell his father that the Lady was most probably coming to kill him for spurning her, that he and Nascha needed to flee the forest as quickly as possible to have any hope of seeing sunrise, but he realised he had more immediate problems to deal with. His father was experiencing a bout of madness again. For all Bradan knew, it was the same one that had almost led to his own death a few nights ago. Lonan was getting ready to pounce.

White shapes erupted from the undergrowth, and all at once the Pale Wardens were around them, Lord Bidzell at their head. He took one look at the fallen guardswoman, and levelled his axe at Bradan's father.

"Time to kill a legend, boys," Lord Bidzell shouted, charging at Lonan.

Lonan's head snapped away from Bradan instantly. In some ways, Bradan was hurt by how quickly his father dismissed him. Instead, Lonan catapulted himself across the forest floor to crash into a wall of pointed spears. As one, the Titonidae cried out.

Remembering Nascha, his friend, Bradan took off into the night again, taking only one short moment to look behind. There, in the midst of an onslaught of whiteness, his father stood screaming, plucking and tossing men and women like twigs, two white-painted spear shafts already sticking from his body.

Bradan turned his back on the conflict and ran, aware of the Vulpe somewhere in front of him, and the Lady somewhere behind.

The knife did not cause pain as it tore. Nascha knew it probably should, and that it certainly would later, if Vippon gave her the luxury of time, but for now she was too tired and the knife was too sharp for the pain to properly register. All Nascha was aware of was her former lover's deep breathing, and the urgency with which he clutched her. Vippon held her so close his face took up the entirety of her vision, his yellow-rimmed eye focussed on his handiwork, intense, passionate.

That eye. The blackness of his eye held so many memories.

So many dreams.

Nascha dove in, escaping from herself. Time slowed; Vippon stopped cutting. Nascha fell into that darkness, losing herself in it.

She collapsed onto the dusty floor of a castle. She grunted, pulling herself up. It was dark here, just as it had been in the forest, but it was colder. The autumn air of the Magpie King's woods had still held warmth, of a sort, but the stones of this floor spoke of winter, and a particularly cold one at that.

Nascha stood, dusting herself off. The air here seemed thick, as if it was an effort for her to move through it. She spun around, trying to figure out which direction would be best for her to travel in. Aside from the long stone windows right beside her – the view of which was revealed by the full moon, though the moon in the forest had waned to a sliver – there were three other doorways out of here, and one staircase heading down, into the dark.

For a moment, then, Nascha thought she could hear crying coming from downstairs.

She took a step towards the stairs, not liking the look of the darkness of that descent. Then she remembered she was in a dream, and that dreams were hers, so she reached into the sky and picked a piece of that full moon, and allowed its illuminated paleness to light the way before her.

Nascha stepped down into that enclosed stairway, and found

that the steps wound their way down the walls of a massive shaft. Even with a piece of the moon in her hand, Nascha could not see the bottom. As she shone the moon down, the crying from below raised in volume. Knowing she would not be happy leaving this story incomplete, Nascha made her way down the staircase, taking care to stay close to the relative safety of the wall.

Eventually, the stairs did reach an end, coming to rest on the floor of a large square room, entirely cut off from any source of light except for Nascha's moon. The floor here, unlike the room above, was hard, compact dirt, but the walls were of black stone, and into these walls were set a multitude of cells, each covered with iron bars. The crying was coming from one of these cells, from the corner furthest from Nascha.

As Nascha walked towards the source of the crying, her moonlight caught glimpses of some of the other cells' occupants. All were corpses, all in different stages of decay. From some the flesh had long since disappeared, leaving only cleaned bone. Not all of the bodies had clothing still attached, but those who did all wore the same type of garment. Nascha had never owned one herself, but they were all clearly wearing wedding dresses.

The final cell, the one the crying was coming from, however, had a very different type of occupant.

It was a small boy. The child – about eight or nine years of age – was naked, covered in nothing except for his wild mane of red hair. The boy shifted away from the moonlight when Nascha shone it upon him, crying out at the sight of her. When he moved away, Nascha was surprised to see something protruding from behind him, almost like a small black stick poking out from the base of his spine where his back met his buttocks. It took Nascha a moment to realise this was the beginning of a tail.

The boy stopped crying, looking at Nascha with blinking eyes.

"Are you all right, Vippon?" Nascha asked.

"I'm lonely," he said meekly, almost frightened to look at her, clutching his knees tightly to his chest. "I've been lonely for so long. I thought… when I saw you, in the forest, I thought maybe we were the same. Maybe we could be lonely together, and that wouldn't be so bad." He looked away, closing his eyes. "But then I messed it up. And the Fox Spirit doesn't like mistakes."

"Lonely together…" Nascha said, softening towards the lost boy, despite the man he had become. "That wouldn't have been the worst idea, if you had just told me before things went bad."

Vippon smiled at her, and this smile was a distant echo of the knowing, cunning grin she was so used to.

Growing in confidence at her presence, Vippon uncurled himself from his fetal position and stood up, walking through the cell towards her.

It was then that Nascha saw the wound between his legs, and she gave a gasp, stepping back from the sight. Where the child's genitals should have been, only a bloody stump remained.

"He said he'd give it back to me," Vippon told her, clutching the iron bars, sadness dripping from his voice. "He'd give it back when I earned it. When I'm good.

"But Nascha," Vippon said, his voice lowering to a whisper, the quivering in it becoming steadier, more serious, "I don't think I know how to be good. Could you teach me, do you think? Is goodness something a boy can learn?"

"A boy had better fucking learn how to be good, and be quick about it," a voice said from the darkness above.

Vippon yelped, throwing himself away from the bars, scrambling back into his ball in the corner of his cell.

Nascha, her heart in her throat, held the moonlight high, watching the figure descending into the castle prison.

Down the steps walked an elderly man, a man whose hair had once been red, but now was mostly dominated by grey. The same could be said of the bushy fox tail that poked out from underneath his long jacket.

The old man, the Gentleman Fox, walked up to Nascha, stepped past her, and held up a small knife to Vippon. "Little boy's pecker will only keep so long before it rots away to look like the blackness within you. So you'd better get good enough to replace me, or I'm going to have to do a whole lot more cutting before you learn that lesson."

Despite all the pain Vippon had caused her, despite the fact that even now he was using a very similar knife to cut her face off, Nascha pitied that little boy as he screamed.

And he did scream.

It was the screams that led Bradan to them, eventually.

At first, he had assumed it was Nascha making the noise, and was surprised at how deep her voice sounded when she was in pain. This made him all the more shocked when he came upon the pair. Nascha was being held up roughly against a tree trunk, but it was Vippon who was bellowing.

"No, no! Get away from me, old man. You're dead. I killed you myself."

Vippon reeled back from Nascha; there was a glint of white as his knife fell from his hand. Nascha, for her part, stood against the tree, transfixed, eyes not breaking from the Vulpe man. In the shadows of the woods, Bradan could not see her properly, but it looked as if something dark covered the left side of her face.

The Vulpe was spinning about himself now, swatting at unseen shapes.

"Out of my head, witch. Out!"

Trying to make as little sound as possible in case the noise broke Vippon from whatever madness had overtaken him, Bradan ran up to his friend, grabbing her by the arm.

It was then Bradan realised there was nothing on Nascha's face. Instead, a sizable flap of skin had peeled back from her forehead, a dark stain of blood oozing from the wound.

Trying to not let his shock steal his precious time, Bradan shook her arm.

"Nascha, it's me. Whatever you've done to him, it's keeping him busy, but we've got to move, now. My father is here, and he's not happy. Also, I think a few more of my demons are on the way, if you're quite done dealing with yours..."

Nascha blinked a few times, moving her eyes from Vippon to Bradan, giving him a lazy smile as she absentmindedly raised a hand to press the flap of skin on her forehead back into place, as if she was just wiping a stray lock of hair from her eyes.

"Your demons?" she said, grimacing as Bradan pulled her from the tree, forcing her to move despite her obvious aches.

"The Lady. Father reckons she's coming for me, that she's close. Knowing our luck, sounds about right."

"Your father? He won't protect us from her?"

"I think the best-case scenario is they'll kill each other to see who gets me first. Vippon pulled you right back down the mountainside." He grabbed her hand, holding tight, just as they had done when entering the church back in Ebora. "I reckon our only chance of survival is to get out of the forest before they're all done beating up on each other."

He saw Nascha look back up the large hill that had taken them hours to climb earlier, and heard her whimper at the sight. He knew how she felt, but the only alternative was—

Movement.

Bradan started, twisting around to look at the trees behind him. They could still hear Vippon's shouts, but that was not what had caught Bradan's attention.

"What is it?" Nascha asked, her nails digging into the back of his hand.

"Not sure," he said, turning back to face the hillside, beginning to march up it as quickly as he could manage, despite the pain in his calves. "Maybe nothing. I'd rather get away from all of this before we have the chance to find out."

As they charged upwards, Bradan's arm ached from dragging Nascha. He was certain there was movement in the treetops around them, but he did not want to alert Nascha to the danger.

Just keep moving, he thought. *Whatever's up there, maybe something else will come along and distract it. That tactic's been working pretty well for us so far, no point in giving up on it now.*

Behind them, Vippon's screams had faded away. Bradan had no idea if that meant the Vulpe was just a gibbering mess on the forest floor, or if he had begun to chase them again. As the shapes above them – he was convinced they were the Lady's barkwraiths – grew louder, either through gathering in numbers or because they were descending towards them, Bradan did not know which foe he would rather face, here on the forest's border.

Ultimately, of course, he had no choice in the matter – as he discovered moments later, when two dark, spider-like shapes dropped on them from above, throwing both Nascha and him to the ground.

Bradan spun onto his back, just in time to see the barkwraith scuttle away from him on all fours. Unlike his first meeting with one, his assailant did not speak to him. Instead, as it backed just beyond the nearest trees, it strained its head forward to hiss at him. This hiss echoed all around them, and Bradan turned on the spot – just as he saw Nascha do beside him – to see a ring of the creatures, at least ten, crouching in the shadows, cutting off all movement.

Nascha's hand found his again, just as the trees downhill began to groan.

Wordlessly, Bradan and Nascha drew close to each other, the bare skin of her arms a welcome warmth against his as a cold wind blew from the north, from the heart of the forest.

Then the oaks in front of them parted, and the Lady appeared.

Just as they had seen her back at the Nest, she was colossal, almost as tall as the trees themselves. Unlike that meeting, however, the Lady's gaze was firmly fixed upon them, and on Bradan in particular. There was no doubting the rage she held for him; the visage that had once been the epitome of rigid beauty was now marred by creases born of hatred and anger.

A multitude of barbed vines fell from the Lady's hair, seeming to run down the entirety of her back. Unlike at the church, however, these vines were not lazily moving through the undergrowth. Instead, they writhed and flicked behind the Lady's back, like the hackles on a cat disturbed during its hunt.

One of these vines whipped out suddenly, catching Bradan on the side of his face.

He gave a cry of pain, raising his hand to it, but the vine had already withdrawn, leaving ruined flesh in its wake.

Nascha raised her own hand to examine his wound, and Bradan turned to her. "We're a matching pair now, aren't we?" he said, eyes lingering on the flap of skin Vippon had almost peeled from her face, doing his best to smile.

Exhausted, defeated, she returned his expression.

"You broke your promise," came a voice from the Lady's foot. It was one of the Children, although it was difficult to tell if this was the same one that had spoken for her back at the Nest. "You broke your faith with Mother. You threw away her gift."

Bradan stepped forward, letting go of Nascha's hand, his eyes on the Lady the whole time. Her look of rage had not diminished.

"I did not mean to offend," he said carefully. In all truth, he had no idea how to survive this. Part of him, from years of habit, wanted to call for his father, although he knew at this point that prayer would go unanswered. Even if it was answered, the response might not be in his favour.

"I thought I would be a good servant for you, that we could both give each other what we wanted. What we needed." He glanced at Nascha. "I don't think that's the case anymore. I'm sorry."

In response, the Lady whipped him again, this time slicing a gouge on his arm.

He cried out, and Nascha threw herself in front of him.

"Don't you dare," she screamed at the goddess before them. "We've come so far. Don't you dare be the end of our story."

"Your story," the Child said again, sounding almost thoughtful. "Your story is the problem. Mother has just begun to rise again in power. It will not do for one of the first stories about her to be one of defiance. No, it would be best if you were both removed, before this story spreads any further."

Bradan felt sick. 'Both,' the Child had said. Although part of him had known it, this was the first time she had confirmed that Nascha was to also be punished for his infractions.

Nascha stepped back beside him, her hand squeezing his again. He turned to look at her, and caught her smiling sadly back at him, their matching ruined faces complementing each other.

Bradan had no idea what was going on here, with Nascha. This was new territory for him. He felt closer to her now than he ever had to anyone, including his own father and the memory of Mother Ogma. Whether that closeness was simple, precious friendship, or perhaps the beginning of something more, he had no idea, and now he would never have the chance to find out.

"I'm sorry," he whispered to her as the Lady loomed down upon them, her fractious vines cracking as they punished the air for his assumed crimes.

Nascha's face froze, then contorted into a mask of dread. She crumpled, collapsing to the forest floor.

"What?" Bradan said, bending down to pick her up. Her reaction was too sudden, such a reversal of the sad smile she had worn only moments ago. Was this because of their impending death? That did not seem likely.

"What is it?" he asked her, lifting her head from the ground.

Her face remained a picture of pale terror, her eyes wide and searching the forest around them, as if dreading what she might find.

She did not seem to be looking at the Lady anymore.

Bradan raised his head to see how close the Lady and his death were.

The Lady's face held the same immovable terror that was carved into Nascha's.

Despite not being able to sense what the others clearly could, a coldness began to bubble in Bradan's gut.

"What's going on?" he asked Nascha again. Finally, she focussed on him, as if seeing him for the first time.

"Spirit, no," was all she said, scrambling to her feet.

Bradan wheeled around, constantly aware of the Lady's presence, and was surprised to see the goddess turn away from them both. Wheeling back, he was just in time to see Nascha making for the nearest tree, a tall elm whose branches stretched into the canopy above.

"Come on," she called. "I have to see. I have to see."

All of Bradan's exhaustion was stripped away by his growing dread, his urgency to follow Nascha giving his limbs the strength they so dearly needed. Despite his stay of execution at the Lady's hands, Bradan felt no relief. He knew that whatever had distracted her was no doubt worse than what had already been due to him.

He did not catch up with Nascha before she broke through the canopy, and she was already perched, muscles taut, peering sentry-like across the treetops when he reached her.

"It's here," she said, her voice a whisper, reminding Bradan of how he had felt the morning he woke to find Mother Ogma unmoving in her bed. "It's found me."

Bradan turned to see what she was looking at.

At first, he thought it was nothing, just a dark storm cloud amassing in the east, a storm that had already passed them by without too much effect.

Then Bradan realised the storm was moving toward them. He saw the dark cloud was not made up of water, ready to pour down on the forest. It was made up of birds.

It was made up of magpies.

Bradan's head swam, and would have caused him to tumble

from the tree if not for Nascha grabbing his tunic at the last moment. He had seen all of this before. After his previous vision, he was not at all surprised when the colossal flock of magpies coalesced into one giant black bird, flapping its wings slowly, soaring across the forest toward them.

"The Magpie Spirit," he said, his voice low, not speaking to anyone in particular. "For the first time in centuries, the Magpie Spirit has returned to the forest."

Beside him, up there in the trees, Nascha shivered.

"I hate it," she said, clutching her branch tightly, eyes squeezed shut as if to ward off the distant vision. "It feels... hungry. It feels like it would pluck out my soul and add it to the multitude that already make it up."

Bradan gave a hollow laugh. "It doesn't care a thing about you, I'd guess. Don't think it cares about anyone here."

Nascha was silent, but bore disagreement on her face.

Below them, something began to roar.

They looked at each other, unsure what they were witnessing. What began as a low, ongoing moan did not fade away. Instead, the sound grew in volume and intensity. The tree they were both perched in began to shake, forcing them to grip tightly to their branch. It felt for a moment as if that would not be enough, as if the tree itself was in danger of being uprooted. All the while, the roaring – clearly a female voice – continued to grow.

Bradan knew it was the Lady of the Forest before her head emerged from the canopy. Still, he was shocked to see her appear. She was, somehow, growing in size. Bradan saw what looked like vines snaking across her body, but then he realised that at that scale, the vines must be the thickness of tree trunks. Those snaking cords were indeed the trunks of trees – the forest around the Lady was somehow being drawn into her, consumed by her, their mass adding to her own, allowing her to grow in stature. She turned to the approaching Magpie Spirit and strode towards it, leaving a ruined scar upon the forest landscape in her wake.

"You dare return?" she bellowed, and Bradan realised it was the first time since the church he had heard her speak without using the Child as an intermediary. "You think to take this place from me again? This time, parasite from Beyond, I am more than willing to fight you back for it, no matter the price my forest might pay."

The Magpie Spirit did not reply in words, but instead a

thousand beaks dived towards the amber and green giantess, the points of them glinting in the moonlight.

THE CLAIMING
OF THE
WOODS

A lost tale of the Corvae

This is a tale of the final meeting between the Lady of the Forest and the Magpie King.

The forest had been invaded. First, by people. They had plundered its goodness, cleared land to live in, and irritated the Great Lady who ruled there, who had raised her kingdom from a single seed.

However, she had not dealt with the infestation of humanity quickly enough. She had not realised what else they would attract to her land.

The Magpie Spirit had found everything she had created, and found that it was good. It wanted everything she had for itself.

And somehow, impossibly, it had taken it.

The Magpie King found the Lady, on that final day, curled up against the final tree that sang to her. The rest of the forest had turned from her rule, the trees had stopped their song, and she was dying. Her creatures, her offspring, who had once existed in great multitudes, now numbered only two. In her arms she cradled a small girl, whose skin had once been green, but was now faded and pale. The child's rust-brown hair had fallen out weeks ago, leaving the sickly thing bald and ugly. On the Lady's back clung the last of her wraiths, crouched as if ready to protect its mistress from harm, but lacking the energy to perform even the simplest of actions.

The Magpie King walked up to his enemy, checking for signs of life.

In response, the Lady turned her head to regard the human who had been responsible for her fall from grace. As she turned her neck to look at him, the bark of her skin splintered, falling from her neck, every movement agony for her now-brittle form.

"How?" she asked, her voice rasping and dry. "I do not understand. The forest is mine. How have you turned it from me?"

"The forest has changed," the Magpie King said. Though the Lady knew better, it almost sounded as if there was pity there, hidden beneath his words. "The forest has changed, but you have not. The forest no longer wants you. It has chosen me and my master instead."

At this, the Lady laughed, but her mirth quickly turned into a painful cough, which rattled about her hollow shell.

"Your master," she spat, once she had composed herself. "You think your master is any better than I for this forest? We want the same thing, your master and I. We want someone to love us. We want to feed from your worship. You think you have improved life in this forest, replacing me with him? We are no different."

The Magpie King shrugged. "Honestly, I do not know. Other than bestowing his gifts upon me, I have had few direct dealings with the Magpie Spirit. What you say could indeed be true. However, what I will say is this: the Magpie Spirit will leave us alone. If we remember him, if we worship him, he will not come to this place, and will allow us to prosper in peace, as long as we do so in his name. So, you see, we are gaining something different by ridding the forest of you. We are gaining freedom."

The Lady snarled, and stroked the still infant in her arms. "You cannot rid the forest of me, not completely. I am bound to it, am part of its story. You would break this place, if you were to wipe me from it altogether."

The Magpie King nodded. "Yes, I believe you. But stories can change, over time, through different tellings. And over time, the story of the forest has changed. You have not been removed from it, but your importance is less. You are a supporting character, now, a minor figure in the background. Perhaps, in time, only a handful in the forest will remember you ever existed. The forest's story belongs to the Magpie Spirit now, and to the Magpie King."

The Magpie King stood, nodded once more at the sight of his broken foe, and then leapt into the air, to establish for himself a seat of power from which to rule over his kingdom.

Under that final singing tree, the Lady clutched her child tight to her breast. Then, with a grimace of pain, she gave a bitter smile.

"Yes, stories can be changed, Magpie King," she said, pulling the child tighter to her. The unmoving infant began to fall apart, to melt, and the Lady fed the small bundle into her chest, becoming one with it. At the same time, the wraith on her back began to enlarge, its spiky limbs piercing the bark of her flesh, it too becoming one with her body.

"It can take years, generations even, but stories can be changed. For one such as me, generations are not that long a space of time. I can be patient, Magpie King, if I know change is waiting for me."

The Lady then was unrecognisable. Her face was a blank canvas, torn skin stretched over roots that writhed just underneath it, her lank, dark hair dripping from her head like moss on a stone.

Wordlessly, looking to the moon above to guide her, the pale thing that was once the Lady of the Forest burrowed into the final singing tree, making it her lonely home, waiting for the inevitable change that would make the forest hers once more.

CHAPTER TEN

The first blow the Magpie Spirit dealt the Lady of the Forest landed like a thunderclap, and Bradan thought the conflict might be ended there and then. From their vantage point high above the forest, Bradan and Nascha could see the ring of devastation around the combatants caused by that first blow – trees adjacent to the Lady were uprooted, blown free from the earth by the force of the explosion. As far as they were from the fight – Bradan estimated that with only a few footsteps the now-gargantuan Lady had travelled at least a mile from them – Bradan and Nascha still had to grip the tree's branches to not be blown away by the force of the attack.

"Spirit's blood," Nascha swore, grabbing onto Bradan's shoulder to right herself.

"Not yet," Bradan said, "but they're just getting started."

Before them, the Lady gave a bellow of outrage. She extended one of her arms towards the nearby Spirit and a stream of braided tree trunks spewed from it, the wood cracking and splintering as it grew at unnatural speed, extending its roots like a spider's web upon contact with the Magpie Spirit. In response, the multitude of birds that made up this manifestation of the Spirit disassembled, breaking formation and spreading out, flocking away from the source of attack. However, even from this distance Bradan could see the Lady's attack had had some effect, as scores of black, broken shapes fell from the sky where the Magpie Spirit had once been.

The Lady's brief moment of exultation ended when the remaining birds flocked together only a short distance from her, the giant, looming shape of the Magpie Spirit reforming, its talons already extended for another strike.

"I can't believe our luck," Nascha said, her hand on Bradan's shoulder again.

He turned to her, frowning. Luck? All their enemies had come upon them at once, and now they found themselves in the centre of a conflict that was well beyond their already stretched abilities.

Nascha extended her hand towards the warring giants, the mockery on her face making him feel like a fool for being slow on the uptake.

"Nobody's going to be paying attention to us now, are they?" she said. Sure enough, neither the Titonidae nor the Vulpe had bothered them since the Lady had appeared, even though both parties would have seen them scale the tree they were now perched in. Bradan imagined that Lord Bidzell and Vippon both valued their own lives over how much they wanted to get their hands on Nascha, and would have fled the scene as soon as matters escalated.

"Time to get to the border," Nascha said, the strength of her grip mirroring her excitement, "before someone remembers us."

Bradan looked behind himself to the hills that rose above the treetops, so close now, such an achievable goal. That way lay freedom, new life, and Nascha. Even thinking about taking that future made his heart flutter, both with excitement at the thought of the adventure that awaited him, and in fear at the total newness that could be in store, so far removed from anything he had ever imagined for himself.

Then he turned back to look at the Lady and the Magpie Spirit warring above the forest. Just like before, the Lady was striding through the woods to hunt her enemy, and as she did so she consumed the greenery around her, presumably to sustain the form she had chosen for herself, and to repair any damage the Spirit's attacks were causing. However, in her wake she was leaving ruin, and the Spirit was doing nothing to contain her, using its flight to manoeuvre around her, causing the Lady to plough through more forest to catch it, leaving only upturned soil in her wake.

Bradan looked at the land that had been his home; it was being torn apart. The land he had thought he would pledge his life to protect, just like his father had.

In the distance – but not too far away to be entirely safe – plumes of smoke betrayed the location of the nearest Corvae village.

"I can't abandon the forest, Nascha," he said finally.

On his shoulder, he felt her hand briefly tighten, then her grip slackened.

"You can't be serious. We only just managed to survive when Vippon and Lord Bidzell were after us. Even your father – and no offense meant to him – is an acorn compared with those two."

She gestured wildly towards the fighters, her fingers trembling as she did so. Bradan turned just in time to see the Magpie Spirit impact upon the Lady's chest, exploding in a hail of black feathers and amber foliage, knocking the Lady backwards, causing her to disappear from view as she fell to the forest floor, the explosion rippling through the sea of leaves before them like a boulder in a pond. Then the trees surrounding the hole she had fallen into disappeared as she regrew herself, just as the Magpie Spirit reconstituted itself, wheeling around the Lady in a great arc, preparing to attack again.

"They're destroying the forest, Nascha," he said, pointing at the village smoke, which the combat was moving toward. "How many people need to die before this fight ends?"

She looked as helpless as he felt. "I don't... I mean, I hate it, of course I do. But I'm not stupid, either. If I thought there was anything I could do to save those lives, of course I'd try it, but I'm not going to throw my life away just because I don't like what's happening. And I don't want you to throw yours away either. Run away with me, Bradan. Let's cross the ocean, and get away from all this."

He set his mind, then. It was the hardest thing he had ever had to do.

"I'm not planning on throwing my life away. The forest needs a Magpie King, Nascha. With him to deal with problems like this, the Magpie Spirit need never come here. The Magpie King existed to protect the Spirit's interests just as much as he protected the people of the forest. The Magpie Spirit told me I wasn't ready, but I'm going to show it it's wrong.

"I'm going to force it to make me the Magpie King – a proper one, not like Father – and then I'm going to stop this conflict before it tears the forest apart."

He looked at Nascha – properly holding her eyes this time, not sneaking a glance and then turning away – and fully expected her to laugh at him.

She bit her lip, opened her mouth as if to protest, then closed it again.

Finally, in a quiet voice, she said, "Okay, then. Where do you need to go?"

They ran through the forest once again, but this time the land around them was punctuated by loud explosions, inhuman screams and the sound of falling trees. Bradan had spotted an outcrop of rock slightly up the hillside, one the Magpie Spirit came close to a few times as it wheeled around the less manoeuvrable Lady. His admittedly uncomplicated plan was to get the Spirit's attention as it flew past. If that did not work... well, at least they would be somewhat up the hillside already, and then he would consider Nascha's proposal.

Nascha gripped his hand, as she had done since they had descended from their tree. She was silent as they ran. Bradan took a brief glimpse at her. She looked so serious, her eyes forward. He assumed she was looking out for her own enemies, wherever they might have fled to. A few times she had to bring her hand to her face, to reposition the piece of skin Vippon had almost torn from it. The act did not seem to faze her.

For a brief moment, Bradan allowed himself to consider what she had meant when she had said 'run away with me.' They had grown close in their days together, closer than Bradan had originally realised, but he had no idea what that word really meant.

Close.

He especially had no idea what it meant where Nascha was concerned.

Was she talking about being travelling companions, or was she hinting at something more? Other than admiring some of the village girls from afar when he visited on his father's business, Bradan had no experience with romance, just as he had no real experience with friendship. He found himself inadequate to judge what he wanted from their relationship, let alone what Nascha desired. Time, he assumed, was required to make sense of this tangle of circumstance and emotions, if Fate was also willing to be generous.

A nearby explosion threw them both to the ground. His head ringing, Bradan grabbed Nascha, checking if she was all right. A smattering of irritation at his attention played across her face as she picked herself up.

"I'm fine," she said. "Haven't you ever been thrown to the ground by warring gods before?" She ran on, no longer holding his hand.

Bradan had no idea who would win if the Lady and the Magpie Spirit were allowed to continue their fight to conclusion. This was the Lady's home, and she drew her strength from the forest, although clearly at a horrific cost to the land around her. The Magpie Spirit, although not native to this world, apparently, let alone the forest, seemed to have diminished little in response to the Lady's attacks. Bradan imagined a score of Magpie Kings, spread throughout the world, gathering worshippers to feed their master's desire for recognition.

A number that Bradan planned to join, if fickle Fate continued to smile kindly upon him.

His heart froze when they came upon the ridge of stone they had been making for. It looked so familiar to him, and then it hit him – he had indeed seen this cliff edge before. He had stood upon it when he had first spoken to the Magpie Spirit, in his vision back at the temple.

He turned to Nascha, a mad grin on his face. "This is going to work. Trust me, I will make this work."

She smiled and nodded, not entirely sharing his confidence.

Bradan gestured for her to stay back, then he stepped forward to the edge of the stone ridge. He looked below him, where the side of the hill was steep, cliff-like, descending in an almost vertical drop to the forest floor far below. Then his eyes travelled across the treetops, to where giants duelled.

The Magpie Spirit was raking at the Lady's face with its massive claws, choosing not to break apart as it drew close to her. This allowed the Lady to work her roots all around the Spirit, capturing it in a net of green, holding it close as her vines grew around it, the blackness of the Magpie Spirit becoming more and more obscured by green and brown. However, the cost to the Lady was great, as this proximity allowed the Spirit's claws access to her face, marring her cold beauty with a patchwork of deep gashes through which green sap began to flow.

At the final moment, before the Lady could fully envelop the Magpie Spirit within her net, the Spirit broke apart, the plethora of black and white birds surging out of the remaining gaps, or creating new holes where the binding was still weak.

Bradan's heart threatened to burst from his chest as the Spirit reformed a distance from the Lady, its wings already spread, moving in a wide circle around its enemy.

As he had predicted, the Magpie Spirit was heading straight for him. As if the vision had been preparing him for this moment, he was exactly where he needed to be to address the Magpie Spirit once again.

Bradan clenched his fists, willing away the sense of failure that threatened to resurface as he considered that previous meeting. It had all been a test. Everything he had been through in the last few days – the beatings at the hands of Vippon and his father – they had all been a way for Bradan to prove he was worthy of becoming the next Magpie King, of following in his father's footsteps.

"Magpie Spirit," he called out as the thing drew near. "It is me – Bradan, son of the Magpie King. Hear me, Magpie Spirit. I am here to prove to you I am worthy of your gift. Allow me to become your servant, and to speak with your voice within the forest."

The black cloud of wings flew on past him, and Bradan sagged, almost dropping where he stood. It had not heard him. Then the Spirit wheeled around, but this time not to attack the Lady. It was turning to face Bradan once more. To fly towards him.

He held his breath. This was it. The moment he was waiting for. The moment he had hoped for his entire life.

As the Spirit flew towards him, it spoke in his mind, as it had done back at the temple.

"I told you you were not ready."

"I've come here to show you you were wrong."

"You have changed. Last time you were unprepared. Now you are… tainted? Why do I feel my enemy's touch upon you?"

Bradan shifted uneasily. For the first time, his nervous excitement drifted dangerously close to outright fear. "I… she offered me power. I did not take it."

"No. Nobody who dismissed her straight away would be as tainted as you are now. You considered her offer. You accepted something from her." Before Bradan, the Magpie Spirit loomed closer. It was not slowing down.

"Yes. Yes, but I changed my mind. I relented. I have turned to you again instead."

"Before, you were not ready. You might have grown into the role. But now? Now, I want nothing to do with you, son of the pretender, betrayer of his name. You will never be the Magpie King. However, there is potential in you, potential that my enemy has recognised.

"I cannot allow you to become one of her tools."

The cloud of magpies hit Bradan with full force. There was no mystical barrier here to protect him. This was not a dream. The birds did not pass through him, or somehow move around him as if he were not there. Instead, a hundred beaks and feathers and claws smashed into him, ripping at his face, tearing at his clothes, and ultimately pushing him backwards, off the cliff he was standing on.

Everything went black when he hit the first rock protruding from the cliff below, breaking his face and shutting off his mind.

"Bradan!" Nascha screamed as the Magpie Spirit hit him. For a brief second she could see glimpses of him within that black cloud, being buffeted by the creatures, a speck of pale flesh within a hail of darkness, and then he was gone.

When the Spirit moved on, wheeling around in the sky, beginning its great arc to fight the Lady once more, Nascha knew there was only one place Bradan could be. She scrambled to the edge of the cliff and looked down it. There, on the forest floor far below her, she saw a lonely figure, splayed out awkwardly in a way no human body should be able to.

Her insides turned to stone. She could not – would not – allow herself to believe that he was dead, despite the knowledge of what a fall like that could do to a person. They had come so far, and Bradan had been willing to give up so much. His story could not end with him being rejected so callously.

Eyes brimming, Nascha looked at the broken form below, willing it to move a little, even just a twitch, to betray the fact that life still clung to it.

An arm moved, barely. It was a gesture that spoke of pain Nascha could only imagine, and it was not the movement of a man who had full control over himself. Still, it meant for now, Bradan still lived. She had a chance to save him. Somehow.

Nascha raised her head, staring at the combatants before her, attacking each other once again, the Magpie Spirit – Nascha imagined it was emboldened by almost taking Bradan's life – raking its claws down the Lady's side, tearing away the amber leaves that made up her now-ruined clothing.

She hated these things. Both of them. Bradan was wrong, and she should have told him so. These creatures would never listen to reason; they would never make deals that did not completely benefit them. They did not care about the people of the forest. Both of them just wanted control, as much of it as possible, and they had no issues with the price anyone else had to pay for them to get what they wanted. The forest did not need either one of them to win. It would not benefit either way – neither the Magpie Spirit nor the Lady would look after the land or its people any better. The forest just needed them to stop fighting. It just needed them to go away.

Nascha looked down at Bradan again, wondering what would be the quickest way down to him. Then she gasped, realising he was no longer alone. A black-cloaked figure stood over Bradan, now carrying his limp form.

The figure looked up. It was Lonan, the pale excuse the forest now had for a Magpie King.

He looked directly at Nascha. There was no humanity left on his face, no trace of the broken, quiet man who had rescued her just a few nights ago. Instead, Lonan's face was that of a wild animal, one that had finally found its prey. Lonan's madness had completely overtaken him now, and there was murder in his eyes.

Taking his prize in his arms, Lonan leapt away into the trees, taking what remained of Bradan far away from Nascha, and from any hope of rescue.

In his haze of pain, Bradan was dimly aware of rough hands holding him.

"Father?" he said, voice quiet, the act of speaking much more painful than he would have thought possible.

His father looked at Bradan in response. Bradan knew fear, then, because he recognised straight away that his father was not in control right now. He had looked at his son as a cat regards a mouse making a final desperate attempt to escape, even after having its neck broken. Lonan was all animal now, all madness. There would be no reasoning with him.

Bradan was thrown to the ground with a thump, letting out a cry of pain as he hit the dirt. All along his body, broken bones screamed as their ruined parts shifted unnaturally, wailing to be left alone.

There was not a part of Bradan that did not ache. His face, he realised, must look terrible. He could only see out of his left eye, and struggled to raise a hand to his right to see what had become of it. Only his right arm would move at all, and he could only close two of his fingers on it.

He tried to shift around to get a better look at his father. His neck, blessedly, did turn, but the movement let Bradan know something was dreadfully wrong with his left shoulder. His back was cold, and felt wet, although he was pretty sure it was not raining.

He could not move or feel either of his legs.

Bradan managed to pull himself around in the dirt, screaming in response to the agony the action caused him. In the distance, he was dimly aware of the sounds of the Magpie Spirit and the Lady still in combat with each other, but his head was ringing so badly he had no idea how far away or in which direction they were. He caught a glimpse of the Pisha Hills looming above, distantly surprised at how close they still were. He was almost at their foot. His father must have carried him along the edge of the forest instead of deeper into it. Still, he knew he must be miles away from Nascha now, as he had felt his father leap more than a couple of times, and Bradan was well aware of how much ground his father was able to cover in a short space of time.

"Father," Bradan said again, hoping to make his voice loud enough to be heard over the distant din of the warring titans. "Father, I'm hurt. I think I'm dying. I need you. Need you to look after me."

Lonan did not react to his son's pleas. Instead, staying hunched in the darkness, shaded from the moonlight, he growled, "You're no son of mine. Sold your soul to the enemy, betrayed me. No son of mine."

Then with one bound Lonan closed the distance between them, kicking Bradan square in the gut, sending him hurtling into the nearby bushes. Inside, broken bones ground in ways they should not have, sending a million spikes of torment throughout his body.

He's going to kill me, Bradan realised. *After everyone who's been chasing us through this forest, it's going to be my own father who kills me.*

"I wish you were never born!" Lonan screamed, hardly sounding at all like the quiet man Bradan had grown to love from afar as they travelled the woods together, saving who they could. "I'll never give you over to her."

Bradan's tears came freely now. He realised he was finding it difficult to breathe, the numbness of his legs spreading up his body. From the smell, he was dimly aware that his bowels had emptied, but he could feel nothing down there to give any other clues.

Hearing his father approaching, unable to even turn properly to face the man, Bradan searched around with his one good hand, desperately seeking for something he could use to protect himself with.

It was no use fighting, really, he knew. He had no chance against his father, even if he was not already broken. Spirit's blood, even if his father did not have the Magpie Spirit's gift in his veins, Bradan was never a fighter.

But if this was it, if he was to die now, Bradan would not lie in wait while death came for him.

His hand closed around a stone in the dirt, a pitiful weapon for a last stand, but all Bradan had available to him.

He would never be a hero. Never be a fighter. But in the Spirit's name – that bastard creature that did not deserve his prayers – if this was his time to die, he would not lie down in the dirt and wait for the end to claim him.

Nascha felt helpless, there on that outcrop, desperately searching the woods in the direction in which Lonan had carried his son. It was no use. She had managed to track his first leap through the trees, spotting him only by the black nothingness of a shadow that he left against the fading purple of the night sky, but she lost sight of him the second time he took to the air. Even if she had been able to find Lonan, he was too far away for her to make any difference now.

In the distance, the Lady screamed, tendrils the size of ancient oaks snaking out from her arms to whip at the Magpie Spirit. Nascha watched the attack with a detached calm, safe in the knowledge that the Lady was not interested in her now, and that Nascha could do nothing against her anyway, no more than she could divert the passage of a thunderstorm. Nascha was aware the combat was moving closer to one of the distant villages, and part of her agonised over that fact, but again she knew she had no chance of making a difference for those people who were about to lose their lives.

Bradan had been wrong. They should have run while they had the chance. Nobody was chasing them now. The hills had been so close.

Nascha turned around, looking at the edge of the forest, looming above her. She was already halfway to the top.

She could see no other option. There was no chance of saving Bradan, no chance of stopping the Lady and the Magpie Spirit from destroying each other and the forest around them. Nascha had tried; she had tried to come back to save Bradan from all of this, but she had failed. The idiot had not listened. Nobody could blame her now for leaving, not now all was lost.

Her face began to ache, pain blooming all around where Vippon had mutilated her with his knife. She suspected the pain from the wound was just beginning, and would get considerably worse before healing truly began. That wound, more than anything, should be proof to her that she had no further contribution to make here, that she had no hope of making a difference to the conflict.

Above her, Nascha fancied she could see a small bird flying just below the clouds, a flash of white briefly visible as its feathers were caught by a moonbeam. It was probably one of the Magpie Spirit's stray birds, but Nascha could not help but remember the Grasslands owl that had spurred her to turn back, to try to save Bradan, to bring him with her.

She could probably escape to the Grasslands now, but was that a life she really wanted? A life of freedom, but a life alone?

The Magpie Spirit wheeled through the air, again approaching close to Nascha and the empty space where Bradan had once stood. This time, Nascha fancied she saw the giant creature turn its head to regard her, briefly, and she felt instantly exposed, naked. The feeling she had in the forest, the feeling of being watched ever since gazing into Lonan's eyes, was intensified – here was something vast, unknowable, and hungry, and it had noticed her. There was no doubt in Nascha's mind that it had always been the Magpie Spirit making its way towards her. Whatever was in her blood, filtered through generations of breeding, was of interest to it.

She should run, even though she felt there was nowhere far enough to be truly safe from that thing in the sky before her. The thing responsible for the death of her friend. The thing Bradan had been so convinced would gift him with the power to make both of them safe.

Inspiration hit Nascha like a raindrop plummeting into a pool, interrupting all other thoughts, sending ripples through all the possible actions she could take next. Her head snapped up, regarding the Magpie Spirit in a new light, more horrible than ever, now. Beyond the Magpie Spirit stood the hateful form of the Lady of the Forest, and beyond her, the forest itself, the place that had been trying to kill Nascha since the day she had set foot into it. The place she had been so close to escaping, the place she could still escape, if she would just shut her mouth, turn away and run.

Instead, she took a step forward, her toes now pointing at the edge of the cliff ledge. She stood tall, much as she had when challenging Lord Bidzell, doing all she could to summon the grace of kings and queens that lurked somewhere within her diluted blood.

Nascha stood on the edge of that cliff, her white hair whipping behind her like a flag on one of the Court spires, and she spoke to the Magpie Spirit.

"Great Spirit of the forest," she said calmly. She did not shout, despite a large part of her wanting to scream and curse at the creature that had taken her friend from her. Instead, Nascha was loud, but calm. Commanding. In control. "Great Spirit, hear me. You know me. You have been searching for me. I am Nascha, of the Titonidae, blessed by the grace of the Great Owl Spirit."

The Magpie Spirit turned its head again to regard her.

"This conflict does not aid your interests here," she continued, tingling with the knowledge that she had this thing's attention. "Your fight with the Lady of the Forest, it brings only ruin to the land you once controlled. You do not wish to fight her here, to win, only to be left with a shell containing nothing worth ruling over."

At the apex of its turn, still a good distance away from her, and from the Lady, the Magpie Spirit stopped and hovered in the air, fully focussed on Nascha now.

She took a deep breath, willed herself to stop shaking, and continued. "This is not how you first won the forest from her, all those generations ago. You did not fight tooth and claw for every inch, every scrap. Instead, you won the hearts of the people here. You showed them that you were a better choice. You did not steal the forest from the Lady. The forest came to you willingly, when the people who lived in it realised life under you would be better for them. It should be this way again. You should not belittle yourself by taking part in this combat. You have other places to be, places worthier of your time."

"It is not how it was before," the Spirit said, a booming voice in the back of her head. Nascha tried not to show her revulsion at the proximity of this creature, how she felt its attention to be almost infecting her, reaching into her mind and leaving parts of itself lodged in her brain as it spoke. She looked across the openness of the forest beneath her feet, at the impossibly large black thing hovering there, looking at her, and she knew it for what it was. The Magpie was just a facade, a face it wore to make it more appealing to her. Just as the Owl Spirit had done for her people, Nascha presumed. Just like the Mouse, the Lion, and the Fox, and all the other great Spirits of the world. The Magpie Spirit was simply a selfish, hungry thing, with no thoughts of anyone or anything other than itself. Looking at it now, the face of a bird was ill-suited to it, like an overweight lordling trying to hide behind the mask of a child at one of the Court's masquerade balls. There was nothing natural about this creature, nothing about it that suited it to working in harmony with the land around it. This thing was hungry, and it wanted to consume, and that was all the motivation that fuelled its machinations.

That was what Nascha had to appeal to.

"Before," the Magpie Spirit continued, "I had my agents, carefully cultivated over generations. They spread my word, turned the people towards me, fed me their attention, their worship. But they are all gone, their line extinguished. Only pitiful, broken remnants limp through the woods now, paying me no real fealty. It would take generations to re-establish such a line of servants. I will not surrender the forest to my enemy for that time. It will take just as long for the forest to regrow after our combat is done. People will find their way to the forest again, in time, and it will be mine once more."

"It does not have to be so long," Nascha said, her heart beating so hard it hurt. "You could have agents in the forest now, tonight, working to turn the people back to you."

"You do not know of what you speak, girl. Without the necessary preparations, all those touched by the finger of one such as me go mad. None remain in the forest who could withstand my gift."

"I could," Nascha said, feeling any possibility of her escape from the forest disappearing as she said it.

The Magpie Spirit said nothing, just hovered in the night sky, regarding her silently.

"For all of my life, I have felt the touch of the Owl Spirit. My blood runs with her gift, and it grows stronger in me every single day. For generations, Owl Queens mixed with Magpie Kings to continue your heralds' bloodline. It would not be such a stretch to allow me, one already blessed by the Owl Spirit, to continue that line for you."

The Magpie Spirit hesitated for a moment longer before speaking. "You would do this willingly?"

"For a price," she said, straight away, "but a relatively small one. Give me your gift, the power of the Magpie King. Allow me to use it to save my friend."

The friend you almost killed.

"Once I have saved him, then I will do your bidding for you, return this forest to your worship."

"Even if I did this, you would not be quick enough to save him," the Spirit said, no remorse at all in its voice. "He is already lost."

"Then hurry up," Nascha screamed, this time doing nothing to hide her anger as she yelled at her patron. "Give me the power to do something other than stand here and imagine his death, and I will win this forest back for you!"

The Magpie Spirit did not speak in her mind again, but instead the black cloud of birds that hung in the sky opened its beaks and gave out a cry, a croak that mirrored Nascha's inner rage, but one that distinctly reminded her of a bird of prey having concluded its hunt. Just as before, as had happened with Bradan, the Magpie Spirit tore through the sky towards her, not slowing, impacting upon her at full force.

Nascha, like so many who lived this close to the forest, knew the stories of how the Magpie King had been given his power. A poisoned flower, lacing his blood with the Spirit's gift. Nothing like this happened for Nascha. Just like with Bradan, the magpies that made up the form of the great Spirit beat into her, pushing her backwards. However, unlike with him, the bodies of those birds did not beat against Nascha and rebound off her. As she was knocked backwards, one foot stepping into only emptiness behind, Nascha felt the bodies of those birds embedding into her, somehow, piercing into her skin as she fell. In a moment of true horror, Nascha was aware of a score of magpies wriggling against her flesh, boring into her, opening her up and worming their way inside.

Nascha screamed.

She fell to the forest floor below, and the world changed.

Her eyes closed, hands embedded in the dirt, Nascha became aware of footsteps running from her. She realised those footsteps were miles away, and as she listened to them, she recognised the gait of the person running. It was Vippon, losing steam, bounding through the forest as only one blessed by the Fox Spirit could, making his way towards a larger collection of people somewhere in the distance. The other Vulpe, Nascha realised, with their remaining caravans. She caught the hint of ashes on the breeze, their distant campfires extinguished half an hour ago; could faintly hear them ordering their ponies to move, still using that guttural tongue that Nascha had never managed to decipher.

Her face, she realised, felt fine. There was no hint of pain from the knife wound she had thought would cause her to suffer for weeks.

She opened her eyes. Despite the fact that it was still night-time, and that the moon was hidden by the trees, Nascha found she could see almost perfectly. She was at the bottom of the cliff; she had landed on her feet from the same fall that had broken Bradan, one hand on the floor of the forest – her forest – to steady herself.

On the ground before her, she picked out details that seconds before would have eluded her. Bradan's blood, one of his teeth, the ground he had landed on, the soil of which had been compacted by his fall. She could also make out Lonan's footprints, leading up to Bradan's body, and from the depth of those footprints she could tell which direction he had pointed himself in before leaping away.

Not too far away, Nascha heard the sound of a body being thrown against a tree, of multiple bones shattering like dry twigs.

Bradan.

"Be quick, my servant," the Spirit said, speaking in her head again. Although she could not see it due to the trees above, Nascha was aware of the Magpie Spirit diving back into its combat with the

Lady. "You are already too late to save him, and I will continue this fight until you intervene, until you keep your promise. If you wish to save the people of this forest for me, you must be quick."

Nascha tensed her legs, aimed herself in the direction Bradan had been taken in, and jumped.

She catapulted herself into the air, propelling herself high above the trees. Dreamlike, soaring through the sky over the forest, Nascha felt almost overwhelmed by everything she was seeing, sensing and doing. The Lady and the Spirit clashed again, and Nascha could sense fear of the conflict ripple throughout the woodlands, deer and rabbits careening through the undergrowth to distance themselves from the fight, villagers sheltering in nearby cellars only just realising that something outside was amiss. Somewhere nearby, she could hear Lord Bidzell ordering his troops to hold firm, despite the fear that laced his commands. More than anything, she was aware of what she had just done. As if it were nothing, she had leapt into the air, reaching heights she would have trembled at climbing in the spires of the distant Court, and already, absentmindedly, she had planned how to deal with her descent.

In just a few seconds, she had received and learned how to control the powers of the Magpie King.

No, not a king. A queen.

Shaking her head, trying to dismiss the giddy realisation of the pact she had forged, Nascha focussed on where she planned to land. Beneath her, a figure stood tall, powerful, staring at something a few feet away from it. As Nascha fell through the air, aiming to land between the figure and whatever it was looking at, Nascha spotted another figure, a body crumpled against a tree, a dark, mangled form slumped against the oak it had been thrown into.

Bradan.

Nascha landed on the forest floor with a snarl. She did nothing to soften her landing; the earth beneath her feet exploded as they impacted into it, causing a hail of mud and stone to erupt as she landed.

"Leave him alone," she shouted at the figure before her, waving her hand behind, indicating the broken body wrapped around the tree. "He is under my protection now, and in the name of the Magpie and Owl Spirits, I will fight you to the death to protect my friend."

It was then that Nascha took a proper look at the figure standing in front of her.

It was Bradan.

Even with the Magpie Spirit's gift running through her veins, it took Nascha a moment to process everything. She spun around, to the body broken against the tree. It was now clear that it was Lonan, the pitiful tatters of the man's black cloak dripping with its owner's blood.

She turned back to Bradan, her mouth open in shock. Minutes ago, she saw his body smashed against the rocks as he fell down a cliff face.

"How?" she said.

Bradan blinked, distracted, as if only just noticing her. Confusion bloomed on his face, like a dreamer waking to an unfamiliar scene. "Nascha," he said, his voice dozy. "Nascha, why do you look... Your hair, what've you done to your hair?"

Using her newly granted strength, Nascha leapt forward, closing the distance between them, grabbing his shoulders with both hands. His clothes were torn, bloody, but he seemed fine. She had not expected him to even be capable of standing – Spirit's blood, she had not even hoped to find him alive – yet somehow he had overpowered his father.

As he saw her move, now powered with the same gift that ran through his father's blood, Bradan's look of confusion gave way to one of horror. "Nascha – what've you done?"

Nascha felt overwhelmed. She had given up her freedom to save Bradan, given her soul over to something she hated to save his life, only to now find that he did not need her.

"Nascha, what did you do?" Bradan said again, his anguish clear in his words and on his face.

Nascha, for her part, could not comprehend what she was looking at. "Bradan, how are you alive?" She turned to look back at Lonan, his form barely twitching, still embedded in the tree trunk. "How did you do that?"

Bradan, his horror-filled face fixed on hers, raised up his right hand, and opened it.

In his hand, he held a plum.

It had a bite out of it.

Nascha gave a cry of anguish, slapping at his hand, causing the plum to roll away into the darkness. She grabbed his shoulders roughly, shaking him hard.

"No!" she screamed. "What did you do? What did you do?"

Bradan opened his mouth to answer, but no sound came out.

Instead, from deep within his gut, and up through his throat, green shoots erupted, exiting his mouth, pulling tight at his flesh, ripping at his jaw to make the hole larger, tearing him apart so that all the greenery inside could burst forth.

He had not known that the thing he had picked up, just before his father had attacked him, was not a stone. It was only when it began pulsing with an urgent familiarity that Bradan realised he had come across the Lady's gift. He had not questioned the coincidence, had not the time to debate if it had been random chance, or some kind of divine intervention. Bradan had recognised the plum for what it was – his only chance of survival.

The moments after taking that bite were unfocussed, sketchy. He remembered the look on his father's face when Bradan stood, his bones no longer broken. No, his bones did not... did not seem to matter anymore. Perhaps they had already been replaced. His father had taken a look at Bradan's hand, then his face had contorted into a mess of rage and loss. Then Bradan had hit his father, there had been a crack, and Nascha had arrived.

Nascha. It had taken Bradan a few moments to realise it was her, not only because of the nature of her entrance – she had seemed to fly down from the sky – but also because of how she looked. It was her hair more than anything. Bradan had grown used to her unruly white locks. Now, her hair was almost pitch black, with only a few specks of white through it to remind him of how she had once looked.

It was clear to Bradan within moments what Nascha had done. To save him, she had bound herself to the Magpie Spirit, had become the forest's first Magpie Queen.

Bradan would never have wished that upon her, not to save him. Especially when he had already damned himself.

All of these thoughts ran through his mind while his body was pulled apart.

It was painful, of course, his deconstruction, but over the last few days pain had been a well-known companion to Bradan. What was more unsettling, however, was the total irreparability of what was happening to him. These wounds were not something time could heal.

It began with his mouth, and his face. The greenery inside him, spawned from the mouthful of the Lady's gift he had consumed, grew at a rapid pace, expanding in his gut and his throat, forcing its way out of his mouth and his nose. It took only seconds for the growth to exceed the little space Bradan's openings afforded it, so the thing birthing within began to pull at his body, stretching it, breaking it. He was aware of the roots inside him gripping the side of his face, pulling his mouth and jaw apart, ripping his flesh to shreds so that more greenery could burst free.

All the while, however, Bradan was captivated by Nascha, and the look on her face. She was a woman who seemed to have lost everything. Nobody would enjoy watching a friend being pulled apart, he realised, detached from his own ruination, but her anguish was more than this. It could only have been moments since she handed her life over to the Magpie Spirit. Nascha must only now be realising what she had condemned herself to.

The pain stopped. Bradan looked about himself, at the shreds of skin on the forest floor around him. He saw part of a face on the ground, an empty eye socket laid out flat on the grass, and realised it was him, looking up at himself. Curious, he raised his hands to his face, and saw that his fingers were no longer pink. Instead, he held writhing green before him, ten digits made up of squirming new shoots, wriggling as he flexed them.

He looked down, and saw no feet. Instead, where his torso — similarly devoid of flesh — met his waist, his form broadened, becoming a trunk of thick roots that dug into the earth. From down there, Bradan realised, he could sense so much. His body did not end where it used to, where feet touched the ground. Instead, in this new form, Bradan extended deeper than he could see. His mind reeled as he realised how far his awareness stretched. He could feel the worms burying beneath him, could feel them niggling at the deep parts of himself. In the distance, he felt multiple cries of agony begin, only to be silenced. A moment later, the sound reached his ears of a large explosion. The Lady had fallen, uprooting and killing a grove of trees along with her. It was the death cries of those trees he had just heard.

Instinctively, as if it was what he had been designed for, Bradan reached out to the Lady, feeling the lines of green that extended from his roots naturally guided towards her.

Her rebuff was like a slap in the face. He took a physical step backwards, forgetting he no longer had legs or feet. Instead, his long roots moved through the earth, propelling him back, keeping him in constant touch with the forest.

Still distracted from his transformation, Bradan was unprepared for when Nascha attacked.

She did not speak words. Perhaps, he thought, she was too enraged to speak properly. He knew of the madness that had infected his father along with the Magpie Spirit's gift. Surely that would be the same for Nascha now.

She screamed with rage, attacking Bradan's new form with both feet and hands, pulling him free from the earth.

For a few brief moments, as the weight of Nascha's impact propelled them through the air, Bradan felt pain in this form for the first time. He realised Nascha had ripped him from the ground, uprooted him, and that lack of contact with the forest was devastating. As they careened through the trees, her impossible strength driving them through the air, Nascha ripped at him, grabbing at the roots and branches that now made up his chest, tearing at them, pulling him apart with her hands. However, those wounds were not what was causing him distress. Losing contact with the forest was like having his head plunged underwater. Bradan could not breathe. His heart, if he had one anymore, had stopped.

And then they hit the forest floor again. The relief was instant. His back, now in full contact with the ground, plunged dozens of new shoots into the earth, shoots that instantly nourished him and expanded, establishing their presence further. Nascha continued to scream, continued to tear at him, but Bradan knew the danger was over. Now that he was with the forest again, he could regrow any damage she was doing.

Gasping for air, Bradan reached up with an overly long arm, took a firm grip of the back of Nascha's torn dress, and flung her away. As he rose, he realised he would never have been able to do that in his previous form, even before Nascha had the Magpie Spirit's gift. He was considerably stronger like this than he had been as a man.

Nascha crouched before him, ready for attack, and Bradan realised he did not fear her. He had what he had always wanted: the power to protect himself, to protect the people of the forest. Finally, he was a force to rival his father.

Why, then, was he so sad?

He raised a hand in a peaceful gesture towards his friend.

"Nascha, it's me. It's Bradan. I know this must be hard, that the Spirit's poison is difficult to resist, but try to listen—"

"I am in control," Nascha said, her teeth gritted.

Bradan struggled to believe her. That look on her face reminded him so much of his father when madness threatened to overcome.

"The Owl in my blood protects me. I've been wrestling against something else in my body my entire life. The Magpie's poison makes little difference."

With that, she leapt forward, fingers extended like claws, ripping again at Bradan's trunk, pulling two handfuls of him away as she leapt.

He looked down at the holes in his chest, already regrowing with new greenery. He should care more about this, he realised. About losing his flesh, about what Nascha was doing to him. However, that emotion was muted, somehow. All emotions seemed to be. For the first time since his transformation, true fear began to blossom in Bradan's breast. What else was changing about him, other than the greenery outside?

"If you're not going mad, then why are you attacking me?" he asked.

She screamed at him then, a howl of uncontrollable rage. "Look at yourself. Look at me. Look what you've done to me," she shouted, pulling at her jet-black hair.

Bradan grew serious. "Nascha, I would never have wished this on you. You must have known that. I'd rather have died than for you to become shackled—"

"Do you think I want you a slave to... to her? Spirit's blood, Bradan, you should never have—"

In the distance, there was a chorus of screams. They came to Bradan through the earth, echoing through his roots. The sound of them was distant, as if the Green only cared half-heartedly about them. They were the screams of people.

Nascha, her head now erect and pointing in the direction of the noise, seemed to have heard them too, though presumably not through the roots as Bradan did.

"A village," she said.

Bradan nodded. "Smithsdown, I think. It's pretty close to here." Also, and he chose not to mention this, Bradan knew there was a copse of alders just overlooking the village, and he could feel them singing through the Green, oblivious to the destruction taking place all around them. "The conflict has woken the village. They know death is coming."

Nascha looked up, and leapt. Bradan saw her alight on the top of a great oak close by, presumably to survey the distant struggle.

He looked back at his own trunk, rooted to the ground, recalling his panic when that bond had been broken. Then, gingerly testing out his new abilities, Bradan moved through the earth again, his own roots carving a gentle furrow in the forest floor until he reached the foot of Nascha's oak. Testing, Bradan placed the palm of his hand on the oak, and felt small roots extend from his fingers, boring through the oak's bark to the flow of sap beneath.

"May I climb you?" he asked the oak.

Bradan received no words in return, only an impression of distinct annoyance. More than that, however, was Bradan's realisation that he did not need permission. This oak could resist him in this form no more than it could a woodcutter's axe. So, doing his best to ignore the oak's growing irritation, Bradan lifted his roots from the earth, curling them around the oak's trunk, pushing himself upwards on them, his trunk-like body still connected to the ground by his parasitic vines that fed from the oak itself, and also extended down the tree's length to plunge into the distant earth.

In this way, Bradan rose to meet Nascha.

On arrival, she looked at him with disgust, but he could tell her anger was beginning to fade. Instead, a haunted look of sadness and pity flashed across her eyes before she turned again to regard the warring titans.

The Lady had managed to grasp the Magpie Spirit this time, a hand on each wing, the tendrils of her fingers splayed out impossibly across the black feathers. The massive bird struggled, pecking at her with its beak, but the Lady held it far enough away that it could not reach her with its claws. Distantly, Bradan was aware of his Lady's sense of victory, and he wondered at the distance of that emotion. It should be closer. She should be closer to him, now, connected through the Greensong. Something was wrong with that.

The Magpie Spirit, for some reason, was not breaking apart into individual birds in response to its enemy's grip. Instead, cawing hoarsely, it flung itself about in the Lady's hands, dragging her with it. Each of the Lady's forced steps was like a thunderclap. No wonder the village had awoken.

From this vantage point, Bradan could still make out the smoke from the village fires he had spotted earlier. The village he had felt screaming was right beside where the gods struggled, now. One wrong footstep for the Lady, and everyone in Smithsdown would be crushed. He did not need to be close to the Lady to realise that the survival of a few humans was very low on her list of priorities.

"It wants to stop," Nascha said, her eyes not leaving the conflict. "The Magpie Spirit, it does not want to be here. Got better things to do, I guess. Part of the... the deal I made with it was that I'd fight its battles for it, here in the forest. Let it get back to whatever it was doing, wherever it was before you called it here."

Bradan opened his mouth to protest at the accusation, but closed it again when he realised he could come up with only a weak response at best.

"Can't see it turning tail and running, though, and can't see me being able to take her on like that, despite what I am now."

Nascha turned to Bradan, and he found her gaze impossible to read. In one heartbeat, he saw all the anger she had shown when facing down Lord Bidzell and Vippon, then a second later he saw the wide eyes of a lost little girl. At no point did he recognise the look of the friend who had run back into the forest to save him, and the sense of loss he felt on realising this was the only emotion that managed to penetrate the veil that was slowly growing over his own soul.

"You've got to go to her," Nascha said, clearly struggling to get the words out. "Get her to back down. Then I can convince the Spirit to leave, too." She waved her hand in the air, and for a brief second Bradan fancied he saw a small smile begin to form on her face, before she recognised and stopped it. "It's up to you to save the village, Bradan. Maybe even the forest. You've got what you wanted. With her power, you're the only one who can do it."

Pride. Pride came bursting through, unabashed, at her words. Yes, Bradan would save Nascha, his father, the village, everyone.

He nodded, and at that she leapt upward again. Not waiting to see where she went, Bradan uncurled himself from the tree, lowering himself to the forest floor and taking off at speed through the undergrowth, grabbing onto any exposed roots or low branches he could find, propelling himself forward as quickly as possible, aiming for the Lady.

The barkwraiths were the first to confront him. Bradan had almost reached her, could see the green of her titanic leg through the trees before him, could hear her distant song, one he had almost been shut off from, before the wraiths formed a wall before him, hunched and packed together, hissing.

Through the Green, Bradan listened for their song. It was like a chorus of strings, plucked hesitantly, waiting. He realised with a smile that they were afraid of him. He moved forward a step, and they backed away, visibly chittering with fear. He was not yet aware of his own strength, of the limits of his new abilities, but clearly these minions knew enough about him to realise they would be no match for him.

He stepped forward once more, willing his roots onward, and the barkwraiths fully parted, unveiling a short, red-haired figure standing behind them. One of the Children, her face still emotionless, looking for all the world like a five-year-old girl.

Probing, Bradan searched the Greensong for the Child. It was his turn to chill when he heard her. Unlike the trees and barkwraiths, and all the other songs he had heard so far, there were no notes to the Child's tune, no lilting, beautiful rhythm. Instead, through the Green the Child gave off a steady drumbeat, stoic, strong. She did not fear him.

They stared at each other for a moment. High in the air, somewhere beyond the trees above the Child's head, the Magpie Spirit gave a squawk of pain. Bradan heard a rumbling that he realised was the beating of a thousand wings, the sound of the Magpie Spirit giving up its struggle, fleeing into its multitudinous bodies.

"Brother," the Child said eventually. "Mother is not happy with you, brother."

Bradan bit his lip, searching through the Greensong for the

Lady, but still struggling to make contact with her.

"She will not speak to me."

"She is not happy with you," the Child repeated.

Bradan nodded. "I can make it up to her," he said, moving forward, making his way around the little girl. The Child did not seem to want to stand in his way. "I have a gift for her."

"What is it?" the Child asked, singing to him through the Green as he left her physical body behind, making his way to where the Lady's foot met the forest floor.

"The forest," Bradan said simply as he reached his hand out to the Lady's foot.

He had expected some kind of aggressive response to his touch. A shock, perhaps, or a physical recognition of his presence. Instead, he was greeted only with a dull window into her soul, one that paled in comparison to the connection he had made with the oak Nascha had climbed.

"My lady?" he sang through the Green, willing a connection to be made between himself and his patron. "Mother?"

Nothing. If she could hear his words, the Lady continued to ignore him.

He looked upward. It was, he mused, the view an ant must have of a normal person. He was able to get only a vague glimpse of her face, and it was not directed at him at all.

If he was to speak with her, he would have to climb.

Resting both hands on her foot, he sent some questing roots inside her, just as he had done with the oak. This was not a similar experience at all. In comparison with feeding from the oak's sap, sustaining himself with its energy, using the Lady as his connection with the Green below was like trying to drink soup through a blanket. It was possible, but it was hard work, with a fraction of the reward for ten times the effort.

But still, Bradan climbed.

When he climbed high enough to clear the treetops, he feared he would be making himself a target for the Magpie Spirit. Weakened, panting from the exertion of trying to feed from the Lady while climbing upward, Bradan took a worried glance about himself for the Magpie Spirit. His heart leapt when he spotted it. It was hovering over the hills to the south, right above the cliff it had knocked him from. There, standing tall at the top of that cliff, her black hair billowing about her like a cloak, stood Nascha, the

Magpie Queen. She had kept her word; the Magpie Spirit had backed off, giving Bradan an opening. He looked upward, at the Lady's face. He could see her clearly now, her gaze fixed on the distant black bird, her face contorted in anger.

Taking a deep breath, Bradan surged upward.

"My lady," he shouted upon reaching her shoulder. "It is I, your servant. I would speak with you."

Lazily, the Lady lifted a finger to her shoulder, flicking Bradan from her, as he would have done to a fly.

"You are no servant of mine, traitor," she said, speaking to him clearly through the Greensong.

Bradan fell, desperately extending the few roots he still had in place on the Lady, pulling himself close to her before all bonds were severed, disconnecting him from the Greensong entirely. He did not have the energy to climb to her shoulder again, so clung there to her back, extending himself into her, searching for more of her strength to add to his own.

He could feel her holding him back this time, deliberately keeping the entirety of her from him.

"My lady, I am yours," Bradan gasped, hanging on for dear life. "I have given my body over to your service. I would win this war for you."

"There is no war to be won, traitor. See my enemy flee from me. I have won today."

"I do not speak of this fight, my lady. I mean the war, the whole thing. The war for the forest."

"My forest," she said, her spite clear in her words.

"Once, my lady. But he took it from you, didn't he? And he'll keep it from you the same way he stole it all those years ago."

"I am as strong as him," she said. "Stronger," she added, but Bradan noticed a moment's hesitation, a break in the orchestra of her song. "I will not back down from this fight."

"But that's the thing, my lady," Bradan said, digging the roots of his fingers under her skin, pulling himself back up to her shoulder. "The fight is not important, and your enemy knows it. The Magpie Spirit is trying to win something else. The same thing it won last time."

He could feel the Lady hesitate at his words, and her barrier keeping him back started to break down. The Greensong became clearer to him, now, and at the heart of it was a sound previously unheard – a voice more beautiful than Bradan could ever imagine, singing a song of war. A tear ran down his cheek as he heard the Lady's song for the first time, crying at how beautiful she was, but equally because of how she wanted to deny him her voice.

"What do you speak of, traitor?"

"The Magpie Spirit won last time because of the people of the forest. It won because it turned their hearts from you."

"Nonsense. The forest is not people. Long before humans lived here, the forest was simply a story of green. Of leaves and flowers and branches. Not even animals, in the beginning."

"But then animals did come, my lady," Bradan ventured. He lashed his roots around her neck, now, and held himself upright, so he could look into her eyes. She looked back, and Bradan's head spun at that gaze, at the attention from a being such as this. Bradan was keenly aware of how vulnerable he was here, of how far he had extended himself from the Greensong, but he felt it was important to make this connection. Through the Green, the Lady was in total control. Out here, in the real world, where people and faces mattered, he was the one with experience.

"Animals came, and the forest added them to its story. And after that, people came too. They were added to the tale, and they became important. Without realising it, my lady, without even your knowledge, they took over the forest's story. So when the Spirit came, and when it realised what was now important to the forest's story, it was able to write you out of it."

"Simple, then," the Lady said. "If I rid the forest of people, I can remove their influence from it. No need to curry their favour."

Bradan's blood chilled as he realised his error. Scrambling for words, he recalled something his father had once told him. "Stories do not like to change, my lady. Not in such big ways, not all at once. If you try to remove people from the tale, you could break it. Instead of doing away with the Spirit, you could cast yourself forever as an enemy, a figure to be demonised for the rest of the forest's history. You could be doing the Spirit's job for it. That was not how the forest's story was stolen from you. It was insidious; it happened slowly, over time. The Magpie Spirit won the people's hearts by giving them a face to trust."

"The Magpie King."

Bradan nodded. "He protected the people of the forest. They learned to love him, to depend on him, when they had previously known only fear. It was only natural they turn to worship him, over time." Bradan bit his lip, aware of the gamble he was going to take next. "The King is dead, my lady, but another has risen to take his place."

Bradan indicated Nascha, standing below the Magpie Spirit, her head held high.

"I could kill her," the Lady said.

"You could."

Bradan dared not respond any further. He had made contact with the Lady; she was giving him trust. She was expecting him to contradict her, to move her thoughts away from killing Nascha. He so desperately wanted to, to protect his friend, but his greater fear was to lose the Lady's ear. Instead, Bradan waited.

"I have already ended the line of the Magpie King," the Lady said eventually. Bradan let out a gasp of air when she spoke. "Yet still the Spirit's favour lingers. If killing her will not win me the forest, what then?"

"Beat her," Bradan said. "Play the game they are playing, but be better at it."

The Lady turned to look at Bradan, her gaze a beacon from the heavens. Under that gaze, Bradan's soul shook like a paper kite flying in a thunderstorm, mere moments away from ripping under the stress of it. "What do you mean, traitor? Speak plainly."

"Win the hearts of the people. Teach them to love you, not fear you."

The Lady looked at Bradan, then back across the forest, towards Nascha.

"Give them a hero, you mean. Protect them."

"Yes."

She looked at Bradan again. "You are talking about yourself."

He hesitated. "Yes."

"And you would do this? Become a hero of the people, dedicate your life to protecting them?"

"It's all I ever wanted," he said, his voice almost a whisper.

"In my name?"

He hesitated again, looking back at Nascha, standing with the Magpie Spirit hanging over her. She had chosen her side already. Time for Bradan to choose his.

"Yes, in your name. As your servant. You had faith in me when others did not. I'm sick of proving myself."

The Lady reached out and grabbed Bradan's head between two fingers. She shook him then, causing his roots to snap, breaking him free from her body, and from his connection to the Greensong. He had been so intent on Nascha, on what he was losing by picking an opposing side to hers, that he had not anticipated the Lady turning on him.

As soon as his connection with the Green was broken, he felt his insides seize up, the life within his body beginning to wilt. His eyes, wide with shock, stared at the baleful glare of the Lady as she brought him closer to her face.

"You have broken faith with me before, traitor."

"I know," Bradan gasped. "I'm sorry. It was a mistake. One I will never make again."

"Oh, I know you will not do so. You are no longer a thing of flesh anymore. You are a thing of the Greensong, and that means you are mine. If you cross me again, Magpie King's son, I need do little more than snap my fingers to break you."

"You will not need to," he said, gasping, his hands fumbling for her fingertips, groping at his own throat in desperation, willing himself to breathe again. "I am yours. In body and soul, yours forever."

Then the Lady of the Forest smiled, and the warmth of that smile made Bradan think of a burst of sunlight, a nourishing brightness that banished away the dark of her anger.

"Welcome home, then, my son," she said, lowering Bradan and clasping him to her chest. Instantly, he extended himself outward, into her, gasping with relief that she no longer held him back, gave him full access to the Greensong inside. Almost crying with relief, he buried his face into the foliage of her skin, drinking deep from the life within her, losing himself within the mesmerising complexity of her song.

"Welcome to our family."

From a distance, Nascha watched the Lady clasp Bradan to her bosom, and then continued to watch as the goddess reduced in size, eventually vanishing from view. She could hear the people of Smithsdown continue to wail, by now out of confusion rather than just sheer terror.

"Go to them," the Magpie Spirit commanded her. "Let them know I am keeping them safe. Make them love me again."

Not quite sneering, Nascha watched as the Magpie Spirit rose in the air, turning away from her, heading east to whatever place of import lay in that direction, leaving the forest behind. There was no embrace for Nascha to welcome her to the fold. Just a command, and then abandonment.

She stood there for a long while, looking over the forest. Her forest, she realised eventually. She knew the hills rose behind her, could recall the flat expanse of freedom beyond them, but knew that was not for her, not anymore. The forest was her prison now, and her jailer was considerably more competent than a greedy nobleman.

As if on cue, a figure in white emerged from the trees below, followed by the few remaining Titonidae soldiers left of Lord Bidzell's band. Nascha could have leapt down to meet them, crossing the ground between them in seconds with very little exertion on her part. Instead, she stood still and watched them climb, watched every aching footstep Lord Bidzell took to reach her. She did not smile at his misfortune, but instead waited, sentry-like, for his arrival.

Eventually, he made his way to the cliff, standing childlike before her. He had lost his white helm, and the right side of his face was crusted over with dried blood. For his part, he stood lost, unsure of what to do next.

"Kneel," Nascha eventually told him.

Lord Bidzell looked at her blankly.

"When presenting yourself before a member of a royal household, it is customary for servants to kneel."

She felt him tense at her words, but then his eyes went to her hair, to the wreckage of the forest beneath them, and to the empty space above her that had recently been occupied by the Magpie Spirit. Then, with a glance at his troops behind, and with a gestured instruction to them, they all knelt before her.

Despite her exhaustion and bitterness at her current

predicament, Nascha found a small sense of satisfaction in that moment.

"I have a message for you to deliver to Laurentina," she said.

Bidzell just looked at her, wisely choosing not to respond.

"Tell her... tell her she has made an error of judgment in sending her dogs to hunt down a harmless slave."

"You were a servant—"

"Slave," she said again, the hardness of her face making it clear she was not to be interrupted. "She has incurred the wrath of the... of the queen. Of the Magpie Queen. And she will have a very hard task repairing that wound."

She felt even more enjoyment from the frustration on Bidzell's face at those words, but she knew he would deliver them exactly to Laurentina.

"Now go," she told them, turning her back on them. "Get the hell out of my forest."

"But... Your Highness, what of the other matters between your crowns?"

Nascha turned, a bemused expression on her face. "There are no other matters. Laurentina has displeased me, and made an enemy of me today. I have the gift of the Magpie Spirit, she has the gift of a greedy old man. That is all we need to know."

Lord Bidzell shook his head, and Nascha was irritated to see his confidence return, to see a hint of the self-assured smirk that had haunted her the length of the forest.

"Now that the Magpie's court has been re-established, now that a new queen has risen in the forest, surely now is time to revisit old bonds between the Magpie's forest and the White Woods?"

Nascha felt her anger begin to bubble as Bidzell's grin broadened. She knew where this was going, and did not like it.

"For every Magpie King, there has always been an Owl Queen bride. It only makes sense for us to provide a king this time—"

"Do not dare," she said, speaking louder than she had intended, taking a step towards him, her fist raised.

Lord Bidzell, to his credit, only flinched from her, did not run away entirely.

"Oh, believe me, I want nothing better than to flee from this wretched place. But I am also loyal to my own people, and I am loyal to the stories and traditions we hold dear. There has always been an Owl in the Magpie's bed. There is no king anymore, but the forest has accepted a queen instead. These stories, they will only allow themselves to be stretched so far. It would not do to break them entirely."

Nascha felt nothing but hate for this man now, and for the whole Titonidae people. Yet despite her hate, part of her saw the truth in his words. If she was queen now, she had to behave like one. That meant making alliances. That meant providing heirs.

Another chain added to her shackle.

She spoke with a lowered voice. "I will never break bread with any from your Court," she said, her voice low, her words measured, doing everything she could to strip them of the anger she was doing her best to hide. "As far as I am concerned, Laurentina does not exist. I do not recognise her as a power in the White Woods."

Lord Bidzell opened his mouth to protest, but Nascha raised her hand to silence him.

"But," she said, eyes locked with him now, "you may send word to the other Courts to expect to hear from me – an envoy – once my House has been firmly established."

Lord Bidzell gritted his teeth, but nodded.

"Tell them it would not be in their best interests to speak to me of betrothal, not in the way some ham-fisted members of that nameless Court have recently done. Instead, tell them that apologising, seeking to make amends for the sins of their neighbour, would be a good way to gain my favour."

Lord Bidzell nodded again, his face white with anger now.

"Good," Nascha said, smiling and turning from him.

"Now, you have three days to get out of my forest," she said, tensing her legs, preparing to jump. "The White Woods are a long journey to the north. I suggest you get started."

With that, the Magpie Queen took off into the night, the specks of white in her jet-black hair melting into the blanket of stars above.

They found each other a week later. Nascha had sensed Bradan only a few times since that night, a burrowing force through the forest floor, but had seen more evidence of his passage through the land they shared. In the undergrowth – never on the main paths or roads between villages – she had spotted long furrows of overturned soil, the way those roots that extended from his waist ploughed the earth as he moved around. More than that, however, she heard about him when she came into contact with the villagers, with the Corvae people.

They had been terrified of her when she had first approached, even those villages who had held true to the worship of the Magpie Spirit. Her first attempt to announce herself to a village had been to alight upon one of their cottage roofs just before sundown, when people were still milling through the village green. There had been a lot of screaming, some commotion, and then all had fled, locking themselves in their cellars, refusing to answer her when she called them. The next village she had just walked into, and of course nobody had taken her seriously, looking as she did, until, through frustration, she smashed a tree in half. Then there was screaming, commotion, locked cellars. Her one bit of success so far had been when she had sensed a remote farmstead in danger of being attacked by some overlarge spiders that had burrowed underneath the building. Nascha had burst into the farmhouse, through the thatch, just in time to pull the legs off a handful of the beasts before the rest ran away. The farmer and her family were very grateful to Nascha, but still raised eyebrows when she told them she was the Magpie Queen.

"I don't know, love, didn't the Magpie King have a mask? If you want to be taken seriously, you should really get yerself one of those."

Nascha supposed the woman might be right. Now, as the sun began to set, not for the first time did Nascha's eyes raise to the Eyrie, to the former seat of the Magpie King's power. It was hers now, she knew, but she was reluctant to begin establishing her home there. It reminded her too much of the Court, and all the rules and regulations that would have to come with it. She also remembered the promise she had made to the Titonidae Courts, the promise that Lord Bidzell must have delivered to most of them by now. "Once my House has been firmly established..."

Nascha shivered, but it had nothing to do with the cold.

"I don't like the night. The sun... I miss the sun. So much more than before."

She turned with a start. It was Bradan. Somehow, he had made his way up the elm she was perched on without her noticing.

She narrowed her eyes. "How did you do that?"

Bradan breathed in a deep sigh, his arms outstretched, eyes closed, drinking in the last rays of sunlight. "Not sure. Still getting used to this. There's a lot I don't understand yet. Must be the same for you?"

Nascha struggled to look at him. She could not think of him as the man she had given her freedom for, the only true friend she had ever known. She had watched that Bradan being torn apart, ripped to shreds by whatever this mockery was that was standing before her.

Still, there was so much of this thing that reminded her of him. Not least of which was how much she wanted to hit him right now.

"I'm getting used to it. Hear you've been busy. Being a hero."

A number of villages she had visited spoke about the Greenman, or the Lady's Man. They all had good things to say about him.

Bradan grinned, opening his eyes and peeking at her. He took a deep breath, the branches that twined together to make up his body creaking with smugness.

Damn, he was insufferable when he was happy.

Bradan's smile fell, however, when he looked at her. Then his face became much more like the man she had travelled with, had learned to trust.

"Nascha, I'm sorry. I never meant any of this for you."

She shrugged. "Seems to have worked out for you, though, hasn't it? Got what you wanted, a chance to be the hero. Doesn't seem to bother you that you look like..." She waved a hand indicating his new form. "Doesn't seem to be a big deal."

Bradan looked down at his body, vines overlapped and interwoven to give it the rough proportions of a human torso. He frowned. "I... It feels worth it, I guess. What's happened to me, not what's happened to you—"

"Forget me."

"I haven't, Nascha. I couldn't. I hate this, you know that. I would never have wished this on you."

"It isn't all bad," she said, her face daring him to believe her. "I mean, nobody's hunting me down anymore, right?" She held a fist in front of her, tensing it. She had crushed rocks with that fist in the past week. "They wouldn't dare. Not now."

"But you wanted to escape—" Bradan began, but stopped when Nascha looked up at him, her eyes dark.

Nascha kept her gaze locked with this thing that looked like her friend, and he gazed right back at her. That was how Nascha knew Bradan was really gone. This thing might look like him, but it did not act like him. The magpie boy had never been able to keep eye contact with her for this long.

"This is magpie territory," she told him eventually. "You should leave."

It was true that the nearest villages were the ones that had retained worship of the Magpie Spirit in the years since the fall of the king.

Bradan looked sheepish.

"The Lady has requested that I reach out to them, try to convince them that turning to her would be best for everyone."

Nascha clicked her tongue. "She's threatening them?"

"No," Bradan said hurriedly, alarmed. "No, she's protecting them. I'm going to protect them."

"They already have protection," Nascha said, pulling herself up tall. "They have me."

Bradan finally looked away from her. "She's not as bad as you think, Nascha. She's listening to me. She wants them to feel safe—"

"All she wants is their worship, any way she can get it. She doesn't care anything for these people, as long as she gets what she wants."

"And you think the Magpie Spirit is any different?"

"Yes. It's different because it isn't here. Until last week, it had been hundreds, if not thousands of years since the Spirit had returned to the forest. If I have my way, it'll never have to come back here again. The people will be safe, the Spirit will be content, and we can all have some peace for a while."

Bradan nodded, still looking at the forest floor. "That isn't going to happen if the Lady keeps expanding her reach."

He looked up at Nascha again, but other than locking gazes with him, she did not respond. She did not need to. They had both made promises to save each other that night, and to save the forest. Promises that now pitted them on opposite sides of a battlefield Nascha had desperately hoped to escape.

There would be trouble, before the peace she longed for could come to pass.

"If you care about the forest as much as you say you do, Greenman, stop the Lady from stealing my villages. Get her to focus on the others out there, the ones worshipping other creatures, and turn them to your flock, if you have to. But stay away from mine."

Bradan nodded. "And you'll do the same? Stay away from us?"

She nodded, pursing her lips, not missing his use of the word 'us'.

But that Lady will have to be dealt with, before the forest is safe. That Lady, and all her creatures.

The thing that looked like Bradan began to retreat, turning away from the magpie villages.

"I'm sorry this has happened to you, Nascha," he said, before turning from her as well. "Sorry this has happened to us both. But I am glad to see you here, in the forest. And I'm glad you're safe now. Our patrons might still be in conflict, but they're trusting us to win this for them. There must be some way we can work this out, some way we can save things, so that both powers are pleased, and we can all exist peacefully together. We can figure this out, can't we?"

She stood, impassionate, as he retreated, watching his smile fade as she refused to answer.

Finally, when the Greenman was long gone, Nascha exhaled, her held breath leaving her as a short sob she instantly cursed herself for.

"I am going to work this out," she said, tensing her legs, looking at the cloud-covered sky above her. "Going to work this out, and rid this forest of all the evil things in it. All the evil things, including the things that took the life of my friend."

She leapt into the night sky, propelling herself high above the treetops. At the height of her ascent, she fancied she saw, to the north, a brief glint of moonlight reflecting off the silver birch of the White Woods. Her former prison, one that seemed so small, and so far from her, now.

Then, as she fell, guiding herself towards the ruined castle in the centre of her forest, the white of her former home disappeared, replaced by the black of her new kingdom as she flew down to meet it.

She had traded one prison for another. However, Nascha's new prison was vast, and for the first time in her life, she was a power within it.

She might be chained to this land, but she was not alone.

This was not the life she had wanted, but Nascha had spent a lifetime already in captivity, and was used to making do with what she had been given.

If she was trapped in this forest now, then she would do everything in her power to make this a land worth giving up her freedom for.

She plummeted toward the Eyrie, and the Magpie King's former stronghold. Above, a bank of dark clouds rolled across the moon, obscuring it from view. The pale moonlight that had painted the forest was scraped away, leaving it a dark and empty place.

A place perfect to hide away in, and to begin plotting revenge.

A WORD FROM THE AUTHOR

I'd like to talk about Knacks, and about Lonan.

In my early twenties (all those many years ago), I had no clue what I wanted to do with my life. I had spent the last few decades working my way through the education system, and I was *good* at getting educated. I had, if you excuse the Yarnsworld pun, the Knack for it.

It was when it came to putting that education to good use that I had a problem.

I felt lost and directionless for a good portion of my early years as an adult. That's where the idea for the Knacks came from, especially for Lonan in *They Mostly Come Out At Night* - he literally had no guidance for where to go with his life, unlike those around him. The theme has continued for the main characters of the Yarnsworld books. Unlike Lonan, both Kaimana and Arturo (and Nascha, in this book) actually had Knacks, but those gifts never work out the way the characters expect them to at the start of the story. Their Knacks might not always affect the plot directly, but they very much define what is going on inside those characters' heads.

And now for Lonan.

I had always known I had wanted to return to the Magpie King's forest, and as I was mulling over where the story was to go, I had always assumed I would be continuing Lonan's tale. I was struggling a lot more than I had expected to when plotting the next part of his story, and that was around the time I discovered *Kubo and the Two Strings*, my favourite film of 2016. I read an interview with the film director Travis Knight, and that cut to the core of the problem I was having with Lonan's story. He said:

"The way we approach our stories is we imagine each film as if it's the most meaningful experience of our protagonist's life. If that's your point of view, your sequel is automatically… going to be a diminishment of that—is it the second most important experience of your protagonist's life?"

That was my problem. Any continuation of Lonan's would diminish the events of *They Mostly Come Out At Night*, and the sacrifices he made at the end of it, especially as his goal in that story would most likely be to undo the effects his choices at the end of *Mostly* had on him.

No, Lonan had already cast his lot. Once I realised the forest's story would continue with different players, the book you have just read began to come into focus…

Some hints of that original tale still exist, and you have already read them. The folktale *The Girl and the Lake*, in particular, hint at the happiness that Lonan was almost given, but I now firmly believe that happiness was never his due.

I don't believe that every story can't continue, by the way. For some characters, the events of their first tale have a knock on effect, and it ultimately becomes the first part of a much larger story. I knew I would eventually return to the Crescent Atoll, but I had thought Kaimana and Rakau's tale was done. They told me otherwise, and the next Yarnsworld book has the tentative title of *The Life and Death of a Taniwha Girl*.

Head to www.benedictpatrick.com to be kept up to date on Yarnsworld news, and to receive some free stories from the Magpie King's forest…

Until then, take care,

Benedict

The standalone fantasy book that readers are calling a delightfully weird, dark fairytale.

The villagers of the forest seal themselves in their cellars at night, whispering folktales to each other about the monsters that prey on them in the dark. Only the Magpie King, their shadowy, unseen protector, can keep them safe.

However, when an outcast called Lonan begins to dream of the Magpie King's defeat at the hands of inhuman invaders, this young man must do what he can to protect his village. He is the only person who can keep his loved ones from being stolen away after dark, and to do so he will have to convince them to trust him again.

They Mostly Come Out At Night is the first novel from Benedict Patrick's Yarnsworld series. Straddling the line between fantasy and folklore, this book is perfect for fans of the darker Brothers Grimm stories.

Start reading today to discover this epic tale of dreams, fables and monsters!

Printed in Great Britain
by Amazon

65249829R00184